Fighting FATE

Linda Kage

OMNIFIC PUBLISHING
DALLAS

Omnific Publishing
10000 North Central Expressway, Dallas, TX 75231
www.omnificpublishing.com

First Omnific eBook edition, July 2013
First Omnific trade paperback edition, July 2013

The characters and events in this book are fictitious.
Any similarity to real persons, living or dead,
is coincidental and not intended by the author.

Library of Congress Cataloguing-in-Publication Data

Kage, Linda.
    Fighting Fate / Linda Kage – 1st ed.
    ISBN: 978-1-623420-29-1
    1. Love — Fiction. 2. Grief — Fiction.
    3. New Adult — Fiction. 4. College — Fiction. I. Title

10 9 8 7 6 5 4 3 2 1

Cover Design by Micha Stone and Amy Brokaw
Interior Book Design by Coreen Montagna

Printed in the United States of America

To Courtney Wyant and Andrea Reed
for always being so positive and funny!
The world needs more people like you two.

Chapter One

Paige Zukowski dressed in the dark, her fingers fumbling over the buttons on her blouse. She tried a breathing technique to calm her rattled nerves. Inhale. Hold. One, two, three. Exhale. Hold. One, two, three. Inhale…

The buttons were mismatched. She frowned and started over, forgetting whether she was on inhale or exhale. Only when she was about to pass out because she was still holding her breath did she let a lungful of oxygen rush from her chest.

Oh, well. Breathing was overrated anyway. She gave up on the entire relaxation attempt and closed her eyes as she worked her way higher. Trace used to tease her relentlessly about fastening things from the bottom up.

"You just gotta do everything backwards, don't you, Pay Day? You're supposed to start at the top and go down. You miss less buttons that way, plus it keeps your gig line in order."

She'd raised an eyebrow at that one. "My what line?"

"It's a military term." He had shrugged with his usual nonchalance. "Something to do with making sure your buttons, belt buckle, and fly run a straight column down the front of your body."

Paige's derisive snicker had told him what she'd thought of that. "Are you joining the Army now? Since when do you know military terms?"

Lying way too comfortably on her bed with his legs stretched out and crossed at the ankles and his arms resting behind his head, he had merely sent her a cocky smile. "I know everything."

And he had. Her brother had been the brightest, most promising member of their family. He was going to go places. Even after his funeral, the college acceptance letters had poured in, inviting him to attend their university with a full ride.

He'd been anticipating the letter from Granton University the most. And it had come with a complete scholarship included.

Two weeks too late.

Her own nostalgic smile dying, Paige tried not to remember his infectious grin, though it was hard, particularly this morning. She left the top two buttons unfastened so she wouldn't feel as if she was choking through the entire day, and cold metal brushed the back of her hand as she manually tried to straighten her crooked gig line. With a sigh, she wrapped her fingers around the cool amulet draping her neck. A ruby embedded in a Celtic-looking cross. Trace had given it to her on her thirteenth birthday since ruby was her birthstone.

It was big, and clunky, and kind of gaudy, but in the three years he'd been gone, she'd yet to take it off. She squeezed the shape of the cross into her palm and whispered into the dim dorm room.

"For you, Bubba. I won't let you down."

A buzz echoed around her. Paige jumped, freaked for a split second that the ghost of her brother was responding…until she realized her cell phone was simply vibrating across the corner of her new desk, announcing an incoming call.

On the other side of the room, sheets rustled from the shadowed corner, giving her another heart attack. Still not used to sharing her space with anyone else, especially a complete stranger, Paige dashed a worried glance in the direction of her roommate's bed as she leaped toward her phone to silence it.

"Hello," she answered in a harried, hushed voice, trying not to wake Mariah, though honestly, Mariah hadn't seemed all that worried about not waking her when she'd come stumbling in at two this morning, cursing across the dark room until she'd turned on the light over her bed and jerked Paige from a restless sleep.

Huddled under her covers, Paige had feigned unconsciousness until Mariah had changed into a camisole and shorty shorts, then passed out face first on top of her covers, the reek of stale alcohol and cigarettes filming the air. Paige had waited five minutes before she'd tiptoed across the floor and killed the lights. It had taken her another hour to fall back to sleep in between counting every time Mariah tossed and turned, making the springs on her mattress screech and moan.

"Hello?" a quiet voice breathed back. "Why are we whispering?"

Paige sat on the edge of her bed, relieved to hear her best friend. "Because my roommate's still asleep."

She squinted through the dark, wondering if she actually should wake Mariah. Her new roomie probably wouldn't like being late on the first day of classes. But if she was the type to habitually come in at two in the morning, then maybe she was smart enough not to schedule an early course.

Paige wiped at her tired, dry eyes, wondering what had possessed her to sign up for anything before nine herself.

Rookie freshman error, she decided.

"Ah. So…how's it going with the whole roommate thing?" Kayla asked. "She okay or what?"

Stray beams of morning light filtered into the room, giving Paige a glimpse of her organized desk. She studied the four-by-six framed photo of Trace nestled next to the television.

"She's…fine." Since meeting only the day before, Paige had really only talked to Mariah a few times. The previous night's conversation had lasted but a couple of minutes before some guy had knocked on their door and whisked her roommate away. But those few moments hadn't been pleasant. "We're still getting used to each other."

"Hmm. So, are there any available hotties there asking you out yet?"

Paige rolled her eyes. "Not hardly."

"What! No available hotties at all? What kind of college are you at?"

With a snicker, Paige corrected, "No one's asked me out."

"Oh." Kayla sighed. "Well, they will."

"Kayla, I didn't come here to date a bunch of—"

"Yeah, yeah, yeah. You're there because of Trace. And I'm telling you right now, that's the worst reason in the world to move so far away from home to attend a school you don't even like."

Paige's back straightened with indignation. "I never said I didn't like—"

"Well, you don't love it the way he did. Paige…" Kayla sighed again, this time sounding like a wise old parent tired of repeating the same lecture.

"Look, I can't talk about this right now." It was her first day of school. Besides, they'd been over it before. A lot. Nothing had changed her mind so far. Nothing would change it now.

So what if her best friend in the world thought Paige was crazy for trying to live a dead boy's life for him? It wasn't as if she had her own future to look forward to. After Trace's funeral, her world had collapsed. Her parents had turned away from her, too entrenched in their own misery to help her deal with hers. Her mother had descended so far into depression she'd looked right through Paige. And after her mom was gone, her father had drowned himself in booze. Paige had lost everything.

The only way she'd been able to dig her way out of the agony had been to focus on Trace's lost dreams, to decide she'd live them for him and become what he'd always wanted to be.

"I really need to get to class," she said, standing up and slipping into the sandals she'd set out last night to wear with her first-day outfit.

Kayla sighed. A third time. Really, it was too much. "Sweetie, you know I love you. I just want you to be happy. But—"

"Love you too," Paige broke in with fake enthusiasm. "Talk later." Disconnecting the line, she cringed, telling herself she'd call back and apologize after she actually survived her first day of school. Right now, she had other worries.

She had college to start, a first class to find, a dead boy's life to fulfill.

Busy, busy, busy.

A minute later, Paige pushed her way from her dormitory and halted in her tracks. The campus of Granton sprawled before her, teeming with activity. Thousands of students strolled the sidewalks while another thousand sat cross-legged in clusters on the grass as bicyclists darted between the foot traffic and an endless amount of cars filed into the parking lots. Half a dozen digital billboards sat perched in front of buildings, scrolling messages and advertisements across their screens. And a marching band practiced the Party Rock Anthem somewhere in the distance.

It was so hectic, so crowded. So intimidating. After living in a town of two thousand people her entire life and attending a school of barely three hundred, Paige huddled against the entrance of her dorm building, tempted to scurry back inside and hide under her blankets for the rest of the semester.

"Trace." She groaned under her breath, squeezing her fingers around his gaudy amulet. "Why'd you have to pick such a huge school to dream about?"

If her brother were here now, she'd be tempted to strangle him... right after she hugged him silly and reprimanded him to never die on her again.

"I can do this, I can do this, I can do this," she chanted as she forced her numb legs to move, trudging down a slight decline to the cafeteria. But when she entered Gibson Hall, the smell of bacon and sausages made her stomach churn, and not in a good way.

"I can't do this." At least not food. Not right now.

She turned around and walked right back out. Okay, so she'd just get to her first class and set up early. Unfolding her map of the campus, she hunted for her eight a.m. course.

As the first to arrive, she selected a seat in the front row, changing spots a few times until she had herself positioned near the exit yet close enough to the center to provide a decent view of the instructor's podium. She wanted to be the perfect, exemplary student.

When a trio of chatty guys entered the lecture hall, she'd already tugged a laptop from her bag and set it on top of the desk. After it booted, the screen lit with its wallpaper. Trace had picked out the M. C. Escher design as the background as soon as he'd bought the laptop, saving all the money he'd made mowing lawns between his junior and senior years of high school.

His computer had only been six months old when he'd died.

A year ago, Paige had decided she wouldn't let his hard-earned mowing money go to waste. She wouldn't let his dream of Granton die with him. She'd taken over his computer, and now here she sat, ready and willing to take over the rest of his life. In another four years, she planned to graduate with a Bachelors of Business Administration and find a job he would be proud of in the marketing world.

Logging into the processor, she pre-saved a word document and minimized the screen, prepared for an hour of copious note taking. Nothing was going to distract her from her studies. She had a goal to meet, her brother's dream to realize, and his future to begin.

"Good morning!" A loud voice ripped her attention from the two Escher hands drawing each other on her computer. "This is World Regional Geography. If you're in the wrong room, there's the door. If you have no respect for professorial authority, feel free to follow the other lost souls out the exit because I will not accept impudence."

Paige gulped and glanced surreptitiously behind her, surprised to see hundreds of other students had arrived while she'd been dazing off. They filled nearly every seat.

When no one stood from the sea of blurred bodies to leave, she slowly swiveled back around to face the professor.

Dr. Presni—as her class schedule labeled him—was a short, stout man with an irritable disposition, thick eyebrows, and a bad comb-over. Without introducing himself, he announced he would take roll call today, but after that, attendance was entirely up to the student.

"Marissa Abbott," he began, starting down his list.

"Here," the return call echoed from the back of the room.

The scratch of a check mark followed as Presni noted her presence. And so it began all the way through the alphabet. With her Z surname, Paige figured she had a while to wait before he called on her. She relaxed, tuning out, and studied the front of the room. A white board and stark, blank walls stared back. Yeesh, maybe she shouldn't have sat in the front row. She felt self-conscious. Singled out. She eyed the exit just to her left. It looked so welcoming.

"Rupert Waltrip...Alison Wutke..."

Paige refocused on the teacher's droning voice—really dry, droning voice. It was going to be hard to concentrate on his lectures with a voice like his, all arid and—

"Logan Xander."

Logan Xander?

Paige stopped breathing. Icicles crystalized on her brain, freezing her motionless.

That name.

Oh, God. That name.

Why would the professor say that name? Of all the names in the world, why—

"Here." A voice answered, claiming ownership of that horrendous name. He sat too close behind her and a tad to her right.

She couldn't help herself. Paige whipped around to look. She had to know.

There he sat.

Three rows back. Two seats over.

Logan Xander.

It had been three years since she'd last seen him. He fixed his dirty-blond hair shorter these days, shaved to a buzz cut. And his face had aged, the planes and angles sharper and more defined. Matured. But there was no way she'd ever forget what he looked like.

He must've caught her abrupt reaction to his name, because he glanced her way. Their gazes caught and held, and all the air in the room stalled, leaving her suffocated.

Dying.

A great, crushing tremble clutched her, wracking a painful shudder up her spine. Immediate tears throbbed behind her eyes. She blinked repeatedly, but her retinas remained scorching dry, giving her no relief from the horror she was beholding.

A bewildered frown wove through the center of Logan Xander's brow as he stared back, obviously not recognizing her.

She clenched her teeth and fisted her hands. She wanted to strike out, physically, verbally, any way possible, to make him remember the way she remembered. How dare he forget her when she would know his face—his name—for the rest of her life!

At the front of the room, the professor called, "Paige Zukowski?"

Finally, Xander reacted. His eyes flared wide and his face drained of color as he glanced at the professor, then back to her. His mouth dropped open, forming a great big dreaded O.

Fear and rage and pain overwhelmed her.

A whimper sobbed from her throat. Humiliated for letting her distress echo into the room, she spun away, fumbling as she grabbed her things off her desk, snapping her laptop shut as she swung out her arm and swiped it into her bag.

People were staring, gasps of surprise coming from her left and right, everywhere behind her. She didn't care. She had to escape.

Run!

A pen fell from her bag, but pausing to retrieve it seemed preposterous. It became collateral damage.

She tripped trying to stand too quickly, her legs tangling in the confining desk/chair combo. The professor lifted his head from his roll call and gaped at her over the top of his wire-rimmed glasses, his bushy brows and mustache twitching with confusion.

She didn't bother to explain herself. Couldn't speak if she'd wanted to.

Springing toward the door, she shoved it open and wheezed for air when she reached the hall. She didn't pause or slow down until she was outside and two blocks from the building containing Logan Vance Xander. All the while, she kept glancing over her shoulder, worried he might've followed.

He hadn't, thank God.

Of course he hadn't. Why would he? But, seriously. What was he doing here? How could he step foot onto the grounds of Trace's dream school?

How dare he?

It wasn't right, shouldn't be acceptable. He'd destroyed Paige three years ago, annihilated her entire family. He didn't deserve a second chance—a college degree—when Trace had nothing but a headstone and silly epitaph.

Tears streamed down her cheeks with a hot vengeance. She sprinted all the way back to her dorm room, her book bag repeatedly clouting her in the spine, spurring her onward. Grateful to find her roommate gone when she got inside, she huddled in her bed and wept hard, her body shuddering with the shock of discovering a murderer attended the same university as she.

And not just any murderer.

Her brother's murderer.

Chapter Two

Logan gawked after the girl as she disappeared from the doorway, the breeze from her passing still causing papers on the front row desks to flutter and dance.

"Lover's quarrel?" Dr. Presni's dry voice made him jump.

Logan jerked his attention to the professor who curiously eyed *him* of all people over the tops of his glasses. Shifting his gaze around him, Logan found an entire room full of curious eyes watching him.

Slumping lower in his seat, he shook his head adamantly. "N-no, sir. I don't...I don't even know her."

Though his words were true, he squirmed inside, feeling as if everyone else saw otherwise, as if they'd suddenly learned every horrible thing about him.

But in all honesty, he *didn't* know the girl with the large dark eyes who'd just stared at him as if he'd ripped out her very soul. If he had three guesses, however, he was fairly certain he wouldn't need two of them to correctly guess her identity.

Logan knew Trace Zukowski had had a younger sister. He'd read about her in Zukowski's obituary, though for the life of him, he couldn't remember her name. He remembered the girl he'd assumed was the sister when he'd gone to the funeral, though. She'd approached him hesitantly only to spit in his face. Hate and damnation had seared him from a pair of tear-stained eyes that had seemed too large for such a small, pale girl. But she'd darted away before he could seal a concrete image of that face in his brain.

He doubted he'd forget what she looked like this time around.

"I'm guessing that was Paige Zukowski," Presni pressed, still staring expectantly at Logan.

Logan shrugged, hoping he looked baffled enough for the teacher to leave off.

But...Paige. He wouldn't forget her name so easily either.

Paige Zukowski. Trace's little sister. All grown up and in college.

At *Granton* of all places.

What was she doing here? He'd been so certain he'd moved far enough from home he'd never cross paths with anyone else from Creighton County again.

"All right, then." Heaving out a disgruntled sigh, the professor closed his roll booklet. "If everyone is done with running from the room bawling, then let's get to some geography, shall we?"

Logan wiped a hand over his face, startled to find his fingers trembling.

Over the last year, he'd actually been able to relax a little, positive no one on campus would ever unveil his secrets. He'd begun to think maybe he could start over and move past the dreaded night that had changed his life forever.

Or at least make a good impression of moving on.

A crazy, anxious breath shuddered from his lungs. He set a closed fist over his mouth to muffle the wheeze even as he glanced sideways to make sure his neighbors weren't staring at him as if they feared he might break out with gunfire and eliminate everyone in class.

Who would expect anything less from a confirmed killer?

No one seemed to pay him any mind, though. They were too busy dozing, or staring off toward the bank of windows at their right, or taking notes as they listened to Presni's lecture. The girl next to him was preoccupied with pressing little butterfly stickers to her fingernails.

It didn't seem real. Shame and fear coursed through him as he sat there stiff as a board, concentrating on breathing through his nose so he didn't have a panic attack, and no one acted as if anything earth-shattering had just happened.

Paige Zukowski was going to tell the truth about him. He'd lose all the acquaintances he'd managed to accumulate over the past few years. He'd have to leave campus in disgrace. He'd have to start over again from scratch.

He wasn't sure if he could pull up roots and try somewhere else. He was tired of running, tired of hurting. He just wanted to feel as if he actually belonged in one place.

But he already knew he never really would because, no matter how far or fast he ran, he wouldn't be able to escape himself. And there lay in the true problem. He was stuck being Logan Vance Xander, the murderer.

An hour passed not in seconds but by the number of nervous sweat drops that leaked down the center of his back. Still dazed as Dr. Presni dismissed class, Logan was dimly aware of the students around him packing their things and shuffling toward the exit. He closed the notebook he'd opened at the beginning of the hour — still new and fresh without a single word written inside — and slid it into his bag before he slung the strap over his shoulder and stood.

He passed the rows of desks until he reached the front. The exit stood open just to his left, but for some reason he glanced right toward the desk where *she* had sat. When he spotted the pen she'd dropped, he paused. He wasn't sure why he bothered, but he neared it slowly, almost cautiously, and bent to retrieve it.

The barrel was cool to the touch and covered with floor dust. Hot pink and infinitely girly, it had sparkled strips running diagonally across the grain. He smoothed his thumb over one sparkled line just as someone passed him and clapped him on the back.

"Hey, Xander man. Try not to make any more girls cry today, will you?"

Logan lifted his face and focused on a guy who'd lived in the same dorm as him their freshman year. "Yeah." He forced an amused smile. "I'll try."

Reggie Oates waved an arm and continued toward the exit. Staring after him, Logan idly shoved the pen into the front pocket of his bag.

He left the room and headed straight to the registrar's department. After waiting in an hour-long line, he dropped World Regional Geography with Presni and headed back outside. It was too late to take another geography class at a different time—the other slots were already full—he'd just have to make up the credits next semester.

If he was still here next semester.

With Trace Zukowski's little sister on campus, he had a feeling the pitchforks and torches wouldn't be far behind, running him off within the week. Maybe within the day. Or the next hour.

Oh, God.

Clenching his teeth, he closed his eyes briefly, panicked what his future—and the rest of his life—held in store for him now. He shoved his way out of the old limestone building, glowering at the flowering ivy growing up the walls, and nearly plowed into a girl hurrying up the wide marble steps. He darted to the side, barely missing her.

She was turned away from him and not paying attention to where she was going. While she glanced behind her as if making sure no one was following, he sucked in a breath.

"Paige," he said, though he couldn't see her face. For some reason, he just knew.

She whirled around, her straight dark hair fluttering out over her shoulders, sending a whiff of her shampoo his way. All spicy and sweet, the mix struck him hard. A wave of awareness cramped his muscles. When she looked up, he couldn't help but notice how pretty she was.

But she obviously didn't return the attraction. Her horrified gasp and wide, frightened eyes, not to mention the way she lurched back with a fearful flinch, pretty much told him she'd just spotted the most ghastly beast on earth.

Helpless anger stole over him. She was going to ruin his life. Before he could even brace himself for the fallout, she'd crush everything he'd worked three years to build. And here she was, acting scared of *him?*

He wanted to grab her and shake her, make her look at the man behind the murderer, and force her to forgive him, tell him it was okay, that she knew he hadn't meant to kill her brother.

"I'm not going to hurt you," he snapped, irrationally insulted by her unnecessary fear.

But when she met his gaze, forgiveness didn't line her wary, darting eyes. Tears did. "Except you already *have*." A frightened tear quivered at the edge of her long lashes.

She was right. Physical pain couldn't match the emotional turmoil he'd put her through. His anger dissolved like sugar in water. Ashamed of himself, he stepped back and tried to swallow the knot in his throat, forcing himself to calm down.

"Look. If you were coming here to drop the class, I already did, okay? You don't have to."

He risked a quick glance up to catch her reaction. She held her book bag in front of her, using it as a barrier against him, even as she lifted her chin, though that only seemed to expose her neck in a more vulnerable way, revealing the rapid beat of her pulse throbbing against tender flesh.

Three years ago, Logan couldn't imagine frightening anyone so completely, especially a girl. But those days were long gone. She looked terrified.

"Did you hear me?" he asked, knowing he sounded brusque, maybe even rude. But he couldn't help it. Seeing her rattled him as much as it obviously did her. He wanted her gone, far and away from Granton.

Though she refused to make eye contact and stared around him as if she still wanted to enter the registrar's building, she nodded with a quick, jerky bob.

"Good," he said, his voice going hoarse. When he felt his chin wobble, he drew in a sharp, horrified breath and added, "I guess that's settled then. We don't share a class any longer; I doubt we'll see each other again. Problem solved."

Her gaze flashed his way, raking him with animosity. And it struck him how her problems were far from solved. Her brother was never coming back, and that was his fault.

He swallowed, his throat so dry he was surprised he didn't choke. He wanted to apologize, but he didn't particularly want her to spit in his face again, so he just stared, waiting.

When she only damned him with her beautiful, dark eyes, he gave in first, jerking his gaze away and blinking rapidly.

"Here," he choked out, grasping at the only thing he could think to provide as a peace offering. He yanked her pen from his bag and thrust it forward. "You dropped this."

She focused on her pen, her eyes dilating with horror.

When she didn't reach for it, he let his hand fall back to his side, feeling like an idiot. "Right," he said, unable to keep the sneer from his voice. "It's tainted now that I've touched it, isn't it?"

He wanted to pound his fists against the injustice of it all, demand that she and the entire world let him back in among the living. The worst part was, though, even if he was welcomed with open arms, he didn't think he could enter, because he knew he didn't deserve normalcy or happiness.

Or forgiveness.

Paige Zukowski sent him one last scathing glower before turning away and dashing down the marble stairs away from the registrar's.

Either she'd decided not to drop the class or she'd return later. In either case, he felt as if he'd actually accomplished a small victory. He wasn't sure why he didn't want her to leave Presni's class when actually he wanted her gone completely, but it had something to do with taking her brother away from her. If he couldn't return Trace, then at least he could step aside so she'd stay in all her classes and attain her college goals.

And maybe in doing so, he'd gain a measure of atonement. Or maybe he was just fooling himself, and he was doomed to live with this guilt for the rest of his life.

Chapter Three

After her second encounter with Logan Xander in the space of two hours, Paige hurried back to her room and missed the rest of her classes on her first day at Granton. Rattled to the core, she camped out on her narrow bed and watched the TV Mariah had brought and set up on Paige's desk, taking up nearly all the space, which would force Paige to do her homework on her bed.

If she stuck around long enough to *have* homework.

God. What was she doing here anyway? This had been Trace's dream, not hers. What did she care about business administration and marketing? And what did she think to accomplish by graduating from *his* college? It wouldn't bring him back.

It wouldn't bring any of them back.

She should just quit now. If her first few minutes on campus were any indication of how the rest of her year would go, she didn't want to suffer through such torment anyway.

But leaving would feel like a defeat. And it would feel like she was giving up on her brother. It'd feel like she was letting Logan Xander win.

That just wasn't acceptable.

Frustrated, angry tears seeped down her cheeks. She wiped at them savagely, cursing their source. After surviving through her brother's death and the funeral her mother had forced her to attend two years later, she would've thought there were no more tears left inside her. But her body just kept producing them, and she blamed each one on the killer who'd invaded Trace's dream school.

She hated Logan Xander, hated him so much. Hated what he'd already done to her. Hated what he was still doing to her. And by all accounts, she didn't even know the first thing about him except he'd been the star basketball player on his high school team and was the son of a lawyer.

It didn't matter. She hated him.

By six that evening, her hate had cooled to a boiling abhorrence. As she paced the floor in front of her bed, she made a decision. She would stay and show everyone—herself included—that she could do this.

So…how was she going to do this? Trace had been a believer in the "keep it simple" motto, so taking it one baby step at a time sounded good. What should she do in the…oh, next five minutes?

When her stomach rumbled, Paige grinned and set her hand over her abdomen. Food was a reasonable step. She hadn't left her room since that morning. Maybe she could go find something to eat. But with a glance toward her door, she shuddered.

Maybe a nice, calming shower would help her build up the nerve to leave her room. Wrapping her toiletries inside her towel, she carried her things into the bathroom and glanced toward the opposite door that led into another room. Her suitemates, Mariah had said. Paige hadn't even known what a suitemate *was* until yesterday, and she apparently had two whom she'd yet to meet.

She took the shortest shower in the history of showers. The temperature of the water changed constantly from scorching to freezing. She had to keep her hand on the control knob even as she lathered and rinsed. It reminded her of her back and forth feelings about whether to stay or leave campus.

After she turned the water off, she stood with her face upturned to the showerhead and her eyes closed as she tried to control the anxiety still plaguing her.

What if she saw him again?

Could she handle that?

Maybe Kayla was right. Coming here had been a mistake. This was a sign, clearly telling her she'd made an extremely bad move. She should just return home to Creighton County tonight, enroll for fall classes at the community college there, and work toward a degree in education. That was probably what she would've done anyway if her family had remained whole and half the members hadn't died on her. She liked kids, liked watching them learn and grasp new concepts. She could've been a grade school teacher. And most of all, she could've stayed close to her safe, comfortable home.

Except her home hadn't felt safe or comfortable for three years now.

Thanks to Logan Vance Xander.

With her emotions bubbling back to the surface, Paige ripped the shower curtain open and reached for the towel she'd left folded on the toilet seat. She snapped it open to wrap around her just as the door from her suitemates' room opened.

With a startled shriek, she covered herself and leaped back into the tub. The wet floor made her slip but she caught herself against the wall.

"Oh my God!" The intruder's red curls bobbed madly as she jerked to a stop. "I'm so sorry. I didn't know anyone was in here."

Paige closed her eyes and pressed her hand against her pounding heart to keep her towel from slipping. Her face heated as she croaked, "I forgot to lock the door."

The redhead instantly began to retreat. "No problem. I'll just... yeah." The bathroom door was quickly shut, leaving a streaming wet Paige alone again.

Though it was too late to worry about lost privacy now, Paige reached out and locked her door. Then she dried herself and her shampoo and soap bottles at warp speed before jerking into her clothes. She barely remembered to turn the handle on her suitemates' room to unlock it again before she fled back into her own.

A few seconds later, her bathroom locked from the inside, telling her the suitemate was now using it. A minute after that, the toilet flushed.

Paige was still blushing over the whole encounter, trying not to feel like such a stupid idiot, when a soft knock came from the bathroom.

Ready to be degraded for her forgetfulness, she hesitantly inched it open.

The redhead inside grinned at her sheepishly. "I'm sorry again," she said. "I really didn't mean to barge in on you like that."

Paige brushed the apology aside. "It's okay. Don't worry. I'm sorry for forgetting to lock the door."

The girl laughed out a full, jovial sound, her blue eyes dancing. "Oh, don't worry about that. I've been so afraid of forgetting to lock it myself and being caught with my pants down, I actually had a nightmare about it last night." She laughed again. "I'm glad you did it first. At least, now I know I'm not the only clueless freshman around. I mean, not that you're clueless, or a freshman. Or—" Her brow puckered as if she was frantically trying to think up another reason to beg for forgiveness.

Paige laughed. The sound felt foreign coming from her throat, it almost startled her, and it did tickle her vocal chords. But this perky redhead made her feel lighter. Freer.

"I *am* a freshman," she confessed with a rueful grin. "And pretty much clueless too. I'm Paige."

She stuck out her hand. The other girl began to reach for her fingers but froze at the last second. "Eww. I haven't washed my hands yet. Sorry. Can I use your—"

Instead of waiting for permission, Red darted around Paige and into her room, immediately making herself at home at the sink, dousing her palms with hand soap and scrubbing them clean. Once she finished, she turned back to Paige with a refreshed grin, and initiated another shake.

"There. Tess Simpson," she said. "Pleased to meet you."

They shook at last, and Paige found herself grinning again at the overly dramatic show of formality Tess put into the greeting.

"You have such a neat, clean room," Tess said, dropping her hand as she glanced around. "My roommate is a total slob. We haven't even been here twenty-four hours yet and she's strewn clothes all over the floor. And, oh my God—" She paused when she spotted Mariah's television on Paige's desk. "You have, like, the biggest TV I have ever seen! Ours is microscopic compared to this. Bailey would just die if she saw—" Without finishing the sentiment, she flew back into the bathroom, calling, "Bailey! You have to see this thing." She pushed open both doors wide only to return to Paige's room.

"It's got to have a fifty-inch screen, I swear to God. Ours is only twenty-two."

The grumbling started before Bailey appeared in Paige's room as well. "Tess, I can't get my ring tone to—oh my God." She froze in the middle of Paige's room beside her roommate to ogle Mariah's television, her cell phone forgotten in her hands. "It's like the Mecca of dorm-room televisions." She turned to Paige, looking dazed. "I so want your TV right now. Hell, I'll trade you Tess for it."

Paige shifted, suddenly uncomfortable. She hadn't even thought of the television's size past how much it hogged all her desk space. Sitcoms, game shows, reality TV, none of those had really reached her in the past couple of years. It felt strange to see someone ooh and awe over the mundane.

"Actually, it's my roommate's." She shrugged. "She just put it on my desk so she could see it from her bed. But she doesn't care if I watch it when she's away."

"Well, that's sweet." Bailey nodded with approval. "You get to watch the roomie's boob tube without the annoying roomie around."

"Hey." Tess frowned at her, slapping her hands to her generous hips. "Is that some kind of dig at *your* roommate?"

Bailey blinked, appearing dumbfounded by the question. She hooked a thumb over her shoulder, motioning to Paige. "No. It was a dig at *her* roommate."

"Oh." Tess immediately brightened and sent Paige a commiserating look. "I do feel sorry for you. We met her yesterday before you arrived. And she seemed a little…"

They all three glanced at each other, and Paige knew exactly what the other two girls were thinking. She felt a sudden kinship with them as she snickered. "Yeah. I noticed."

She clearly remembered the wrinkled-nose look of disdain on Mariah's expression after Paige had declined Mariah's invitation to go to the clubs together last night.

"Thanks, but I think I'll get a good night's sleep before the first day of school," Paige had politely answered.

And Mariah had snorted, making a prude face. "Aww, you're a good girl, aren't you? That's so…sickening." Then she'd dragged her boyfriend across the room to the door, calling, "Don't wait up, grandma," before disappearing until the wee hours.

"When she found out we were both freshman, she gagged aloud and asked if the entire building was infested with us." Tess's eyes grew big as she nodded, drawing Paige from her memories. "And, yeah, she actually used the word *infested* like we're some kind of bug."

"I told her not to breathe too deeply because we might be contagious," Bailey added with a grin.

Bailey and Tess laughed, nudging each other with self-congratulations.

Noticing the easy companionship between them, Paige studied them a little more closely. "Did you two know each other before coming to Granton?"

"Oh, sure." Bailey slung her arm around Tess's shoulder. "We've gone to school together since Kindergarten."

Tess tipped her cheek toward Bailey's. "We're actually best friends when she cares to claim me."

Envy nipped at Paige as she watched them hug. "I wish I could've been able to do that."

She missed Kayla already and wished she could've convinced her to come to Granton too. But not only was Kayla totally against the idea of Granton, she had no use for any college at all. She'd worked as a waitress ever since she'd graduated from high school and acted as if she was perfectly satisfied right where she was.

Bailey skimmed her gaze over Paige's still-wet hair. "So you're the one Tess just caught naked in the shower, huh?"

"Bailey!" Tess squawked, blushing. "Oh my God. How many times have we talked about your subtlety issues? Besides, I didn't *see* anything. She had a big, fluffy towel on."

Not sure whether to duck her head in embarrassment or slap her hands over her ears from the overwhelming inflow of conversation, Paige mumbled, "Yeah, that was me."

Then her stomach growled, butting in on the conversation, and all three of them laughed. It wasn't that humorous really, but with these two around, everything seemed suddenly entertaining. She couldn't recall feeling so carefree in a long, long time.

"Hey, we were about to head down to Gibson Hall and scrounge up some supper," Tess said. "Want to come with us?"

She murmured her acceptance, even as she swallowed down a rash of tears.

It had been forever since she'd felt like a part of anything. Aside from Kayla, she'd been disjointed from reality since Trace's death. She hadn't cared about clothes, or televisions sizes, or much of anything. Tess and Bailey's overly easy acceptance of her was too touching to properly digest.

Tucking her still-damp hair behind her ear, she snagged her room key and student ID and followed them out the door. She didn't even remember Logan Xander's existence until she stepped into the warm evening air.

Then everything came flooding back. With a vengeance.

She faltered behind Tess and Bailey, scanning left and right to make sure she couldn't spot him nearby.

Bailey glanced back at her and paused. "You coming?"

Not spying the murderer anywhere, Paige nodded and forced a smile. "Uh, yeah. Right behind you." But when she followed, she did so with reservation, all her carefree emotions from a moment before shattered and blown away.

Baby steps, she reminded herself, as she forced her feet to follow her new friends. If she could get past supper, she would already be closer to attaining her goals.

If, being the key word.

Chapter Four

Logan headed straight to Gibson Hall as soon as he clocked out at the juice bar. He'd worked through lunch, and after serving other people drinks and snacks this afternoon, he was starved.

His muscles ached too. All morning, he'd tensed up every time he'd entered a classroom. After running into Paige Zukowski twice, he'd waited until the last possible second, then slipped in right before the class started to scan the faces first and make sure they didn't share another course together before he tiptoed to a seat. He'd looked for her when he exited every building and had even held his breath whenever he spotted a dark-headed girl getting into his line at the juice bar.

Almost too hungry and exhausted to care where she was now, he entered the campus's main student dining hall, ready to visit just about every food station they had to offer. He paused in line at the door to pay his entrance fee. He pulled a thin wad of cash from his pocket, wondering not for the first time if he should've roomed in a dorm this year. Meals had been free here when he'd been a dorm resident his freshman year.

But so much close proximity to so many other people had nearly suffocated him. Three years ago, he'd actually been looking forward to living with a large group and maybe trying to get into his dad's old fraternity. But one fateful night had changed all that. These days, he couldn't handle crowds. It would be too easy to hurt someone else.

After a year of surviving in the dorms, he'd rented an apartment and rested a little easier with his solitude.

"Yo! Designated Dave," a voice called as soon as he paid his discounted student price.

Since Dave was what pretty much everyone called him, Logan lifted his face to acknowledge the greeting. Jerod, a member of Phi Gamma Delta, drew near with a welcoming grin, holding out his hand to fist bump with Logan.

Having given up trying to correct people that his name was not Dave, Logan obligingly rapped his knuckles against Jerod's. "What's up?"

"We're having our Fiji Islander this Saturday and need to hire a DD. You in?"

Logan nodded. "Yeah, sure. I don't have to work at The Squeeze that night, so, I'll be around."

He'd purposely asked for the first weekend of school off at work. That was when all the raging parties took place. And there were never enough willing people to stay sober and play the responsible designated driver for them.

"Cool, man. Thanks. You're a life saver."

Jerod took off again without sticking around to make small talk. Not that Logan minded. He'd grown used to the whole loner thing. If he didn't play the dopey DD at every mixer on campus, he doubted anyone would bother talking to him at all or even know who he was — wrong name or not.

He shuffled a step forward in the pizza buffet line behind a group of jock-looking guys discussing the next football game. Logan didn't listen as he scanned the crowded tables, scouting for an empty place to sit once he filled his plate.

Skimming his gaze past a small round table where three girls sat, he did a double take when glossy black hair captured his attention.

Paige Zukowski picked at her salad and side of fruit like a girl with no appetite. Sitting between two other ladies who talked animatedly around her, she listened to their conversation without adding a lot of input.

He wondered how well she knew them. Had she already told them about him? Had word spread far?

Jerod obviously hadn't known; otherwise Logan doubted the fraternity brother would've asked him to DD. But who *did* know?

His muscles seized as more tension filled him. A headache was beginning to throb behind his eyes. Watching Paige, he scowled, wanting to hate her.

He didn't know a thing about her. But that didn't matter. She was going to ruin him as surely as he'd ruined her when he'd taken her brother away. He deserved it, yeah, but he didn't have to like it.

He'd thought all afternoon of where he'd go next, but his mind kept coming up blank. He didn't want to leave Granton yet.

A girl with a wild mess of curly red hair said something to Paige, making her smile shyly. Color heightened the tops of her cheeks as she gave a soft blush. Logan sucked in a breath, unable to look away.

Damn, she was pretty, no matter who she was.

Tucking a piece of her long, dark hair behind her ear, she nodded and answered the redhead. He couldn't hear anything they were saying over the racket in the busy dining hall and from his distance away, but he really didn't need to. She didn't seem all that familiar around her acquaintances. They must've just met.

He hoped she wasn't comfortable enough to tell them about her brother's murderer whom she'd almost shared a class with earlier in the day.

He froze, petrified, when she glanced toward the line of people waiting to sample the pizza buffet.

She didn't spot him, thank God, before she turned to say something to the girl with the multi-colored hair. Maybe his ball cap had helped disguise him. He had no idea, but he considered it a close call. Too close.

"Hey, it's your turn." A finger poked him in the back, reminding him where he was.

Logan stepped aside to let the guy pass him. "Go ahead. I'm not hungry."

Ducking his chin, he hurried for the exit. Once he made it to the outside air, he stopped to close his eyes, drawing in a deep breath.

Frustrated curses rose in his throat. Seeing her three times in one day was not good. If this was how the rest of the semester was going to progress, he was screwed.

Digging back into his pocket, he counted his cash and wondered where he could go near campus to get a two-dollar meal. With a sigh, he shoved the pair of bills back into his pants and decided it was going to be another ramen noodle night.

Oh, the joy.

Didn't matter. At least he was still here. He hadn't caught any rumor about his past, and no one had chased him off campus. That was something to celebrate.

One day down, only six hundred and thirty left to go—give or take a few—before he could graduate and leave of his own free will.

Chapter Five

Paige's second day at Granton went much smoother than the first. She actually attended every class on her schedule, and she didn't spot any tall guys with nearly-shaved heads anywhere. But every time she left her building, her gaze continued to dart back and forth, searching for him, knowing he was out there somewhere. Too close for comfort.

When she didn't spot him again by the end of the first week, she finally began to relax—at least, she didn't flinch whenever she saw a guy out of the corner of her eye. She made her decision to stay permanent and official by hopping online and scouting for a decent part-time job.

Tess and Bailey invited her to eat with them each evening, and she looked forward to that. But she didn't grow any closer to her roommate, Mariah.

Paige had assumed that the guy Mariah was with the first day was her boyfriend. But now she had no idea who that dude had been. Mariah went out every night that first week…with a different guy each time. And she'd only stayed in one evening, which had been to lead some aggie boy in a cowboy hat, boots, and a big belt buckle to her bed, where they'd made sounds under the covers that Paige wanted to erase from her memory for the rest of her life.

She didn't like to judge, but she was a little scandalized her room-mate could be such a ho-bag and act so proud of it.

On the first weekend of the semester, Mariah dressed up in a long grass skirt, a fake coconut bra, and sandals. She'd looped half a dozen leis around her neck before she trooped out the door, snidely telling Paige to have a good night *reading.*

Since Paige really had planned on reading, she knocked on Tess and Bailey's door to engage them in a little non-ho-bag fun just to spite Mariah, only to learn her suitemates were leaving to head home for the weekend.

So she stayed up late watching TV by herself instead of crack-ing open her book. Mariah hadn't made it back by midnight, which didn't surprise Paige in the least. She climbed into a comfortable pair of jammies, doused the lights, and hit her pillow. She wanted to call Kayla, just to hear her voice but knew her friend would be able to detect Paige's loneliness, so she nixed that idea.

Staring at the dark ceiling above her, she lay in bed, wondering what she'd do with a marketing degree. Like magic, the boring subject rendered her unconscious almost immediately.

A loud thud tore her from troubling dreams where she'd just walked into some hazy corporate office wearing nothing but a bra and panties while everyone else in three-piece suits gawked and laughed at her. Instantly awake, she tightened every muscle in her body as a strange scratching followed, accompanied by high-pitched giggles.

"Here. Let me." A muffled male voice joined the muddled sounds, stopping the eerie scratch.

Orienting herself, Paige realized she was hearing a key in her door lock. Mariah must be home. With company. Again.

She craned her neck to get a glimpse of her alarm clock.

Three a.m.

"Whoa. No, don't sit down out here, Mariah. I almost got you inside. Just wait a second."

The door floated open. The light from the hallway blared against Paige's face where she lay. Wincing, she drew up the blanket enough to shade her eyes. But curiosity caused her to peek out, hoping to catch a glimpse of the stranger bringing her roommate home tonight. Mariah did tend to draw a lot of hotties; Paige would give her that. If nothing else, the continuous stream of guys Mariah paraded through their room was nice eye candy.

Though she could see out of her hole in the blanket, she doubted anyone could see in simply because of the way she'd covered her head. She could freely gawk at tonight's hottie without anyone being the wiser.

The figure of a guy took Mariah's arm and carefully looped it over his shoulder. He wrapped one hand around her waist and walked her into the room. She slumped against him, her cheek pressed flush to his shoulder.

Wow, that must've been some party. Paige had never seen her roommate quite this wasted before. Weekends apparently brought out the best in Mariah.

Still wearing her Hawaiian-theme costume, Mariah giggled as she tried to take the plastic garlands from around her own neck to loop them over the guy's.

"There. You just got leied." She tittered at her own pun.

Enough hall light flashed over their faces for Paige to see Mariah being nearly carried to her bed by Logan Xander. She stopped breathing, though her blanket literally covered her from head to toe. Embarrassed, vulnerable heat coated her body like a rash. She could not believe he was in her bedroom standing mere *inches* away from where she lay in her pajamas.

"Thanks for bringing me home, Dave," Mariah cooed, nearly drooling on him as she pressed her face so close to his. "I 'ppreciate it *sooo* much."

Dave? Paige squinted, hoping she was wrong and her brother's murderer wasn't really in her dorm room about to sleep with her roommate.

He sounded winded as he wheezed, "Well, it's my job." He took her wrist, unwrapped her arm from around his head and gently lowered her onto her bed against the far wall — away from Paige's bed, and yet way too close to Paige's bed.

Paige saw his face clearly as he shifted, and there was no way he was this Dave character Mariah mistook him for. He was definitely Logan Xander.

"I don't understand why you're always the DD at every party," Mariah slurred, plopping down so hard she dragged him onto the mattress right along with her.

He grunted as he landed. "Someone has to be." He tried to untangle himself, but Mariah wrapped her arms around his neck, only ensnaring him more. "I should get back," he added desperately.

Relieved he wasn't going to start groping her roommate, Paige winced when Mariah caught his arm and pulled him to her. "Kiss me, Dave."

He drew his face back hard, turning his mouth away from hers as he tried unsuccessfully to unclamp her hands from him. "No. Stop it. *Mariah!* Your roommate is like five feet away."

"Who cares? She'd dead asleep."

Logan gave an uneasy laugh. "Yeah, I somehow doubt that."

"So *what*," Mariah tossed out defiantly, once again moving in, trying to force a kiss. "It'd be good for the innocent little virgin. We could teach her a few things about the birds and the bees."

"No thanks." Logan struggled with renewed fury to free himself. "Trust me. I'm no tutor."

The light from the opened door leading out in the bright hallway sprayed directly on him, and from her spying spot, Paige could see his face clearly. He looked almost scared in his frantic struggle to escape Mariah.

"I said no," he growled, finally using just enough force to push himself away from her. Instead of shoving her back though, he propelled himself off the side of Mariah's bed and landed on the floor with a thump.

Mariah scowled down at him. "What the hell is your problem? I'm throwing myself at you here, Dave."

"I'm sorry." He sounded truly apologetic as he glanced at the floor between his sprawled legs. "I just…don't want to."

"So you never drink. You never kiss girls. What do you do then?" She tipped her head sideways as she studied him. "You do like girls, don't you?"

Logan looked up at her, and the expression on his face had Paige holding her breath. She couldn't remember if she'd ever seen anyone look so tormented before. Watching him made her chest tighten as if she actually shared his agony with him. For a split second, she hurt. For him. For both of them.

His voice sounded rusted over when he answered. "Yes, I like girls."

Paige's body heat ratcheted to an unbearable temperature. She wanted to shove the suffocating blankets off her she was so hot. But there was no way she was uncovering herself with him around.

"Then why don't I ever *see* you with any?" Mariah reached out slowly, almost gently and touched his hair, running her fingers over the short, sandy, prickled strands. "You're the best looking guy on campus. I'm sure girls throw themselves at you constantly. Why don't you ever take what's offered?"

Tipping his head away from her touch, Logan cleared his throat and mumbled his answer.

Paige had to strain her ears to hear.

"Because I don't deserve it."

Her breath caught in her chest. Had he really just confessed that?

He pushed himself to his feet and dusted off his jeans. "My name isn't Dave, you know?" Then he turned away and walked out of Paige's view.

Blood pounded through her veins, whooshing though her eardrums so loudly she couldn't hear his footsteps. But she knew he must've stopped because the light from the hall continued to shine into the room.

Curious as to what he was doing, Paige shifted just enough to see him again. He'd stopped with his back to both beds and stood in front of Paige's desk, or rather in front of the four-by-six picture sitting beside the television. In the portrait, she and Trace posed for the camera, giving each other bunny ears as they tilted their heads together and grinned.

Realizing he must now know who Mariah's roommate was, Paige held her breath and let the blanket fall from her face, revealing herself.

Slowly, he turned, as if something beyond his power was forcing him around.

When their gazes met, a shockwave of emotion passed through her. She hated him more than she thought it was possible to hate, because for a brief moment, he'd actually made her feel sorry for him. He'd actually made her respect him.

Unlike her father, he hadn't turned to alcohol to deal with his problems. He'd done the opposite, becoming the sober designated driver. And he'd freely admitted he'd done something worthy of never deserving happiness again. He seemed remorseful as if he wanted to somehow make up for his past sins.

After living for three years in a house where no one wanted to deal with their problems, she was awestruck by the courage and strength it must take for Logan Xander to admit daily he was flawed and for him to actually do something to correct his character.

But she didn't want to feel awe or respect for him. She wanted to keep hating him. Blaming him.

He stared at her, looking frozen and vulnerable, his eyes large and his bottom lip occasionally jerking.

This boy was capable of murder, of murder with his bare hands. He'd killed her brother with a single punch, the force of his fist knocking Trace unconscious until he'd fallen backward and landed on the ground where he'd split his head open against a broken bottle.

Trace had been strong too, so much stronger than Paige. And if Logan Xander could outmuscle him, who knew how much damage he could do to her?

But she didn't experience an iota of fear. She glared at him, daring him to come at her, to attack, to try to hurt her more than he already had.

"Dave?" Mariah called, sounding confused.

He glanced at Paige's roommate before he tripped backward and bolted for the door, slamming it behind him.

Paige shuddered and squeezed her eyes closed, telling herself it had all been a horrible, awful dream. She hadn't just felt sorry for Logan Xander. She hadn't respected him, and she never would.

"What a strange guy," Mariah mused from her bed.

As snoring rose almost immediately from the other side of the room, Paige pulled her blanket back over her head and squeezed her eyes shut, but hot tears of humiliation still managed to trickle through the cracks of her sealed eyelids. Mad at herself for the complete malfunction of her emotions, she brought up a picture of Trace in her head. He was nine and she was six, maybe seven, and he grinned up at her from the base of a tree as he held open his arms. *Go ahead and jump, Pay Day. I'll catch you.*

Love for her lost brother helped her antagonism for his killer level itself back to healthy proportions. Settled once again in her bitter comfort zone of animosity and blame, she fell asleep with no more dreams for the rest of the night.

Chapter Six

"Is that your boyfriend?"

The question yanked Paige's attention to her two suitemates as nothing else could. "What?"

Her second week at Granton had gone much better than the first. Dr. Presni still glanced warily at her every time he started Geography class, no doubt expecting her to run away weeping again, but she kept her expression blank and her attention alert. And everything seemed to go okay.

Her classes progressed without a hitch, except maybe Chemistry. She did not get chemical equations at all. She'd only enrolled in the core requirements this semester and hadn't actually taken a "marketing" seminar yet. She kind of dreaded the day when it came to that. Marketing wasn't in her blood. But if fulfilling Trace's dreams were the only way to keep a piece of him alive inside her, she'd learn the marketing world, scraping by until her fingers bled.

"Wow." Tess snagged the picture Bailey had been holding and pulled it to her face for a closer study. "He's freaking gorgeous. What's his name?"

A white hot needle of pain and memories pierced her chest as she watched her suitemates play tug-a-war over the framed photo. "Thanks, but…no. That's not a boyfriend. He…he's my brother. Trace."

She had invited the two over to watch a movie after supper since she'd finished all her homework and wanted a little company. Since they still talked about how much they loved Mariah's television, they'd readily accepted. But now, she wasn't so certain if having them around was a good idea, not with them both ogling her picture of Trace.

She'd yet to tell anyone in Granton about him or about any fragment of her life, really. And it had been nice. She could pretend to be a normal college student with a normal past full of two normal parents and a normal, live sibling.

With no murderers lurking in any of her classes any longer, she'd been able to pass herself off as a real girl.

But she couldn't pretend forever.

"He died a few years ago."

Both Bailey and Tess lifted their faces to gape at her, their mouths dropping open in harmonized horror.

"Oh my God, how awful." Tess quickly set the picture back where it had been resting on top of the desk.

"Geesh." Her face bright red, Bailey stuffed her hands into her back pockets and shifted her weight from one foot to the other. "I…I'm sorry."

Paige shrugged, practically tasting the awkwardness in the air and regretting that she'd opened her mouth. "It's okay. It happened three years ago."

She decided not to bring up her mom, or her dad's addiction, or Logan Xander's existence. One uncomfortable issue at a time.

"Hey, you know, there's this guy in my World History class," Tess blurted out. "Kevin. He's super cute. Dark brown eyes. Wispy blond hair." She sighed with longing as she fanned herself. "Give me minute here."

Bailey rolled her eyes. "Okay, if that's your idea of a conversation changer, it kind of sucks, hon."

"No, no." Tess blushed and waved at Paige to make her listen. "I actually have a point. Anyway, I built up the nerve to, you know, talk to him today before class started. When I asked if he was going to movie night out on the football field tomorrow, he said he couldn't because — " she grinned and wiggled her eyebrows, letting Paige know she was finally making her way to the point of her story " — he has grief group every Tuesday night at seven over in the Crimson Room of the Student Union."

Bailey opened her mouth again, but Tess hushed her by slapping her hand over her friend's mouth, all without taking her attention off Paige. "When I asked what grief group was, he said it was this student organization for people who've lost loved ones. He was really excited about it and told me how much it had helped him." She shrugged. "I guess he lost his dad in a car accident when he was eight."

"That's awful." Paige knew how crushing it was to lose a parent. But she'd been a teen and somewhat self-sufficient by the time she'd been abandoned. Her mom had virtually disappeared from her life before she'd actually died. But poor Kevin with the dark brown eyes and wispy blond hair had been so young and probably very dependent upon his father.

"Yeah, well…" Tess motioned uneasily to the image of Trace. "Maybe you'd like this group too." She flushed. "I mean, I hope that wasn't too intrusive or anything. I only thought—"

"No." Paige stopped Tess's blustering with a big smile. "I think it sounds great. I'll give it a try."

In high school, everyone had pushed her toward counseling, but talking about her pain, sharing her story with anyone else, had just been too much. But hearing Logan Xander openly admit his haunted feelings to Mariah had shaken her. She couldn't bear the thought of him being more courageous than her, of embracing his suffering and accepting it when she couldn't do the same.

She wanted to be better off than he was, and if counseling got her there, she'd at least try it.

Tess looked surprised. "Really?"

With a nervous laugh, Paige nodded. "Sure."

When she didn't say anything else, Tess cleared her throat. Bailey ducked her head and drew a circle on the carpet with the toe of her shoe.

Wishing she could bring the buoyancy back into the room, Paige opened her mouth to say something silly, but nothing came to mind. Grasping her cross amulet, she ran her thumb over the smooth surface of the ruby.

Bailey looked up and glanced around until she spotted a microwave sitting on top of a plastic crate. "Is that yours?"

"No." Relieved for a shift in topics, Paige slid open a drawer in her desk and yanked up a package of movie theater butter microwavable

Orville Redenbacher. "But the popcorn is." She winked and put on a great, goofy grin. "So…you guys want some?"

"Hells yeah." Bailey snagged up the TV remote and clicked on the channel guide. "You make the food, and we'll see if there's anything good playing."

And just like that, the tension oozed out of the room.

As Bailey manned the remote, Tess camped out on Paige's bed, making herself at home. She flipped open the novel Paige had left on her mattress while Paige popped the bag into the microwave. "Is this any good? I haven't read it yet."

Paige glanced over and shrugged. "It's okay. But I liked the first book in the series better."

"Oh, I loved that one too!"

Bailey paused her channel surfing to see what book they were discussing. "I heard the third one's the best, but I can't imagine why. Caleb's the hero in that story, and he's a total tool."

Realizing they shared a love for the same type of books, Paige gave a big internal sigh and relaxed even more. By the time their snack was ready, they'd found an old movie they all wanted to watch.

Twenty minutes later, Tess stuffed her mouth with a handful of popcorn. "I still can't believe he died from cancer. He was such a good dancer."

From the floor where she'd stretched out, Bailey tossed a popped kernel into the air and caught it in her mouth. "How in the world does good dancing have anything to do with not getting cancer?"

Tess shrugged, looking momentarily puzzled. "Hmm. I don't know."

Paige grinned and tucked her knees up toward her chest where she was sitting against the wall. "If I went to summer camp with my family, I think I'd fall for the dance instructor too. Especially if he looked like a young Patrick Swayze."

"I'd totally jump his bones in that water scene where he teaches Baby how to do the leap. He looked so hot all wet and slippery."

"Oh whatever." Bailey chucked popcorn at Tess, catching her in the cheek. "You so would not. You can't even talk to a guy without blushing and blabbering like a baboon."

Instead of growing irritated, Tess merely shrugged and picked the popcorn off her shirt to toss it into her mouth. "Okay, so I wouldn't jump him. But I'd totally dream about it."

Paige laughed. "Yeah," she agreed. "Me too."

After *Dirty Dancing*, they found the original *Footloose* playing on another channel and started to watch it.

It had nearly finished when the door to her room opened and Mariah stumbled in, a new guy plastered to her as he kissed her throat, leaving a trail of hickies in his wake. Paige held her breath until she saw his face. When she made sure he wasn't Logan Xander, she finally exhaled.

"Whoa," Bailey yelped, jumping to her feet and dodging out of the way to keep from getting trampled. "People here!"

Mariah lifted her face. "Oh, good. The freshmen have gathered." She giggled at them and fisted a handful of the boy's shirt, tugging him close, while he ducked his head and nibbled on her ear. "Ready for a different kind of Granton education, girlies?"

She and her boy-toy stumbled to her bed and fell onto the mattress, neither coming up for air. Paige cleared her throat and winced apologetically.

"Sorry. I…she…"

"Want to come to our room and stay the night?" Bailey asked over the sounds of sucking lips and disturbing moans.

Paige didn't hesitate. "Yes." She snatched her pillow and the top cover off her bed. Clutching them close, she followed Bailey and Tess through the bathroom and into their room.

The scent of apple cinnamon candles wafted out to greet her and enfold her with a warm, unpretentious feel. She felt like she'd come home. Both girls had pictures posted to their walls of family and friends from home.

Tess and Bailey chipped in an extra blanket each for her to build a nest on the floor, and it ended up actually being comfortable once Bailey shoved all her dirty laundry out of the way.

Even after they turned out the lights, the three of them continued to talk and make jokes. Paige had a feeling she'd be staying over here a lot.

"So how many times has she brought some random guy back to your room to screw him in front of you?" Bailey asked.

Paige sighed. "Too many for my taste. Though usually they have the decency to turn out the lights first."

Tess sighed wistfully—at least Paige assumed it was Tess since she couldn't picture the ever-sarcastic Bailey making such a longing sound. "You know, I'm kind of jealous of her."

"Of what?" Bailey squawked. "Possibly catching an STD or risking pregnancy every other night?"

"I don't know. Of her freedom, I guess. Her confidence. Her vivacity. I wish I could just flirt with any guy I found attractive."

"You could," Bailey's dry voice answered. "You just gotta do it."

Paige didn't join the conversation. But she had to side with Tess on this one. Though Mariah's personality rubbed her the wrong way, she did kind of wish she had that kind of confidence. She wished she wasn't so afraid of her own shadow. She wished she could be bold.

With her own wistful sigh, Paige stared up at the ceiling, barely making out light shadows coming in through the windows from the streetlamps outside.

She stayed awake awhile, listening to the muffled sounds of Mariah and her friend soaking through the thin wall.

For some reason, she thought of Logan Xander.

She wondered what it would have been like to listen to *him* and Mariah together if he hadn't turned Mariah down the night he'd brought her home.

For the most part, listening to Mariah "entertain" was straight up disgusting. But occasionally, some of the sighs and gasps she heard had made Paige warm in the most uncomfortable places, made her wonder what exactly was happening over there on the bed located less than ten feet from her own.

Would Logan have made the more interesting sounds or would he have made the disgusting ones?

She slammed her eyes closed, commanding herself to *never* wonder that again.

If only he wasn't so attractive, though. If only Trace had permanently disfigured him or disabled him before he'd been killed. Logan Xander didn't deserve looks that made him in any way appealing, that made her want to stroke him when he looked sad.

Monsters weren't supposed to come in pretty packages.

But even with his hair buzzed so close to his perfectly shaped skull, his facial features were utterly compelling. And his body? Sweet

Lord. There was no way to deny he had a nice body, all tall and sleek and graceful. Like Channing Tatum hot.

She groaned to herself and wrapped an arm over her closed eyes, hoping to dispel the image of him sitting on the floor by Mariah's bed a few nights before. He'd looked so vulnerable, so touchable. Lost and alone. Why did she always feel compelled to comfort tortured souls? She *wanted* Logan Xander to be tortured, to stay tortured.

For the rest of his life.

When she finally fell into a troubled sleep, she dreamed of him. He sat on the floor by *her* bed and looked up at her with troubled eyes that begged her to help him.

Coerced by a force she couldn't control, she reached out to touch his face. His skin was warm. Real.

A pleasant heat traveled up her arm and stirred an achy tightness in her chest.

When she gasped awake, dawn was barely beginning to filter in through the closed window blinds. Tess and Bailey lay sprawled on their beds. From her pile on the floor, Paige wept silently, horrified by the direction of her dream.

Feeling as if she'd just betrayed her brother, she folded Bailey and Tess's blankets and dragged her own back to her room.

Mariah's visitor had left, so Paige quickly gathered her shower supplies and spent the next half hour bawling under a scorching hot stream, trying to scrub the disturbing images in her sleep from her very soul.

Chapter Seven

Logan showed up half an hour early to his Tuesday night meeting. The group's counselor had already arrived and was setting the last folding chair in the center of the room to form a complete circle.

Samantha grinned when she saw him. "There's my helper. Early as usual."

He waved a brief hello. "Hey, Sam. Want me to set up the refreshment table?"

She snorted. "Have I ever turned down your offer of help before? I think we'll only need one though. They're having a movie night in the stadium, which will probably lower our turnout."

Logan nodded and got to work. He found a long table folded in a nearby closet. He lugged it into the Crimson Room and pulled open the legs, and situated it where Sam wanted it to go. Setting the paper bag he'd brought on top, he unloaded the baked goods inside.

"Mmm." Sam paused by him to breathe in the aroma. "Did you bring something from The Squeeze again?"

He nodded. "I just came from work. Gus was going to throw the blueberry muffins out, and they're only a day old."

His boss didn't believe in letting anything go stale. Gus refreshed his small stock of pastries daily. Logan often made a complete meal from the free castoffs, which was helpful during those times when his grocery fund was exhausted.

"Bless him." Sam snatched a muffin and moaned as she chewed.

Logan watched her, amused by the exaggerated way she let her eyes roll into the back of her head. As the leader of the group, she was the only non-student. He didn't think she could be much older than thirty, but he could detect a sprinkling of gray in her dark hair, probably from the stress of losing her husband two years before, which left her raising two young sons by herself, working a full time job, and still slotting in a couple hours each week to lead this group.

He came early to help her set up as much as he was able.

"Is there anything else you need me to do?" he asked.

"Nope." Sam picked up a napkin and dabbed her mouth. "I think we're good to go."

Not the answer he wanted to hear. He preferred to stay busy. With nothing to do, his mind tended to wander, and it never strayed toward good memories. Not anymore.

Though he wasn't a fan of idle conversation, he forced a tense smile and asked, "How are the boys?"

Thankfully, Samantha loved to talk about her children. She went off onto an entertaining tangent about the latest potty training adventures with her youngest. "The kid's almost four years old," she said, completely exasperated. "At this rate, I swear, he's going to graduate from college in diapers."

The image actually induced an amused grin to quirk one side of Logan's mouth.

When another girl arrived, Sam stole one more muffin and meandered to the circle to greet her while Logan lingered by the refreshment table, helping set food out whenever someone brought more in.

Just about everyone who arrived called a friendly greeting to him. He waved an acknowledgement back but didn't engage anyone in conversation. It was nice they all knew him as Logan — not Dave — but he purposely kept himself a step removed from the other members of the group, mainly because he was a fraud.

He felt guilty he hadn't shared a personal story the way everyone else had shared theirs. Then again, he didn't have a story of loss to share, so that was never going to happen anyway.

The truth was he was using them, using their personal accounts to heal himself while he gave nothing in return. And that made him feel vile. Just not vile enough to leave and never come back. Without them, he knew he'd be worse off than he was. So he kept returning each week, complete fake that he was.

"Anything good to eat tonight?" a voice asked beside him.

Logan glanced around to spot Kevin Lloyd, who'd lost his dad when he was eight.

"I've been eyeing those wrap things," Logan answered. "Jamie just brought them."

Kevin took two for himself. "Oh, God. These are amazing." He moaned between bites. "Jamie sure can cook. But then, she's a culinary major, isn't she?"

Logan eyed the blonde they were discussing as she sat in the circle talking to another girl. "English," he corrected.

Kevin frowned. "Really? Well, she *should* have a culinary degree." He licked his fingers clean and reached for another wrap when something caught his eye on the other side of the room. "Whoa! Dude, check it out. New girl." He hitched his chin toward one of the many doorways leading into the Crimson Room.

The back of Logan's neck prickled. A strange warmth spread through his veins. Before he even turned, he knew. When he glanced around, he wasn't at all surprised to see Paige hovering shyly in the entrance. A powerful jolt of shock passed over him. Or maybe it wasn't shock.

Ducking his chin just enough so she wouldn't immediately see his face from underneath his ball cap, he clenched his teeth and gave a silent curse. He should've known she would show up to one of these meetings sooner or later. Why hadn't he thought of that?

God, she looked good. He loved her silky dark hair, her dark soulful eyes, the way her clothes accentuated her lithe frame.

Kevin nudged his arm. "Smoking hot, huh?"

Logan cleared his throat and jerked his attention away from Trace Zukowski's little sister.

Her presence was a total disaster. Panic leaped into his veins. If she saw him, she could cut him off from his only line of emotional support with one sentence.

She might as well cut off his air supply.

"Uh…yeah," he mumbled, scanning for the nearest escape route. "She's…cute." Cute for a girl about to destroy him.

"*Cute?*" Kevin's jaw dropped. He stared at Logan as if he was insane. "Puppies are cute, man. That goddess is flat-out gorgeous."

Logan silently agreed, his gaze locking on a doorway to his left. But gorgeous or not, she was going to flay him alive. He couldn't make any sudden movements and outright dash for the exit; she'd see him. He'd have to be stealthy about his escape.

Keeping perfectly still, he held his breath and waited for an opening. His insides tightened as he prayed she wouldn't spot him. She didn't seem to be aware of his presence yet but she hadn't moved from the doorway either.

"Looks like she needs a friendly welcome," Kevin murmured.

Logan and Kevin both glanced at Samantha, the one who usually welcomed fresh recruits to the group. But buried in a one-on-one conversation with some guy, she hadn't noticed Paige's arrival.

"Well." Kevin breathed into his palm to check his breath before he straightened his shirt and stepped away from Logan. "I guess that's my cue."

The urge to grab Kevin back and keep him away from her nearly overwhelmed Logan, but he fisted his hands down at his sides and managed to restrain himself. He crept backward, slowly and inconspicuously nearing the closest escape while Kevin called out to her, distracting her attention.

This was his chance to leave without her ever being the wiser. But for some reason, he couldn't go quite yet. Watching her and Kevin together held him entranced.

She jumped and spun toward Kevin, eyeing him warily, even as she offered a tentative smile. "Hi. Um…is this the grief group?"

"Sure is." Kevin held out a hand for her to shake. "I'm Kevin."

"Oh!" A bright smile of recognition bloomed across her face. "How lucky is that? It's so nice to meet you."

Shifting into a shadow, Logan sucked in a breath as he watched her. An ache started in his breastbone as she smiled prettily at Kevin. He'd never seen her smile before. It was…devastating. He wanted her to aim that bright, beautiful, dazzling smile at him.

"I think my suitemate has a class with you," she told Kevin. "Her name's Tess. She said she met you in World History, and you told her about these meetings. That's how I learned about them, incidentally."

Kevin stared at her blankly, looking utterly awed, probably held under the spell of her smile as well. Then his face flushed, and he cleared his throat. "Tess?" he repeated only to nod. "Yeah. Yeah, sure. I know Tess."

"I'm Paige." She relaxed her stance, showing Logan how much she already trusted Kevin. "I'm glad I met you first thing."

Logan's throat burned. She knew next to nothing about Kevin, had no idea what horrible things he might have done in his life, and yet she automatically liked him more than she would ever like Logan, on principle alone.

"Help yourself to something to eat," Kevin offered, leading her over to the refreshment table.

Again, Logan realized this was another timely moment to flee without getting noticed, but he wanted to watch her, just a little longer. She held so much power over him, could decide his fate with a few simple words. It made him strangely curious about her. Like an idiot captivated by the lethal beauty of a cobra that was poised and ready to strike.

"Oh, yum." She brightened as she scanned the food. "Blueberry muffins. These things are my absolute favorite food."

Sensations roared through him as he watched her pick up one of the muffins he'd brought and sink her teeth into the tender breading. He could almost taste the tart berry on his own tongue as he watched her close her eyes and moan. It made his mouth water, but not because he was hungry.

He wondered what she'd do if she knew her favorite food had come to this table courtesy of him. He hoped no one told her; he liked watching her enjoy the pastry. He liked it a little too much.

"These wraps are really good too," Kevin told her as he picked up another and popped it into his mouth. He grinned as he chewed as if sharing some kind of inside joke with her. Then he shifted just so, blocking Logan's view.

Logan frowned, disappointed yet relieved the spell she held him under was broken. He wanted to keep staring but with his sanity returned, he decided to make a break for it.

Until Samantha spoke up. "Looks like we have a newbie tonight," she called, thankfully interrupting Paige and Kevin's moment. "And more of you showed up than I was expecting. Logan?" After a quick glance around the circle, Sam looked at the faces of the members as if searching for someone. "Could you get us another handful of chairs please?"

Logan froze only two steps from the doorway.

Sweating like crazy, he looked over just in time to catch Paige's face drain of color. She swerved around and spotted him. As their gazes connected, he felt struck hard in the chest, watching the dazzling smile she'd flashed a second before disappear as if it had never existed.

Sick about sucking the joy out of her, he waited a beat, braced for her to point and scream, "Imposter!"

But when her face only darkened with silent hate, he yanked his stare away and gave Sam a tight smile. "Sure."

As he stumbled from the Crimson Room, he knew this was his last opportunity to run. But Sam was counting on him to return with more chairs. He couldn't let her down.

He couldn't let anyone down. Not ever again.

Not even to fetch some stupid chairs.

Gritting his teeth, he silently cursed his overwhelming need to be responsible all the way to the supply closet. Running was meaningless now anyway. Paige knew he was a member of the group; she was going to out him whether he stuck around to watch the horror or not.

He'd rather not, but Sam was still waiting on him to return.

A cold kind of numb coated his skin as he lugged four chairs from the supply closet. By the time he returned to the Crimson Room, everyone but he and Sam had found a seat. She took one from him and sat down.

He put all his attention into unfolding the other three just a little behind Jamie and Brenda. Then he paused, making his final decision to stay before slipping into one of the three empty seats. When he looked up, he found himself directly across the circle from Kevin.

Who sat beside Paige.

He exhaled deeply through his nose, trying to control the panic, but he couldn't stop the crazy jump in his pulse. It was like watching a train wreck from the viewpoint of a passenger, waiting for the impact, braced for the explosion which would surely slay him. His life flashed before his eyes.

She was going to destroy him in mere moments. He could probably start the countdown.

A little startled to see she hadn't left either—since that had seemed to be her standard reaction around him—he held her gaze for longer than he meant to.

"Logan?" He jumped at Sam's call. Clearing his throat, he tore his attention from Trace's little sister to the group's leader. Sam smiled. "You were out of the room when we all introduced ourselves. So… this is Paige. Paige, Logan."

Slicing his gaze back to Paige, he managed a greeting nod but didn't even try to speak. She didn't respond past staring at him as if he was insane. Logan jiggled his leg, couldn't stop his bobbing knee if he tried. His anxiety needed *some* kind of outlet.

No one else seemed to sense the animosity and terror bouncing back and forth between them. It was all so surreal. Save for the heavy, frantic thump of his heartbeat grounding him inside himself, he felt almost as if he were watching the scene unfold from outside his body.

Sam started group as she always did, with a bright, rather forced smile. "Tonight, let's go around and share one thing we miss most about our loved ones. I'll go first." After a bracing breath, she said, "I miss seeing my husband stretched out on the couch, watching football." After a humorless laugh, she added, "I used to razz him mercilessly when he was alive about being a couch potato. But now… I'll walk through the living room and it'll look so…bare. I'd give anything to see him lying there again."

Jamie went next, talking about her grandmother's snickerdoodle cookies.

Then Brenda spoke of her best friend she'd lost to leukemia.

After her, everyone turned to Logan. He shook his head and hoarsely rasped, "Pass," as he usually did. He'd never been urged to share anything, and he couldn't explain how much that relieved him.

But tonight, as soon as he croaked the word, Paige raised her hand immediately from across the room. "May I go next?"

When he met her blazing, condemning glare, sweat trickled down the side of his face. Dear God, it was time for impact. The breath shuddered from his lungs and his flesh went clammy.

"Yes, of course you may." Sam's voice was soothing, which only made Logan feel worse. "Feel free to jump in whenever you like, Paige. We're a very laid-back group."

"I miss my brother's laugh," Paige said, her gaze still on Logan.

The pain on her face made his bones shudder with regret. He closed his eyes, unable to hold her accusing stare, wishing he could do something—anything—to take her anguish away, to take it all away.

"How long has he been gone?" Sam asked softly.

"Almost three years."

It'll be three years exactly on February fifth, Logan silently added.

"He was killed," Paige said.

Logan flinched. Though the air conditioning had just turned on, blowing a cool breeze across the back of his neck, his body heated uncomfortably, sweat seeping from his brow. He opened his lashes to find Paige still watching him from her beautiful, hate-filled eyes.

He wanted to bolt, to dart away and never look back, but fear paralyzed him. He couldn't budge, couldn't even break eye contact as she kept talking.

"My brother died when I was fifteen and he'd only been eighteen for a week."

He deserved this, Logan told himself. But, God, he felt sick. He wasn't sure if he was going to vomit or pass out. Maybe both.

Though his body went into full panic mode, he stayed horrifyingly conscious as she continued.

"He was a basketball player and had just led his team in winning the most important game of the season against our biggest rivals. Afterward, he went out celebrating with his girlfriend and their friends, and ran across a couple members of the losing team."

Shoulders lifting and lips parting, Logan sucked in an unsteady breath. He tore his gaze away from her and stared blankly at a spot on the floor in the center of the circle, lost in his own memories of that night.

"When he got into a fight with the captain of the opposing team, he was knocked unconscious and hit his head on a glass bottle when he fell. He died instantly."

Instantly was right. It still traumatized Logan to realize just how instantly a person could die. How unexpectedly.

"I'm so sorry, dear," Sam murmured. "It must've been tragic."

Paige nodded once. "The boy who killed him never saw the inside of a jail cell. His father was some rich, fancy lawyer who got him off without a trial. He convinced everyone who was there that night, even a couple of my brother's *friends*, to say Trace had started the fight and thrown the first punch. My poor dead brother couldn't defend himself, so they made him out to look like some kind of hot-headed delinquent."

Logan couldn't decide what was worse: Paige Zukowski publicly condemning him to everyone in the group or his waiting for her to publicly condemn him. Yet, with each word she spoke, his name didn't cross her lips, and he decided the anticipation would take him long before the revelation would.

Why wasn't she pointing at him already and telling everyone *he* was the murderer?

"After that, my entire family fell apart. My father started drinking, more and more each night until he became a mean drunk. He lost his job within a couple months of Trace's death. My mom disappeared into some dark place inside herself."

She paused with a ragged shudder. For a brief moment, Logan thought she was going to start crying. He panicked. He wouldn't be able to handle seeing her cry.

But then she fisted her hands and gritted her teeth before she snarled, "She killed herself. Two years after Trace died, she put a gun in her mouth and pulled the trigger."

Say what?

Logan jolted, ready for her to laugh and say *Gotcha*, but the dull agony in her eyes, the icy whiteness of her skin let him know this was no joke.

He'd had no idea her mother had committed suicide.

Forget merely puking, he felt as if every particle of his being was going to explode.

But to learn he had not just one death on his conscience now, but two, was more than he could take. And there was no way he could deny culpability for the death of Trace's mother. No way would she have killed herself if he hadn't taken her son away first and destroyed her family.

Paige sat stone still across the circle from him, staring a hole into the back wall. He couldn't imagine what she was going through. Losing two people so terribly in the space of three years was simply unbelievable.

Beside her, Kevin reached out to take her hand in a sympathetic squeeze. Logan stared hard at their connection, hoping she found some measure of comfort from the contact. But Paige politely slipped her fingers out from under Kevin's and folded them in her lap.

Silence echoed through the large Crimson Room. Logan wanted to shout for someone to console her already. He couldn't handle watching her hurt, knowing he was the reason.

"I sense a lot of anger still in you, Paige," Samantha finally said. "You sound mad at your mother for deserting you as much as you sound upset with the boy who fought with your brother."

Logan held his breath as he watched Paige meet Samantha's stare. "I am," she said simply. Her shoulders shuddered as if it took everything she had to contain her rage. He closed his eyes, unable to watch.

"And if this boy or your mother were here right now," Sam pressed softly, "what would you say to either of them?"

Oh God.

Opening his lashes, he glanced up and found her looking directly at him, dooming him with her glare.

Here it comes.

Chapter Eight

This was her chance. Paige could tell him whatever she wanted. She could say she hated him, she wished he'd gone to jail for what he'd done and been gangbanged by a crazed group of tattooed skinheads every night, or that she wished it had been him instead of her brother. She wanted him to pay for hurting her. She wanted him to hurt as much she hurt.

But when their gazes met, all she felt was sick.

He knew what she could do to him, what she planned to do to him, and he just sat there, accepting it, his expression bleak and so freaking desolate, she could only shake her head, confused. This wasn't how he was supposed to react at all.

"I don't know," she choked out, her voice barely a whisper. "I don't know what I'd say."

Across the circle, Logan Xander's chest heaved. Looking up at the ceiling, he blinked repeatedly.

"Would you tell them you forgive them?" Samantha asked.

She shook her head, making a tear slither down her cheek in a crooked trail. "No."

Lurching upright, Xander startled the two girls on either side of him. "Excuse me." He lifted an apologetic hand to them. "I need to…"

His voice cracked. "Bathroom." Stumbling to the exit, he slapped a steadying hand against the wall just as he turned and disappeared from the doorway into a hall.

His departure broke the spell inside her. As if returning to her body after a long vacation, she blinked and glanced around, realizing what she'd just done. The other students and even the group leader stared as if she was an alien being. Spilling her entire sordid story had been to torture Xander, but in doing so, she'd shared everything with a roomful of complete strangers.

She hadn't even told Bailey and Tess this much.

"I'm sorry," she said, wincing and wishing she could take back the last few minutes. Not only had she not meant to share so much so soon, but torturing Logan Xander hadn't been as fulfilling as she'd always dreamed it would be. "I didn't mean to say so much."

Samantha shook her head. "No, no. This is healthy." She laughed. "It may not feel like it now, but you'll feel it later. Trust me. And honestly, I'm proud of you for admitting your anger and telling us you're not ready to forgive yet. It's a very positive step in the right direction."

Kevin leaned toward her and nodded with a glint of admiration in his eyes. "It really is," he said for her ears alone.

Her face heated at his praise, and she forced a smile, hoping he didn't hold anything against her for pulling away from his touch. He seemed really nice. And Tess had been right; he had gorgeous brown eyes and amazing wispy blond hair.

Around her, grief group continued. Paige remained silent for the rest of the session, and her nerves eventually loosened with each passing minute, feeling closer to the other members than she thought should be appropriate. But they *understood*. They honestly knew some of the pain, anger, and denial she was going through.

Logan Xander didn't return. She kept waiting for him to blow back into the room and spill some big tragic story — all lies — about his own past. But he didn't. And by the time the meeting let out, her anger at him for even being at a grief group meeting had unwillingly drained from her.

"Paige." Samantha approached as soon as everyone stood and loitered around the refreshment table. She set a sturdy, comforting hand on Paige's shoulder. "I really want to thank you for coming tonight and for telling us your story. I think you're going to work through this and be just fine. But if you ever find yourself needing to talk, please don't hesitate to call me."

A business card appeared between her index and middle fingers. Paige accepted the generous offer, grateful the group's leader wasn't irritated with her for sending another member racing from the room.

As if reading her mind, Sam sighed and slipped her hand off Paige. "Well, I better go see if I can track Logan down and talk to him. He looked pretty affected by your story, but I doubt he's gone far. He always sticks around to help me put things away after every meeting."

Paige's brow crinkled, a little confused to hear about such a considerate quality in him. So he drove drunk girls home from parties and didn't take advantage of them, plus he cleaned up after grief counseling meetings? Neither aspect fit with the boy she'd built him up to be in her head. Rich, spoiled lawyers' sons didn't do such things.

They didn't take responsibility for their actions and they didn't act sorry for what they'd done.

Shaking the thought away, she watched Samantha leave through the same doorway Logan had earlier. But she turned left at the exit when he had gone right.

Not quite sure what possessed her, Paige followed, curving right when she left the Crimson Room. She honestly didn't want to come across him. As she'd already said in the meeting, she didn't know what she'd say to him if they did meet up. But she wanted to know if Samantha had been right. Had he stayed close by to help put away the tables and chairs?

Was he really that kind of person?

It didn't seem possible.

She wandered through the halls, feeling like a fool on a meaningless mission. From the way he'd left, there was no way he was still in the building.

The Student Union was quiet, most of the rooms darkened, and even the passageways were barely lit by the occasional red glow of an exit sign or emergency light. She was about to turn around and try to find her way back to the Crimson Room, because she only knew how to get out of the building from there, when she went around a corner and came to a shuddering halt.

He sat on the floor, his back propped against the wall, his knees bent as his legs sprawled in front of him. But he'd crossed his arms over his chest as if he was cold, and he'd tilted his head back so his face was upturned toward the ceiling. With his eyes closed, he swallowed, the muscles in his throat working through the motion.

One overhead light caught his cheek perfectly, reflecting a glistening track of skin from the bottom of his eye and down along his jaw. Recent tears.

Slowly, he opened his lashes and rolled his head against the wall, lulling it her way until their gazes met. He looked exhausted and beaten.

Broken.

It wasn't satisfying at all to realize she'd made *anyone* look broken—no matter who he was or what he'd done.

He didn't seem surprised to see her. He appeared to be actually waiting on her.

"You didn't tell them it was me," he said, his voice so dry and raspy, it croaked.

Damn it. This was all wrong. He wasn't supposed to be so ruined. He was supposed to be cocky and arrogant, boasting about defeating her brother in that fight. Smug he'd gotten away with murder without any punishment.

Suddenly angry with him for toying with her feelings, for confusing her, she hissed, "No one here knows, do they? No one knows what you *are*."

He jerked, every muscle in his body seeming to torque at her accusing tone. When he shook his head, she exhaled harshly and knotted her jaw. "Well, isn't that just convenient for you?"

He squinted, staring at her as if he had no idea what convenient meant.

"Why didn't you tell them?" he asked, his eyes bright with what looked like another batch of approaching tears. "Why didn't you point at me and tell them everything?"

She didn't know. She'd started out with every intention of revealing him to everyone, but when it came down to it, she hadn't been able to. It would've united them together if she had. Everyone would see her as her brother's survivor and Logan as her brother's killer. People would automatically think of him when she was mentioned and vice versa. She didn't want to share that kind of link with him, didn't want to share anything with him. It would be too intimate. Too binding.

When he shifted, slowly pushing off the floor and to his feet like a drunk old bum, she skittered a step back, realizing she hadn't answered him yet. Stiffening her jaw, she tilted her chin up defiantly.

"Who says I won't?"

Even standing, he continued to lean against the wall. Gulping loudly, he nodded, once again accepting her condemnation. Sweat coated his forehead with an unnatural gleam. He looked like he might be physically ill. But he didn't beg her to keep quiet about his identity.

Closing his eyes, he asked, "Do you want me to drop out of the grief group?"

"Yes," she said. No way could she go to another meeting, knowing he'd be there. And she desperately wanted to attend another meeting.

He inhaled a sharp, pained breath but nodded his compliance. A split second later, his expression crumpled and his gaze clashed with hers, begging. "I don't think I can."

Her mouth fell open, incredulous. "What do you mean, you don't *think* you can?"

"This group has helped me a lot." He looked embarrassed to admit it.

She shook her head, confused. "Helped you with what? You didn't *lose* anyone."

His jaw bunched as if offended.

Angry heat surged through her veins. "What are you even doing in this kind of support group anyway? No one in your family died, did they? You've never experienced *loss*." She lifted one eyebrow, daring him to admit he was a total fraud.

His face cleared, and he shook his head. "No," he confessed quietly. His eyes narrowed almost defiantly. "But all the Murderers Anonymous groups were full up, so I had to make do with the grief group."

Spinning away, he stalked off, swerving a wide berth around her so they couldn't come into any kind of contact.

She fisted her hand, wanting to punch him. "Hey," she growled.

He barely paused. "I'll quit the goddamn group, all right?" His stiff back still faced her as he jerked around the corner, disappearing.

Paige stared after him, her emotions a confusing mix even she couldn't discern. She wanted to rejoice in her small victory. She'd gotten him out of the group so she could attend another meeting. But instead of victorious, she felt kind of crappy.

It's helped me a lot, his rueful confession echoed through her.

As much as the group had helped her already, she had to believe he'd been telling the truth. But the meetings had helped him with *what?* Who had he lost?

He and Trace hadn't been close. He couldn't possibly be mourning her brother too. They'd been adversaries, attending separate schools. The only times they'd ever met up were at ball games, where each of them had been the star player of his team.

She'd loved going to the games when her school had played against Village Heights. Logan Xander had given her brother better competition than anyone else in the division. The games between them had always been exciting, especially since they'd defeated Village Heights more often than not.

Paige had been a sophomore in high school when they'd been seniors, and she'd always viewed Logan Xander as the Village Heights version of Trace, except Xander wasn't her brother, so he'd seemed a lot more dazzling from afar. Half the girls in her school—her included—had let out a dreamy sigh whenever he would step onto the court.

But the defeated shell of a human being who'd just slunk away from her did not resemble the self-assured pretty boy who'd played in all those basketball games during high school.

She wasn't sure what was going on with him, but she didn't like how it affected her. Hugging herself, she retraced her steps back to the Crimson Room, but she didn't go inside. She found her way out of the building from there and hurried back to her dorm room.

Logan Xander was dangerous on every level possible. It would do her good to remember that. Whatever happened next, she wanted to stay as far away from him as possible.

Chapter Nine

Logan plucked the front of his shirt, letting warm September air stir inside the fabric, barely cooling him. He arrived early for his Sunday evening shift, wishing chillier weather would move in soon, so all his long-sleeved shirts wouldn't feel so suffocatingly hot.

When he passed the front entrance of the juice bar on his way to the back door, he noticed the help wanted sign was still posted in the window for the fourth day in a row, which surprised as much as it depressed him. He had thought the position would've been snagged within the hour around this neighborhood. Shoulders sagging a little heavier, he wondered how short-handed they'd be tonight. Would he even have anyone else around to help him?

Grabbing his waist apron off a hook as soon as he entered, he paused after tying it in place to punch his time card.

Gus had closed his office door until it was just barely cracked. Being that Logan's boss always left it hanging open wide, Logan assumed Gus was in the middle of something important.

"...have any experience with food service?" Gus's rich, thickly accented voice floated into the hall.

Logan paused when he realized his boss was in the middle of an interview.

Please be someone hirable, please be someone hirable.

A part of him craved a little relief from the hectic schedule he'd been working since the onset of the fall semester, while another part of him knew he needed the extra hours — or rather, the extra income — to keep himself afloat. His apartment manager had raised the rent last month, and his textbooks had cost almost twice as much this semester as they had last. Even the price of the e-book texts he'd ordered had been more expensive.

"I worked at a small ice cream parlor in high school," the interviewee — a female — answered Gus's question. "For about…six months, I think."

Her voice floated out, stirring something in Logan. Vaguely familiar, it drew him. The texture, the tone, the rhythm of her words were so lulling, he half-closed his eyes, feeling almost drunk from listening to her.

"But the manager liked my work performance so much he gave me a raise before I had to leave for college."

Something about her dialect — the way she strung her words together, the pace and rhythm with which she spoke — reminded him of Creighton County. A homesick ache split a huge gash through the center of his chest before he could rein it in. Her mention of ice cream parlors stirred an image of that old-time shop called Dairy Delight in Landry, the biggest town in Creighton County. They made the best orange cream sherbet; his mouth watered just thinking about it.

"And this was at…Dairy Delight, right?" Gus asked.

"That's right," the girl answered. "It's legendary in my area."

Frowning, Logan moved closer to the cracked opening. When he made out the back of the girl's head, he caught his breath. The silky dark hair falling midway down her back revealed exactly who was interviewing for a position.

He yanked himself backward and bit out a silent curse, not sure what to do. Karma definitely hated him. With the size of Granton, he was never supposed to see her around campus again. So what was with seeing her every time he turned around?

He couldn't quit. Every college-student friendly job was probably already snagged since school was back in session. His chances of finding another anywhere in town were probably zip. But he couldn't take Paige's opportunity for a job away from her either.

He knew Trace hadn't come from a wealthy family. She probably needed an income as badly as he did.

Maybe he could wait to see if Gus actually hired her, then take his boss aside and beg him not to schedule them with any shifts together. Of course, then he'd have to explain *why*, and Logan wasn't sure how to finagle a convincing lie.

He pinched the bridge of his nose, hurrying away from the train wreck—er, interview—in progress and Paige Zukowski's enticing voice.

Only one guy manned the counter when Logan hurried into the front.

"We need more large latte cups, medium smoothie cups, long spoons, and straws," Ricky called as soon as Logan appeared, the rest of his attention focused on the blender where he was mixing something pink. A small line of customers had formed at the counter, waiting to be served.

"On it," Logan answered, letting his co-worker know he'd heard him. He disappeared into the back, hurried into the storage closet, and hunted up the requested supplies. His arms were full when he elbowed the door open and entered the hall.

"Logan!" Gus's voice stalled him, making him jump and almost drop the box of straws. Fumbling to catch them and not drop the spoons as well, he didn't notice the girl at his boss's side until he finally glanced up.

"This is Paige," Gus said, setting a hand on her shoulder and squeezing with a measure of what looked like fatherly pride. "She's going to start tonight. And I want you to train her."

"Are you crazy? I'm not working with *him*." Paige whirled to gape at Gus Winders, hoping he was joking.

This all had to be a horrible, awful, terrible joke.

She'd gotten such good vibes about working at The Squeeze. How could Logan Xander be an employee here too? And how could anyone suggest he actually *train* her?

Mr. Winders pulled back, his eyebrows arching with startled disbelief as he glanced between her and the murderer. "You two know each other?"

"No!" she spat out, appalled by the very idea at the same moment Logan Xander declared his own emphatic, "No."

Gus blinked, showing his blank confusion.

"I...she..." Though his hands were full, Logan tried to point and motion to her. He lost his hold on a package of green cups and jiggled his shoulders to secure them back into place. "Her brother and I...fought."

He looked her way, his face pale and desperate, his gaze begging her for something she didn't understand.

Returning his attention to Gus, he added, "I think she's required to hate me on principle alone."

Again, her new boss glanced between them, looking utterly pole-axed. "Well, you're just going to have to put all the family rivalry aside. We have a juice bar to run and customers waiting."

Paige's mouth fell open.

Family rivalry? Family rivalry, her butt.

Since Xander had been the one to speak up about their enmity in the first place, Paige sent him an expectant look, waiting for him to correct their boss.

But he didn't say a word.

"Good," Gus announced with a wide smile as if everything was settled. "Get back to work then." Turning away from them, he left her alone...with Logan Xander.

"Uh...grab a time card and clock in," Logan told her, trying to motion her in the right direction with his arms full, all the while looking as rattled as she felt. After he told her to sign her name at the top of the card and to tie on a tiny blue waist apron with a *The Squeeze* logo splashed across one of the pockets, she followed him toward the front of the juice bar...where she was going to be *trained* by Logan Xander.

It didn't seem real, but it was most definitely happening.

"You lied to me," she hissed into his ear after hurrying up a step. "You said we would never cross paths again. And look. Every time I turn around, there you are!"

"I've worked here for almost two years," he growled back under his breath. "How was I supposed to know you'd apply today?"

She snorted. "So, what? Just because you were here first, I should automatically back out, then?"

"I didn't say that." He glanced back at her with an incredulous expression, which she knew she deserved. She knew she was being totally unreasonable, glaring at him for already working where she wanted to work. But she *could* blame the inability to control her emotions on him. He tended to bring out the unreasonable in her.

Grr. She should've done a little reconnaissance and discovered the fact that he already worked here before applying, though honestly, she never would've thought a high-and-mighty lawyer's son would need to lower himself to being a beverage server.

The whole situation had her utterly unbalanced. But on the plus side, it totally negated her new job nerves. She was too busy glaring at the back of his head to worry about messing up her first night.

When they entered the front, stepping directly into chaos behind the counter where one tall, lanky college student manned the counter, she pulled to an abrupt halt and found herself actually starting her job.

"This is Ricky," Logan said, brushing past her to restock the supplies in his arms in their various locations.

Ricky—with a huge, black button-looking things for earrings, a chain hanging from his skinny jeans, and a blond Mohawk—barely looked her way as he rushed from one of the many beverage machines with two cups overflowing and whipped cream on top to the counter.

"About time you came back," he muttered to Logan.

Logan had all the supplies in order before she could properly orient herself, digesting the scene in the tight, cramped space behind the counter.

"This way," he said as he swept by.

She scowled after him for his brusque command. But since he was apparently her trainer for the next few hours, she reluctantly followed.

When he approached the line of impatiently waiting customers, she gulped, her new-job jitters roaring to life.

As the two girls and one guy at the front of the line gave their order, Logan nodded without writing a single thing down, his attention on finding something under the counter. Spotting a laminated sheet of paper, he handed it to Paige.

"Cheat sheet." Then he repeated verbatim the order back to the customers.

He brought her around to face the back wall full of foreign machines. Leading her to one, he explained in hyper speed how to make each drink, barely pausing his demonstration to point out the recipes for them on her cheat sheet before completing the order.

"Don't worry," he added as if reading her mind. "When things slow down, we can go through them again, one step at a time."

As he picked up two of the three drinks he'd fixed, Paige snagged the third. He looked momentarily startled by her helpfulness but didn't say anything.

Again, he rushed when showing her how to run the cash register. She understood the hurry. She didn't want to bottleneck the flow either, but she hoped he hadn't been lying when he'd said they would go back over everything later, one detail at a time.

He nearly bumped into her as he spun to retrieve the next order. It was more than she could take. Jerking backward away from him, she motioned toward Ricky manning the second register.

"Why can't *he* train me?"

"Uh…" Logan blinked, looking taken aback. "He hasn't worked here very long." When Paige just stared at him, he blew out an irritated, yet surrendering breath. "Fine. I'll ask him."

Chapter Ten

Ricky had to be the lamest flirt Logan had ever seen. If it had been any other situation, he would've laughed aloud as he watched his co-worker's awkward attempt to put the moves on Paige Zukowski.

The lanky, pimple-faced sophomore stood entirely too close to Paige as he showed her how to work the meat slicer once the rush of customers had subsided. They didn't serve a lot of food at the juice bar. Mostly muffins and baked goods, but they were quickly growing famous for their Deli Deluxe Sandwich, which required a lot of slicing and blade changing.

"So this little doohickey goes here." Ricky demonstrated by showing Paige how to screw the new blade into place. "And voilà!" He flared out his hands, using an awful French accent. "Our masterpiece is complete."

Logan arched an eyebrow, wondering if that was supposed to be funny.

Paige smiled vaguely, looking more sick to her stomach than amused by Ricky's theatrics. "It looks…nice."

A snort worked up Logan's throat. He jerked his face away and covered the beginning of his laugh with a cough, surprised by how much the whole thing amused him. But her overly polite answer was just too much. Poor Ricky didn't impress her in the least.

He wanted to snicker some dry, sarcastic crack about how Mr. Mohawk captivated all the girls with his meat slicing abilities. But Paige then flashed Ricky a genuine smile, and a fresh wave of grief gripped Logan, pulverizing his cheer to pieces.

As pathetic as he was, Ricky could still flirt with her. He could press up close to her and try with all his might to win her favor. It was a heck of a lot more than Logan could ever attempt, *if* he felt so inclined, which — after a brief glance her way — okay, he kind of did. Nevertheless, he could never flirt with her. In another life, he'd probably be macking all over her, busting out his mojo and —

But that Logan was long gone. Even if the situation were appropriate for him to act, he hadn't flirted with a girl since...not for three years now. Whenever one smiled and fluttered her lashes at him these days, he usually just felt clammy and panicked. Swallowing hard, he looked away from Trace Zukowski's little sister.

What in God's name was wrong with him? Why didn't *she* make him feel clammy and panicked? Sure, she was pretty, in an ethereal way, with her glossy dark hair and eyes against the stark contrast of her pale skin. But there were a lot of visually pleasing ladies on campus. And he hadn't taken this kind of notice of *them*.

Why her?

It didn't matter anyway. Nothing was ever going to happen there. Feeling centuries old, he rubbed his hands briskly over his face and checked the counter, wishing someone would approach and make an order already.

Where had everyone gone? It was never this slow around here.

"And now we're ready to slice and dice." Ricky had transformed his act into some kind of chef impersonation.

Unable to stop himself, Logan glanced over and immediately spotted what Ricky had failed to show Paige.

"You forgot the guard," he groused under his breath.

Paige glanced at him, her beautiful dark eyes instantly narrowing. "What?"

He gulped and pulled his attention away from her to Ricky, since Ricky had stopped talking to look at him too. After clearing his throat, he raised his voice. "You forgot to show her how to put on the safety guard."

Ricky stared at him blankly. "Huh?"

Was he serious? With a sigh of disgust, Logan marched over and yanked up the plastic shield lying forgotten on the sidebar. "The safety guard," he repeated.

Paige shifted a step away from him, nearly bumping into Ricky. Logan barely refrained from rolling his eyes. He'd like to see how close she cuddled to Mohawk when he got her finger sliced off because of his neglect.

"I never use that thing," Ricky said, making a face at the guard as if it was contaminated. "It just gets in the way. And I've never gotten cut."

Logan opened his mouth to argue. But a ding came from the counter by his register. Three people stood in line, waiting for service. Of course. *Now* they showed up.

Grinding his molars, Logan reminded himself she had *asked* for Ricky to train her. Whatever came from it could be on her conscience. Putting his back to them, he returned to the counter.

"What can I get for you?"

"And that's a wrap. Let's clock out."

At Ricky's announcement, Paige frowned, sending a short a glance away from her trainer and across the shop to Logan. With his long sleeves rolled up to his biceps, he'd buried his hands elbow deep into a sink full of sudsy water. She watched the muscles in his back stretch under his shirt as he scrubbed. Blinking, she tore her gaze away and focused once again on Ricky as he hefted a book bag onto his shoulder.

"But don't we have to help clean up?" she asked.

He shrugged and cast his own appraising glance toward Logan. "Why? Looks like Xander has it under control." Then he flashed her a grin and waved. "I'll see you next shift we work together. It was great to meet you."

She could only gape as he took off down the hall to the rear of the restaurant. When the clunk of the time clock echoed back to her, her mouth dropped open. He was seriously just leaving without cleaning anything up.

What was worse, he'd just left her alone with Logan Xander.

Unease swamped her. She cast another quick peek at his back. This time the bunch and flex of his muscles underneath his shirt looked a lot more threatening. He could overpower her so easily, kill with one punch.

She sucked in a breath through her nose, commanding herself not to panic.

But, hello. She'd just been freaking left *alone* with Logan Xander.

She should go. She could leave and clock out right along with Ricky. Except, what kind of lame co-worker left you alone with clean-up duty? Though honestly, the guy who was currently stacking a line of cleaned plates onto the rinse rack didn't seem to mind the added burden. Logan said nothing as he turned on the hose and sprayed the suds off each plate, creating a hot steam of fog to float up around him.

Paige shifted uneasily. She couldn't just leave him.

"What do I need to do?" she called when he stopped rinsing and had returned to washing.

He whirled around as if surprised anyone was still present. Looking almost horrified to see her, he opened his mouth but no words came out. Then he pressed his lips together, and his throat worked while he swallowed.

Looking away, he mumbled, "You can go ahead and go home. I got this."

Now she really couldn't go. Leave him alone to clean the mess she'd helped create so she'd forever owe him one? Not going to happen.

Straightening her shoulders, she narrowed her eyes. "But how will I know what to do on the nights I *don't* work with you and my other co-worker flakes off as soon as we close?"

He looked conflicted as he stared at her. Then he winced and muttered, "Right," as he scratched his scalp with a sudsy hand, leaving a white glob of bubbles clinging to the side of his head. It looked so ridiculous, she simply blinked.

Whenever she envisioned her brother's killer, she always saw this cool, collected lethal guy in black leather and dark pants, with not a hair out of place. He was the spoiled rich son of a spoiled, rich lawyer, too arrogant and smug to tip his nose down enough to notice the little people he squashed below his name-brand boots. But there Logan Xander stood, humble and oh-so-human with whipped topping splattered across his waiter's apron and soapsuds in his hair.

"You can, uh, wipe down the tables in the front." He dunked his hand into the water and pulled out a dripping washcloth for her to use. After wringing it semi-dry, he held it out to her.

Paige stared at it. They worked the same job, wore the same kind of apron, went to the same school, had even shared a class for the space of thirty seconds. It was unnerving.

Logan suddenly sniffed out a sound of disgust and smacked the wet cloth against the counter beside him. "There," he growled and promptly turned away to shove his hands into the dishwater and pull out a serving knife he must've forgotten to run through with the rest of the dishes. Or maybe he'd purposed left it out to clean by hand to intimidate her.

In either case, she jolted at the size of the blade, but he didn't seem to notice her apprehension as he scrubbed it clean with a scouring pad. He seemed upset.

She swallowed, swirling in her confusion when it struck her; he'd been offended that she hadn't taken the wash cloth from his hand. Quickly snagging it off the counter, she hurried to the front and wiped every horizontal surface she could find, even a couple vertical surfaces like the chair leg where a smoothie splatter caught her attention. Then she turned the chairs over and set them upside down on the tabletops.

After hunting up a broom and dust pan, she swept the floor and threw away the dirt, stray napkins, and extra trash.

Logan had finished the dishes and drained the water by the time she returned. He was cleaning out one of the large juicers, his back toward her. She glanced around, looking for something to do.

"I'll get the slicer," she said.

His brief nod was the only response he gave. Clearing her throat, she approached the slicing machine.

Logan Xander was dashing every preconceived notion she'd made about him. All evening, he'd been tidy and efficient, quick to do any job that needed done, and courteous to every customer. His patience surprised her when he'd handled a complaint from an order Ricky had made. When he'd given the upset man a refund, he'd even apologized for the error.

He didn't complain, didn't whine, just did his job.

She liked that. A lot.

Shaking her head in confusion, she unscrewed the blade, working in reverse of how Ricky had showed her to put it together. Behind her, Logan walked past, making her muscles clench with anxiety. But he kept going until he disappeared into the back. A split second later, she heard him rustling around in the supply closet.

She exhaled, commanding herself to stop acting so jumpy. Logically, she knew he wasn't a cold-blooded killer. Trace's death had come in the heat of the moment; he hadn't pre-planned anything. But the mere fact he'd taken so much from her — he'd ruined her life — she just couldn't relax around him.

Focusing on the noise he made in the supply closet and bracing for the moment he would return to the intimate space behind the counter with her, she sucked in a breath when a sharp, slicing pain carved across her thumb.

Jumping away from the slicer, she dropped the blade, letting it clatter to the floor, and gaped in horror at the blood welling from her skin.

Dear God, she couldn't stand the sight of blood. There had been so much blood. It had flared out from under her mother's body like a scarlet cape.

The cape of death.

Dizziness swamped her. She was going to pass out. Her vision grayed at the edges. No wonder she refused to even think about her mother anymore. Even the mere memory made her want to faint.

"Wha—"

She looked up to see the stacks of cups in Logan's arms tumble to the floor as his eyes widened with shock. He leaped toward her, making her jump back and ram her hip into the side of the counter.

Her need to swoon vanished, replaced by the shock of her brother's murderer charging toward her.

Without speaking, he snatched her hand and pressed his fingers hard against the knuckle of her thumb, making the cut pulse with pain. She gasped and tried to pull away. Ignoring her, he looked both directions before glancing down and burying her thumb into his apron. The cloth instantly soaked up her blood.

After mummifying her thumb, he kept a tight hold of the wrap as he untied his apron strings with his free hand, untethering her from him.

Again, Paige tried to wrench free. "That *hurts.*"

"No, wait." He tugged her closer. "We need to keep pressure on it to stanch the blood flow. Your cut looks pretty deep."

Blood flow. Deep cut.

The words made her blanch.

He lifted his gaze to her face. "There's a medical kit in the supply closet."

She heard him but what he said didn't make a lot of sense. When he nudged her along, she fell into step, drifting in whichever direction he prodded.

In the surprisingly roomy supply closet, he instructed her to sit on a sealed box full of Styrofoam cups. She eased down gingerly, not about to risk the chance of falling through the unstable makeshift stool.

After showing her how to hold her wrapped thumb tight so he could let go, Logan turned away and scoured the shelves until he located the medical kit. By the time he turned back, her heartbeat throbbed into her thumb with the force of a sonic boom.

"How're you doing?" he asked, his calm voice somehow stabilizing her.

She could only nod, her tongue too thick with pain and dizziness.

The kit clanged open, and she winced against the crack of sound it made in her pounding head.

"Okay," he said, easing her hand off the offended area. "Let's take a peek. I need to clean it first to see what we're working with."

She closed her eyes and turned her head aside, knowing better than to look at the damage while he carefully removed the apron bandage. But she could practically taste the metallic flavor of blood, making her tongue tingle and her jaws ache, and knew it wasn't good.

Paige concentrated on breathing through her nose. When an entire palate of scents entered her nostrils, she inhaled more, feeling strangely comforted. Who would've thought a musty old supply closet could smell so nice?

When she realized the smell wasn't coming from the room, but from the boy tending to her, her eyes flew open in horror.

Oh God, she must be totally out of it if she thought Logan Xander smelled good. Clean. Like mountain spring fresh dryer sheets and spearmint gum.

He winced as he removed the apron. "This is deep. It might need stitches."

Slamming her eyes closed again, Paige swayed.

"Hey, are you okay? *Paige?*"

His voice. Her name. They sounded so strange together.

"No hospital." She slurred out the words.

"But—"

She flashed her lashes open just long enough to glare at him. "I don't have insurance. My father can't afford it."

His bright sky blue eyes caught her off guard. She'd had no idea his eyes were so…blue. His mouth snapped shut as his blue, blue eyes studied her. "Okay. I'll see what I can do."

He cleaned the wound first, apologizing softly as he poured the antiseptic over the cut, filling her entire hand and half her arm with liquid heat. Hissing out a strangled exhale, Paige grabbed a nearby shelf and held on for dear life.

Logan cursed quietly under his breath. "I should've forced him to put that safety guard on. You wouldn't have gotten cut if it had been on. What was I thinking?"

Shocked he wanted to take responsibility for her stupid mistake, Paige shook her head and began to say, "No. No, you're not—" But a second later, she realized what she was doing. She scowled and quickly added, "Yes. Yes, you should have. You owe me a new finger."

He glanced up and his mouth fell open. His blue eyes blinked twice before he murmured, "Uh, how…how about I just patch up the one you have?"

She wanted to giggle. For some reason, the whole encounter seemed hilarious. A murderer was actually taking *care* of her, and she was damn near flirting with him, demanding new fingers as she fought back the gray fringes of unconsciousness that kept nudging at her brain.

She tossed out her unharmed hand with a sloppy flair. "Whatever. Fine. Do your best."

He nodded and went back to work.

It took everything she had to stay conscious. She concentrated on him, reminding herself why she hated him and what he'd taken from her. Meanwhile, he tended to her the same way he worked his job: with quick, precise efficiency. Keeping his touch tender, he—

Wait. *Tender?*

Paige furrowed her brow in confusion. Yeah, she must be totally out of it. She stared hard at that place where their hands stayed in constant contact to find he'd already cleaned her up and was wrapping the area with a wad of sterile, white gauze. His warm fingers grazed hers with every rotation.

"This doesn't mean I forgive you."

He paused before continuing with his work. "Don't worry. No one else has either. I wouldn't expect you to be the first."

She wrinkled her eyebrows, wondering what he meant by no one else. Had he been to see her father recently, begging for forgiveness? She could only imagine how well Dad had received him.

Probably by throwing a beer bottle at his head. He was kind of famous for that these days.

"I didn't know…about your mom," he said into the silence, his voice low and clogged with emotion.

Paige swayed. She didn't like to think about her mom. Ever.

He kept his attention lowered as he worked, using a pair of scissors to neatly sever the gauze wrapped around her from the roll it had come from, cut a piece of surgical tape, and fastened the wrap.

"You didn't have a picture of her on your desk in your dorm room like you did Trace."

Trace.

The entire reason why she hated Logan Xander.

Immediate rage engulfed her, once again reminding her she did not and never would like this guy. Paige snapped her hand away from him and surged to her feet. "Don't you dare say his name!"

Startled blue eyes popped up to gawk at her.

She glared at him. "Don't…don't *talk* to me about any of this like we're besties or something. I only stayed to help clean up because I want to be a good employee, not because I wanted to hang out with my brother's *murderer* and share my feelings, okay?"

His expression fell blank. But he opened his mouth to respond.

She didn't think she could handle hearing his voice, so she pushed past him. "And I only let you near my finger because the sight of blood makes me pass out. So can we please *not* talk?"

"Okay." His voice was defensive as he lifted his hands, showing his surrender. "Okay, I get it. No talking."

But with his hands in the air and his palms facing her way, the un-cuffed sleeves of his shirt sagged down, exposing his wrists...and the multitude of scars slashed over his veins.

He'd cut himself. A lot. Had probably even tried to commit—

Her mouth fell open as she gasped, unable to take her eyes off his ruined flesh, unable to believe the pampered, got-everything-his-rich-heart-desired lawyer's son had actually tried to kill himself.

It took him a second to realize what she was ogling, but when he caught her expression, his face drained of color and he yanked his hands down, burrowing his mangled wrists against his waist and out of sight. But those scars continued to blaze through her mind's eye as clearly as if she was still looking at them.

He backed up from her, looking more afraid of her than she'd ever been of him.

When he whirled away and staggered from the closet, Paige remained frozen, staring at the spot where he'd exposed what might possibly be his deepest, darkest secret.

Seeing him looking all depressed on her dorm room floor might've stirred the tiniest bit of empathy in her. Knowing he'd cried at the grief meeting had been unsettling. But this...this blew her away.

For the first time in three years, she actually felt completely aware of another person—outside her family—hurting. Suffering.

Logan Xander had definitely suffered.

She plopped down hard onto the box she'd been sitting on before... and promptly fell through, landing in a pile of plastic and Styrofoam.

Chapter Eleven

Paige had no idea how long she sat in the supply closet of The Squeeze among scattered and squashed cups, staring dazed at the doorway where Logan had disappeared. Could've been twenty seconds or twenty minutes; her brain was too dazed to keep track of time.

But seriously, what was she supposed to make of this new development?

Logan Xander was no longer just a name to her, the name of the evil being who'd taken away her brother. He was a person with feelings, lots of feelings. Reserved and moody, hard-working and keeping to himself, he wasn't anything like she had assumed he'd be. He seemed more like a guy who'd made a horrible mistake and was constantly struggling to make some kind of amends. Full of an inner strength and sturdy determination she wished she could have.

And he had beautiful, sad, blue eyes.

A sound from the front of the store jolted her out of her rambling thoughts. Blinking, she glanced around her and scrambled to her feet. After setting the broken cardboard box and stacks of cups back to rights, she hurried into the main area, certain Logan couldn't be lingering around.

From the way he'd lit out of the supply closet, she would've thought he had escaped the building without even bothering to punch his time card. Wondering if it might be a burglar, she snatched up a broom and crept down the hall. After peeking around the corner, she stopped short.

Logan had already finished cleaning the meat slicer of doom and was wiping down all the countertops. Keeping his back to her as he scrubbed with a vengeance, he said, "Go ahead and go. We're pretty much done here. I'll lock up."

She shook her head in disbelief. By the tense set of his shoulders, she could only imagine how strongly braced he was, ready for her to mention his scars.

She didn't think she could, though. She knew why he'd done it. He was sorry for Trace's death. *Really* sorry. He wasn't all oops-my-bad kind of sorry or I'm-only-sorry-I-got-caught; he was filled with bone-deep regret.

How was she supposed to configure this into her brain and slot it in with the anger and hatred she'd always felt for him? "Th-thanks for wrapping my thumb." She pushed out the words awkwardly, feeling lame because she couldn't summon the courage to outright apologize for her behavior.

He paused in his scrubbing, glancing over his shoulder at her as if he couldn't believe his ears.

It was more than she could handle. Their gazes met, and an awareness she wanted to deny rocked through her; she gasped and whirled away. Her attraction to him was the straw that broke it all. Hurrying down the hall, she cradled her stomach and silently punched her time card before fleeing back to her dorm building through the dark evening.

Every muscle in her body ached by the time she reached Grammar Hall. Temples throbbing, she unlocked the front door, ready to collapse onto her bed and bawl, when she entered madness.

Startled by the yelling and things flying by her head, she instantly ducked and wrapped her arms over her face.

"Suck on this, Einstein!"

A bulky football player-looking guy, his expression contorted into an evil, taunting sneer, wound his arm back and threw something into the shadowed space under the stairs.

A second later, the item was lobbed back and landed on the floor not two feet from her shoes. Paige squinted and made out what looked to be a baby's pacifier.

Laughing and jostling against half a dozen replicas of himself, the football player hurried up the stairs with his friends, leaving her alone in the foyer.

She knew who Einstein was. She'd seen the boy around and heard the rumors. Nearly every university had one of them—a genius kid who'd enrolled in college way before he was old enough to graduate from high school.

His real name was Anthony something-or-other. Anthony…Morris, that was it. But everyone made fun of him, calling him Einstein. He was sixteen, if the rumors she'd heard were correct, and he was already a junior. What's worse, the poor kid was small for his age, so he looked closer to twelve.

When he didn't emerge from under the stairs, she inched forward to check on him. But as soon as she got too close, he threw a jar of baby food at her. She jumped back to save her sneakers from getting splattered as the glass shattered against the floor.

"Sheep," a young voice jeered from the shadowed nook. "You're all sheep. *Baa.*"

At his exaggerated bleating, Paige snickered. "Yeah, they *do* kind of act like a big dumb cluster of sheep, don't they?"

"Flock." The voice turned sullen as it responded.

"What's that?" she asked, trying to sound as polite and non-threatening as possible. Stepping around the puddle of strained carrots, she cradled her wrapped hand protectively closer to her chest and approached the nook again, much more cautiously this time.

"A group of sheep is called a flock. Or a herd, a trip, or a drove. Sometimes a mob. But never a *cluster.*"

She flushed, a little indignant he'd corrected her vocabulary when she was the only person trying to be nice to him. "Oh. I like a mob then. They looked like a big group of dumb mobsters."

"I said *mob*, not mobster. There's a huge difference." He appeared, frowning at her with impatience. A green glob of peas had been smeared across his youthful face. When he saw her, he stopped dead and his pale brown eyes flared open wide.

She cringed at the torment he'd received. "Oh, you poor thing. Here. I think I have some wet wipes in my bag." Unzipping her purse, she fished around until she found her package of wipes, wincing when her injured thumb bumped her compact.

She pulled a single sheet free and handed it to him, but he backed away, scowling. "*Diaper* wipes?"

Great. Now he thought *she* was making fun of him. "No, actually, they're face wipes. I use them to take my makeup off each night."

When he didn't reach out to take the cloth from her, she sighed and stepped closer to dab the smudge off his face for him, hoping he didn't take insult from her motherly treatment.

But instead of pushing her hand away, he tipped his chin up, encouraging her ministrations. Logan had wrapped her cut thumb so snug that she couldn't bend it. Sticking out awkwardly, its gauze surface brushed Anthony's cheek as she scrubbed. He didn't seem to notice, however, he seemed more concerned about trying to keep his fluttering eyes open as Paige pampered him.

She slowed as she removed the last little bit of peas. "There," she murmured, forcing a bright smile. "All clean."

When he simply studied her, looking utterly awed, she shifted her stance, uncomfortable by such intense scrutiny. "You're Anthony, right? Anthony Morris."

"Einstein," he corrected, his wary frown returning.

Okay, so he actually liked his derogatory nickname. She supposed she could deal with it if he could. "Right. Sorry. I think I knew that. I'm Paige. I live up on the—"

"Third floor," he finished for her in a trance-like state as if he was reading her stats verbatim. "Room three-oh-eight with that rude tramp named Mariah. Suitemate to Bailey Prescott and Tess Simpson."

When her mouth dropped open, he shrugged. "It's incredibly easy to hack into the university's database."

She nodded, gulping down her instinctive need to flee. But the genius sixteen-year-old definitely had a creepy vibe about him.

"Well…" She floundered, not sure how to tie up this little conversation and flee, yet somehow show him she wasn't like the mob who'd just harassed him. "Don't let those bullies get to you, okay, Einstein? Someday when you're a successful billionaire, they'll be too busy begging you for a job to laugh. You can get your revenge then."

Einstein snorted. "If I survive until then." He lifted his hands to show her his wrists.

She reared back, stunned to see a copy of the same marks she'd seen not-so-long-ago on a different pair of wrists.

"Who did that do you?" she demanded, instantly wanting to beat up whoever had hurt him.

Einstein, blinked, looking confused. "No one. I did it to myself."

She furrowed her brow. "But—" Why wasn't he hiding them in shame the way Logan had?

Einstein sniffed. "Yeah, I doubt you know what it's like to be made fun of at all. You don't know true pain. You're too *pretty*." He spat the word as if it were a curse.

Paige took another step back and slipped in the carrots on the floor. Waving her arms and making a dull throb arch up her arm from her cut thumb to her elbow, she caught herself and hopped over the pile until it lay between her and the eerie little genius.

People didn't call her pretty. Not as a compliment, and certainly not a curse. To hear such a word applied to her felt strange all by itself, but to be labeled the kind of person he seemed to think she was piqued her to no end.

Anthony "Einstein" Morris filled her with all kinds of confusion. She wanted to protect him, to mother him, to yell at him, and run from him all in the space two minutes. It had to be some kind of record.

Stiffening her back, she straightened her shoulders and lifted her chin. "Actually I *do* know what true pain is like."

He studied her a moment before saying, "Oh, right. Your mom." When she gasped, he shrugged. "Your record said your dad is the only contact you have, so I figured she was already—" He shrugged again. "My mom ran off with a rock star when I was five. They died in a car crash together."

Paige squinted at him, wondering if this kid was for real. A rock star? That was something a seven-year-old would concoct.

His brain might challenge that of a college student, but he was sadly lacking in the social skills department. She wondered if he was even sixteen yet. Immediately, her emotions reverted back to pity. She was going to have to take this poor child under her wing.

"So why did you hurt yourself?" she asked, motioning to his wrists.

For some reason, she knew she could ask him that question. Unlike Logan, Einstein showed off his scars as if he were proud of them. He probably had a big, crazy reason for cutting himself, like—

"I wanted to see what it felt like." He grinned and showed her the marks again. "The vertical slashes here that run the length of your arm are actually more painful than the traditional horizontal cuts. They must hit more nerve endings. But these others bleed more."

Slightly ill from even the mention of blood, Paige cuddled her own injury to her chest and winced. It pulsed with more pain, reminding her how fresh and deep it was.

"Did you have to go to the hospital?" she asked.

Einstein rolled his eyes. "Yes. You should've seen my mom when she came across the mess. Totally freaked out. Would've thought I was dying or something."

Probably because he *had* been dying. So many things about his story rang false. For one, his reason for cutting himself. She doubted Logan Xander had sliced his own skin open purely because of academic curiosity. She doubted anyone would, even Einstein.

Tilting her face to the side, she blinked. "So you did this *before* your mom ran off with the rock star?"

His cheeks flushed as if he'd been caught in a lie. But he smoothly revised his story. "I meant my stepmom. My stepmom freaked."

That was totally plausible, but she still didn't believe him for a second. She nodded as if she did, however. "Oh. I see."

She wondered if anything that came out of his mouth was true. Again, sympathy struck her deep in the chest. She was probably the first person he'd talked to all year that hadn't thrown something at his head. He no doubt wanted to impress her with some grand story just to keep the conversation flowing.

Bending to clean up the broken jar between them, she pulled out another wet wipe and listened to him brag about his trip to the hospital, where they'd sewn up his wrists with an unprecedented amount of stitches. It made her glad she'd talked Logan out of rushing her to the hospital earlier. Even the idea of one stitch made her woozy.

But Einstein's ramblings successfully drew her away from such thoughts. She actually appreciated his non-stop chatter. It gave her something almost frivolous to focus on. After the night she'd had—first night of work and so many new revelations about Logan Xander—frivolous was good.

Self-consciously tugging his long sleeves down until they nearly reached his knuckles, Logan glanced both ways at the crosswalk before stepping into the street. Though he wasn't scheduled to work that evening, he headed toward The Squeeze as soon as he finished his last class on Monday.

Passing the front of the juice bar, he snuck a discreet sideways peek inside to make sure *she* wasn't working and hurried around to the back. As soon as he slipped inside, he headed straight to his boss's small, square office.

The office didn't have a window or even much circulation, and the smell of body odor struck his nose as soon as he tapped on the doorframe.

"Gus?"

The voluptuous man wedged behind the desk glanced up from a laptop he was typing in. "Logan. What's up?"

Logan slipped off his ball cap and fingered the brim nervously. "Do you have a minute?"

Gus's attention had already fallen back to his screen. Backspacing over what he'd just entered, he waved Logan forward with a free hand. "Sure. Come on in."

Logan took two steps inside and sank into the folding metal chair opposite Gus.

"I can't work with her," he blurted. "Please don't schedule me to work with her again."

He gritted his teeth, deriding himself for saying that. For the past hour, he'd been practicing a completely different line.

I quit.

There, how hard was that to say?

Gus stopped typing, his fingers freezing over the keyboard, and looked up. "You can't work with who?"

Logan's mouth moved as his face flamed. But he couldn't say her name. Every time he said her name, he felt like he was going up in flames, and he wasn't entirely certain if they were good flames or bad flames.

"The...the new girl," he croaked.

Gus blinked. "*Paige?*"

Wow, even hearing her name affected him. Ignoring the prickling heat just under his skin, Logan nodded.

Steepling his hands, Gus cocked his head with a puzzled squint. "Why not? Didn't she do a good enough job her first night?"

Logan paused. For a brief, guilty second, he considered lying. He could say no. It'd be so easy. Gus would believe him. And he'd never have to worry about working with her again. He'd never have to feel any of those things he felt whenever he got close to her. No guilt, no shame, no panic, no fear, no desire.

The last thought made his insides seize. He needed to cut that kind of thinking out right now. Just because a girl was pretty, and had a smile—for other people, certainly not for him—like an angel's, and a voice that caressed his ear with a carnal awareness, and beautiful glossy hair he wanted to sink his hands into every time he saw her, and—

Okay, okay. None of that should induce him to feel interest or desire.

In a normal world, yes, but none of this was normal. With her, he should feel…well, probably nothing.

"Logan?" Gus said, a strange frown on his face, reminding Logan he'd been spacing out big time.

Clearing his throat, Logan ducked his face. "Yes," he admitted. "Yes, she did a fine job." And if she were anyone else, he'd probably be begging to work with her every shift instead begging the opposite. She hadn't passed the buck on any of the workload—even though it had been her first night—and she'd dealt with the customers surprising well, plus she caught on fast and hadn't messed up one order. Frankly, she'd been remarkable.

"I just can't work with her," he mumbled to his lap.

With an impatient sigh, Gus growled, "Does this have anything to do with that family feud you two are having?"

Logan jerked his face up, his eyes burning, and he stared at his boss hard.

"I killed her brother." The words slopped from his mouth like spilled acid, fast and deadly.

Gus physically lurched back in his chair. "Excuse me?"

Logan's throat was so dry it hurt to breathe. This was the first time he'd told anyone in this town what he'd done. At home, everyone had known, so he wondered if this was the first time he'd ever actually uttered the words aloud.

Bowing his head, he squeezed his eyes closed. "We were in high school. Rival sports teams. We got into a fistfight, and he hit his head." When he built the courage to look up, Logan found Gus's jaw had gone slack and his eyes were open wide.

"It was an accident," Logan added. "I didn't even go to jail. But he's still dead, and she's still his sister. We absolutely cannot work the same shift together. She *hates* me. Please, Gus."

Gus swallowed, then wiped a hand over his face and blew out a breath. "Yeah," he said looking dazed. "No, yeah, you're right. You two definitely shouldn't work the same shift." After filling the air with a fluid curse, he shook his head as if trying to clear it. "Wow, this was not what I was expecting to hear. Why didn't I know any of this before?"

A defensive streak in Logan made him knot his jaw. "I'm not an ex-convict. I didn't have to report it to you."

When his boss narrowed his eyes, Logan's muscles tensed. He braced himself for the inevitable. He was about to be fired. It should be okay; he'd come into this room to quit anyway. But the thought of losing his position terrified him. What if his next place of employment demanded a reference? The only person he could name as a source was Gus, and Gus would definitely tell them what a murderer he was.

If he couldn't find another job, what would he do then? How would he—

"You're right," Gus finally said. He let out a soft chuckle. "Hell, I doubt I'd be able to talk about it either."

When Logan opened his mouth, Gus waved him quiet. "Okay, okay." With a weary sigh, he grumbled, "I understand and agree. This will be a challenge, but I'll make sure you two never work together or even cross paths. God knows I don't need that kind of drama hanging over my business."

"Thank you." Logan exhaled, though strangely as disappointed as he was relieved. What if he never saw her again? The thought of never setting eyes on that hair, those eyes, her smile, left him feeling glum and lost.

Though he'd gotten what he wanted, it didn't seem to matter how he viewed the situation. His future still looked as bleak as it had been for the past three years.

Chapter Twelve

By October, Paige had slipped into a routine.

Monday, Wednesday, and Friday evenings, along with early Saturday mornings, she worked at The Squeeze. Miracle upon miracles, but she didn't work any day of the week with Logan. She didn't even spot him on shift changes. A guilty part of her wondered if he'd quit there too, just as he'd dropped out of Geography class and the grief group.

She told herself it didn't matter; he'd find another job. But that small, sympathetic side of her that could no longer hate him felt bad about making him change so much of his life just to accommodate her. She'd had no idea trying to live Trace's dream for him would affect anyone else.

Not that she was doing very well in *that* department. Classes were progressing passably. But the thought of taking an actual business course in the spring scared the bejesus out of her.

And Chemistry still sucked. Then again, another part of her routine involved doing homework with Einstein, which helped her immensely. He hung out a lot in the game room of their dormitory, and sometimes he still loitered under the staircase in the main foyer.

When he popped out of either place to greet her each time she entered the front door, she felt obligated to stop and talk to him for a while. Their visits grew so long she finally asked if they could just work on homework together in the game room so she couldn't fall behind in in her classes because of her attempt to befriend him.

She hadn't asked him for help on her Chemistry—honest—he had simply looked over her shoulder and said, "That answer's not right." It bothered him to no end when she came up with the wrong equations, and since he constantly looked over her shoulder at what she was studying, he was bothered a lot.

But at least she was rocking a nifty B in the class because of him.

Mariah continued to shuffle men through their room, and Paige continued to camp out on Bailey and Tess's floor. Though her suitemates went home every weekend, whenever Paige wasn't in class, at work, attending grief group, or studying with Einstein, she spent her free time with them.

Phone calls to Creighton County grew fewer and fewer, and Kayla's stories about people from their hometown began to sound more like tales of complete strangers.

All the while, her Tuesday night meetings became as important to her as her classwork. Within a month, she'd accumulated the position of *caller*, someone Samantha referred to as a person anyone could call whenever they were feeling particularly down. Two members had called Paige already in the middle of the night. After talking to them and listening to their heartbreaking accounts, she began to wonder if social work or psychology might actually be her life's calling.

She knew she helped others by simply listening to them, yet ever since the first meeting she'd attended, she still couldn't mention her mother or Logan Xander's tie to her to anyone. Not to Tess or Bailey, and not to the members of the grief group.

Although…Xander's tie to her no longer seemed like an issue. It was as if he'd dropped off the face of the earth. If she hadn't seen him so much that first week of school, she might've convinced herself he didn't exist at all. She knew he hadn't left Granton, though. She'd finally checked the time cards at work and seen how he punched his regularly.

But it was possible he'd dropped out of school, because she hadn't spotted him on campus. She didn't want to care whether he had or not, but late at night, when she found it hard to sleep, his face would drift into her head. His desolate blue eyes would look at her, and she just wanted to comfort him, kiss his short crop of hair, and wrap her arms around his neck to press their cheeks together. Share the loneliness and pain that plagued them both.

Her mind wandered to him as she walked to class one day. She hadn't seen him in a good six weeks, not since the night he'd wrapped her thumb, which had healed nicely due to his thorough administrations.

She wished she would've at least apologized for being so rude, so —

With a gasp, she paused in her tracks. Logan Xander sat about thirty feet away. She slipped into the shade of a nearby tree and stared covertly at him. It was as if her thoughts had conjured him. But there he was, across the lawn, sitting on a bench and —

What was he doing? Drawing, maybe?

With an ankle crossed over one knee, he'd perched a large pad on his lap and was bent over it, scrawling madly. Every couple of seconds, he'd pause and glance up, staring across the campus lawn. Following the direction of his gaze, Paige spotted a couple camped out on the short grass, lying on a blanket. The girl read a book and rested the back of her head on the guy's chest as he sprawled out perpendicular to her, playing with her hair.

Returning her attention to Logan, Paige watched him pause and simply study the lounging students with a wistful sort of smile. Then he glanced down at his pad, and the smile died. Scowling, he ripped the large sheet from the pad and tore it in half before chucking the paper into a nearby trashcan. After glancing at his watch, he stuffed the drawing pad into his book bag, hooked the strap over his shoulder, and pushed to his feet.

As he started off in the opposite direction, Paige's curiosity got the best of her. She darted forward and headed straight for the trash receptacle. The torn sheets lay right on top, so she pulled them out, ironed them as best as she could with her hands, and held them together to see what he'd created.

It was astounding.

Logan Xander would probably never be an artist, but the stark representation of his subject matter left her breathless, her chest tight with emotion. Using straight blunt lines, he'd sketched a Cubism picture of the two students. But it wasn't the lack of realism that struck her with awe; it was the passion in the scene. The couple with their heads close together and the guy gently touching his woman was love in its purest form.

Remembering the achy, wistful look on Logan's face as he'd watched them, Paige pulled in a shaky breath and gently set the picture halves back into the trash. Dazed, she walked away, because deep inside she knew she'd found a completely unacceptable connection with someone who was completely unacceptable.

But he was someone who ached for something more. Just as she did.

She couldn't concentrate in her next class, and once it let out, she raced back to that trashcan, but someone had already emptied the contents, and the drawing was gone.

She was still wishing she'd kept it the next morning as she sat in World Regional Geography class, waiting for Presni to make an appearance.

"Morning, gorgeous." Slipping into a chair next to her, Reggie—who had become her Geography buddy in the past couple weeks—grinned as he slumped into a comfortable sprawl in the seat beside hers. "Did you get your assignment finished?"

Pushing troubling thoughts of troubling guys from her mind, Paige gasped. "Assignment?" When Reggie's eyes flashed open wide and he opened his mouth to explain what she'd forgotten, she relaxed and grinned. "Of course I finished it."

Strangely enough, she was making better grades in all her classes at Granton than she'd made in high school.

Reggie rolled his eyes. "That's right. You got the little boy genius doing all your homework for you, don't you?" Winking, he bumped his elbow into her as if congratulating her. "That's pretty brilliant actually."

She gritted her teeth and scowled. "Einstein does not do my homework." But a second later, her shoulders collapsed. "He does seem to go over everything I do and pre-grade it, though," she had to admit.

With a chuckle, Reggie stuck out his fist for her to bump. "Hey, I'm not hating, girl. I say, right on. Milk it for all it's worth."

Compelled to clash her knuckles against his as she sighed and rolled her eyes, she sucked in a sharp breath when he caught her fingers before she could retract them.

"Ouch," he murmured on a low whistle while he ran his thumb over the angry red scar on her thumb. "How'd you get this beauty?"

Suddenly uneasy, Paige wanted to pull her hand away. She pictured Logan bending over her as he gently wrapped gauze around her finger, and she didn't want anyone else filling that memory or touching what he had taken care of.

"I…I cut it at work."

"Wow, I didn't know the juice bar was so dangerous."

And she hadn't realized he knew where she worked. His touch slid away from the old cut and down the side of her finger, sending prickles of warmth up her arm.

But she wasn't sure if she appreciated the sensation or not.

Reggie Oates had flawless looks, gorgeous dark skin and eyes, with cheekbones to die for along with the widest, most charming grin on campus. But something about him told her he probably ran wilder than she did. She was actually surprised he hadn't shown up in her room attached to Mariah yet.

She managed a carefree laugh. "Oh, well, I usually find danger everywhere I go." Total lie, but it sounded good in the heat of the moment. Okay, it sounded corny, but at least it made him smile that delicious grin of his.

"So I gotta know; if I come visit you sometime at The Squeeze, you going to give me a free smoothie?"

It took everything Paige had to keep her mouth from falling open as his fingers wandered down to the back of her wrist.

He was flirting her with, *openly* flirting with her.

Thrilled such a hottie thought her flirt-worthy, she swallowed, feeling her entire face flame with jittery excitement.

She quipped back, "Only if you make my tip the price of your drink."

Reggie chuckled and wrapped his entire hand around her wrist. "Deal." Before she realized what he was about to do, he brought her fingers to his mouth and kissed her knuckles as if to seal the agreement.

She fluttered her lashes, unable to look away.

"So there's this costume party I'm going to on Halloween," he murmured against her knuckles, his breath washing across her skin. "Do you already have plans that night?"

Paige opened her mouth, but she couldn't even manage a croak. Her first impulse was to decline. Sure, flirting had been exciting, but it didn't seem fair to go out with one man when she couldn't stop thinking about another. Then again, she shouldn't be thinking about the other. In fact, the best thing she could do to get him out of her brain was fill her thoughts with someone else.

Right?

Hoping this worked, she shook her head back and forth, letting Reggie know she was totally free.

He winked, his wide smile full of all the confidence in the world. "Well, you have plans now."

Dear God. She finally had a date with an available hottie.

Score!

If he didn't hurry, he was going to be late.

Logan dashed down the last flight of stairs in McCuffrey Hall — the math department — and shoved his way outside the building.

His Linear Algebra professor had kept him a few minutes after class, asking if he'd like to become a tutor. Thrilled by the opportunity since math was his thing, Logan had readily agreed, but he'd shuffled his feet anxiously the entire time Dr. Cookson spent going over his requirements list.

Time ran precariously limited as Logan found his usual bench already taken. Scanning quickly, he tightened his hold on his bag and found another unoccupied bench about thirty feet away.

Paige would pass through this courtyard in moments, and he didn't want to miss it.

Plopping down, he set his bag beside him and searched for his lunch inside. Finding the PB&J squashed flat at the bottom, he pulled it out along with the envelope Cookson had given him to look through.

Unwrapping his pancaked sandwich, he tore off a hearty bite with his teeth and slid out his new tutoring instructions with his free hand. As he chewed, he read through the curriculum plan Cookson wanted him to follow. It seemed pretty straightforward and simple. He was actually growing excited about this new venture when that familiar prickle of awareness danced across the back of his neck.

Linear Algebra instantly forgotten, he lifted his face and scanned the courtyard.

When he spotted a flash of silky dark hair, he tracked the movement until he caught sight of her.

The breath caught in his throat. And so did his dry sandwich. Groping for the half-empty bottle of water he knew was in his bag, he kept his gaze on her and hastily unscrewed the cap to chug, wetting his suddenly dry throat.

Paige had her own drink and was sucking through her straw while he drained his water. She must follow her own obsessed routine. She always carried an iced caramel latte across the courtyard when he watched her on these days. He could tell what flavor she drank by the color of the cup. The Squeeze had a strange system of color-coding their cups to fit the drink.

He should probably feel guilty about stalking her, finding a spot to camp out every Monday, Wednesday, and Friday just to see her for fifteen seconds as she walked across the main courtyard, drinking her iced caramel latte with a smile on her face. But she had bloomed in the past few weeks. Every day he caught a glimpse, he swore she walked with a little more buoyancy in her step, her chin notching just a little bit higher and her smile spreading a little bit wider.

Seeing her transform from a shy freshman too hesitant to enter a room to this stunning beauty striding confidently across campus helped him heal.

Granton had been good for her. And he was eternally grateful his presence here hadn't chased her off. Whether she realized it or not, she was getting over her brother's tragic death, maybe even her mother's too. And that filled him with a certain peace.

He was so lost in watching the healthy stain of contented color splashed across her cheeks, he almost missed the guy walking alongside her until she looked up and said something to him.

A sharp pain exploded within his ribcage as he turned his attention to Reggie Oates, who looked as vividly excited as Paige did while they strolled together.

They liked each other. From clear across the courtyard, Logan could see it as plain as day. Reggie was as into her as she was into him.

He told himself this was good. Paige was moving on, dating guys. It was all part of the healing process. And Reggie was okay. Though

Logan couldn't guess what they'd ever have in common, he at least knew Reggie would treat her right.

He looked away because watching the animation on their faces as they flirted hurt more than he wanted to admit. But when he realized he would miss the last few seconds of seeing her until next Monday, he turned back just in time to see Reggie put his arm around her shoulder and tug her tight against his side.

Together, the pair walked past a building, blocking Logan's view, but he continued to stare at the spot he'd last seen her.

She was happy. So he should be happy for her. But as he looked down at the flat, half-eaten stale sandwich in his hand, all he felt was empty.

Chapter Thirteen

"This is so lame." Bailey yanked down a dress from her closet, rolled her eyes, and shoved it back onto the rack. "I can't believe I'm actually getting excited about living vicariously through you. I think it's about time some guy asked *me* out."

"Well, I don't see how that's going to happen if you never leave our room," Tess tossed back, burrowing a path through her own closet.

Bailey flipped her the bird. "Like you go out all the time either, loser."

"What?" Tess batted her lashes a little too innocently. "Someone has to stay behind and keep you company."

Amused, Paige munched from a bag of popcorn on Tess's bed as she watched her suitemates banter back and forth.

"Hey, what about this one?" Bailey spun toward them with a black flash of material in her hand.

Tess let out a happy squeal. "Oh, your little black dress. What a good idea. Why didn't I think of that?" Abandoning her own closet, she hurried to Bailey and snagged the dress away as she whirled to Paige, excitement glittering across her face. "This looks absolutely adorable on Bailey. It'll look so cute on you too. Now, up!"

"Uh…okay." Realizing they wanted her to try it on that very minute, Paige reluctantly set her popcorn aside. To her surprise, Tess and Bailey each grabbed her arms, helping her off the bed.

Together they stripped her of her shirt and jeans. Feeling more like their play doll than a human being, Paige shifted awkwardly as they pulled the black swath over her head.

"Arms," Tess commanded.

Obediently, Paige lifted them and her hands poked through the armholes. The dress slid down over her body, the clingy synthetic blend feeling deliciously soft as it fell around her knees. Without checking a mirror first, she lifted her face to gauge Bailey and Tess's reactions.

Both girls frowned.

"You've gotta be freaking kidding me," Bailey muttered.

Tess covered her mouth with one hand. "Oh, my. The only place it fits is in her boobs."

Confused, Paige glanced down. The waist and hips were a little loose, but it felt nice on her. Comfortable. Then she turned and looked at her reflection in their mirror.

"It looks like you're wearing a black potato sack," Bailey wailed.

Tess clucked her tongue. "I didn't realize you were quite that skinny, Paige. Or chesty. You are so not trying on any of *my* dresses."

"Maybe we could pin the waist in." Bailey gathered a handful of cloth, then another. "Good God, is your waistline, like, ten inches around?"

Paige blushed, humiliated. "No."

"Um…" Tess tapped her finger against her chin and cocked her head to the side. "I don't remember it looking that short on you either," she told Bailey.

"That's because she's like five inches taller than me. And it's all in her legs. Ugh!" Scowling at Paige, Bailey set her hands on her hips. "I officially hate you. Pretty face *and* killer body. It's just not fair."

"Okay, take it off," Tess ordered, looking away as if disgusted. "It hurts too much to see you in that."

"And it's *my* dress." Clearly offended, Bailey helped Paige rip it off over her head.

Scurrying to put her shirt back on, Paige mumbled, "I'm sorry, I — " In an attempt to make them feel better, she wanted to tell them she never looked good in black anyway; it washed out her already pale complexion completely. And with Bailey's multi-colored hair cropped short in varying lengths to frame her pixie-cute face with a stylish flare and her tanned skin, Paige was sure her suitemate really did look nice in this dress.

"Sorry?" Bailey yelped, glancing at her incredulously. "Why are you *sorry?*"

Tess laughed. "Sweetie, you're gorgeous. Own it."

Nodding in agreement, Bailey grinned. "Totally."

Immediate relief swamped her; they didn't hate her for being a little taller and slimmer than them.

Through the bathroom, she heard her room door open. Hurrying even faster to yank her jeans on because Mariah rarely came home alone, she was just fastening the top button when Bailey called, "Hey, Hooker. Do you have a decent dress Paige can wear tonight?"

"Oh my God," Tess hissed, slapping her roommate's arm. "I can't believe you just called her that."

Bailey blinked, looking confused. "What? We always call her that."

"Not to her face."

Mariah appeared in the bathroom, scowling at all three of them. "And why does Paige need a dress?"

"She's going on a first date with some hot guy to a costume party," Tess promptly answered, smiling engagingly at Mariah. "And we're fresh out of costumes over here."

Paige soon learned there was one universal thing no girl could resist: playing dress up on another girl.

As Mariah dragged her into their room, Bailey and Tess eagerly padded along behind, but they froze in the doorway when they saw the guy lounging against the door, waiting for Mariah. In cowboy boots, lean blue jeans, a shiny brass belt buckle, and a Western pearl-snapped shirt, he'd crossed one booted foot in front of the other.

"Howdy," he greeted with a Texas twang as he tipped his cowboy hat to them.

Covering her heart with one hand, Bailey sank against Tess as she gawked.

"All you really need for a costume party is some kind of ears and a kickass skanky dress," Mariah instructed, pulling Paige along.

Reaching into her closet, she tugged out a pair of bunny ears and set them on Paige's head.

"Oh, those are perfect." Tess clapped, skipping closer. "So do you think you have a kickass skanky dress that'll work?"

Mariah rolled her eyes. "Look who you're talking to here. Of course I do."

And she did. It was red, sinfully tight, and short enough that Paige wouldn't dare bend over while wearing it.

"It's stunning," Tess said, her voice awed. "Let's try it on."

When she reached for the hem of Paige's shirt, Paige skipped backward and sent the cowboy a leery glance. "Umm…"

He grinned at her, flashing a pair of deep dimples. "Don't stop on my account, darlin'."

Bailey whimpered.

"Try it on after we're gone then," Mariah said with a sigh that told Paige what a prude she thought she was. "If that one doesn't work, try this." She shoved an emerald green dress into Paige's arms. After grabbing up the overnight bag she often took with her when she stayed out all night, she strutted toward the cowboy. "Come on, handsome. Let's go have some fun."

With a nod, he pulled open the door, and let her precede him into the hall. As he stepped from the room, he glanced back, tipping his hat again to Paige, Bailey, and Tess.

"Ladies."

The three waved as if in a trance, watching him shut the door. Slowly turning toward Tess and Paige, Bailey gulped down an audible swallow. "I cannot believe what I just saw."

"I know, right?" Paige shook her head, a little flabbergasted herself. "That's the first time I've ever seen her with the same guy more than once."

With a gasp, Bailey clasped her arm, hanging on tight. "He's been here before? Do you know him? What's his name? Is he single?"

"Hello." Tess waved a hand in front of Bailey's face. "You just saw him with the *hooker!*" She snorted. "And you ask if he's single?"

"You're right." Bailey slapped the palm of her hand against her forehead. "Of course he's single."

Tess turned to Paige. "Is she for real?"

Paige had to bite her lip to keep from laughing.

"I wonder if he's a real cowboy or if he was just wearing those clothes to look like one." Bailey stared longingly toward Paige's door as if she wanted another look at his…spurs. "Oh, what does it matter? He filled out those Wranglers like *oh…my…gawd!*"

Paige arched her eyebrows Tess's way. "I'm going to go out on a limb here and say Bailey's got a thing for cowboys."

Tess sighed. "How'd you guess?"

As if she heard neither girl, Bailey glanced at Paige. "So do you think you can introduce us?"

"You are so pathetic." Groaning, Tess put her back to her roommate, dismissing her as she faced Paige. "Let's try on the red one first."

It fit. A little too well. Her suitemates cheered and wolf-whistled as she spun in a circle before them.

Paige winced. "You don't think it's too —"

"You are wearing that dress and that's final." Bailey pulled out a chair from Mariah's desk and dragged it to the sink. "Now sit. We'll do your hair and makeup too."

While Bailey curled her hair into ringlets and pulled it up, Tess applied her new face.

"Now remember." Bailey nudged Tess's elbow. "It's Halloween so it's perfectly fine for her to look like Hooker. Don't be afraid to put it on thick and slutty."

Tess paused to send Bailey a dry frown. "I was gonna."

"Oh. Well…continue then."

The two worked in quiet efficiency for a few minutes, and Paige found herself wishing they'd say something. When her hands began to fidget in her lap, Tess patted them in a motherly manner.

"When's he going to pick you up?"

Paige drew in a breath. "He's not. I'm supposed to meet him there."

Both girls paused to stare at her. Then Bailey folded her arms over her chest. "You mean, you're supposed to prance all the way across campus alone on Halloween dressed in *that?* Oh, hell no."

Siding with her roommate, Tess nodded. "It really would be safer if he picked you up." Her bottom lip suddenly pouted. "Plus I want to see his face when he gets his first look at you."

Paige glanced between them. She hadn't been looking forward to the trip there and home by herself, but Reggie had told her he needed to help organize the party so he wouldn't have a chance to get away and come pick her up.

"You know," she said, thinking up the perfect plan. "Why don't you two just come with me? I don't think the party's invitation only or anything, and I'd certainly feel better with you there."

Wearing his regularly issued bright red t-shirt with *Designated Driver* branded across his front and back in huge white letters, Logan crossed his arms over his chest and watched a bunch of costumed drunks party around him.

"Hey, Designated Dave," someone called. "Have a beer."

He ducked as some idiot lobbed an empty, crumpled can at his head. He offered the guy a tight smile. "Thanks."

Deciding to loiter in another room and wait for someone to require his services, he waded through a pathetic attempt at a mosh pit and pushed into the main living room of the fraternity house only to stop dead in his tracks. Arriving in the entrance opposite from him, a trio of lovely ladies dominated the scene.

Fifty people had to be mingling between them, but all he saw was one girl. He couldn't look away from the tall, slender one in the middle with the gorgeous mass of dark hair piled on top of her head and stray coils corkscrewing around her face. A crooked pair of bunny ears had been stuck on top, making her look as sexy as it did innocent and adorable.

Nothing south of her neck was innocent, though. Especially his thoughts.

Her dress was small, tight, glittery red—

His brain short-circuited at her legs, too long and shapely to be anything shy of amazing.

He actually recognized the redhead on her left before he realized whom he was ogling. The muscles in his stomach clenched hard and heat spread though his center. A ribbon of awareness curled up his spine, consuming him, until he had to remind himself to breathe.

She was the most—

"Paige!" Hearing someone else call her name over the thumping music and people shook Logan from his stupor. He jerked himself toward a shadowed corner so she wouldn't spot him and watched as Reggie Oates approached her and took her elbow.

Jealousy ate at him like an acid as they talked. When Oates led her into the kitchen where the drinks were being distributed, Logan didn't follow. He forced himself out of the house and down the front steps past a couple making out in the porch swing and a game of washers going on in the yard.

Positioning himself as far from the party as he could get, he found the designated driver's car and leaned against it, closing his eyes and wishing someone would need a ride soon.

Knowing she was here—with someone else and wearing that dress—was going to make this one painfully long night.

Chapter Fourteen

"Thirsty?" Holding up two cups, Reggie turned from the keg he'd led Paige to. When he handed her one full of frothy amber liquid, she stared at it bleakly for a moment before gifting him with a tight smile.

"Thanks." Taking one of the Solo cups from him, she held it high in front of her chest in an unconscious attempt to cover the girls and felt lame as her date took a hearty slug from his beer.

With a refreshed sigh, he grinned and took her elbow. "Let's mingle."

Paige nodded. "Okay."

She'd lost sight of Tess and Bailey as soon as Reggie had arrived and rushed her into the kitchen. He hadn't even given her enough time to introduce them. She'd tried to wave goodbye to her friends, but when she'd glanced behind her, they were already gone, swallowed by a sea of head-banging bodies.

Reggie slid his hand down her arm to her hand and interlaced their fingers so they wouldn't get separated, but she still felt lost and overwhelmed as she trailed him down a jam-packed hall and into another enormous room.

Someone rang a bell as soon as they entered, and everyone in room cheered, lifting their plastic red cups before chugging. When

Reggie noticed she wasn't following along, he yelled into her ear, explaining it was the house rule to drink whenever someone rang the bell.

As if on cue, the bell rang again. Paige didn't lift her cup.

Reggie leaned in again to speak into her ear. "Don't worry. Campus cops never bust these parties. You won't get into trouble."

That wasn't exactly her problem. Leaning in close to his ear, she lied, "I don't like the taste."

A light dawned in his eyes as he nodded his understanding. Taking the cup from her, he held up one finger, motioning her to stay put. Abandoning her in the middle of a horde of strangers, he disappeared.

Her heart immediately dropped into her stomach. Paige wrapped her arms around her middle, glancing left and right, hoping to spot someone she knew. When she saw Kevin from her grief group, she waved and tried to make her way to him, but he didn't even glance in her direction. He was so busy talking to the girl with him, focusing all his attention on her, he didn't notice Paige.

She paused, watching him. He didn't act like someone who attended a regular meeting to get over the loss of his father. He didn't act as if he felt like an outsider among the world of the living.

Suddenly self-conscious because she obviously hadn't healed as much as he had, she turned away and almost ran into Reggie as he returned with a glass bottle in hand. "Here you go."

He gave her the wine cooler, and she sighed aloud, though he didn't hear her disappointment over all the commotion. Maybe she should've just been honest and said her father was an awful drunk and she didn't want to be anything like him.

Holding the bottle as if she had every intention of drinking from it, she followed Reggie as he circulated the party, shouting good-mannered insults to his friends. He never introduced her or included her in his conversations. He simply held her around the waist as if she was an accessory.

When she tried to smile at another piece of arm candy dangling off another guy's arm, the girl with devil horns in her hair scowled back. Paige gulped and looked around for an ally. A couple of guys were checking her out, running their gazes appreciatively down Mariah's tight red dress. But none of them made eye contact. Adrift in a sea of strangers, loneliness crept in, squeezing her lungs and making it hard to breathe. She wondered if her suitemates were having a good time.

After an hour passed of Reggie ignoring her except to yell into her ear to direct her to another part of the party, Paige was ready to go home.

When her date leaned in to asked, "Having fun?" she didn't bother to hide the boredom on her face as she lifted her eyebrows his way.

He grinned, sliding his hand down from her waist to cup her butt. "Want to go somewhere private?"

Right. What girl didn't *love* being ignored all evening only for her date to haul her off to a dank corner where he could grope her for the rest of the night? She shook her head and refrained from slapping him away as she answered. "Is there a bathroom around here?"

He pointed and gave her a bunch of confusing directions. She smiled, nodding her fake thanks. When he let go of her butt with a degrading pat, she took off with no intention of returning.

Tess and Bailey had to be somewhere. She rambled through every downstairs room, and had to wallop three drunks with wandering hands. When she didn't spot her suitemates anywhere, she began to feel a little frantic. Had they abandoned her? She escaped out the front door, nearly running right out of her borrowed heels in her haste.

Finally, she caught sight of bouncing red curls. Some guy in a ball cap and a bright red shirt was helping Tess and Bailey slide into the back seat of an old, huge boat of a car. Upset they were deserting her and even more leery of whose car they were climbing into, Paige hurried after them.

"Bailey! Wait!" Waving her hand, she raced to catch up. What were they thinking, getting into a car with a complete stranger? But she barely glanced at the words *Designated Driver* branded across the guy's chest before relief swamped her. Oh, what a good idea. And in that case...

"Can I ride back with you guys?"

Bailey frowned. "What about your date?"

Paige made a pained face. "He's lame. I'm ready to leave."

Scowling as if she wanted to say something snide, Bailey studied her a moment before rolling her eyes and muttering, "Okay, fine. Get in."

When she disappeared into the car, Paige hurried to follow her. The designated driver continued to hold the door open for her, and she managed a winded, "Thanks," as she brushed past, ducking her head before crawling into the backseat as well. When the door shut, Tess squealed out an excited sound.

"*Paige*, oh my God. There you are! I'm so happy to see you." She leaned across Bailey to send Paige a huge, sloppy grin. Then she began to crawl over Bailey's lap. "I want to sit by Paige."

Paige's mouth fell open as she watched the show. "Wow. You're, like, totally drunk."

"Gee, you think?" Bailey sent her a dry look, and then nudged Tess along when she got stuck trying to wiggle across her knees.

So busy watching her friends, Paige didn't even notice the driver had gotten in and put the car into the gear until he turned a corner and Tess lost her balance. She tumbled off Bailey's lap and began to roll into Paige's.

"Whoa. Easy there." She caught the drunk girl and deposited her back in the middle of the seat.

Satisfied with taking the opposite window seat as Paige, Bailey scooted to her new spot and arched a brow as she watched Paige try to keep Tess from rolling around. "So you'd seriously rather help me babysit Miss Lush here than stay at the party with your date, huh?"

"Yes." Paige wrapped a seatbelt around Tess, fastening her in.

"But—"

"Where to?" the DD asked, his voice barely audible over the hum of the engine.

"Grammar Hall," Bailey answered, not taking her gaze off Paige. "What happened, Paige?"

Smoothing her hair back behind her ear, Paige shrugged and turned to stare out her window. "What do you mean? Nothing happened."

"Ooh, is *that* why you wanted to leave?" Tess asked with a messy giggle. "Because nothing happened and you *wanted* it to?"

Paige wrinkled her nose. Maybe she'd been hopeful something might happen *before* she'd left this evening. But actually being in Reggie's company outside of the classroom for more than five minutes had cured her of that. They totally did not mesh.

"Not hardly," she muttered. "I was ready to leave because he was too busy socializing with everyone else and ignored me pretty much the entire evening. I didn't know anyone but you two, and you all disappeared about as soon as we got there. Where did you *go?*"

Bailey sighed. "I don't know. But this hot guy invited us into some room where a bunch of people were taking Jell-O shots. No way could we actually to say no to him. He was just so…hot."

"Then Derick showed me how to properly take a Jell-O shot," Tess announced, speaking up as she nodded enthusiastically.

Paige blinked. "Who's Derick?"

Looking momentarily blank, Tess murmured, "I don't know."

"It was Dorian." Bailey rolled her eyes. "Not Derick. And he's the star quarterback of the football team. You know, Dorian Wade. I didn't like how he kept looking at her, so I got us out of there."

Tess puckered her brow in confusion. "How was he looking at me?"

Bailey sighed and stared at her window. "Like he wanted you for breakfast."

"Oh God, I think I'm going to be sick."

"I know. It was so gross I —"

"No, I'm going to throw up. For realz!"

Instantly, Bailey and Paige hugged both backseat doors, one taking the left, the other taking the right.

"Driver, could you pull over?" Paige asked as Tess leaned over her lap. "*Now!*"

But it was too late. Even as the car swerved to the curb and screeched to a halt, Tess vomited all over the front of Mariah's sparkling red dress.

Closing her eyes so she didn't join in, Paige tried to hold Tess's hair back by feel alone. When the car jarred to a halt, she fumbled blindly for the door latch and spilled onto the sidewalk, gasping in a lungful of fresh air.

Tess and Bailey tumbled out behind her. Though it was virtually impossible to shake out such a tight skirt, Paige tried to grasp hold of the hem and shake the bile off her dress while Bailey hustled Tess to a row of nearby bushes. Unable to believe her ears because she'd thought everything inside Tess now dripped from her lap, she listened to her suitemate retch some more.

The driver had already gotten out of the car and popped the trunk. When he emerged with a spray bottle and thick roll of paper towels, Paige pounced. Turning to him, she opened her mouth to ask if she could borrow some paper towels.

But he was already lifting them, offering them her way. "One step ahead of you."

She grinned and lifted her face to thank him. But when she focused on a familiar pair of cerulean eyes, she stumbled in her heels, gasping.

"What're *you* doing here?"

"Um…" Logan sent her a strange look, and she wanted to slap her palm to her forehead for such a stupid, here's-your-sign question even as he answered, "I'm designated driving."

A month's worth of thoughts and daydreams about him rushed to the surface. A hot flush instantly coated her skin as her gaze gobbled him from head to toe. She couldn't believe she hadn't recognized him immediately outside the party before she'd even gotten into his car. Then again, she'd been a little preoccupied and hadn't bothered to focus on the face below his hat or above the DD shirt.

Though the red shirt was short-sleeved, he wore a white thermal underneath, the sleeves long enough to cover his wrists. She paused at his veiled wrist as he silently held out the bottle of disinfectant, then moved on to his fingers. Beautiful, long fingers that sketched his deepest desires for love on paper and had tended to Paige's injury with such gentle kindness. And had balled into a fist to kill her brother.

"Uh…thanks." She quickly accepted his offering even as her stare moved up to his face.

He didn't make eye contact but stiffly turned away to fetch more cleaning supplies from the trunk. As he leaned into the back seat, she watched him wipe away the mess Tess had left.

Something inside her seemed to click into place. Looking at him, standing near him. It just felt right. Even if it should be wrong.

Disturbed by the direction of her straying thoughts, she whirled away to find both Bailey and Tess watching her.

"You *know* him?" Bailey asked.

"Uh…yes," Paige answered vaguely as she put all her attention into tearing off a handful of paper towels and scrubbing at her stained dress.

"But he's so gorgeous." Tess squeezed her eyes closed and gave a low moan. "Oh, how horrifying. I just barfed on the side of the road in front of a totally gorgeous guy."

She promptly turned back to the bushes as if she was going to be sick again.

Drawn back to Logan, Paige watched him duck his head out from the back seat and straighten, both his hands full of dirty, wadded paper towels.

Over the past few weeks, she'd actually been planning what she wanted to say to him if they ever crossed paths again. But when he looked at her now, her mind went blank.

"If that doesn't work." He motioned toward her spray bottle. "There's an entire crate full of stain removers in the trunk you could choose from."

Paige frowned slightly, confused. "You have a crate full of stain removers in your trunk?" As soon as she quirked an eyebrow, thinking that was the strangest thing she'd ever heard, Tess heaved out an awful sound, emptying more of her stomach.

On the other hand, if he played DD a lot, it might be the smartest thing she'd ever heard.

Still, Logan flushed at the question. "It's not my car." After tossing his cleaning supplies into the trunk, he rubbed the back of his neck, looking embarrassed. With his hat on, he looked so different; she could almost pretend he was someone else. Someone she was allowed to smile at.

She nodded. "Oh, so then you're stealing cars now, huh?"

The words spilled out before she could stop them. They were meant to be a joke, and her teasing smile supported that.

But his eyes widened to nearly the size of golf balls. "What? No! I—the fraternity house got a grant to buy an old clunker for designated driving use only."

She bumped his elbow. "I was teasing."

"I—" He cleared his throat. "Thanks for telling me." But a moment later, one corner of his mouth hitched up and the skin around his eyes crinkled with amusement.

His crooked half smile was so charming she felt the impact of it directly in the center of her chest. And she knew instantly she'd gone over the line. Just because she didn't outright abhor him any longer didn't mean they could become friends.

Like ever.

God, what was she doing, trying to make a joke with Logan Xander? It had just felt so nice to see him again after so long…and she had no idea why. Their last encounter hadn't been pleasant. However, it had been eye-opening. It had changed her entire perspective of him. And strangely, of herself too.

But just because she didn't out-and-out hate him now didn't mean she could become friends with him.

His blue eyes warmed as he scrutinized her, melting to an almost smoky gray. When he seemed to shift closer, she skittered back a step. "You know, I think I *will* try a different spray." Clutching the spray bottle in her hands to her chest, she veered past him, hurrying toward the opened trunk of the car that wasn't his.

Chapter Fifteen

Logan stared after Paige as she hurried off. He wasn't sure what shocked him more: the complete lack of loathing in her gaze when she'd looked at him, or the fact she'd actually teased him.

Teased!

Him!

Too unbalanced to make heads or tails over what this meant, he glanced at the two girls still huddled by the bushes.

The sober one shook her head and snorted. "Don't look at me. I didn't think it was that funny of a joke either."

But Paige had actually *tried* to make a joke. With *him*. Utterly boggled, he stared at her friends until the drunk one sat back on her haunches as if she was finally finished being sick.

Feeling like an ass for not checking on her before, he hurried forward and knelt beside her. "How're you doing down here?"

Her head fell back as if she'd lost all control of her neck muscles, and she looked up at him, studying him from glassy, dazed eyes and slightly parted lips. "It's all good," she slurred and smiled dreamily. "I'm Tess."

When she held out her hand, he shook it, charmed and beyond grateful she was a cheerful drunk instead of the other kind. "Logan."

Her brow wrinkled. "I thought they called you Dave. Yeah, they pointed and said you were Designated Dave."

Logan sighed. "That's part of another joke I don't get. Trust me. My name's Logan."

With a sigh, she swayed toward him. "Hi, Logan. You're really pretty."

Her friend gasped. "Tess!"

Tess glanced at the sober one. "What?" Then she smiled at Logan and pointed to the other girl. "Oh, and she's Bailey." Leaning closer to him, she lowered her voice. "But she doesn't think I should call you pretty."

Feeling a grin coming on, Logan shook his head. "You can call me whatever you want, but I'll warn you, I tend to look better through beer goggles. Here. Let me help you up." When he held out his hand, she took it, and together they pulled each other upright. Remembering he'd snagged a bottle of water for her, he pulled it from his pocket and passed it over.

"Oh God, I love you." She snatched it without hesitating. "Will you marry me?"

His lips twitched once again with amusement as he watched her chug. "That depends. Do you like shoes?"

She swallowed and lowered the bottle. "Yeah. I'm a girl, aren't I?" She looked baffled by the question.

He gave a sad sigh as he gently grasped her elbow and escorted her back to the car, where all the doors hung open as it aired out. "Well, we have a slight problem then. I live in a dinky apartment where the only closet is smaller than the trunk of this car. I'm afraid too many shoes just wouldn't fit at my place."

Face falling, Tess nodded as if she completely understood. "Yeah," she mumbled. "You're right. It'd never work out."

"Probably not."

Bailey, who'd gotten up when they had, was keeping pace with them. Holding onto Tess's other arm, she pulled a fingernail she'd been chewing on from her teeth. "Do you own a cowboy hat?"

Huh? He glanced her way to find her studying him intently. "No. Why?"

With a wave of her hand, she sighed and turned away. "Yeah, I give up too."

When he sent Tess a baffled glance, she gave his arm a sympathy pat. "She only does cowboys."

Ah.

Busy by the trunk, Paige moved to join her friends. "I think I got it as clean as it's going to get. I hope Mariah isn't too upset."

Even with a wet spot covering a good portion of her dress, she looked amazing. Logan forced his attention away as he helped Tess into the back seat.

"Yeah, well, Hooker should've known she might get a few stains if she lent her things out." Bailey climbed in next, following Tess, and Logan suddenly found himself alone outside the vehicle with Paige looking up at him from her gorgeous dark eyes. With so much makeup lining her lashes, she looked different and yet exactly the same, like a more intense version of herself. It gave him a more intense reaction to her.

"Whatever the fraternity pays you to DD," she said, "you should ask for a raise."

His throat felt dry, burning. He didn't understand what was happening. What had he done to deserve her kindness? The last time they'd spoken, she'd made it clear she hated him and would continue to hate him.

"I…I volunteer," he croaked, feeling lame.

Her eyes flared with surprised. She opened her mouth as if to ask him why. But then she pressed her lips back together and glanced away. "Well…thanks for being so patient with us and pulling over for Tess. She…"

She motioned into the car but didn't seem to know what to say about her friend. He didn't know what to say about her gratitude. Had he just fallen down a hill and landed on his head? Paige Zukowski was not supposed to be *nice* to him. To tease him.

"Yeah, well…" He rubbed at the back of his neck, utterly uncomfortable, out of his element, and not sure what to do about the girl he was obsessed with actually smiling at him. He was used to her hating him. "At least she's a happy drunk. A lot of them aren't."

Her gaze touched on his and something dark and knowing swam in the depths of her brown eyes. "How well I know that."

At first, he thought she was referring to him. The last time he'd been drunk, he'd killed someone. That was about as far removed from being a happy drunk as a person could get. But then, in an unconscious gesture, she touched the side of her shoulder and rubbed one specific spot. He tracked the movement with his gaze, seeing a half-moon shaped scar embedded in her perfect skin.

"Wha—" Shocked, he lurched forward to help her, much the same way he'd done at The Squeeze when she'd cut her finger. Not that he could do anything about a scar that had healed long ago, but his body reacted before his head did. He wanted to fix anything wrong with her.

But she jerked back, her eyes flaring with fear. He stopped himself, realizing what he was doing. Body going into a hyper-aware kind of shock, his epidermis heated and chilled at the same time, making his entire system feel as if he had ants crawling on him.

She knew pain at the hands of a nasty drunk and bore a scar to prove it.

That wasn't acceptable.

He wanted to act. He wanted to hurt whoever had hurt her. Fisting his hands at his sides, he let his system prepare for war even though it was too late to do anything about it now.

Feeling as useless as he'd ever felt, he whispered, "Your dad?"

Of course it had been her dad. She'd already admitted as much at the one group meeting they'd attended together, talking about how her father had turned into a drunk.

Without answering, Paige jerked away and jumped into the back seat with her friends, slamming the door.

Logan stood there, hollowed out and numb. Tempted to stumble to the bushes and borrow Tess's sick spot, he covered his mouth with one hand because it struck him how much this was his fault. His actions had turned her father into a morose alcoholic, and she had suffered the consequences.

"So how do you guys know each other?"

Logan glanced over his shoulder to find Bailey perching herself on the edge of her seat so she could rest a forearm on the back of his and lean in toward him with an expectant look.

He cleared his throat and shifted, casting a quick darting peek in his rearview mirror to meet Paige's gaze. He still couldn't believe her dad had actually hit her. And left a scar.

"We, uh, we work together at The Squeeze," she said, looking straight at his reflection, her gaze demanding he keep silent about everything else, which baffled him.

"Really? Hmm. Paige has never mentioned you before." The way Bailey said Paige's name told him Paige was getting a stern, reprimanding look. He slid another quick glance into his mirror, amazed she hadn't told her friends about him. Amazed she didn't *want* them to know.

She'd told no one. Anything.

When she looked up and made eye contact, he realized she *wouldn't* say anything, either.

Why hadn't she fed him to the wolves already and gotten him chased out of Granton? He appreciated her silence more than he could say, but he had a sinking feeling it was for her own protection, not his. If she spoke of his relationship to her, she might have to keep talking, and reveal her mother's suicide and father's abuse.

Dawning realization struck him. That had to be it. He clenched his teeth, not liking this insight at all. He didn't like thinking she couldn't talk to anyone about her scars — physical and emotional. Maybe he should go see Samantha and ask her to seek out Paige privately and — but no. Every time he'd butted into Paige Zukowski's life, he'd only left her hurting more. He needed to mind his own damn business.

Blinking rapidly, he forced his attention to the road and slowed to turn down the street toward her dormitory. Okay, so he finally understood her silence concerning him. But why was she being so pleasant when he knew she hated him and still blamed him for Trace's death?

As he pulled alongside the curb in front of Grammar Hall, a group of guys had gathered around a small tree on the front lawn and were launching things into the branches at something cowering above them.

"What *is* that?" he said, squinting as he leaned forward to see better. It looked as if they'd treed some kind of animal.

In the back seat, Paige gasped. "Oh my God. *Einstein!*" She pushed open the back driver's side door before he'd even come to a complete halt.

"Paige!" He slammed on the brake, though she was already out and sprinting a lopsided dash in her high heels across the front lawn.

Approaching the largest guy in the group, she dived at him, shoving him square in the chest with both hands and making him falter backwards away from the tree.

Logan's jaw dropped. "*Holy*—is she completely insane?"

"Yes," Bailey moaned. "Yes, she is."

Ripping open his door, Logan got out of the car and sprinted toward the action, hearing her friends scrambling after him.

"How many times have I told you to leave him alone already?" Paige roared to the big fellow, pushing him again. "Don't you have anything better to do, like get a *life?*"

"Maybe I would, if you'd ever go out with me." Instead of looking insulted, the guy appeared as if he'd just accepted a challenge. Stepping right up to her until he was entirely too close, he reached out and ran his fingers over her bare shoulder, playing with the thin red strap holding up her dress.

Logan moved to intervene, his teeth clenched with fury.

But with a growl of repugnance, Paige grabbed the bully's hand off her shoulder, by his thumb, and twisted hard, making him grunt out a sound of pain as he doubled over. "Are you *trying* to make me sick?"

Stumbling to a halt, Logan's mouth dropped open. Paige must've applied more pressure to the guy's thumb because he bowed down nearly onto his knees before her and whimpered.

"No, ma'am," her victim rushed to croak. "But he…the little homo was watching me take a shower."

"I don't care if he was trying to *join* you in the shower. No human being deserves to be chased up a tree like an animal. Leave him alone."

"Yes, ma'am."

"Next time, just tell him to stop." Releasing Einstein's tormentor, Paige pushed him back and stepped toward the tree, opening her arms as if prompting a kitten to jump down to her.

"Okay, everybody clear out," Logan called, deciding to clean up while she was preoccupied. "Now! Get going."

He waved his arms wide, corralling the spectators away from Paige. Surprisingly enough, they followed his orders, slowly shuffling toward the entrance of the building. One person was even nice enough to pause and help the sore-thumbed bully up from the ground.

Inside of a minute, the only people left around the tree were him, Paige, and her two friends.

"Holy guacamole, Paige." Bailey gaped at her. "Where'd you learn a move like that?"

Paige shrugged, her attention still up the tree. "My brother taught it to me when I was little. Okay," she called softly. "They're all gone. You can come down now."

"You're sure?" a timid voice asked.

"I'm sure. All the mobsters have fled."

"It's mob," the voice muttered.

When Paige only chuckled, the dark mass in the tree deftly leaped down, landing on the grass with ease. A young boy straightened and hurried from the shadows and straight into Paige's arms. He buried his face in her shoulder as she hugged him close, and Logan shook his head, certain he was seeing things.

What was a *kid* doing on campus?

"I can't believe she's so nice to that freak," Bailey hissed beside him. "Look at him. He's gawking down her cleavage while she's trying to pamper him like some kind of concerned mama bear."

"Did they get you anywhere tonight?" Paige asked, pulling back just enough to look him over.

The boy shook his head, long dark bangs flopping into his eyes. "No." After giving his sullen answer, he scooted back to her for another hug.

Paige lifted her face to her friends while she wrapped one arm around the boy's shoulder and turned him toward the dorm building. "I'm going to take Einstein up to his room. I'll see you guys later, okay?" Her gaze touched briefly on Logan. "Thanks again for the ride."

Einstein yanked to an abrupt halt, looking up at Logan with sudden suspicion glittering in his eyes. "Who's he?" he demanded, then he turned to Paige and looked her up and down. "Where *were* you?"

"We went to a Halloween party," she said, tearing the bunny ears off her head as if she suddenly decided they must look lame. "I would've invited you, but you weren't by the door when we left."

As they started toward the entrance of Grammar Hall, Bailey groaned. "She *would* have invited him too." After rolling her eyes, she gave a dreaded shiver. "Paige pampers the creepy little weirdo like he's actually normal."

"She does," Tess agreed sadly, tipping her head to watch them leave. "I tried to be nice to him once. Told him I liked his shirt. He said it wasn't for sale and was too small to fit me anyway." She harrumphed. "The jerk."

"You mean, he's a *student* here?" Logan asked. "But he looks like he's ten years old."

"Looks ten. Acts eight." Bailey sighed. "He's sixteen and some boy genius or something like that, except the kid's cracked if you asked me. He spies on everyone from under the front stairs, and if you try to talk nicely to him, he always ends up insulting your intelligence. Paige is the only person who can get him to behave slightly normal."

"Who else here thinks he's exactly like Plato off *Rebel Without a Cause?*" Tess asked, raising her own hand.

"Off what?" Bailey arched her strange look.

"*Rebel Without a Cause.* You know, that old classic movie with James Dean."

"Yeah. Who here has actually seen *Rebel Without a Cause?*"

This time, no one put a hand in the air.

"Well, the day we find him on the top of a roof, waving a gun at everyone, don't you come running to me and say I told you so, because...because I told you so."

After sharing a look with Logan, Bailey cracked off a laugh. "Oh my God, you are so drunk you said that all wrong."

Tess frowned. "I did?"

Looping her arm around Tess's shoulder, Bailey chuckled again. "Yeah, you did. Come on, lush. Let's get you inside." Gesturing at Logan, she said, "Thanks for the ride, Dave, or Logan, or whoever you are."

He watched them head in and then glanced around the now-deserted yard. He definitely couldn't claim it had been a boring evening. Looking up at Grammar Hall, he wondered which room Paige was in now. He pictured her tucking the strange kid college student into his crib and telling him some kind of bedtime story.

This nurturing side of her was a new development. The lady certainly came in many layers, and he'd seen his fair share of them tonight alone. Jokester, warrior, temptress, nurturer.

What was worse, *all* of them intrigued him.

As he returned to the DD-mobile, he shook his head, his mind wandering back to that costume she'd worn.

Reggie Oates had to be the biggest idiot on earth. He'd had the most gorgeous girl in all Granton by his side tonight and he'd blown it. Logan knew he should feel bad that her date had bombed, but he just couldn't summon the oomph. Whistling quietly to himself, he climbed into the car.

If he'd been honored enough to go to a party with her, he certainly would have paid attention to her.

Hell, he felt honored just getting to drive her home. His lips twitched with pleasure because not only had she been around him and not hated on him, but she'd actually smiled, *teased* him, and thanked him for the ride. Things were definitely looking up.

If he'd never learned her alcoholic father had physically scarred her, tonight might actually have ended up a being spectacular.

Chapter Sixteen

October worked its way into November, and the weather grew colder as the days grew shorter.

Reggie stopped flirting with Paige in Geography. Either he must've known he'd lost her after the Halloween flop, or he'd lost interest himself. Whatever the case, he now sat by a stunning Latina near the back of the class and made her giggle all hour while Presni tried to give his dry lectures.

Despite all that, she wasn't depressed. Her B in Chemistry rose to an A. And Einstein's tormentors gave up on him altogether, finding fresh prey in another dorm building.

Mariah met a guy she liked enough that she actually entered a monogamous relationship, and her rare visits to the dorm room stopped altogether after she packed all her clothes and moved in with Gavin.

Bailey became determined to find Mariah's castoff cowboy. She dragged Tess and Paige outside every free evening they had together so they could walk the campus, scouting for him.

And all the while, Paige looked for Logan Xander. She didn't spot him once. Her obsession had gotten almost as bad as Bailey's. She scanned for even a glimpse of him everywhere she went, and it wasn't to hide from him either. There was just something about the hard-working, protective, strong-willed, tortured loner that drew her, like they were kindred spirits, though that couldn't be possible. They were supposed to be complete opposites.

When Thanksgiving break rolled around, she packed a few days' worth of clothes into her beaten down old car and limped it five hours back to Creighton County.

Though she still talked to Kayla over the phone, she'd spoken to her father only a handful of times all semester to check in on him. But every time she had called, he'd seemed too inconvenienced to hear from her. She'd finally stopped altogether and didn't even bother to let him know when she'd get home for the holiday.

The house was quiet when she slipped in the back door late Tuesday night after she'd driven straight from her last class.

Too quiet. It reminded her of the day she'd come home and found her mom lying in a pool of her own blood.

"Hello?" she called in a small voice as she flipped on a light.

The sight that greeted her made her catch her breath.

Lord above, had he cleaned at all since she'd left?

"Who's there?" a gruff voice bellowed from the living room. It didn't really sound like Paul Zukowski, but she knew it couldn't be anyone else.

Relief swamped her. At least he was alive. "Dad?"

A pause. "Paige?"

Footsteps slugged through the house until he appeared in the opening of the kitchen, grease and sweat stains marring the dingy off-white tank top he wore. His ragged, saggy blue jeans didn't look any better. A half-empty beer bottle dangled loosely from one hand as if the two had grown attached to each other.

Paige wanted to weep when she saw what he had become. She could remember when he'd been the most hygienic man she'd ever known. He'd had such particular grooming habits; he used to put his hair comb in the dishwasher at least once a week to keep it sterilized.

But she found she couldn't shed a single tear for him.

"What're you doing here?" he grumbled, eyeing her as if he was trying to figure her out.

Paige forced a smile. "I'm home for Thanksgiving."

He gave a grunt of acknowledgement and turned away. "Didn't think you'd come back for that nonsense."

As he began to shuffle off, she lifted onto her toes. "Kayla invited us to eat with her family this year. I thought you and I could ride over there together."

He paused but didn't turn around. She knew good and well that Kayla was his soft spot. "Oh," he mumbled. "Well. I guess that'd be okay, then."

Her shoulders relaxed as he left, but she really didn't feel as if she'd accomplished much. Glancing around the mess that had once been her family kitchen, she blew out a long, tired sigh. Then she rolled up her sleeves and got to work.

After cleaning all of Wednesday from sunup to sundown, trying to put the house back together, Paige was sore and tired, and kind of irritable. She was beyond ready for Thursday to roll around. Still, she climbed out of her childhood bed early to make a dish to bring to the Hashmans' house for dinner.

When the oven dinged, telling her the pumpkin pie was ready, her father appeared in the doorway. This time, he'd at least attempted to tidy himself. He wore one of the shirts she'd laundered and hung in his closet the day before, and his wet hair was combed sloppily over his bald spot.

"About time to go, is it?"

Paige nodded, feeling a stirring of the doting love she'd once felt for him. She kept glancing at him from the passenger seat of his truck as he drove them to Kayla's.

"What?" he asked with a scowl when he caught her peeking.

"You need a haircut," she said, her lips twitching with the desire to smile.

Grumbling something incompressible under his breath, he pulled into the Hashmans' driveway and slapped at his hair before he got out of the car.

Kayla didn't wait by the door to greet them; she dashed outside and met them at the truck. It was strange and yet familiar for Paige to hug her. They'd been apart for so long, everything felt different. She still smelled like Kayla's minty fragrance and felt like Kayla. Except she didn't.

Kayla clung to her tightly. "You will not believe how much I missed you."

Then she pulled back to hug Paige's father. Watching them together, Paige tried to remember the last time she'd hugged him herself. Certainly not since her mother's death, maybe not even since Trace's.

She wondered why he could still be affectionate with Kayla and yet his warmth for his own daughter was nonexistent. Maybe he wished she had died instead of Trace. Or instead of her mother.

Tearing her thoughts from such a troubling decline, Paige focused on Kayla's parents as they stepped outside.

The Hashmans were wonderful, pleasant hosts and made sure to include everyone in every part of the dinner. But Paige still felt disconnected, a spectator more than a participant. She wanted to return to Granton.

After dessert, Kayla hooked her arm through Paige's and led her back to her room. It looked the same as always, sending a wistful pang of nostalgia through her. She remembered the first time she'd been here. With Trace.

He'd let her tag along with him so Kayla's parents wouldn't make a fuss about him being in Kayla's bedroom without parental supervision. And while Kayla had let fourteen-year-old Paige paw through her jewelry, she and Trace had made out all evening on her bed.

Kayla had been devastated when he'd died. Though she and Paige hadn't exactly been close before the accident, they'd become inseparable afterward. Kayla had been there when it had happened and had told Paige he'd died instantly without feeling any pain whatsoever.

And she'd been able to share Paige's grief like no one else. Paige sometimes felt Kayla had taken Trace's death the hardest.

Sitting at Kayla's old dressing table, Paige studied her own reflection in the mirror and wondered if she should ever tell her friend about Logan Xander's presence at Granton.

"I love this vanity," she murmured instead, running her fingers over the gray marble top.

Behind Paige, Kayla scooped up a handful of Paige's hair and began to play with it. "I can't believe I'm actually going to say this, but…you look great. I think Granton agrees with you."

Closing her eyes against the soothing effect Kayla's fingers had on her scalp, Paige tilted her head back and sighed. "It does. I went there looking for a way to reconnect with Trace, but I ended up reconnecting with myself." She opened her eyes and met Kayla's gaze in the mirror. "I think I was able to let go of him." She smiled. "It was past time."

Kayla dropped Paige's hair and propped her hip against the vanity so she could face Paige directly. "I think I was able to let go too."

Worrying her bottom lip between her teeth, she rushed out her next words. "I met someone."

Paige's mouth dropped open. After the way she'd mourned Trace, Paige had worried Kayla would never move on again. Maybe her leaving had helped Kayla too.

Popping to her feet, she took a relieved breath and hugged her friend. "That's wonderful."

Kayla squeezed her tight and didn't let go. "You're not mad?"

Paige frowned. "Why would I be mad? It's been three years, Kayla. Way past time for you to date again."

"But—"

"Look at me." Paige pulled back enough to catch Kayla's shoulders and stare her in the eye. "Trace would want you to be happy."

Kayla looked sick to her stomach. She shook her head and opened her mouth, no doubt to argue, so Paige quickly spoke over her. "And *I* want you to be happy."

Paige had debated with herself numerous times over the years whether to tell Kayla about the engagement ring she'd found when cleaning out Trace's room after his funeral. He really had loved Kayla; he'd wanted to marry her.

In the end, Paige had decided against mentioning it; it'd only hurt Kayla more to know. Looking at her friend now, she was doubly glad she'd made the decision she had.

"Now spill all the details," she demanded, grinning. "What's this guy's name? What does he do? When can I meet him?"

Watching Kayla blush and gush about her new love interest was almost surreal. Since they'd become *real* friends, Paige couldn't re-member a conversation about something positive or the future. This felt…normal. Good.

Her attending Granton really had been the best thing. For everyone.

Paige returned to Granton first thing Sunday morning after Thanksgiving. Her father made no move to stop her or coax her to stay a couple hours longer. She wondered if he was relieved to see her go.

When she returned to her dorm, she felt better. At ease. She had no idea when this one room had become more of a home to her than her own, but she was glad to be back.

It was lonely, though. She knew Tess and Bailey wouldn't show up until after dinner, and Einstein wasn't in his usual haunts. She was actually relieved when Gus called her later that morning.

"I'm sorry to bother you, Paige, but Lynne called in sick, and I can't find anyone else to fill in for her tonight for the closing shift. I tried, I really did."

Curious why he sounded so apologetic since he called her all the time, asking her to fill in for someone, she assured him, "That's fine. I can come in tonight, no problem."

"Uh…"

Seriously, what in the world was going on?

"Yes?" she prompted.

"You'd be working with Logan."

Her heart gave a jolt. Suddenly, everything became clear. Logan must've said something to Gus. She wondered how exactly he'd worded his request. No way would he have told their boss about Trace. Would he?

"Tha — that's fine," she said, still flabbergasted about this revelation. "I don't mind."

"Really?" Gus sounded startled. "Oh, thank God. I promised my wife I'd take her out for our anniversary. She would've killed me if I'd had to cancel on her to fill in for Lynne."

"It's fine," Paige repeated, even though her heart rate jacked up a little too fast. "Really."

Chapter Seventeen

Paige clocked in ten minutes early for her shift with Logan. As she slowly wrapped her uniform apron around her waist, she drew in a bracing breath. She was about to see him again. Her pulse had been jackhammering through her bloodstream for the past hour since she'd hung up with Gus.

The idea of getting to see him animated her from the inside out. She couldn't pinpoint why it had her so restless; she barely knew him outside their history together. Maybe it was because every encounter with him had been so intense, it was hard for her body not to expect a little more intensity when she saw him again.

Forcing herself to exhale, she moved into the front, where Debra, who was obviously about to leave, gave a happy squeal and ripped off her apron. "Thank God you're here. I was about to go crazy."

Preoccupied with blending up a smoothie, Logan didn't notice her arrival.

Paige tore her gaze away from him and sent Debra a smile. "Been a busy night?" she asked. She would've thought things would slow down during the holiday break.

Logan whirled around, lost his grip on the cup he held and nearly dropped it. While he fumbled to straighten it, he choked out, "What're you—"

She breezed past him to the register where she would be working for the rest of the night. "Lynne called in sick. Gus couldn't find anyone else to fill in."

He didn't have an opportunity to respond, customers were flocking to the counter, so he let her explanation go for a good five minutes before they had a break in traffic.

Paige turned to him and set her hand on her hips. "You talked to him, didn't you? About making sure we never worked together?"

Logan studied her a moment before inclining his head. "Yes."

Her lips parted. "What did you tell him?"

"The truth." He glanced away, though she still caught the swirling look of anguish in his azure gaze.

Amazed and shocked he'd done something she instinctively knew he dreaded most in the world, she shook her head to deny it. But what was more unbelievable was he'd done it for her.

"You know, I, um…I really appreciate what you did," she murmured. "But honestly, it doesn't matter anymore."

At first, his only reaction was the flickering of his eyelashes. Then he frowned. "What doesn't matter?"

She shrugged and shifted by him to find a rag and wipe up a spot she saw on the back counter. "It doesn't matter if we work together or not, or if we're, you know, in the same room. Or same class. I know I used to freak out whenever you were…close, but that's not the case anymore."

He went very still, focusing intently on her. "It's not?" He shook his head. "I don't understand. Why not? What's changed?"

"Nothing changed." Paige put her back to him as she rinsed out the washcloth. "Except me, I guess. I just…I've worked through my issues a little. My issues concerning you, anyway."

Behind her, he remained quiet, though she could almost hear his thoughts whirling, trying to figure out what this meant for them now. She would have liked to answer him, but she wasn't too certain what it meant either. She only knew avoiding him at all costs was no longer necessary for her well-being.

When someone approached the counter, she rushed in front of Logan to take the order.

His mind still spinning as Paige stole his customer, Logan cocked his head to the side, trying to figure her out. She really was a different person than she'd been a few short months ago. He'd seen the transformation from across campus, but up close like this, it was… breathtaking.

He was so busy staring at her he didn't realize he needed to intervene until she muttered a curse under her breath. Scowling at the whipped cream dispenser, she jiggled the nozzle, trying to get it to work.

"Oh, I forgot to warn you." He hurried forward. "It's on the fritz."

"Again?" Paige spun to send him a frustrated frown. "What're we supposed to use then?"

When he motioned toward the dozen cans of whipped cream Gus had run to the store and bought earlier, her mouth dropped. "Are you freaking serious?"

He shrugged and held up his hands. "I know."

She shook her head and sighed. He helped her with filling the rest of her order, and together they worked in efficient silence until the counter was free of customers.

"Thanks," she murmured, glancing up at him from her lovely, dark eyes.

He glanced away because sometimes she was just too beautiful to look at. "Mmm hmm."

"So…" When she didn't continue, he gave in and cast a peek her way. She was still watching him, looking intent, like she wanted to say something. Her mouth opened. Then closed.

He turned to her fully, giving her his complete attention and that seemed to intimidate her even more. Ticked at himself for scaring her off of what she'd wanted to say, he began to turn away again, and finally she rushed out, "How was your Thanksgiving?"

He had a feeling that's not what she'd really wanted to say, but he didn't question it. She was talking to him. Life was good. But no way was he going to tell her how badly his holiday weekend had sucked.

He'd sat in his apartment alone, watching the Macy's parade on TV and wondering how she was, who she was with, if she was having a good time.

He nodded and murmured, "Mmm," to tell her it was fine without technically lying. "You?"

She nodded too. "Mmm."

Logan squinted, studying her hard enough to catch the gleam of amusement in her gaze. Was she…was she teasing him…again? For his non-forthcoming answer?

Obviously catching on to his suspicious gaze, she rolled her eyes and twirled away, leaving him breathless…in too good of a way.

She'd definitely been teasing him.

"So is there any castoff food we can snack on today?" she asked, busying herself by tossing away empty whipped topping cans. "I'm starving."

He watched her a moment longer before answering. "Uh, yeah. Actually, there is. Gus left a plateful in the break room. I'll go get it."

Before she could respond, he escaped down the back hall, hurrying to the break room. The tightness in his chest didn't come from leery anxiety about having to work with a woman who hated him. Instead it came from a leery anxiety about having to work with a woman who *didn't* hate him.

Because he didn't hate her right back.

And that could be very dangerous.

He'd composed his heart rate to a steady thump by the time he returned. Paige was busy with another customer, her back was to him, so she didn't see it when he stole a blueberry muffin from the for-sale bin and add it to the castoff plate, reminding himself to pay for it later.

It took everything he had not to grin smugly to himself when the blueberry muffin was the first thing she went for after her customers were taken care of.

"Mmm. Oh God, this is so good." Her eyes nearly rolled into the back of her head as she moaned, and his nearly rolled to the back of his as the sound she made pinged against every hormone in his body, stirring them all to life with painful awareness. "You know what would go great with this?"

He couldn't think up a non-naughty answer, so he merely lifted his eyebrows in question.

"An iced caramel latte." Then she brightened. "I'm buying one. We're not that busy."

After she pulled a bill from her pocket, she tossed it to him. "Could you ring me up, please?"

Catching the fluttering five from the air, he nodded. "Sure." When she began to make her own, he added, "I think I'll have one too," and pulled some money from his own pocket.

Her wide smile about undid him. "Cool."

Once he'd paid for her drink with her cash and the blueberry muffin and his drink with his, he approached her from behind, holding out her change. "Here's your change. Hey, you didn't have to make my latte too."

"It's okay; I don't mind." In the process of opening a new whipped cream can, Paige turned to smile at him as she struggled to pry it off. When she finally picked the lid free, it flew in a fancy arc straight toward Logan, beaning him right between the eyes.

She slapped her hand over her mouth. "Oh my God. I'm so sorry. Are you okay? Let me see." She grabbed his wrist of the hand he was holding over his face and yanked it down. "Oh, no. It left a mark. Logan, I can't believe I almost took your eye out."

He couldn't believe she looked so concerned about his eye. Or was holding his hand.

His face heated as he shrugged. "It's okay. Really. I have another one."

Dropping his wrist, she snorted out a laugh. "Yeah, I guess you do. Hmm." Her eyes continued to gleam with amusement as she watched him. "I wonder why people *do* have two eyes. I mean, we only have one nose and one mouth. Why two eyes? Or…why not three or four?"

He blinked, wondering where the heck that thought had come from. Instead of telling her how adorable he found her weird, philosophical pondering, he scratched his temple. "I've always wondered the same thing."

She lit with excitement. "Really?"

Oh, crap. He deflated and came clean. "No. Not really."

Giving him a sideways smirk, she pushed playfully at this arm. "Are you calling me weird?"

"No." He unconsciously reached for his sleeve where she'd touched him. "I wouldn't dare."

"You better not." Grinning, she nodded in approval.

Then she turned away to help a group of guys who came into the shop. They didn't have a chance to tease and play around for the rest of the night, but Logan still felt high from their brief encounter. By the time closing rolled around, he still had this euphoric surge of adrenaline pounding through him, like he could pick up the entire building and twirl it around on his pinkie.

As soon as Paige turned the *Open* sign around to display *Closed*, her nerves kicked in. She'd wanted to talk to Logan about his wrists for a while. After chickening out earlier, now was her last chance. But since "now" was actually here, saying what she wanted to say seemed awkward.

She cleared her throat as she hurried back the counter. "Do you mind if I turn on the radio? It helps me work better." Maybe it'd help ease her nerves into saying what she wanted to say too.

He glanced at her with the most inscrutable expression, and then gave a slight shake of his head. "I don't mind."

She tried to smile and found it strained. Her chest felt full, crammed with anxiety. "Thanks."

Gus kept an old alarm clock radio sitting on top of the tallest juice machine. Ricky had taught her she could turn the radio on after hours. Stretching up onto her tiptoes, she reached for the power button, her fingers stumbling blindly for the knob.

"Here." A long arm swooped above her head and flipped the switch.

A low, slow melody flowed over them. Paige lowered her hand and turned, finding it difficult to breathe as she caught Logan's gaze. With his arm still stretched over them, he asked, "Is this station okay?"

Her voice had definitely gone on vacation. She opened her mouth, tried to speak, and got nothing. Pressing her lips together, she nodded.

He lowered his arm, and she released her breath in a shudder.

When he shifted away, she felt a little lost. Pressing her hand against her heart, hoping to calm the rapid beat pouring through her, she closed her eyes, and steadied herself.

"I call dish duty."

He'd have to roll up his sleeves to do the dishes, and she'd caught him more than once this evening tugging them down. He'd probably done it before around her, but now she noticed it. She wondered if he realized how hard he constantly worked to hide them though.

Logan moved to the meat slicer and began to disassemble it. They worked together in companionable silence, the radio lulling her as it played the top forty hits.

When they finished, she glanced around. "Wow. I don't think I've ever finished clean up this fast before." Tossing him a pleased grin, she added, "We make a good team."

A choking sound came from his throat as he seared her with a dumbfounded glance.

She drew in a long breath, glad she had his attention, yet dreading the next few minutes.

"Actually, I'm glad we were scheduled together tonight," she pushed out, ready to get her speech over and done with. Ignoring the shock on his face, she smiled again, hoping to reassure him that she wasn't going to say anything rude or hateful. "I've been hoping to run across you for a while now. There was something I wanted to say. And I was going to do it on Halloween when you drove me and my friends home, but then Einstein got into trouble and sidetracked me, so..." She shrugged and sent him a rueful smile.

He blinked. "Okay." When he just watched her, his face frozen as if he was reserving his reaction until he heard her out, she glanced away, suddenly self-conscious.

"Anyway, I wanted to tell you I...that is, it wasn't fair of me to kick you out of the grief group. I shouldn't have done that."

He stared at her a moment longer, still frozen. Then he shook his head and frowned. "You didn't kick me out. I left voluntarily."

She frowned right back. He wasn't going to make this easy on her, was he? "But you wouldn't have left if I hadn't—"

He lifted his hand to stop her. "It's okay. You don't have to—"

"No," she pressed, remembering Einstein's scars, not just on his skin but on his soul. She didn't like the thought of someone else suffering that way too. Not even Logan Xander. "I *do* have to. When you said the group had really helped you, I didn't get it. Not then. But I know what you mean now, because the group's really helped me too." She flushed. "I mean, I haven't been able to talk about my issues with my mom's death yet or anything like that, but I just...I can tell that it's working...somehow."

She bit her lip, hoping that made some semblance of sense to him.

Logan gave a slow nod. "Yeah, I can tell too." When she looked up, he was the one to glance away and flush. "I mean, you're definitely different than you were at the beginning of the semester."

She smiled. "As in, I don't run wailing from the room whenever I see you now?"

His lips did that crooked hitch in one corner, as if he wanted to smile but wasn't quite capable. "Among other things."

His low voice moved through her, spreading a strange heat into all her limbs. Looking down at her hands, she pushed at her cuticles.

"Well, I *feel* different," she announced. "In a good way." When he didn't answer, she dropped her hands. "I guess we don't have to stand around here all night if we're done." Spinning away, she reached up to turn off the clock radio, except she couldn't reach it.

"Let me." Awareness curled up her spine as he stepped in close behind her. His arm brushed hers as he reached past her. She dropped her hand and lowered her face. The radio fell silent and her own thoughts seemed to echo around the quiet shop like a sonic boom.

When Logan stayed directly behind her, she swallowed and shut her eyes, hoping and praying he wouldn't do what she actually wanted him to do.

"You found her, didn't you?" he said. When she frowned and turned around, not comprehending, he winced. "Your mom."

He stepped back as if to give her space to run if she wanted to, but she didn't move. His face was now flushed. "It's just...I assume it has to be something even more traumatic than what happened with Tra—with your brother, since you still can't talk about her."

"Yes. I found her." She'd never told anyone that. "Why are you asking about this?"

"Because I need to know." His throat worked as he swallowed. She knew exactly what he was thinking. He wanted the details so he could share the pain with her. He felt responsible. She had no idea how she knew that just by looking at the bleak desolation in his blue eyes, but she was more certain of it than she was of anything.

"It must've happened on some big day," he went on, his voice hoarse. "A holiday, or...or the anniversary of your brother's death?"

"New Year's Eve," she whispered, closing her eyes, reeling in the fact she was sharing this...with Logan Xander of all people. "She left a note saying the thought of suffering through another year of life was more than she could handle."

"I'm sorry."

His quiet, heartfelt words didn't even reach her. She'd shifted to the past. "I'd just spent the night at my best friend's house. When I came home, she was…in the kitchen. I saw her as soon as I opened the back door."

Logan nodded. "Where was your dad?"

"In the living room, passed out on the couch. I don't know why he hadn't found her yet or heard the gunshot, but when I screamed, he came tearing into the kitchen, an empty beer bottle in his hand. After…after he saw her, he roared out this sound like an enraged animal, and he threw the bottle against the wall. But I was standing too close. Some of the shattering glass ricocheted and caught me in the arm." She rubbed the side of her shoulder where the half-moon scar was hidden under her long sleeves. "So much happened that day, I didn't even realize I'd been cut until late that night when I changed into something to sleep in."

With a sad sigh, Paige kept talking, the words spilling from her without her permission.

"Sometimes I wonder if she thought of me at all when she put the gun in her mouth. And I can't decide which would be worse, that she did consider my feelings in all this and hated me so much, she didn't care how it would affect me. Or that I meant so little to her, I didn't even cross her mind."

A sudden anger rose in her throat. "I mean, how *dare* she do this to me? To my dad? To herself? She planned it, probably for days. It was purposeful. It was even worse than what *you* did."

She knew she'd gone over the line when Logan wrenched back, his face saturated with pain and shock. And guilt.

Opening her mouth to instantly apologize, "Logan, I—" she stopped when he shook his head.

"No. I don't know if it was worse or not." He ducked his face as it flushed with color. "Maybe it wasn't. I definitely meant to hit your brother." Just as abruptly as the color had highlighted his cheeks, it fled, leaving him shaken and wan.

Reading his expression, she knew he was remembering. He was seeing Trace die at his feet all over again.

"But you didn't mean to kill him." She kept her voice low. Apologetic.

He closed his eyes and shuddered. "No. From the bottom of my heart, no. I didn't mean to kill him, I swear to you. I never meant it to go that far." When his lashes lifted, his piercing gaze begged her for forgiveness. "I never meant it to go that far."

For the first time, she actually wanted to give it. But letting go of the bitter anger toward him scared her, even though she knew she'd already absolved him in her heart over a month ago.

Clinging to her denial like a security blanket, she realized forgiving him would open the floodgate for other emotions to enter, emotions she knew she shouldn't harbor for Logan Xander.

Needing space from the overly personal conversation they'd started, she backed up and glanced around. They were still at The Squeeze, clocked in and discussing her mother of all things, a topic she'd refused to discuss with anyone.

She shook her head, dazed. "Why did I tell you all that?"

He shrugged. "Because I asked."

She knew it was more than that. She felt a connection with him. They had both suffered from the same event. They were both scrambling to find a way out of the misery. They were both lost but desperately seeking a purpose.

"Do you know why I came to Granton?" she asked, pretty much out of the blue.

Logan shook his head. "Did you know I was here?"

"No." She gave him a sad smile. "Not at all. It was actually because of Trace. This was his dream school."

"Oh, God." Face once again blanching of color, Logan leaned against the opposite counter and swiped a hand over his short crop of hair. "I had no idea."

"He wanted to get a business administration degree in marketing. So I majored in business administration." Paige gave a short, harsh laugh. "But the thought of actually taking a business class scares the crap out of me."

Logan peered at her. "Then why did you—"

"Because I wanted to live his life for him." Her shoulders lifted and fell in a helpless shrug. "It seemed easier than living my own life. Yet once I got here, I found I *could* have my own life. And slowly,

I started living for me instead of him. It was so strange. At home, everything fell apart around me, and no matter how hard I tried to fix it, it just got worse. But here...here I actually help people. I make a difference. I'm somebody. And I like it."

Glancing at him to gauge his reaction, she found him profoundly affected. Though he wasn't technically crying, his eyes looked wet. "That's...that's great, Paige," he whispered as if he was honestly proud of her.

"Yeah." She wiped her damp palms on her thighs before dropping her next bomb. "I think subconsciously, you and I both came here, to this college, for exactly the same reason. To start over fresh. But if not attending those grief group meetings prevents you from doing that, if it keeps you from your own healing process, I won't be able to move on quite so well either. I like helping people, and if I do something that purposely blocks you from being helped, it's going to bother me. A lot. So I really need you to come back to the meetings. Okay?"

The breath shuddered from his lungs before he answered. She knew how big a decision this was for him. But she didn't back off. She stared at him hard until he nodded.

"Okay," he said, his voice quiet. "I'll be there."

Chapter Eighteen

Logan approached the Crimson Room the next Tuesday evening with his nerves on edge. Just because Paige had *told* him she was fine with him returning to the grief group didn't mean she honestly *was* fine with him returning to the grief group. He knew he'd said he was fine plenty of times when he hadn't been.

But there was only one way to find out the truth. To show up at a meeting. Besides, he'd missed it. A lot. He missed Samantha, and Jamie's weekly treats, and Kevin's goofy comments. The members had become his pseudo family these last few years, and he looked forward to seeing them again.

Most of all, he looked forward to seeing her.

He fully realized he had to be the biggest loser on earth, crushing on the most forbidden girl he could possibly dream about. But Paige was so…

She was just so Paige.

She could put her own abhorrence for him aside so they could both move on with their lives. There was something precious about that. He wished he could be more like her.

Smoothing his long sleeves as far down over his wrists as he could get them to go, he paused just before the entrance, working himself up for the big moment. When he felt ready enough to proceed, he blew out cheeks full of air and stepped into the room.

"Oh my God. *Logan?*"

At Samantha's astonished cry, Paige lifted her face. She turned slowly from talking to Jamie and watched from across the room as Samantha rushed to him and hugged him hard. Others flocked forward to welcome him back as well, and not one person asked why he'd been absent for so long.

Logan smiled timorously at the hearty greetings and murmured one-word responses to each person who spoke to him.

It struck her then how quiet he was. Not even at work when he had to talk to customers did he speak a lot other than what needed to be said.

There went another misconception she'd made about him. Before, she'd always pictured him as a conceited loudmouth, spewing out a bunch of vain nonsense just to hear his own voice. But her assumption couldn't have been further from the truth.

Paige sighed. She'd been so wrong about him on so many different issues.

When he glanced up and caught her gaze, she felt captured. Her breathing stumbled through her lungs at the hesitant, questioning look he sent her, silently asking if she was certain about his presence.

In answer, she smiled and nodded her own greeting.

He stared at her another moment longer before turning back to Sam to respond to whatever she'd said to him.

The leader of the group seemed happier to see him than anyone. Samantha hooked her arm through his and led him to the circle, talking animatedly. Paige hadn't realized just how much she'd taken away from everyone here when she'd forced him to leave. He might not have been a loquacious member, but sometimes silent support was equally important.

She was glad she'd grown up enough to make him come back.

"Okay, everyone," Sam called, clapping her hands. "Time to get this show on the road. We have lots to do tonight." Her cheeks were flushed with pleasure and her smile full of joy as she gathered the college students to the circle.

To show her support, Paige made sure to slip into the empty seat next to Logan.

He didn't glance her way, but she heard his sharp intake as she sat.

Keeping her voice quiet, she murmured, "Welcome back."

He gave a slight nod, letting her know he'd heard her.

She had never been so aware of the person sitting next to her before. Paige held her breath as she stared at his knee, barely making out the jean-clad joint in her peripheral vision. They sat only inches apart. If she wanted to, she could probably swing her leg to the side and bump it into his.

Why she was even thinking about this, she had no idea. But it was hard to concentrate on anything else.

Samantha cleared her throat, gaining the room's attention. "First of all, I wanted to let everyone know I got us some hour-long slots to visit the children's ward at the cancer center next month. So I have a clipboard here with the sign-up sheet. Once everyone interested in participating writes down their name, I'll split you up into groups and let you know which dates you have."

She handed the clipboard to the girl on her right.

"And since finals are next week, this is technically our last meeting before winter break. So, I'm making it our Christmas party of sorts. Because our group uses the Crimson Room more actively than any other group on campus, we were asked to decorate it for the holidays. Which means, no group sharing tonight. We're hanging decorations instead!"

Christmas.

The word sent a lonely flutter through Paige's throat. She'd have to go home for a few weeks following finals since the dorms closed during the winter break. After spending two days home during Thanksgiving, she wasn't looking forward to Christmas at all. Her dad hadn't said a total of five sentences to her the last time she'd seen him. She wondered if he'd bother to talk to her at all this time.

Realizing most of the grief group had already shifted to the boxes full of decorations lined against the wall, Paige looked up when the girl on her left handed her the sign-in sheet.

"Thanks." She studied the list, a little disappointed so few had volunteered to visit the sick children. Wanting to write her name in huge, bold letters, she frowned when she realized she didn't have the proper equipment.

"Does anyone have a pen I can borrow?" she called, lifting her attention from the clipboard.

"I think I do."

When she realized Logan still sat beside her, waiting for his turn to sign while everyone else had wandered toward the decorations, her muscles tensed.

Ducking his face, he dug through his backpack. Paige grew fascinated watching the crown of his head where she could see his scalp through his trim, buzzed hair. She wondered why he cut it so short. Did it have anything to do with this penance thing he seemed so determined to put himself through?

When he came up from the depth of his bag with a pen in hand, he sucked in a breath the same moment she recognized it. It was her pen, the very pen she'd dropped the first day of classes when she'd learned he was attending the same university as her.

"Oh." The word puffed from his lips as he gaped at the pen in horrified embarrassment. "Sorry. I have another…" He began to retract it and slip it into his bag when she decided they were being silly.

For crying out loud, it was just a pen.

"This one will do." She plucked it from his hand before he could tuck it away.

His head snapped up, blue eyes startled.

Turning away before she could read too much into his expression, or he could read too much into hers, she scrawled her name on the sheet, ignoring the way her hand shook slightly.

Plastering an overly grateful smile on her face, she said, "Thanks," and tried to give the pen back to him.

His eyes flared wide, and he pulled back as if scared of the pen. Shaking his head, he waved her to keep it. "It's yours anyway."

"Don't you need it to sign in?" she asked.

He stared at her a moment as if he wanted to figure out what was going on in her head. Then he apparently gave up trying and lowered his gaze as he nodded. "Thanks."

The pen slipped slowly from her hand. She had no idea why she stuck around, but she remained seated beside him while he signed in his name and set the clipboard on Samantha's vacated seat.

He stared at the pen in his hand. She could almost hear the inner debate in his head, wondering if he should try to foist it back on her or just keep it.

Deciding to save him from such daunting indecision, she reached out and tugged it from his fingers.

Though he let her take it without a word of protest, he tracked the departing tool as if silently saying goodbye to an old friend. Then his gaze shifted to her.

She held her breath, knowing she should really stand up and go now, but she couldn't seem to move.

"I didn't know if you'd really show up tonight or not."

One corner of his mouth hitched in amusement. "Neither did I."

Paige patted his knee. "Well, I'm glad you did." She realized she shouldn't have touched him when he immediately focused on her hand. She'd been attempting to be friendly—and nothing more—but even a friendly touch was too much between them. She pulled her fingers back to her own lap.

Needing to escape, she surged to her feet and hurried to the main event of the evening. When Kevin called her over to the imitation tree that was rapidly growing from the floor up, she joined him, grateful for the distraction.

While others strung vines of holly and festive streamers around the room, she and Kevin buried themselves in the tree project. Though she made sure not to look his way, she heard Samantha call to Logan for assistance with untangling a huge ball of lights.

Always aware of where Logan was, she cracked jokes with Kevin as they put their heads together and hooked faux tree limbs around the metal-pipe trunk.

Stepping back after they finished, Kevin scratched his head and made a face. "There's just something about imitation trees that looks so…"

"Fake?" Paige supplied with a grin.

"Exactly." When he caught her teasing smile, he smirked and bumped his arm against hers. "Smart aleck."

Chuckling, she bent down and fiddled with the tree's skirt. "Don't worry. Once we get the ornaments and lights put on, it'll look better."

Finishing her task, she glanced up at Kevin because he hadn't responded yet. He was absorbed in looking at her butt, making her self-conscious, hoping she hadn't sat in something earlier and had a huge stain or nasty smear across her back pockets.

Quickly darting his gaze away, Kevin cleared his throat and tugged at his ear, pasting his attention back on the limp, tilted tree.

"What's wrong?" she asked, straightening and wiping at her knees she'd been sitting on before discreetly brushing off her backside.

Face infused with hot, embarrassed color, Kevin mumbled, "Nothing. Uh…I think I know what this thing needs." Holding up a finger, he instructed, "Wait right here."

As he darted toward an opened cardboard box full of decorations, Paige frowned after him, confused by his odd behavior. Then she checked on Logan, telling herself she needed to know if he had a row of lights strung out yet for them to wind around the tree, though really, she just wanted to peek at him.

His attention was already on her, and his lips twitched, his expression gleaming with amusement. When their gazes met, his blue eyes flared. He jerked away to focus on his job where he already had two series of lights unraveled and strung across the floor.

"What's so funny?" she asked, utterly confused.

First Kevin. Now Logan. What the heck? She had sat in something, hadn't she? She swept a hand over the back of her jeans again, wishing *someone* would tell her if she'd made a mess of herself.

"Nothing," he said, only to chuckle under his breath.

If she had one nearby, she might be tempted to throw an ornament at him. "*What?*" she hissed.

His grin spread, and he shook his head. "You don't even know when you're being hit on, do you?"

Totally not expecting him to say something like that, Paige blinked, dumbfounded. "Huh?" Had he just confessed he was hitting on her?

Her heart lurched erratically in her chest.

She opened her mouth but had no idea how to respond.

"I've got tinsel," Kevin said, returning to her and sounding breathless as if he'd run the entire way. He looked so eager to please she gaped at him a moment before realization hit. "I swear tinsel can make anything look better," he added as he playfully tossed a strand onto her hair.

Oh. *Ohhhh…*

Holy guacamole, *Kevin* had been hitting on her this entire time. And no, she *hadn't* realized it. Geesh, it hadn't even occurred her that he'd been *appreciating* the view when she'd bent over to straighten the tree skirt.

She flashed a quick, censorious look Logan's way, but he suddenly seemed overly involved in his menial task.

"Here you go." Kevin offered her a handful.

With a weak smile, she accepted the sparkly silver tinsel and sparingly began to spread it over the tree.

"How're we doing getting the lights unwound?" Samantha asked, approaching Logan to assist him. When he pulled a pentagon from the tangle of green wires, she gasped. "Oh, you found the star. Great." Taking it from him, she smiled fondly. "My husband and I always made a ritual out of putting the star on last." Then she laughed as if amused with herself. "As I'm sure most people do."

When her smile fell, Paige paused in her tinsel draping to watch the leader of their group look momentarily lost, no doubt mourning the love of her life.

She wanted to give Sam a hug, but the woman pulled herself back under control too quickly. She cleared her throat, forcing cheerfulness. "Does your family do that too, Logan?"

Logan began to shake his head but paused. "No, but uh…every year, my family would wait until Christmas Eve before we went to the Christmas tree farm and picked out our tree. I always thought of it as Christmas Tree Night instead of Christmas Eve. I remember anticipating Christmas Tree Night almost as much as Christmas morning. Both my parents would be home. My brothers and I would crowd into the back seat, always arguing over who had to sit in the middle." A wistful smile crossed his face.

"What made your family stop them?" Sam asked softly.

He jerked his face up, looking guilty. "What? Oh, no. They haven't…they haven't stopped."

Sam wrinkled her brow. She looked as confused by his statement as Paige felt. Paige watched his expression go shuttered as Samantha pressed, "But they're not the same anymore?"

He offered her a tight smile. "No, you're right. They're still…it's still the best night of the year."

As the leader of the group lifted an untangled line of lights and carried it off, Paige continued to study Logan's face. Something was very off about what he'd just said, but she couldn't figure out what.

As if sensing her stare, he looked up. Not bothering to mask his emotion, he stared at her, and she could see from his face how much he hurt inside. He appeared so vulnerable, she actually stepped toward him.

But Kevin turned to her, asking if she needed more tinsel.

"What?" She blinked and looked at her tree-decorating partner. "Oh. No. No, I think I'm good over here. Should we put the lights on next?"

He agreed, and having heard them, Logan lifted an unraveled strand to help them wrap the tree.

They'd just finished when Jamie called Logan away, needing someone tall to climb a ladder and hang ornaments from the ceiling tiles.

Paige managed to deflect Kevin's attempts at flirting for the rest of the meeting. After her dud date with Reggie, going out with another guy didn't seem so exciting anymore. She'd decided she wanted to really feel it before she accepted another date from anyone. And though she liked Kevin enough, the zing of chemistry didn't ricochet through her system like a hyper bouncy ball whenever she saw him. Not the way it did with —

Realizing who she was thinking about, her gaze zapped to the tall figure standing on a ladder stretching his arms over his head to hang a tiny angel.

Oh, this wasn't good.

Releasing her hate was one thing. But actually liking him — as in, *liking* liking him — was something totally different. Something disastrous. Like spitting on Trace's grave.

She needed to nip this in the bud right now.

Determined to avoid him, she strayed to the other side of the room from him for the rest of the decorating party. And she was successful, keeping her distance...until Samantha called it a night.

"Oh, I've gone through the sign-ups for the cancer center visits and paired everyone into groups of two or three. Make sure to check your dates before you leave tonight."

Paige fell into line behind the handful of others who'd signed up. When she reached the schedule, she ran her finger along the sheet until she found her name. Her first visitation would take place right after the New Year with Jamie and...Logan.

She dropped her hand from the sheet and jolted backward, unable to believe her eyes.

Great. How was she supposed to elude him if they were scheduled to attend a hospital together?

"I can ask Sam to change the group assignment," a low voice murmured beside her so only she could hear him.

Paige jumped and swung around to gape up at Logan. His eyes looked remote as he studied her. She could tell from his expression he knew exactly what she was thinking.

Drawing in a deep breath, she shook her head. "No, don't...don't worry about it. It'll be fine."

His lips parted and his eyes narrowed as if he didn't believe her.

Flushing, she realized she must appear as horrified as she felt about seeing their names side by side.

"Are you sure?" he pressed.

Gah, what was wrong with her? All they'd be doing was entertaining a bunch of sick children for an hour. It wasn't the end of the world.

Stiffening her shoulders, she nodded. "Yes. I'm positive. It's fine."

He studied her a second longer before he gave a single nod. "Okay, then. I guess I'll see you at the children's ward in four weeks."

"This doesn't mean..." She rushed out, only to realize what she'd almost said. She wanted to tell him she still hadn't forgiven him, but the words wouldn't come, probably because they weren't true.

His azure eyes filled with bleak acceptance. "Trust me; I *know*." Turning away, he marched off, his stride stiff and angry.

Paige stared after him, feeling awful. That fine line where she no longer hated him but knew better than to actually like him seemed impossible to find. No matter how hard she tried, it always came out as stark black or white with him.

Chapter Nineteen

"Have you been home yet?"

Paige's fingers paused over the metal jewelry tree of rings she was examining on Kayla's dressing table. Lifting her face, she met Kayla's gaze in the mirror as her best friend came up behind her.

"Not yet." Promptly dropping her gaze again, she picked out a silver ring with a turquoise stone embedded in a coiled design. "I came here to see you as soon I made it into town."

"And I'm glad you did. I've missed you so much these past few months." Kayla set her hands on Paige's shoulders and gave an encouraging squeeze. "But seriously, do you want me to go with you? I know things between you and Paul aren't...close. Maybe a third party will help things feel..." she shrugged "...not so awkward."

Paige slipped off the turquoise ring and sighed deeply. "Thanks for the offer, but it's fine. I can handle it."

Besides, she hadn't been home since Thanksgiving. She didn't want to think of how messy the place was by now. And she didn't want Kayla to see what had become of it...or of her father, though she suspected Kayla already knew how far Paul Zukowski had declined.

"I don't mind," Kayla said. She smiled brightly as she took off Paige's ruby cross amulet to sling another bedazzled necklace around her throat. "I bought Paul a gift for Christmas anyway."

Without saying a word, Paige shook her head, once again declining Kayla's efforts. "I'll gladly deliver Dad's present for you, though." She tried to soften her refusal.

Winding Paige's hair into one large coil, Kayla curled the dark mane into a makeshift bun on top of her head. "Is it that bad between you two?" she asked quietly.

Paige sighed again, not even wanting to think about her and her dad. "No, it's not so bad. I mean, we don't talk at all when I'm gone and barely at all when I'm back. But other than that, things are…manageable. Civil."

Kayla dropped Paige's hair as if giving up on it. As the dark strands fluttered down over her shoulders, she met her best friend's gaze in the mirror.

"Then why do you look so sad, sweetie? At Thanksgiving, I swear you seemed like the old you, the Pay Day you were before—" She shook her head, refusing to mention *the before*. "Is Granton not treating you right after all?"

"No." Paige shook her head. "No, it's nothing like that." Feeling naked without Trace's necklace against her skin, she slid off the one Kayla had tried on her and returned the cross where it belonged. "I still love it there. I'm making friends and fitting in, and—" she blushed "—flirting with guys."

"Ooh, now you have my attention." Kayla wiggled her eyebrows and nudged Paige to scoot over and give her room on the small stool so they could sit beside each other. "Tell me more about these guys."

Paige groaned, wishing she'd kept quiet about that part. "There's nothing to tell really. I already told you about Reggie. But…a couple others have shown their interest."

"And?"

Paige shrugged. "And nothing. I haven't felt a spark back toward any of them. Well, except for—" When she realized whose name had almost spilled from her mouth, her lips slapped together tight and her eyes flew open wide with horror as mortified heat covered her from head to toe.

Kayla pounced. "Except for who?"

Wagging her head back and forth savagely, Paige squeaked, "No one."

"Oh, no you don't, girlfriend. Spill it. Every detail."

"I can't...there's nothing to spill. Honest. He's no one." Except the person she had once upon a time blamed for taking Trace away from them and destroying both their lives.

Kayla bumped Paige's shoulder insistently. "So what's no one's name?" she sang out the question.

All feeling and warmth leached from Paige. No way could she tell Kayla his name.

"Okay, fine," Kayla gave in, leaving that question alone. "Just tell me he's super-hot and likes you as much as you like him."

"I can't...it doesn't matter. Nothing can ever happen between us. It's impossible."

"Why? Is he married? A professor?" Kayla gasped. "Oh my God, he's a married professor."

Paige snorted, then laughed. "No. Neither. But he is forbidden. *Really* forbidden."

Chewing on her bottom lip, Kayla looked momentarily stumped. "Yeah, those forbidden boys do tend to look more appealing, don't they? There's just something about being told to stay away that makes you want to climb all over 'em."

Mouth dropping open, Paige turned to gawk at her best friend. "You sound a little too much like the voice of experience there."

Kayla blushed and picked up a tube of lip-gloss. Averting her attention to the mirror as she screwed off the cap and applied it, she said, "What do you think Trace was? My dad had heard of his wild reputation and told me to stay away."

Paige gasped. "Oh my God."

How could Mr. Hashman think of Trace as wild? He'd only been outgoing with a mischievous side, and okay, sometimes he said the most outrageous, controversial things just to stir up a commotion. And maybe he'd driven too fast and had spent his fair share of time in school detention. But he'd been harmless.

"Why have I never heard this before?" Paige demanded.

"Probably because I totally ignored my dad's warning and started dating him anyway." Kayla shrugged. "Dad didn't really object that loudly, and he ended up *adoring* Trace once they finally met." She laughed and rolled her eyes. "I swear, Trace could charm anyone."

"Wow." Dazed, Paige glanced at her own reflection in the mirror. "My annoying brother was actually your forbidden taste of bad boy. Weird."

Kayla giggled. "And he did taste mighty fine, thank you very much."

Pretending to gag, Paige gasped, "TMI! TMI!"

Both girls shoved at each other, laughing uncontrollably, and ended up booting one another off the stool. After landing on the floor, they curled into balls and gripped their stomachs, giggling.

But after the moment passed, Paige grew serious and closed her eyes. "So how do I know if it's this guy's forbidden status that has me fascinated or if it's just plain him I like?"

"Well…" Sprawled on the floor, Kayla kicked out her legs and found a relaxed incline as she tucked a hand against her cheek and studied Paige. "How well do you know him?"

Paige blinked, not quite sure how to answer. She knew more about him than anyone else at Granton knew about him. She also knew how he volunteered his time for good, honorable acts. He worked hard. He faced his biggest fears on a daily basis. He put others before himself. He'd been willing to sacrifice things he loved so Paige could get whatever she wanted without having to deal with his presence. He cleaned and wrapped bloody fingers. She felt connected to him as she did no one else since they shared some of the same aches and loneliness in life. She could tell him things she couldn't tell anyone else. He took life too seriously and hardly ever smiled. He had the saddest yet most beautiful blue eyes she'd ever seen, and a crooked half grin that made her tummy clench with the urge to touch him. And he handled her corny teasing with a dry wit she loved. And he was too freaking gorgeous for his own good.

"I guess…I guess I know him better than I thought I did, but we haven't…we haven't really *tried* to get to know each other." They'd been a little too busy trying to *avoid* each other.

Groaning over the entire messed up situation, she rolled onto her spine and thumped the back of her head on the Kayla's bedroom carpet, once, twice, and a third time for good measure. "Not that any of that matters. Nothing will ever happen. I don't want it to happen. I don't even want to consider it happening."

"Which is exactly what you're doing now." Kayla grinned.

Paige rolled onto her side to lob Kayla an irritated scowl. She really hated it when Kayla was right. "Nothing's going to happen," she stated firmly.

"Well, then I guess we should just stop talking about him then, huh." With an impish grin, she fluttered her lashes. "Though you will name your firstborn after me, right? And it goes without saying I'm going to be the maid of honor at your wedding."

"Oh, shut up!" With a laugh, Paige grabbed a stuffed teddy bear lying at the foot of Kayla's bed and chucked it at her.

Kayla's arm shot up, shielding herself, and the padded toy bounced unharmed off her arm. "Ooh, what a deadly comeback. I'm shaking in my jammies over here."

Challenged, Paige grabbed a sock monkey. And the giggling fight was on. As immature and silly as it was, the stuffed animal war soothed Paige's nerves. Ducking and swinging, she laughed, throwing out empty threats and basking in Kayla's company.

But deep inside, she still worried. If Kayla knew who she was talking about, would she be so open to the idea? Would she still tease Paige about marriage and babies?

Paige didn't think so.

She kept her brewing dilemma to herself, determined to push her growing feelings for a forbidden boy as deeply inside herself as they would go and not let them spread any farther.

Avoiding the moment she had to drive home to her dad's house, she lingered at Kayla's, doing total girl stuff together like painting toenails, checking out famous gorgeous guy pictures on line, talking movies, and snacking on junk food.

When she finally called it a night, Kayla walked her to her car. "Thanks for stopping by, sweetie. And call me in the morning. I want to know how the homecoming with Paul went. Besides, I want to spend every possible second with you while you're home, maybe introduce you to my man, Archer, and go last-minute Christmas shopping together."

"It's a deal." Paige hugged her friend and started home.

Chapter Twenty

Logan couldn't pinpoint exactly what prompted him to drive home on Christmas Eve. He told himself it wasn't because of Paige; just because he knew she was somewhere in Creighton County, he wanted to be here too. But deep inside, he recognized she was definitely a factor.

He was drawn to her light.

He drove his old secondhand truck slowly through his hometown, feeling nostalgia, depression, and a strange disconnection. While most things were exactly how they'd been before he'd left, little changes here and there made it look foreign.

He wondered when someone had torn down that old barn at the north end of town across from the school. And had the house next to the post office always been such a gawd-awful green?

Everything seemed so small. Even the streets looked narrower.

Sighing, he drove past his parents' house. Did they still live there? They'd been there all his years of growing up, but things changed.

He'd certainly changed.

The lights were off inside; with dusk approaching, it looked empty. But he already knew it would be. He knew where his family was.

He drove to the only Christmas Tree farm in the county.

Pulling over into the drive of an abandoned gas station that had been running when he'd lived in the area, he killed the engine and slid out of his truck. Across the street, the tree farm looked busy. Festive holiday music played from speakers strategically placed along the rows of perfectly-formed firs and spruces.

Logan scanned the cars in the parking lot, but he didn't spot his mother's Land Cruiser. Then again, she tended to trade in every other year, so he wouldn't know what she was driving now.

After zipping his coat up against the winter chill, he stuffed his hands into the pockets and leaned against his tailgate as he watched families leave and arrive. It amazed him how many people waited until the night before Christmas to get their tree. He'd always thought his was but a few to do this.

But seeing a young dad struggle to roll his Douglas fir onto the roof of his car while his wife held back their three toddler children told Logan how wrong he was. Many families held the same tradition as his. Twitching with the need to race across the street to help the poor guy out, Logan pulled his hands from his pockets and straightened away from his truck. He actually took a step in their direction when another family hauling their tree to a sleek black Mercedes SUV caught his attention.

For a second, he froze as he watched them, feeling royally exposed where he stood. Crouching slightly, he slunk backward along the side of his truck until a shadow concealed him.

His two younger brothers—God, they'd gotten tall—carried their blue spruce with ease, one holding onto the base, the other carrying the front. Under the instruction of their father, they lifted and effortlessly plopped the tree onto the roof.

Chest growing tight as he watched, Logan swallowed convulsively. His mom wore her hair different these days, longer and straighter. She looked lovely. Elegant. Fisting his hand, he brought it to his mouth, feeling like an invader for spying on them during their family time. But he couldn't bring himself to look away.

They definitely hadn't stopped tradition just because he'd left.

"You lied at the meeting."

When the soft accusation came from beside him, Logan whirled around. Focusing on the new arrival, he dropped his hand from his mouth to press his open palm flush against his erratic heartbeat.

"Paige!" He drew in a deep breath. "What...what're you *doing* here?"

She shrugged, her eyes sad as she glanced past him toward his parents and brothers, who were now tying their tree down with bungee cords.

"I just wanted to torture myself, I guess." Her smile was anything but happy. "With it just being my dad and me, Christmas is pretty dismal around my place. It depresses him a lot, so he mostly just drinks. I...I guess I wanted to see what your Christmas Tree Night was all about and feel envious over here across the street by myself while I hated you and your perfect family from afar."

Logan didn't know how to reply to that. He understood her sentiment too well.

"Is that them?" she asked, hitching her chin to point out his family.

He glanced over and watched his brothers pile into the back of their car as his parents got into the front. "Yeah."

Paige nodded. "And why aren't you with them?"

He drew in a long, deep breath. "Because they kicked me out."

"*What?*" Paige seared him with an incredulous glance before she shook her head vigorously. "No...that can't be. Your dad was your lawyer. He got you out of jail. He supported you."

With a bitter laugh, Logan shook his own head. "Of course he got me out of jail. Do you know how mortified he would have been if a Xander, one of his own, had been imprisoned? It was bad enough his son had already embarrassed the family by killing someone, but for me to actually pay for my crime was unheard of. To preserve the family name, he got me off, and then he told me once I graduated from high school, he wanted nothing to do with me."

Paige's mouth fell open as she gaped at him. "And what did your mom say?"

Logan shrugged as he turned his gaze back to watch his family's SUV back out of their parking spot. "She didn't say anything. She agreed with him."

Stepping up beside him as his family disappeared down the street, Paige said nothing.

He wondered what she thought of him now. That he was a pathetic loser who deserved what he got? She'd lost most of her family over what he'd done; it was only fair that he lose his too. She was probably smug and overjoyed to learn he'd lived alone these past few —

"What're your brothers' names?" she asked so quietly he barely heard her.

He glanced at her, astonished to see her eyes downcast with empathy.

Swallowing the knot of shock in his throat, he fumbled to answer. "Uh...Caleb. Caleb and Jake. Jake is sixteen now and Caleb is...wow." Logan shook his head, depressed to realize how much time had really passed. "He's eighteen. Already a senior."

Paige nodded as if soaking in the information. "Have you seen any of them? At all? Had any contact with them?"

Logan began to shake his head. "No. Well...Jake keeps his Facebook account public. I check his page...a lot." He sent her a grin. "Looks like he might be better than me on the basketball court."

Instead of smiling back, Paige looked crushed. His words had reminded her of her own star basketball player of a brother. Dizziness wavered through him, and everything came flooding back. The reason his family had rejected him. The reason he'd never have a future with this wonderful person. The reason he was so broken.

He'd killed Trace Zukowski. Taken a life. Stopped a beating heart.

Forcing himself to breathe through his nose before he had a panic attack, he looked up at the clear sky. Half of a moon dangled among the glittering stars, just like half a man stood next to the most dazzling female he'd ever know.

"You were right, you know," he confessed, still gazing out above them. "Your brother didn't start the fight that night."

He wasn't sure why he told her. But with the memory of Trace lying dead at his feet so fresh in his mind, he wanted her to know the truth. Everything.

Paige gasped. From the corner of his eye, he saw her whirl toward at him.

"So you *did* hit him first?"

He shook his head. "No. No, he threw the first punch. That was true." With a deep breath, he added, "But I made very certain he would."

"What happened?"

Finally, he turned to look at her. With dark eyes intent on him, she'd drawn both her hands up to just below her chin and held them together, almost as in prayer. He could see on her face how much she yearned to hear this story. But if he told her, she'd probably hate him again afterward.

He didn't like it when she hated him.

"Are you sure you want to know?"

She gulped as if she fully comprehended the consequences. Then she nodded. "Yes."

"Okay." He closed his eyes, prepared to regain her absolute abhorrence. "After we lost the ball game that night, my friends and I drove into Landry and got stupid drunk. We were hanging out in our usual spot when your brother and his crew happened by. I was still in a raw mood after losing to him, so I called out something, some kind of sarcastic congratulations. I don't exactly remember what I said. But he had some witty comeback that ticked me off."

Logan scoffed and glanced askance at Paige. "He *always* had a smart aleck response for everything. Even on the court."

Paige's grin was immediate and watered with nostalgic tears. "That was Trace for you. A great big smart-mouthed know-it-all."

"Yeah, well it drove me crazy," Logan muttered. "And he knew it, so he did it every chance he got. What was worse, he was so good at everything. I just wanted to beat him at *something*. And that was when I focused on the girl he had tucked under his arm."

Paige perked to attention. Dropping her hands from her chest, she frowned. "Say what?"

Logan turned back to the stars. He couldn't look at her for this part of the story. "I waited until she was off away from him…and then I struck."

"Oh, my God." Paige covered her mouth with both hands. "What did you *do?*"

Sending her a brief scowl, he sniffed. She didn't have to make it sound as if he'd accosted the girl against her will.

"Nothing *bad*. I just…flirted mostly. She was as drunk as I was, so it wasn't too terribly hard to charm her. When your brother caught us kissing, though, he was—"

"*Kissing!*" Paige jerked her hands down to her abdomen as she sucked in large breaths through her mouth. "You kissed…you kissed Kayla? Oh my God. *Kayla?*"

Kayla? "Yeah," he said on a grimace. "I think that was her name."

"No, no, no," Paige insisted. She shook her head resolutely as if denying it enough would make it not so. "You're mistaken. Not Kayla. You don't understand. You can't mean Kayla. He *loved* Kayla."

When Logan just stared at her, she balled her hands into fists. "You don't understand," she repeated, her voice raising an octave. "He bought her a *ring.* I found it when I was cleaning out his room. But I couldn't tell her about it because I didn't want to hurt her. He loved her *so* much."

A ring?

Falling back a step, Logan gawked, unable to digest this properly. Reaching out, he caught hold of the bed of his truck, needing the support.

"He was going to marry her," Paige hissed, making him flinch.

Looking away, he cursed aloud. "I didn't…I didn't know."

"She…she's my best *friend* now." Paige sobbed in a dry heave.

He glanced up and saw the look in her dazed eyes, the sick disdain on her face.

"God. I shouldn't have told you that part."

"Yes. Yes, you *should* have." Hysteria filtered into her words. "Someone should've told me a long time ago. Oh my God."

"Paige." He stepped toward her, lifting his hand, only wanting to comfort her. "She didn't do anything wrong. She was so out of it. She didn't know what she was doing. It was all me. I did everything I could to steal her away from him. In fact, I swear she was starting to push me away when he caught us."

"I don't care," Paige nearly screamed, slapping his fingers away before he actually touched her. Tears streamed down her cheeks. "He *loved* her. He wanted to marry her someday. And she let another guy *kiss* her?"

He watched her curl into herself, cradling her arm around her waist as she bowed her face and clenched her eyes shut.

Agony tore through him. He didn't want to watch this; he ached even knowing he'd started and couldn't stop it.

"Paige, please," he begged with no idea what he was actually begging for. "No matter what happened that night, she's *still* your best friend. Hating her now is only going to hurt both of you. I guarantee you one hundred percent she is sorry for what happened, and if she could take it back, she would in a heartbeat. I mean, the way she cried over him…" He shook his head. "I swear I've never seen anyone cry like that before. She refused to leave his side. She was…she was *devastated*."

Paige wiped her wet face and looked at him. He tensed under her all-knowing gaze, and everything became clear. He wasn't just pleading her friend's case; he was pleading his own. By the look in her eyes, he could tell she knew that.

"I don't know," he mumbled, suddenly uncomfortable. Hugging himself, he glanced to where his family's car had sat minutes ago. "Or maybe you'll do just fine without her."

His family seemed perfectly fine without him.

"No." Paige sniffed back a few more tears. "No, I wouldn't. And I'm sure your family is *not* fine without you either." Turning slightly away from him, she brushed her hands off onto her thighs as if needing something to do. Then she drew in a deep breath, collected herself, and looked at him over her shoulder. "Thank you for telling me."

He nodded, unsettled by how easily she'd been able to find composure. Holding pain inside couldn't be good for a person. If she was repressing anything, it'd hurt her more in the long run.

Not sure what else to say, certain anything that came out of his mouth would only induce her to hold more in, he reached for the handle of his truck door. "I should…I should go." He'd already done enough damage. He couldn't handle the thought of doing more. Especially to her.

But she stopped him with a single word. "Logan?"

He paused and heaved a shaky breath, afraid to turn around. "Yeah?"

"The night I cut my finger at The Squeeze and saw your wrists…"

When she didn't go on, he swallowed and rotated to face her. She was going to ask about his cut marks; he just knew it. He didn't want to talk about them. Ever. He'd been in a dark place then, so dark he wasn't sure how he'd ever climbed out of all that black. He couldn't reasonably explain why he'd done it, couldn't rationalize the overwhelming necessity to end everything. He'd just needed to stop the pain.

"I was so messed up." He breathed out the confession. "I don't know why I cut them. I'd just gotten my life back on track. It didn't make any sense."

Paige merely watched him. So he kept talking, blurting it all out.

"After…after my parents kicked me out, they let me keep my car. So I drove it as far as I could on a tank of gas. Then I sold it for cash. It was just a quirk of fate I landed in Granton. But I found a job, a crappy place to live, and since the entire town centered around the university, I eventually enrolled. But it was like I was on auto pilot.

"Inside, I knew I didn't deserve any of it. And every day I attended class, I would see all these *normal* people around me, going to classes, living their lives, like nothing…nothing wrong had ever happened in the world. I just didn't belong, so I tried to take myself out of the equation."

Paige shuddered, wrapping her arms more tightly around herself, but let him keep talking.

"When I woke in the hospital, Sam was my state-required counselor. She's the one who convinced me to attend the grief meetings. She thought…" He chuckled derisively to himself. "She said that she could tell just by looking into my eyes that I'd lost someone close."

He glanced at Paige, expecting her to share the irony with him. But she just stared up at him from her own beautiful, dark, grief-stricken eyes.

"You told me once you didn't expect me to forgive you because no one else ever had," she said.

Nodding, he watched her intently, waiting and hoping, yet dreading too.

She gave him a tremulous smile. "I didn't understand what you meant. I didn't know your parents had kicked you out and cut you off. I didn't know you hadn't seen them since graduation, or how much you had struggled to get your life back on track. I didn't know you'd fallen so low you wanted to end it all."

He squinted, wondering what she was getting at. "You couldn't have known. It's fine. I didn't—"

"No." Her lips tilted in a somber smile. "It's not okay. I understand what it's like to lose all my loved ones so suddenly, but I never felt *guilty* about it. I never thought I *deserved* to be cast out of their lives. Not the way you did. And maybe still do." She drew in a large breath. "I think you have suffered just as much, if not more, than I have since Trace died, so I'm going to tell you something and I'm going to mean it, but I think the real person who needs to say this to you is yourself."

Logan frowned, not comprehending at first. When it struck him what she was about to say, he panicked.

No. No, he wasn't ready to hear this. Not from her, not after he'd just hurt her by revealing what he had about her friend.

He began to shake his head, his eyes begging her stay silent. But she reached out anyway and took his hand. It stalled his resistance as nothing else could. Her fingers were warm and stable and they made him want to fall to pieces.

"I forgive you," she whispered.

His shoulders shuddered, and he dropped his chin to his chest. As his fingers began to shake in hers, she tightened her grip.

"I know you never meant to kill him. I know it was an accident. And I know how much you regret it. I forgive you for having any part in Trace's death. It's not your fault he's gone, and I'm sorry I'm admitting it three years too late."

Too late? She was still too early. Way too early. It *had* been his fault. Trace wouldn't have fallen, wouldn't have hit his head if Logan hadn't punched him. He deserved a lifetime of hatred and disgust from her. He deserved eternal punishment and…and…

"I'm sorry I ever blamed you."

When he tried to pull his hand away, a freaking embarrassing sob tore from his throat because she wouldn't let him go. "Paige," he gasped, pleaded. "Don't…"

She shouldn't be the first person to forgive him. It wasn't right. She should keep blaming him.

But she stepped toward him and pressed her forehead to his. With the hand that wasn't holding him prisoner, she reached up and wiped at his damp cheeks.

God, how horrifying. He hadn't even realized he'd begun to bawl.

"As soon as you can forgive yourself, I think you'll be ready to move on with your life completely. And I think you'll be just fine."

Unable to stop the tears, he interlaced his fingers through hers and held on for dear life, breathing her in. Their bodies barely grazed as she hugged him.

In those few precious moments, she was his entire universe, what grounded him and also what helped him float up with a freedom he couldn't explain. He wasn't sure how long they stood there like that, but it wasn't nearly long enough. He wanted more time. He wanted to press closer to her and hug her. He wanted forever.

A brisk breeze swept in around them, but Paige's small soft hand was warm in his. He didn't think he'd ever be cold again.

He sniffed and tilted his face slightly away in a hopeless effort to hide the fact he was still crying. But in doing so, he only slid his cheek alongside hers. Their flesh brushed and one of his tears sealed their skin together, compressing it as someone would press a sentimental flower petal between the pages of a book.

He wanted to kiss her. His mouth watered as if he could already taste her and he licked his lips, tasting salt from his tears.

But he'd kissed her best friend, turned her father into an abusive alcoholic, started the wheels in motion to make her mother commit suicide, and he'd murdered her brother.

With a sigh, he stepped back. She let him go so he could scrub his face with both hands. When he looked at her, he realized she was right. He might not have quite forgiven himself yet, but he found he did want to move on with his life. Except who he wanted to move on *with* was unfeasible.

His lungs heaved for more air. After a sniff and another palm-brush across his eyes, he forced a brave smile. "Thank you. You'll never know how much this means to me."

Chapter Twenty-One

Shaken and emotionally drained, Paige pushed into the back door of her childhood home. She paused half a second before looking around and stepping inside. When she didn't see a dead parent sprawled on the floor in a puddle of his own blood, she breathed out a relieved breath and silently shut the door behind her.

She waited a beat, keeping her back to the exit, and watched the occasional flash of colored light spray into the kitchen from the living room where her father had left the television on.

In the few weeks she'd been home for Christmas break, she'd yet to talk to her dad aside from a greeting hello and to ask what he'd like to eat at mealtimes.

Relieved he hadn't made a mess of the kitchen while she'd been out, she treaded quietly down the hall and peeked around the corner into the living room.

A half empty beer bottle clutched in one hand and cradled almost lovingly to his chest as a sleeping child might cuddle a teddy bear, her father lay passed out on the couch with his head tipped back and his mouth hanging open.

If she tried to talk to him the way she'd just spoken to Logan Xander — if she tried to tell him she forgave him for abandoning her these last three years—she knew he wouldn't thank her the humble, honored way Logan had thanked her. He'd probably deny ever leaving her, saying something along the lines that *she* was the one who'd left and gone to college.

Shaking her head, Paige took a throw blanket off the back of the rocking chair and gently draped it over him.

"Good night, Dad," she murmured. "Merry Christmas Eve." *Or Christmas Tree Night as Logan would call it.*

When he didn't even alter the tenor of his snore, she found the remote and turned off the television.

After changing into some warm pajamas, she crawled into bed and thought of Logan Xander. And Kayla.

She knew exactly why Kayla hadn't told her the truth. And she knew why Kayla had acted as if she'd been doing her own penance these past three years. It was the very reason Logan had been doing the exact same thing.

Guilt.

But had Kayla grown closer to Paige only because of her guilt? Or had Kayla truly come to care about her?

Squeezing her eyes shut, Paige refused to think about that. She felt sore and tired. Drained.

She'd be lying if she said she didn't feel any anger, or blame, or betrayal where her best friend was concerned. She did. But she was so weary of those emotions and didn't want to think about them. She'd deal with them later.

Falling asleep with a numb kind of emptiness inside her, Paige dreamed of Logan and how she'd held him after she'd forgiven him at the Christmas Tree farm. But in the dream, she didn't stop with a hug. She kissed him. And he kissed her back. Then Trace came along and caught them. With a roar, he launched himself at Logan, and the two started to fight.

She woke on a guilty gasp, curled in the same tight fetal position as she'd been when she'd conked out. Sunlight streamed through her window, telling her it was morning. Christmas.

She dragged herself from bed, shuffled through the house, past her dad still unconscious on the couch, and into the kitchen.

It was always a test for her, a challenge she felt compelled to pass, whenever she entered this room. She'd never forget the morning she'd found her mother in here and she'd never like crossing this floor — new tile or not — so she did it as often as possible, on purpose, to show herself she could.

Paige opened the refrigerator and pulled out a carton of eggs, trying to think of happier times when she'd seen her mom hum as she cooked instead of seeing the phantom image of her dead body. She was scraping the last of the scrambled eggs she fixed onto a second plate when her father stumbled in, bleary eyes blood shot and face unshaven.

Forcing a smile, she called, "You're just in time. Breakfast is ready."

"Already got my breakfast," he answered in a guttural voice as he opened the refrigerator.

When he came up with a beer, Paige clenched her teeth but refused to show her irritation.

"How about you not drink today," she suggested with an encouraging grin. "It's Christmas."

"How about you get off my back," he sneered, raising an eyebrow in challenge as he looked her in the eye and intentionally popped off the cap. "It's Christmas." Then he tipped his head back and took a long guzzle.

Sighing quietly as she forfeited the fight, Paige set down the spatula she'd been holding. She'd learned a lot about herself and a lot about grieving in the past couple months. Her group at Granton had healed her in ways she hadn't even known she'd been hurt. And she just wanted her father to experience a little bit of the same ease from his own suffering.

If she didn't at least try to reach him, no one else would, so she set her shoulders firmly. "Dad, I know this is the first year we've had to go through the holidays without Mom but — "

"I don't want to talk about it." His voice was harsh and commanding, leaving her no room to respond without outright pushing. He flung a single glare at her and turned away to leave the kitchen.

She followed him. "Well, I do. You are the only family I have left, Paul Zukowski. And I can't just give up on you the way you've given up on yourself."

"I said I don't want to talk about it!" he roared. He swung around with his bottle pointed at her.

She must have miscalculated how close she'd moved to him, though. Instead of pointing, he cracked her in the cheekbone hard with the side of the glass. The bottle shattered from the force of his swing, and Paige was pitched to the floor, momentarily blinded as pain streaked across her jaw.

Crouched on her hands and knees among the broken glass, she trembled for a good second before sitting up and hesitantly lifting her hand to her face. When her fingers came away wet and sticky—and red, she gaped at them before looking up at her father.

He stared back, obviously dumbfounded. Then he shook his head, bunched his jaw with rage, and yelled, "Damn it, now! Why were you standing so close?"

Too flustered to answer, Paige moved her mouth without actually speaking. But the action shot white-hot heat through her jaw, so she winced and cupped her cheek to keep it still.

After running his hands through his hair and looking wild and undecided about what to do, her dad belted out a couple more curses and staggered from the room.

Paige remained on the floor, sitting only a few feet from where her mother had last lay. When a drop of blood splattered to the tile, her teeth began to chatter.

Pushing clumsily upright, she tripped toward the counter and grabbed a paper towel. She hurried to her room, shut the door silently, and collapsed onto her bed. The mirror next to her closet beckoned her, but she refused to look, couldn't bear to see how bad it was.

The injury throbbed through her head, making one side of her face feel swollen and inflamed.

She blinked repeatedly. At least her vision wasn't harmed.

When her cell phone rang, she jumped, quickly checking the ID. She hoped maybe Bailey or Tess was calling to wish her a Merry Christmas. She needed a dose of Granton like she couldn't believe. But when she saw Kayla's name, she closed her eyes and sniffed.

She couldn't talk to Kayla right now. Kayla would know something was wrong and come racing over. And not only did Paige not want Kayla losing her affection for Paul, but she didn't want to go through the confrontation over what she'd just learned. And she knew the next time she saw her friend, she'd have to confront her. Otherwise, she'd never be able to forgive her.

When the phone stopped ringing and dinged, telling her the caller had left a message, Paige finally cried.

She wanted to go back to Granton, the only place she really felt like herself. But the dorms wouldn't open again until after the new year. She'd have to wait at least ten more days before she could leave.

For some reason, she thought about Logan Xander, wondering what he did by himself on holidays without his family. Did he feel as alone right now as she did? At least his father hadn't physically struck him.

Her brain wandered to the night before. She'd hugged him, actually wrapped her arms around him and felt safe and content in his warm, solid embrace.

The way he'd whispered "thank you" into her ear haunted her as much as it invigorated. Despite how horribly wrong her attempt to reconnect with her father had gone, at least she'd been able to reach Logan and give him a certain peace of mind.

But what would Trace think about all this warmth she was feeling for his arch-enemy? For the guy who'd kissed Kayla?

God, she couldn't think. She just wanted to stop thinking forever. Closing her eyes, she forced herself to fall asleep, where she didn't dream at all.

A splitting headache woke her from her midmorning nap. Finding the courage to face a mirror, she stumbled into the bathroom and checked the damage. The paper towel she'd pressed to the cut while she'd fallen asleep had dried to her skin. Dampening a washcloth, she dabbed the area until she was able to peel the tissue away.

Thankfully, the cut wasn't all that deep; it had just bled a lot. Only a thin slice marred her skin. Well, a thin slice along with a healthy, bright red bruise and puffy cheek.

She cleaned it as best as she could, sucking in a sharp breath whenever she tried to scrub away the dried blood. Her entire body throbbed by the time she finished. After taking two capsules of painkillers, she returned to the kitchen to find her scrambled eggs gone and the pan she'd cooked them in washed and put away. Her father was nowhere on the property.

Realizing how truly sorry he must've been to actually clean up her mess, she sat at the table and cried some more, wondering how in God's name she was going to make it through another ten days like this.

She couldn't go to Kayla without stirring up a huge fight she wasn't ready to have. She couldn't call Tess or Bailey because they knew nothing about her home life and she wanted to keep it that way. She couldn't call home, since she *was* home.

She couldn't turn to anyone.

So she just kept on and suffered through. Her father stayed scarce for the most part, staying out of her way. She only saw traces of his comings and goings and heard him walking through the house late at night when she was in her room, trying to sleep.

When Kayla called the day after Christmas, Paige finally answered and made up some lie about how she and her dad had gone for a drive around the county, talking about old times. Kayla had oohed and ahhed as if it was the sweetest thing she'd ever heard. Then she'd invited Paige to come with her to meet her boyfriend.

It seemed so easy to act as if she didn't know anything about Kayla's involvement in Trace's death, so Paige pretended ignorance. Confronting her didn't seem so important anymore. She said nothing about it and came up with a convincing lie for her cut cheek. When she met with Kayla to meet Archer, she said she'd tripped over a laundry basket in the dark when she'd been going to the bathroom one night.

Kayla had no reason to suspect a lie, so she rolled her eyes and threw an arm around Paige's shoulder. "You can be the most graceful person I know sometimes. But put a laundry basket in your path at night, and you're a total klutz, sweetie."

Paige forced a laugh and bumped her hip against Kayla's. "Yeah, you gotta watch out for those night-stalking laundry baskets. Now where's this guy I'm supposed to meet?"

As the two girls neared the front entrance of the restaurant where they had agreed to hook up with Kayla's boyfriend, the door opened to reveal a short, stocky blond with a goatee.

Face lighting with pleasure, Kayla pointed. "He's right there."

Archer Bloom was nothing at all like Trace. He was laid-back and calm with a polite, almost dry attitude. But he knew how to make her best friend glow.

Paige studied them snuggled together in the booth across from her and tried to feel happy for Kayla. But the pangs of bitter blame kept lapping at her ankles and occasionally she wanted to snarl and demand that her best friend never get over her brother, not after what she'd done to him. Not after whom she'd kissed.

Heat boiled into her belly as she tried to picture Logan and Kayla kissing. A part of her knew she wasn't feeling indignant on Trace's behalf. She was straight-up jealous. Kayla knew what those amazing lips felt like. And Paige never would.

That was in no way fair.

Closing her eyes, she shoved the blame, and anger, and jealousy back down deep inside her and tried to act as if nothing was wrong. Thank goodness Kayla was so wrapped up in her boyfriend she didn't notice, because Paige knew she wouldn't be able to come up with a good lie about what was wrong if Kayla *had* noticed.

Again, she survived.

The days passed until New Year's Eve. The approaching first anniversary of her mother's death wasn't any easier to deal with than the first anniversary of Trace's death. But when Kayla invited Paige to spend New Year's Eve together, Paige almost felt sick from the déjà vu. She agreed, though, because it was a good — okay, her only — reason to get out of the house for a while.

The party was awful, thrown by a bunch of Trace's old friends. The people who didn't shy away from her tried to give her their best regards as if he'd just died yesterday. Kayla seemed too busy with Archer to notice Paige's discomfort, so Paige took off about an hour before the ball dropped.

It was fifteen minutes after eleven when she slipped into the front door, not brave enough to face the back entrance tonight. But when she stepped inside, the sight of her father sprawled on his stomach on the living room floor, face planted in the carpet, almost made her throw up.

She yelped out a horrified screamed and jumped backward, bumping into the wall of the foyer. But as soon as she yelped, the mass on the floor lurched. She screamed again, not expecting him to be alive.

Paul rolled onto his back with a curse. "What the hell are you yapping about?" He groaned and clutched his head as he struggled to sit up.

Her hand pressed solid against her thumping chest, Paige closed her eyes. "What're you doing on the floor?" she demanded right back, her fear urging on her angry tone. "I thought you were *dead.*"

He scowled at her. "What? You thought I offed myself or something?"

Glaring right back, she hissed, "Well, isn't that what you've been doing for the past three years? Drinking yourself to death?"

He opened his mouth to snap something back but stopped in the last second. His gaze settled on the bright purple bruise on her cheek just under her left eye, and he cringed. With a whispered curse, he collapsed backward and rested his spine against the couch as he cradled his head in his hands.

Paige continued to huddle against the closed front door, not sure if she dared go near him.

"Paige, I…" His voice sounded broken.

She slid down the wall, wilting to the floor so she could sit too. No matter what had become of their relationship, he was still her father. She couldn't ignore that.

"I know this is hard for you, Dad. I know you didn't mean to hit me, and it was an accident. I know you're sorry, and I know it's impossible for you to say that out loud. But I forgive you anyway. And I love you, no matter what."

For a heartbeat, he didn't respond. He acted as if he hadn't even heard her. Then his face screwed up into a tomato red and his lips pulled away from his teeth to show just how hard he was gritting them. Eyes squeezed closed, he began to sob.

To Paige, it sounded like his soul was tearing itself away from his body, desperate to escape such agony.

She watched him, dry eyed and perfectly still as he cried in great heaving moans.

"I think you need to change your lifestyle before you really do kill yourself," she said when he'd quieted to silent, streaming tears. "I think you should sell this house and move away from Creighton County. I think you should get out and do things with other people. I think you should live again."

He didn't respond, but she knew her words had sunk in. Sensing he wouldn't be able to accept any kind of physical comfort, Paige slowly pushed to her feet.

"Happy New Year," she murmured before shuffling from the living room. When she lay in her bed that night, she didn't fall asleep until well after midnight.

Nothing felt new or fresh about the new year though. And when she left three days later to return to Granton, nothing had changed between her and her father. But she knew the seed had been planted.

And fully watered with both their tears.

Chapter Twenty-Two

Logan paced as he waited just outside the cancer clinic of the hospital where nearly a month ago Jamie, Paige, and he had had been assigned to meet for their initial visit to the children's ward.

He hadn't intended to be the first to arrive, but he'd been so anxious, and afraid, and eager to see Paige again, he'd been ready since about five minutes after his eyes had snapped open.

He hadn't been able to stop thinking about her. Since their run-in at the tree farm, his little crush on her had bubbled over into huge, undeniable obsession. It had been agony not being able to see her cross Granton's main courtyard every Monday, Wednesday, and Friday. And once the spring semester started next week, he doubted he'd see her then either. New classes, different schedule. He'd be lucky if he caught a glimpse of her anywhere.

But they would still have the grief group together. And today.

Where was everyone, anyway? Had she forgotten? How could she forget when he'd been counting down the days, the very hour—okay, okay, the very *minute*—until he saw her again?

Glancing to the right, down the sidewalk and toward the visitors' parking lot, he blew out a breath and peered through the vapor cloud he'd made. But he didn't spot her.

When a prickle of awareness curled up his vertebrae, he tensed and turned slowly the other way to see her trotting up the sidewalk. She looked adorable bundled up in a black coat with a hot pink stocking cap on her head, knitted tails falling down over her ears, swaying to her harried rhythm. Her long, dark hair streamed over her shoulders, and her hands were stuffed into thick gloves.

"Sorry, I'm late." She panted as she approached, her nose red from the cold. "I forgot to set my alarm and slept in."

Logan began to smile. He'd actually woken up a good hour before his alarm had gone off, too eager to sleep. "Don't worry. Jamie hasn't gotten—"

The words strangled in his throat when he saw her bruise. A greenish violet shade, it had to be a few weeks old. Since she hadn't had it on Christmas Eve, he had to guess she'd gotten it not long after he'd seen her that night.

"Oh my God." Heart pitching into his knees, he gulped. "Are you okay? What happened? Were you in an accident?"

He reached out before he could stop himself. But Paige cringed away, and he immediately jerked his hand back before touching her.

"I'm fine," she said and shook her head. "It's fine."

Logan opened his mouth to once again ask what had happened but the dark, warning glance she shot him said everything. This hadn't been an accident. His sympathy tumbled into blank shock, then outrage. He snapped his mouth shut.

But he couldn't stay silent. "How many times has he done this?"

Paige took a deep breath as if she needed to calm herself before answering. "Look, nothing happened. Yes, he had a bottle in his hand. Yes, he was drunk, and we were arguing. But he didn't mean to hurt me. When he swung around to face me, I-I was standing too close, and the bottle cracked me in the jaw. That's all."

"So, it was an accident," he bit out, not believing her at all. To have enough force behind a swing to break skin could *not* be an accident. "Just like the first time, huh?"

When he reached for her arm to remind her of the crescent-shaped scar on her shoulder, she yanked away and glowered at him. "I told you it's fine."

"Fine?" he repeated incredulously before growling out his frustration. "Do you hear yourself right now? Do you even understand what you sound like?"

"Yes," she hissed and glanced away. "I sound like a battered daughter trying to make excuses for her abusive, alcoholic father and deny that there's any kind of problem. But I'm not! Those were the *only* two times anything has ever happened. And I swear to you, they were both complete accidents. No, our relationship is not perfect, but my father does *not* beat me. Okay?"

He stared out at her a moment longer before he blew out a hard breath. "Okay," he said. But his body still shook with the need to seek vengeance.

How could anyone hurt her? Accident or not, he wanted to find her father and beat him senseless. He wanted to —

Catching his breath, Logan ran a trembling hand over his hair. He hadn't wanted to hit anyone for three years. The thought of physical violence against another member of her family nauseated him.

Stomach heaving, he turned his back to her and sucked in an icy cold breath through his teeth. "I don't know where Jamie is," he said, somehow stepping away from the situation and trying to ground himself in the reason they were actually here. "Should we go ahead and go inside?"

Paige nodded, looking relieved. "Yes. Probably."

He stepped toward the glass door until it automatically slid open. When he stood aside, letting her precede him into the clinic, Paige murmured a surprised thank you and brushed past, her posture rigid and stride stiff.

He followed her, wanting to beg her forgiveness for his reaction to her bruise, though he wasn't sorry in the least. He still wanted to hurt her father. But he couldn't handle her being so formal and rigid with him. But Lordy, she smelled good. Cinnamon and vanilla and pure Paige. Keeping just enough distance so he couldn't drive himself crazy inhaling any more of her heavenly scent, he paused when she did as they reached a nurse's station.

An attendant in bright blue scrubs glanced up from checking a monitor and eyed them curiously. "Can I help you?"

Logan shoved his hands into his back pockets while Paige spoke up. "Yes. We're with the Granton University grief group to meet with some patients in the children's ward."

"Oh." A welcoming smile spread across the nurse's face. "You're just in time. They're already in the playroom, waiting for you."

As she moved out from behind the counter, Paige glanced hesitantly toward Logan. He cleared his throat and turned to the nurse. "Um, excuse me. But what exactly are we supposed to do?"

The nurse shrugged, her grin amused. "Just...entertain them. It doesn't matter, really. They love any kind of company." She moved off, hurrying down the hall before either Logan or Paige could ask anything else.

Paige looked up at him, her eyebrows arched in question. "I guess we're just supposed to *entertain* them, then."

"Entertain them," he repeated. "Right."

Looming large and awkward beside Paige, Logan shifted his weight from one foot to the other in the middle of the children's ward playroom. A roomful of small, expectant faces peered up at him, assembled in a half circle around them. About a dozen sat cross-legged on the floor while another half dozen watched him from wheelchairs, and two more from beds they'd been rolled in on.

None of them had hair.

He gulped, certain he was going to mess this up no matter what he did. "Uh...hi, everyone." He made a big, slow wave, only imaging how lame he must appear. "I'm Logan."

"And I'm Paige," she chirped with a bright, cheery smile.

He sent her a brief, grateful look, glad someone else was there to bumble through this with him.

"So, umm, I guess we're supposed to entertain you guys." Lowering his voice, he stepped closer to them and cupped his mouth with one hand to speak confidentially quiet. "So, even if we totally suck, please at least act entertained. 'Kay?"

They laughed, and somewhere inside him, he glowed with pleasure. There was just something about making a group of sick children laugh. It almost shocked him how good it felt.

Beside him, a sharp elbow dug into his ribs. "Excuse me?" Paige set her hands on her hips and sent him a scowl. "I don't know about you, but I personally don't plan on sucking at all." She put on such an overdone look of outrage, the children giggled again.

He blinked, stunned to realize she was playacting. And after what they'd just gone through outside too.

"Oh, I beg your pardon, my lady." He swept a low bow, jumping into his own role, and was relieved when more giggles arose. "I forgot you were incapable of suckage."

After a brief, forgiving nod, she sniffed and lifted her chin, assuming the station of princess—or queen, or whatever she wanted to be—and waved out one regal hand with a flourish. "Think nothing of it, peasant. Just make sure it doesn't happen again."

Unable to stop a wide grin, he turned to his audience. "I guess we have an hour to not-suck then? What do you guys want to do?"

When no one immediately raised a hand or suggested anything, Paige jumped up and down, clapping her hands. "Oh, I know, I know! Let's ride unicorns across a magical meadow full of pretty, colorful flowers that smell like fresh roses."

Logan arched an eyebrow. The kids laughed and cheered her idea on. At least the girls did. Most of the boys booed. When they settled, Logan made a face. "Why don't we read a book or something instead?"

"But we *always* read books with visitors," one boy grumbled.

"Yeah. I want to ride a unicorn," another girl piped up.

Suddenly, the room was full of impossible suggestions. Climbing mountains, magic carpet rides, fighting zombies, swimming in the ocean, going to Disney World.

After a see-what-you-started scowl for Paige, Logan sighed and set his hands on his hips. "Well, I'm sorry, but my unicorn is in the shop right now, and I don't think they'll let us out of this joint for the rest of that stuff."

A bunch of grumbles answered him, and Paige led the rebellion as she hooked her thumb over her shoulder and motioned to him. "Boy, does he know how to shoot down some perfectly awesome suggestions."

Not sure how he'd become the fuddy-duddy of the group, Logan glanced around the sterile playroom, determined to redeem himself. Trying to come up with something—anything—the kids could safely play, he paused briefly when he spotted an old leather trunk sitting against the far wall.

"Hey, what's in that trunk over there?"

No one knew.

"How long has it been there?" he asked next.

"It's always been there," one shaved-head, bruised-eye little girl answered.

Logan lifted his eyebrows. "Well, isn't anyone curious what's inside?"

"We're not allowed to touch it," someone else spoke up. But since he had mentioned it, the children eyed the trunk, all of them looking decidedly interested.

"I'm going to check it out," he announced and started boldly for the trunk.

"Wait!" Paige grabbed his arm in a light but cautious grip.

He gaped at her fingers before looking up at her face. He had no idea if he'd ever get used to her voluntarily touching him, but he did know he liked it. A lot. A sudden desire to pull her into a fierce hug and press a soft kiss to her bruised, cut cheek overwhelmed him. When was the last time someone had coddled her and kissed away her boo-boos?

Logan restrained himself from doing just that, mainly because he knew she'd push him away if he even attempted it, but also because it'd break up playtime and wipe that refreshing look of vivacity off her face.

Her eyes glittered with amusement even as she showed her teeth as if they were chattering with fear. "I don't know. What if it's full of... of flesh-eating *dragons?*" she asked, her voice going hushed with worry.

Inspired by her act, he patted her hand lightly in reassurance and kept his voice quiet. "Do you really think I'd let a flesh-eating dragon past me...not when I have my handy..." He paused to dig a hand into his pocket. When his fingers latched around something, he pulled it out to show all the children. "...gum with me."

The kids roared with laughter.

Paige glanced at the gigglers and promptly turned back to him, arching her eyebrows. "Gum? Is that all you got?"

He gave a serious nod. "Didn't you know dragons were afraid of gum? Especially spearmint flavor. It takes the fire right out of their breath."

She promptly held out her hand, palm up. "In that case, I'll take two pieces please."

After that, everyone in the room needed a piece of gum to ward off all possible flesh-eating dragons. Logan had to tear the sticks in half so he'd have enough to go around. By the time he had the kids munching contentedly, he and Paige approached the trunk.

"Let's drag it closer so everyone can see inside," she suggested.

He took one end, she took the other, and they worked together, heaving the heavy old thing to the center of the half circle.

"Oh, I'm so scared," Paige told the kids as Logan undid the latch. When she hid behind him and clutched at his shirt, ducking her face against his back, awareness prickled his scalp. He knew it was all an act, but God, he loved having her close to him. Touching him.

Holding back his hand as if to shield her, he paused dramatically and eyed the patients. "Are you ready?"

They cheered out their enthusiasm. Logan slung open the lid, only to yank out...a dress from the top of the pile.

"Clothes?" a crew of disappointed little voices chorused.

He wrinkled his nose. Old and tacky, and gagging him with its overpowering musty perfume, the dress seemed to be made of hot pink gossamer tulle, a little silk, and not much else.

"And I think it's just your size," he told Paige with a taunting grin, though it was obviously way too big for her.

She shook her head. "Umm. No. Pink's not really my color." Her dark brown eyes sparkled with mischief as she added, "But I think it'd look simply fabulous on you, Logan. With your sky blue eyes, you'd be *sooo* beautiful in it."

His smile dropped flat, all joking aside. "I'm not wearing a dress."

But all the kids rebelled, urging him to put it on. Paige pooched out her bottom lip and gave a fake pout, setting her hands on her hips and everything.

"Fun hater," she charged.

He closed his eyes briefly and prayed no one had a camera phone on them.

Chapter Twenty-Three

An hour later, still decked out in a frilly pink dress over his clothes, Logan accepted a hearty hug from the last kid in line to wish him a farewell and thank him for coming. As an attendant rolled the little boy from the room, Paige straightened from dumping a pile of shoes into the trunk and called goodbye.

They'd gotten a small lecture from the nurse who'd caught them playing in the chest, something about letting unknown molds and mildew into the air for even unlatching the lid. So their time with the kids had gotten cut short. But Logan still considered it worth it. Every child had left the room grinning. To see those sick, sunken faces so alive with joy, he'd gladly break the rule again.

Feeling very full inside with a positive, glowing kind of energy swirling through him, he turned to grin at Paige.

She beamed back. "So, did that totally suck or what?"

He chuckled. "Yeah. Totally."

Spinning away, she made a sound of absolute delight. "Oh my God. I had no idea playing with a group of sick children could be so…so fulfilling. Wow." She whirled back to him, her gorgeous, dark eyes sparkling with her elation. "I haven't had so much fun in…I don't know. A long time."

"Yeah, well, you didn't have to wear the dress," Logan reminded her.

Rolling her eyes, she playfully nudged his arm. "Oh, whatever. You know you liked it."

Stuck in the playful disposition from their hour of silliness, Logan primped for her, cocking out his hip and cradling the back of his head as if poofing an imaginary mound of hair. "I am totally rocking this dress, aren't I? Pink really is my color."

Paige threw her head back and laughed.

The sound wavered through him. Captivated, he stared at her, enthralled by every facet of her being: the wash of healthy, laughing color on her cheeks, the liquid flow of her hair as she tossed it over her shoulder, the way her lashes swept low over her dark eyes and barely rested against the tops of her creamy cheekbones.

"I was so right," she admitted with a smug sniff and a lift of her eyebrows. "It does match your eyes brilliantly."

And her visual beauty only mirrored what lay deep inside her.

He couldn't say the way she'd handled the kids today surprised him in the least. The two times he'd worked with her at The Squeeze, he could tell she was good with people. But watching her in action still left him reeling and in awe.

There was just something so amazing about her.

She made him feel—

Oh.

Wow.

Realizing exactly what she made him feel struck Logan like a thunderbolt. He'd always been attracted to her and had formed that strange obsession thing for her, but this...this was worse.

He was in huge trouble.

Paige noticed his horrified stare a moment later.

She did a double take before focusing on his face, knitting her brow as her smile faltered. "What's wrong? Are you okay?"

He shook his head, utterly bowled over. He'd killed her brother, been indirectly responsible for the death of her mother, turned her dad into an abusive drunk, ruined her relationship with her best friend, and had permanently altered the course of her life. She should hate him, but there she stood, looking worried.

About him.

He was in more than just huge trouble. He was totally screwed.

This wasn't some stupid, misdirected crush anymore. It wasn't some mild obsession. He'd fallen irrevocably flat-out in love with Trace Zukowski's little sister.

"Logan?" She stepped toward him, lifting her hand as if she wanted to touch him, maybe feel his brow for a fever.

He shook his head, commanding himself to get a grip. "It's nothing," he assured her.

Deciding he no longer needed to wear the dress, he turned away and went about shrugging it off over his head. As he rolled it into a ball around his arm, he caught her watching him, skimming her gaze down his physique with the gleam of sexual interest in her expression. And just like that, heat ran over his body, prickling his skin, making all his hairs stand on end, aware of nothing but her assessing eyes.

He told himself it didn't mean what he wanted it to mean. But, oh, how he wished. How he envisioned the whole thing.

It'd only take him two, maybe three, steps to reach her. He'd cup her face in both of his hands and tilt her chin just so to align their lips perfectly. She'd kiss him back, willingly, gently. His mouth watered, already imagining what she'd taste like, how she'd feel against him.

Soft. She'd be so soft. That gorgeous hair of hers would slip over the backs of his fingers as he cradled her face. Like silk.

He jerked his attention away and tossed the balled dress into the opened chest.

She wandered closer to him, or maybe she was heading toward the trunk. But to him, it felt like she was the fly unknowingly heading straight into his tangled web.

"I can't believe you actually wore the dress. For some reason, I always pictured you as a snob, all conceited and full of yourself, too good for the rest of the population. Certainly too good to wear a pink dress for a group of sick children."

He glanced at her. Nothing malicious lurked behind her statement, but it pained him anyway. Because it had been a little too true.

"Yeah. Well, you're not too far off the mark. Back in the day, I *was* pretty full of myself."

Kneeling before the trunk, he reached out to collect the clothing accessories strewn across the floor. When he realized tossing them haphazardly into the trunk wouldn't allow everything that had been in there before to fit, he rearranged items, slotting them in in a more organized manner.

He was busy piling the shoes on one end when Paige closed in.

"Well, I think the Logan Xander you are now is a remarkable person."

And all he'd had to do to become this way was eliminate one of the most important people in her life.

Sadness and regret cramped his stomach muscles. "Yeah," he mumbled, keeping his attention on the shoe arrangement.

Paige leaned past him to pick up the pink dress he'd worn. And as she did, her hair fell down in front of her face, cascading before him to dangle into the depths of the chest. Those glossy black strands swayed inches from his nose. He held his breath, but a whiff of her shampoo — that alluring cinnamon and vanilla — had already fluttered up his nostrils, captured in his heightened senses.

He closed his eyes, commanding himself not to react.

All too soon, she straightened and began to fold the wadded dress into a neat square. He exhaled, air whooshing from his lungs in a rush, making him dizzy.

Then she did the unthinkable. She leaned down *again* and set the folded dress neatly in the bottom of the trunk, only to pick up a black cape, probably to fold it too.

Once, he could handle. Twice, he was doomed.

As the tempting tendrils of her dark, glossy mane floated before him for a second time, he leaned into them, breathing deeply, consuming their silky texture into his very essence as they barely brushed his cheek.

Oh, God, her hair was even softer than he'd imagined.

He was so entrenched in his reverence he didn't immediately notice how she'd frozen. He felt too drugged, too high on her nearness to care about anything else. As long as she kept letting him breathe in the scent of her hair, life was perfect.

When he realized he was making a worship-service out of the act and she was watching, he yanked himself back, abruptly returning to reality.

Busted.

A pair of startled, dark eyes slid his way, and she straightened just as quickly as he'd pulled away.

For the space of two seconds, they just stared at each other, their gazes wide with a shared shock.

"I — " He tried to apologize. But he wasn't sorry. If given another chance, he knew he'd do the same thing again, maybe even try for more. Skin to skin contact. A kiss. Anything she'd allow.

The fact that she wasn't running away right now gave him foolish hope. She looked so vulnerable and scared, and her bruised cheek dragged out the protective instincts in him. It all spurred him into the reckless act of reaching for her, his fingers stretching for the impossible.

"Paige."

She jerked back before he could touch her cheek. "I should go." Pale and trembling, she spun away and rushed from the room.

Rocking back on his haunches from where he'd been crouched on the floor, Logan sat hard on the cool tile, staring after her as she disappeared.

All that progress they'd made from the start of the school year was shattered. She was back to running away from him. He'd managed to sever the tender threads of their precarious friendship with one stupid move. She'd never talk to him again now, never smile at him, never sit by him at another group meeting.

He'd just ruined everything.

"You're such an idiot," he hissed to himself. After sitting there, cursing his own stupidity for a good thirty seconds, he shoved the rest of the contents into the trunk, compressing them with both hands until he was able to slam the lid closed.

He was latching the trunk's buckle into place when the back of his neck tingled as it always did right before he saw her. Great, now it was happening just from thinking about her.

Rubbing at the irritating sensation, he muttered, "Stop it," under his breath and picked up one end of the trunk to drag it back to its position against the wall.

He only got two feet before he realized she'd returned. Standing in the doorway of the playroom, she twisted her hands at her lap as she watched him. He stumbled to a stop, still holding onto one end of the trunk.

"I…I forgot my coat and hat."

With a single nod, he began to turn away, but she hurried forward. "Here. Let me help."

"It's okay. I got — "

She picked up the other end of the chest. He drew in a lungful, telling himself to calm down. This didn't mean anything. But after they dropped the chest back into its original spot, he couldn't help but send her a curious glance as he brushed his hands off onto his thighs.

"Thanks."

She nodded, not making eye contact as she retrieved her coat. She slipped it on, then tugged that adorable hat over her head before she turned to him, her gaze darting and wary.

"So, um…see you at the next meeting?"

That's how they were going to play it, then? Pretend it never happened?

Since he knew this was the only way he'd ever get anywhere near her, he silently acquiesced to her wishes. With a nod, he answered, "Yeah. See you then."

Chapter Twenty-Four

Paige actually looked forward to the start of spring classes. Though she enrolled in more core requirements, steering clear of anything pertaining to her degree, she visited her advisor a week before the new semester started.

"I want to change my major," she announced, releasing the pent up air she'd been holding since she'd initially enrolled at Granton.

Dr. Carrel studied her a moment before chuckling. "Well, it's about time. I knew after our first meeting, business marketing wasn't the path for you. So, what's it to be, Miss Zukowski? Education?"

Paige grinned and nodded. After tacking on another two classes to her spring schedule, she thanked her advisor for all the help, and skipped from the building, feeling much lighter.

When she returned to her dorm, she was still smiling. But as soon as she shut herself in her room, the sheets on Mariah's old bed rustled, making her scream.

Her roommate winced against the sound as she sat up. "Nice to see you too," Mariah grumbled, her voice slightly hoarse.

"Oh, my God. *Mariah!* What're you doing here?" Paige pressed a hand against her chest, trying to beat back the heart attack she wanted to have.

Mariah scowled at her from bloodshot eyes. "It's my room too, you know."

"But…" Paige frowned when she realized the red around Mariah's eyes were from recently shed tears, not some kind of hangover. "What's wrong?"

"It's over, that's what's wrong." Mariah sniffed and wiped at another tear dripping down her cheek. "Gavin and I. He cheated on me. The rat bastard." When she buried her face into her hands and began to weep in earnest, Paige's pity kicked in. She hurried across the room to sit on the bed next to her roommate and wrapped her arms around Mariah.

Mariah curled toward her and rested her cheek on Paige's shoulder. "I loved him so much."

As she blubbered, detailing everything she missed about her boyfriend, Paige listened, thinking Mariah's boyfriend's best attributes didn't sound all that appealing. Logan outshone him in every way. As his face popped into her head, her thoughts wandered to him. She couldn't count the number of times she had replayed that moment in the hospital when she'd realized he was smelling her hair.

The way his lips had parted and nostrils had flared exposed a look of utter ecstasy that couldn't be faked. Then his lashes had parted, and his eyes had been glazed with pleasure as if he were drugged and high off her scent. He'd gazed at her blindly for a moment, all his emotions etched onto his face. He had wanted her.

The muscles deep in her belly had clenched with utter awareness, and she'd wanted him back, wanted to kiss him and touch him. She'd wanted everything he had to offer. She'd never felt so attracted to another person in her life.

Then his gaze had cleared, and her mind had cleared, and horror had filled her.

Escape had been the only viable option, because remaining anywhere near Logan Xander after that would've been epically disastrous.

As Mariah sobbed in her arms, swearing off all men, Paige silently swore herself off one man. Trace would roll over in his grave if he knew what she was thinking.

Besides, up until a few months ago, she'd hated Logan. From absolutely loathing him to wanting to jump his bones just seemed wrong, unfair to him, and…and really, really wrong. The attraction couldn't be trusted.

She decided avoiding him at all costs was out of the question since doing that would only prove how much she was running from her attraction. Befriending him was also out of the question. But kind, distant, polite courtesy she could handle.

At least she hoped so.

Paige spent the rest of the day helping Mariah get through her breakup and trying to convince herself with every excuse she could concoct why Logan was bad for her.

When Bailey and Tess arrived later that evening, finally moving back in after the holiday break, Paige was beyond relieved to see them, though actually she had somewhat welcomed Mariah's breakdown. It had marginally helped distract her from everything she didn't want to think about.

She winced inwardly when she had to lie about her bruise to Bailey and Tess, using the old laundry basket story. But after Logan's response to the truth, she decided she liked her fib much better, even if she wished she didn't have to tell her closest friends a lie.

Wonderful support that they were, Tess and Bailey swallowed her story whole and then helped her cheer up Mariah. By Friday, Mariah was back to her regular self, ready to go out and find a party.

Paige and her suitemates wasted most of the weekend before the spring classes started catching up. Bailey had actually met a guy back in her hometown, but Tess heartily disapproved of him. Entertained by watching them argue about him, Paige was thrown for a loop when Tess turned from Bailey, ignoring her insults, and blankly asked, "So, how was your winter break, Paige?"

"Oh…" Flashes of her few tense confrontations with her father, of learning the truth about Kayla, of realizing how much she liked Logan struck her cold in the chest.

She smiled vaguely and answered, "It was fine. My friend Kayla got me a pair of ruby earrings to go with my cross necklace."

"Oh, they're cute." Neither suitemate asked anything else, and she breathed a sigh of relief, glad her moment in the spotlight had passed.

She started back to work the night before her first class began. Thankful and yet disappointed to learn she didn't share the shift with Logan, she went through the motions, more distracted than paying attention to what she was actually doing.

When the next day began, she was up early and ready for some good hectic chaos, which she got. Her new schedule was much tougher this semester. But it still didn't keep her mind from straying at the most inopportune moments, like the first Tuesday her grief group meetings resumed. She was so preoccupied about seeing Logan again she was lost in her own thoughts as she hurried down the front steps of Grammar Hall to the exit.

Einstein popped out from behind the staircase. Paige screamed.

"Oh my God." She closed her eyes and waited for her heart to settle. "I swear, Einstein, you just scared ten years off my life."

"Where're you headed?"

"My grief group." She glanced at her wristwatch, knowing she didn't have time to small talk. "It starts in five minutes."

His shoulders deflated. "That's right. It's *Tuesday*, isn't it?" His depression tugged at her sympathies and reminded her it had been a while since she'd hung out with him. Suddenly remembering his story about his mother — though she still didn't believe it — she said, "Hey, why don't you come with me? You could talk about your mom."

Instead of brightening, his scowl grew darker. "I don't need a room full of strangers picking at my brain, telling me what I should and shouldn't feel. I'm not a *freak*." Brushing past her so hard he actually knocked her back a step, he rounded the staircase and hurried up to the second level.

Startled, Paige gaped after him. *Well, okay, then.* He must think she *was* a freak, then, because she *did* need help. She made an immediate note to herself never to mention counseling or group therapy to Anthony Morris again.

When she slipped into the Crimson Room five minutes later, she scanned the circle until she spotted Logan. Though his back was to her as he spoke to some guy who'd lost his sister in a car accident, he reached up and touched the back of his neck before he turned and looked directly at her.

Longing swirled in his gaze, and suddenly she couldn't breathe. *This is bad, this is bad, this is bad.*

Jerking her attention from him, she jumped when Sam descended upon her. "What happened? Were you in an accident?"

Paige had no idea what she meant until Sam winced and brushed her fingers delicately across Paige's cheek.

Gritting her molars hard, Paige silently cursed that stupid shiner. After three weeks, the cut had healed and was barely noticeable, but the bruise had gone through every color of the rainbow already. Though it had faded a lot, it just wouldn't disappear.

"Oh, I tripped over a laundry basket in the dark one night when I was trying to find my way to the bathroom."

Holding her breath as she spilled out the lie, her gaze unconsciously sought Logan. By the way he watched her, she knew he'd heard her story. His lips tightened with disapproval, but he said nothing as he turned away.

And he wouldn't. That was just the kind of person he was.

Glancing away, she focused on the group leader just as Samantha clapped her hands and called the meeting to a start.

After going around and sharing what they'd done for their winter break—Logan quietly passing his turn, and Paige merely saying she'd spent it with her dad—Sam cleared her throat once everyone had gotten a chance to share. "All right, let's have a cancer center visit report from—" she checked her schedule "—Jamie, Paige, and Logan."

"Oh my God." Jamie gasped, slapping her hand against her forehead. "I totally forgot about that." She turned toward Paige who sat beside her. "I'm so sorry I didn't make it. I owe you big time."

"It's okay," Paige said, waving her apologies aside. "We managed." Glancing across the circle toward Logan, she grinned. "Just the two of us. Though, a warning: don't open the old wooden trunk sitting against the wall. It's only there for looks."

Logan held her gaze a moment, his eyes glittering with amusement. As if on cue, her body lit up, her nerves tingling out of control with an overdose of awareness.

He gazed back, blue eyes going heated. She knew he was remembering the same exact moment from that day that she was.

Clearing his throat, he glanced away and flushed. "Yeah. The trunk is a definite taboo."

Paige turned away too, guilty and yet giddy. She couldn't control the stir of excitement swirling through her.

"Well," Sam encouraged. "What happened? Stand up, you two, and share."

Together, Paige and Logan dragged themselves upright and met in the middle of the circle. Facing Samantha, Logan scratched the back of his neck as Paige gripped her hands at her waist.

"We, uh, well, we found this old trunk full of dress up clothes," Logan started haltingly, "and spent most of the hour playing make-believe with different costumes."

"Hey, now that sounds fun." Samantha nodded in approval.

"Yeah, the kids really enjoyed the outfits we put on them." Paige grinned big and risked a knowing peek at Logan, wondering if he'd flip out if she mentioned *his* outfit. "And ourselves."

He narrowed his eyes in warning, silently demanding she keep quiet. Then he turned back to everyone and dryly confessed, "I wore a dress."

Kevin snickered. "Dude."

"He made a very cute girl," Paige immediately defended.

He sent her a scowl but ended up cracking a grin a second later. "I did, didn't I?"

"Incredibly." She smiled back, aching to simply reach out and touch him.

"Aww," Jamie spoke up from her chair. "You two are so cute together. Seriously, when are you guys going to stop fighting it and just hook up already?"

Paige gasped while Logan's mouth fell open. Her face drained, and she felt suddenly very faint.

When nothing but silence followed Jamie's comment, and everyone in the room stared at her and Logan standing side by side as if they wanted to know the answer too, Paige slapped her hands over her mouth and ran.

Frozen in place, Logan stared after Paige as she rushed from the Crimson Room. He wanted to go after her and soothe her, but since he was the source of her distress, he knew he was the last thing she wanted.

And he hated that.

After he sent a glare to Jamie for opening her mouth, she shrugged. "What? What'd I say?"

"Jamie—" Samantha started in a warning voice, but Logan spoke above her.

"I killed her brother. Okay?"

This time, the silence in the room was more stark and echoing.

"You *what?*" Kevin finally said, his voice halting and disbelieving.

"I…we grew up in the same county," Logan explained. "Neighboring schools. Biggest rivals. Everything she told you about his death was true. I got into a fight with him, and after I hit him, he fell and hit his head, and he died. Then my lawyer dad got me out of trouble, and I never spent a moment in jail for killing him."

As he finished, he closed his eyes, braced for the fallout.

Samantha was the first to react. "Well? Keep going."

"Keep going?" Logan opened his eyes and frowned, confused.

Sam waved out her hand, signaling him to continue. "Yes. Keep talking. I know your story doesn't end there. What happened after your father cleared your name?"

She didn't look at all surprised to learn he'd murdered someone. It sent off alarm bells in his head. But everyone else was gaping, clearly not in the know.

Since he still stood in the middle of the circle, the center of attention, he kept going as the leader had instructed him to.

"After…after he cleared my name, my dad told me to leave and never come back." He looked up, straight into Sam's sympathetic gaze. "I haven't seen anyone in my family since then. I moved away and ended up here where no one knew who I was or what I'd done. I just wanted to start fresh with a new life, as a new person."

Swallowing down the hard lump in his throat, Logan looked down at his hands. "I know I didn't lose anyone like everyone else here did. I don't belong in this group. I…I'm sorry for deceiving you and misleading you into thinking I was…grieving."

Wiping at his dry face, he lowered his head and started for the door.

"Logan, stop," Sam said.

He paused and glanced back, ready for her to rip him a new one.

"But you *did* lose someone," she told him softly. "You lost yourself."

Chapter Twenty-Five

Sam went directly to Logan as soon as the meeting let out. Wrapping an arm around his shoulder, she hugged him to her side. "I'm so glad you talked to us. After you left for a couple months in there, I was worried you'd never be able to get this off your chest. I kept waiting for you to return, hoping you'd come back." Tightening her grip with encouragement, she smiled proudly. "And now look at you. Maybe it'll be easier for you to share the little things from now on too."

He blinked, bowled over. "You actually *want* me to keep coming to the meetings?"

She laughed heartily. "Yes, I most definitely want you to keep coming. And — " she glanced around before leaning in close to whisper " — I have a little confession."

When she winced, he frowned. "What's that?"

"The first night Paige showed up to the group, I went looking for you afterward. Took me a while to find you, but when I did, I overheard a little of your conversation with her…in the back hallway."

"Holy — you mean, you *knew* about me all along?" he realized with startling clarity. His mouth dropped open. "But why — " He gasped. "Is that why you signed us up for the cancer center's visit on the same day? To force us together so we'd work out our differences?"

Sam winked. "Guilty."

He shook his head, rattled by this revelation. "And Jamie?" he asked. Had she convinced Jamie to no-show at the children's ward and then to tell them they needed to hook up?

Sam snorted and waved a hand. "She forgets to show up for everything she volunteers for. I was just banking on the odds there."

This was almost more than he could take. Samantha had known about him for months, and she'd forced him and Paige to be together. He wondered how Paige would take such knowledge.

Jumping when Samantha slapped a quick kiss to his cheek, he blinked when she patted his arm and moved off only for Kevin to hedge closer, looking decidedly uneasy.

"Yo, man," he said, not making eye contact.

"Hey," Logan said and bit the inside of his cheek. He hadn't been all that worried how the group would receive him when he'd blurted out his story. He'd been too busy trying to defend Paige and explain why she would never want anything to do with him. But now...now he worried.

"Damn." Kevin blew out a long breath as he glanced askance to Logan. "And I thought I'd had it bad losing my dad and all, but for your entire family to drop you? That's harsh." He clapped Logan on the shoulder in companionship. "I got into a couple fights in my day. I can't even imagine what it would've been like if any of them had ended the way yours had. I'm sorry you had to deal with that."

Kevin's total acceptance of him caught him hard in the chest. For the first time in his life, he wanted to hug another dude.

Resisting, he nodded stiffly. "Thanks."

Kevin nodded back, his brown eyes full of understanding. "Catch you next week."

As he wandered off, a couple more people approached. Dumbfounded by all the support, Logan thanked everyone and escaped at his first opportunity. For three years, no one had accepted him, no one had forgiven him. And now, to have an entire group of friends at his back...it was overwhelming.

He was worried how Paige must feel, though. He glanced back once to make sure no one was following him, then he exited out the doorway she'd dashed through. It was the same door he'd used to escape the first time she'd come to a meeting.

He knew where he'd find her. And when he approached the entrance of the same dead-end hallway she'd caught him sulking in that first night, he heard her sniffles.

Bracing himself, he turned the corner and came to a stop. When he dared to look, he found her sitting exactly where he had sat, her back to the wall, her knees folded up to her chest, her misery etched deeply into her face.

Her dark eyes were the only thing that moved as she looked at him.

"I told them," he said, hoping to reassure her. "I told them everything."

She shook her head. "You didn't have to do that."

He shrugged. "It was past time. And if Sam were here, I'm sure she'd say I *needed* to talk about it." He smiled, hoping she would too.

She didn't.

His soul cracked open and started to bleed. He couldn't handle seeing her miserable.

"About what Jamie said," he choked out awkwardly. "She didn't mean anything. It was just—"

"Don't." Her voice was so hoarse it was barely a whisper. Stumbling to her feet, she shook her head fervently. "Please don't do this."

He stood stock still, not stopping her, as she fled past him, racing down the hall. When he heard her turn the corner, he closed his eyes and fisted his hands down at his sides, telling himself to let her go.

But he couldn't let her go.

Whirling after her, he started running too.

"Paige."

At Logan's call, Paige quickened her pace.

"*Paige*," he growled impatiently as he caught up to her. A warm hand wrapped around her elbow.

He didn't make her stop, but she jerked to a halt, anyway, and spun around. "What?" Horrified by the crack in her voice, she gritted her teeth and commanded herself not to cry. "What do you *want* from me?"

"I…" Agony contorted his features. He looked so upset, she actually wanted to hug him, comfort him.

The very guy who'd taken her brother away, the guy she had forgiven and no longer blamed. The guy she should still avoid.

She pressed a closed hand against her aching chest, digging up the last reserve of her anger. "Look, just because I don't…hate you anymore doesn't mean…we're not…we can't be…"

God, she couldn't even say it. When she was looking at him like that, and with him looking back at her the way he was looking at her, she couldn't reject him.

Couldn't bear to hurt him.

A weighty breath shuddered from his lungs. He gave a single, humble nod. "I know."

Great. She was going to start crying again. Tears slipped from the corners of her eyes, wetting her cheeks. "Then what do you want from me?"

"What do I want?" When a sad smile flittered across Logan's lips, Paige shuddered, practically tasting his misery. Closing his eyes, he confessed, "Everything I know I shouldn't, I guess."

She closed her eyes too. "Logan…"

"I know," he said again, his voice rustic. "I *know*. When I look at you, I should feel nothing but guilt and remorse. I should close down and burrow into that wretched place inside myself. But I can't. I just…I feel so *alive*. You've made me smile and laugh and…and want."

Her eyes flashed open. When his gaze darted down her body, her skin warmed and her pulse throbbed in the most wicked places. She curled her fingers into her palms to keep from reaching for him.

"I can't remember the last time I really wanted a girl. But I want you, Paige. In every way possible. I know it hurts you to hear this, but you've healed me like nothing else has. You've made me feel… forgiven. And hopeful. And complete."

"But I can't just…it wouldn't be right. I couldn't ever be with you; it would totally disgrace Trace's memory. It…it…"

"I know."

God, she hated how lost he sounded whenever he said those two words. Why did he have to keep saying them?

He gave a bitter laugh and ran his hands over his face. When he dropped his fingers, he looked up at the ceiling, addressing the white tiles. "Wow. Who knew falling in love would be so gut-wrenchingly disastrous?"

Paige choked out a sob and covered her mouth with both hands. Logan focused on her, his brow knit with worry. When he took a step forward, she countered with a skip backward.

Shaking her head, she muffled out her command from between shaking fingers. "Don't say that. You don't mean…you can't—"

"But I do." Misery filled his eyes. "And I don't regret it. I've fallen in love with you, Paige. I just—"

She couldn't listen to any more. Whirling away, she took off, but he caught her arm two steps into her flight. She gasped as he spun her back to him. When they literally bumped into each other, he caught her shoulders and coaxed her in reverse until her spine met a wall. Then he pressed his forehead to hers and simply held her there.

The press of his body against hers, the fall of his minty breath on her cheek, the warmth of his fingers as they barely slid across her cheek, just under her bruise, was too delicious to resist. She closed her eyes, her chest heaving from the anticipation racing through her. She wanted this, wanted it so bad.

He caught a piece of her hair. "I could count the reasons you made me love you, one for each strand of beautiful hair you have. Or…or I could show you."

He kept his brow pressed to hers as he tilted his face just so until his breath fanned across her lips. Less than an inch away from kissing her, he paused and cupped her face, his fingers trembling against her skin.

"Paige?"

So tender and uncertain, his voice coaxed her into lifting her face to meet his mouth, greedy to taste him.

But at the last second, she pictured him and Kayla locked in this same embrace.

And Trace's roar of outrage as he discovered them together.

With a sob, she tore her mouth away. "I can't. I just—I can't." Ducking under his arms, she escaped and sprinted away. He didn't take up the chase this time, and she knew he wouldn't. But she didn't slow down until she reached Grammar Hall.

When she shut herself inside her room, she was more than relieved to find Mariah absent. Tess and Bailey might've been around, but if they heard her come in, they didn't pop over.

She sat on her bed, trying to regain her breathing—and her composure.

Logan loved her. Her chest swelled with euphoria. The first guy to ever really hit her radar felt the same intense awareness of her as she did for him.

But logically, she was all kinds of confused. Being with him had to be taboo. Didn't it?

Then again, if she'd honestly forgiven him, then it shouldn't matter what had happened three years ago. And in a way, it didn't.

But what would Trace think of her?

What would Kayla think, or her father?

A small part of her brain said she didn't care about her dad's opinion; he could rot in his alcohol for the rest of his life. But she really did care. She loved Paul Zukowski, knew how tormented he was. She didn't want to lose what little affection her only family left had for her. And she would if she started anything with Logan.

Wouldn't she?

God, she was so confused.

Maybe she'd been the sole person who'd found Logan culpable for the past three years. Maybe her father had never blamed him. Maybe Kayla didn't blame him either. Maybe Trace wouldn't have blamed him.

Except his own family had kicked him out. If his own flesh and blood could do that to him, her family probably wanted much worse.

She winced. She wanted to call her best friend. She needed Kayla's advice. But she'd never confessed what she knew about Kayla's involvement that night. Unable to deal with more than one problem as a time, she cradled her head in her hands and came up with no easy solution.

Chapter Twenty-Six

"Are you sure you can't come with us this weekend?" Bailey begged. Beside her, Tess fluttered her lashes. "Please, please, please come, Paige. We already told you we'd both chip in to pay your way."

Paige chuckled as she sat curled on Bailey's bed. It was only the second Friday into the semester, and her suitemates had plans to go skiing with both their families over the weekend.

Watching them pack, she shook her head sadly. "I have to work." When Tess opened her mouth to protest, Paige quickly added, "And I have a test first thing on Monday. A big test. I need to study."

Bailey wrinkled her nose as she stuffed bras and panties haphazardly into her suitcase. "A test already? But it's only —"

"World history with Daley," Paige spoke over her.

Since Bailey had just taken that course with the same professor last semester, she snapped her mouth shut. "Oh."

"Well, one of these days you have to promise to come home with us. We want you to meet our families." Neatly folding her undergarments before placing them precisely in her own bag, Tess sent Paige a stern look, waiting for an answer.

Paige nodded. "I promise."

She stayed with them, chatting until it was time for them to leave. Then she helped carry their luggage to Bailey's car. "Have fun and be safe," she warned as she hugged both girls goodbye.

After they left, she returned to her own room, morose and lonely. Without those two around, she always had too much time to think. And thinking was the last thing she wanted to do.

When Mariah blew into the dorm, instantly ripping off her shirt and digging through her closet for something else to wear, Paige welcomed the distraction.

"Going out again?"

"Yep." Mariah sounded sidetracked as she found a slinky, glittery, backless party top to wiggle into. "I've decided the only way to get over one man is to block out his memory with a couple more. And I've met this guy named Reggie. He's so hot. Dreamy hot."

Paige perked to attention. "Reggie? Reggie Oates?"

"Mmm hmm. Do you know him?"

"Yeah. We had geography together last semester. He's really nice." And she could totally see Reggie and Mariah hitting it off.

Wrinkling her nose, Mariah sent Paige a disappointed look over her shoulder. "Nice?"

"I mean—" Back peddling, Paige thought quickly. "Nice in a total player, party-animal, hottie kind of way."

Mariah thought that through. "Oh." With a grin, she winked. "Cool."

With her vertebrae resting against the wall, Paige sat on her bed and hugged her knees to her chest as she watched Mariah get ready for her night out.

An evening in alone, thinking about Logan, might kill her. As Mariah slipped on a pair of black leather boot stilettos, an idea hit Paige, and she spoke before she could stop herself.

"Hey, can I come with you?"

Mariah paused and gaped at her. "What?"

Paige shrugged. Hadn't she been the one to tell her father he needed to get out and meet people? Well, maybe she should listen to her own advice. And what if Logan was there, designated driving again? Maybe she could catch a peek of him.

She quickly dismissed the idea. Grr. She was supposed to be avoiding him. *That* was why she wanted to go tonight. To block out his memory with more guys, like Mariah had said. He probably wouldn't be there, anyway; he couldn't attend every party. Besides, if she wasn't scheduled to work at The Squeeze, that meant he undoubtedly *was*.

"Are you serious?" Mariah demanded.

"Only if you have something I can borrow to wear." Thank goodness Tess's vomit had laundered out of the last dress Mariah had loaned her. Her roommate had no idea how close it had come to being ruined.

A proud grin splitting her face, Mariah rubbed her hands together with relish. "Oh, have I ever."

The party was loud and rowdy and took Paige's mind off pretty much everything. Mariah ditched her the moment they arrived. Reggie appeared, greeted Paige with a grin and a quick hug, and then he whisked Mariah away.

She meandered through the different rooms, surprised at how similar the only two fraternity houses she'd ever been inside were to each other. Spotting Logan nowhere, she relaxed a little even as she tensed more, not sure how to engage anyone in a conversation.

Not that she had to worry about that.

A large form loomed in front of her, hazel eyes glittering with approval as the behemoth grinned and checked her out from head to toe. "Hey, I'm Dorian."

She nodded. "I know. I've seen you play football."

The star quarterback of Granton's football team brightened. "Have you? And what'd you think?"

They'd lost the one game she had attended with Tess and Bailey, and Dorian Wade had thrown two interceptions along with getting sacked four times. Not wanting to hurt his feeling, she nodded and smiled politely. "It was fun."

His gaze slid back down Mariah's outfit. The emerald dress hugged her frame like a second skin and the spaghetti straps barely held her bust up. Self-conscious under his intense scrutiny, she wiggled her fingers at her sides. Why couldn't he just look her in the eyes?

"Ever had a Jell-O shot?" he asked, finally lifting his gaze.

She shook her head. He grinned and wrapped a meaty hand around her elbow. "We got a bunch in this other room here. Strawberry flavored."

Her taste buds despised beer; the rotten barley scent of it reminded her too much of her father. But strawberry flavor she might be able to handle. And she could do with a little bit of liquid courage at the moment. Tess had seemed pleasantly happy after doing Jell-O shots with Dorian Wade—before she'd gotten violently ill, anyway. Paige just wouldn't let herself drink that much.

As soon as he led her into another room and ordered a round of shots, everyone around her cheered and about five co-eds scurried forward to offer her tiny plastic cups of red Jell-O.

With a shy smile, she accepted from one of them. Dorian took another. They faced each other, and she tried to drink hers as if it was a liquid, getting nowhere.

"No, honey." Dorian laughed and took the shot from her hand. "Here, like this." He slowly demonstrated the proper procedure by wrinkling the bottom of the cup to dislodge the gelatin. "Then you wrap your entire mouth around the rim and suck it out with your tongue."

He brought it to her lips, and she opened her mouth, trying his suggestion. He moved in closer beside her, his chest brushing her bare arm. A warm hand settled on her lower back as he leaned in to watch her in action.

She flushed but wiggled her tongue into the small shot cup and sucked out as much Jell-O as possible.

"That's more like it." He grinned.

The helpful co-eds cheered her on and offered her another. Since it tasted just like strawberry gelatin, as Dorian had said it would, she took one. Vaguely she wondered how many Tess had swallowed until she'd gotten as drunk as she'd been. But it didn't really matter. Paige would stop as soon as she began to feel the effects.

Two shots later, she found herself sitting on a couch with four guys, Dorian among them, and turning down a fourth.

Dorian tugged on her hand. "I love this song. Let's dance."

She nodded and let him pull her to her feet. But the music was too loud and the gyrating bodies were too crowded for her to move much. Plus all the active people crammed into the room exuded a humid heat that made the Jell-O in her stomach gurgle in a nauseating way.

Leaning up into Dorian's ear, she called, "I think I hit my limit."

He must've thought she meant alcohol-wise and not dancing-wise because he gave her a strange look before his mouth tipped into a big smile.

"Want to get out of here?" he called back.

She nodded, so he took her hand and led her through the horde. Once they reached the back door and stepped outside, she sucked in the cool January air. Though she wished they could've stopped to grab her coat, she welcomed the much-needed space.

Instead of stopping just outside the door, he led her around an outbuilding that abutted the fraternity house to an open area that held a fire pit and a couple of picnic tables. Tiled with cobblestones, the clearing was undoubtedly a popular spot in the warmer months. But tonight it stood deserted.

"Brr." She hugged herself and rubbed her bare arms briskly.

"Cold?" Dorian shifted closer. "Here, let me help with that." With a smile, he tugged her to him and wrapped his arms around her. Heat poured off his large body, and she soaked it up gratefully, burrowing closer to him.

He chuckled and tucked a piece of her hair behind her ear. "Better?"

She sighed. "Lots." Closing her eyes, she focused on the generous warmth he was sharing. "Though I always thought quarterbacks were a lot smaller than you."

Laughing again, he nuzzled his nose against her hair. "They tried to make me a lineman my first year I tried out, but I was so good at throwing the ball, I became the quarterback."

"Hmm." She could fall asleep like this. It was so cold, and he was so warm.

"I'm going to kiss you," he murmured in her ear.

She didn't say anything. It had been far too long since she'd kissed anyone. When he tilted her chin up, she let him. She wanted to see if he could make her heart race like a certain other person she didn't want to think about.

His mouth was pleasant enough, and she definitely wasn't repulsed. But he seemed to like to take control, which was a little unsettling right out of the gate. After she let him open her mouth, he became even more enthusiastic and backed her against the wall of the outbuilding until they were framed by the ivy growing up the vinyl siding. And it didn't shoot a single spark of chemistry through her.

Depressing.

But maybe if she imagined he was Logan...

Just thinking that name launched a bolt of heat straight down the center of her spine. She moaned, and a hand began to wander up from her waist, cupping her where she didn't let just anyone cup her, especially on the first kiss.

She broke her mouth away from his. "Okay, that's enough." She nudged him in the chest to get him to step back.

He didn't. If anything, he moved in closer, trapping her more firmly against the wall.

Paige frowned. That was not how he was supposed to respond.

"Stop." When she shoved against him again, he caught her hand and tugged it close, wrapping his fingers securely around her wrists, imprisoning her. She didn't like that and frowned her disfavor. "Dorian. Stop. I said stop."

He grinned smugly. "But we're just getting started."

Dipping back in, he kissed her neck, giving the sensitive skin a sharp, painful nip with his teeth just as his hand caught the hem of her dress and started working its way up.

Startled by his audacity, she lurched so violently in his arms she was able to dislodge him enough for her to gain a bit of breathing space.

As soon as she slipped out from between him and wall, she took off running, but tripped in the heels she'd borrowed from Mariah. She got another awkward fumbling step away before a big meaty hand hooked her around the waist.

"Hey!" She flailed in his arms as he picked her up off the ground. "Dorian. This isn't funny. Let me go."

"Not until I'm finished with you."

He spun her around, the vertigo catching her unaware. The wall he shoved her into smacked her hard and fast in the face, cutting her scream short. Sharp pain spiked through her cheek and rattled her brain.

Dorian snickered as he pressed against her from behind, grinding roughly against her bottom. "Know what I like most about skirts?"

he rasped into her ear, his breath sticky on the back of her neck. "Easy access."

Panic gripped her. Fingers on the back of her legs tugged her dress up. She felt sick. She swallowed and tried not to lose the Jell-O shots she'd slugged down. "No," she moaned. "Stop. *Somebody help me!*"

Dorian slapped his hand over her mouth. She couldn't even bite him, he held her so hard. She tried to scream for help, but his fingers gagged her.

Bitter cold air rushed up her legs, letting her know he'd exposed her. Her panties tore next, but the sturdy waistband caught and held, keeping him from shredding them off her hips. He cursed under his breath, and she bucked and wiggled, making him lose his grip before he caught her again and tried once more to rip her underwear off.

Terrified tears stung her eyes. Her esophagus burned from the screams he trapped in her throat with his hand. She tried to swing her arms behind her to fight him off. She tried to lever her legs up and push from the wall in front of her. But the attempts were useless. She couldn't even slam her skull back and hit him in the face; he held her head too firmly against his shoulder.

Just as the fabric of her panties began to tear, Dorian leaped backward away from her, releasing his grip. Relieved, she sank to the ground and shimmied her skirt back down over her thighs. Still in a crouch and not sure if she could stand on her shaking legs, she spun to face him, prepared to fight him off again…when she realized he hadn't voluntarily left.

Someone had ripped him away. Her savior spun Dorian to face him, putting Dorian's back to Paige, a split second before he reared his fist back and cracked the star quarterback in the jaw.

From her huddle on the cobblestones, Paige couldn't see her hero's face…until Dorian crumpled, revealing a livid Logan Xander, decked out in his bright red Designated Driver shirt.

She gasped as he reached down and picked Dorian up again by the front of his shirt.

Chapter Twenty-Seven

So furious that he shook, physically shook, Logan jerked Paige's attacker off the ground, manually picking him back up by his shirtfront.

Glancing over Dorian's shoulder, Logan checked on Paige. The tears streaming down her cheeks gave her raccoon eyes while a red smudge rimmed the corner of her lip. And one side of her face — the opposite side of her already bruised cheek — looked significantly darker than the other, as if she'd been hit or slapped. Huddled on the ground, she fumbled to yank up the broken strap of her dress, covering herself.

When a terrified hiccup escaped her, he saw red. Literally. A red haze of anger clouded his vision. Returning his attention to Dorian, he saw the bleeding man in nothing but shades of crimson.

"You need to leave. Now."

Gripping his nose with his hand, Dorian Wade didn't leave. He snarled and shoved Logan. "Who 'da fuck do you think you are, hitting *me?*" When he focused on the red shirt in front of him, he slurred, "Oh, hell no. Designated Dave is not going to kick *my* ass."

He swung but missed when Logan ducked out of his way. Then the drunk idiot came back for more. When one of his swings was lucky enough to catch Logan in the temple, Logan reared his elbow back and punched forward. The satisfying crunch of knuckle into jaw actually sounded good to his ear.

But it caused Dorian's head to snap back and his legs to go limp. Behind him, Paige screamed as Dorian slumped to the ground.

And didn't stir.

He blinked at the unmoving body, reality seizing him. A flicker of Trace Zukowski's dead eyes staring up at him as he lay crumbled in nearly the same limp position.

"Oh, God." He rasped a terrified curse, and spun around to face Paige when her soft hand touched his elbow. "Is he dead?"

She shivered without answering and didn't take her horrified stare off Dorian's crumpled form.

Logan broke away and dropped to his knees in front of a potted plant, where he emptied his stomach.

"Hey, what just happened?" someone asked from behind him.

"Dude, I think Designated Dave just beat the shit out of Dorian Wade."

"Paige? Oh my God, Paige. Are you okay? What happened?"

"What's going on out here?"

When Logan stopped vomiting, he sat back on his haunches to find the small backyard patio packed with people. Looking for Paige in the crowd, he found her with her roommate as Mariah corralled her back toward the house. Then he checked on Dorian just as one of the onlookers finally darted forward and knelt beside the prone quarterback.

He held his breath, waiting, ready to learn he'd killed again, when Dorian groaned and rolled onto his side, curling into the fetal position to hug his ribs. Logan exhaled, so relieved he almost passed out. He slumped onto a picnic table bench and cupped his head in his hands.

Time passed, but he wasn't sure how long. No one approached him, and he didn't want to be approached. When someone shouted, "Campus police is here! Who called the cops?" he lifted his face and stood up.

He watched dispassionately as a receiver for the football team helped a barely conscious Dorian stand upright as he spoke to a pair of uniformed men. When he turned and pointed at Logan, Logan braced himself, wondering if he was going to spend the night in jail for assaulting the star quarterback.

The two officers approached him, their stern expressions masked with disapproval. Dazed that this was happening again, he answered their questions, gave his account, and kept glancing around for Paige. When he realized he wasn't going to be incarcerated, he lost a little of his patience.

"Have you talked to the girl yet?" he had to ask in the middle of his interrogation. "Is she okay?"

One officer nodded. "She's fine. A little shaken. Her roommate's already taken her back to her dormitory."

Logan nodded, slightly relieved. "Is Wade going to jail?" he asked, narrowing his eyes as he glanced across the crowd where a group of fraternity guys were trying to take care of Dorian as they helped him stumble inside.

Both cops paused and shared a look. That would be a no, Logan decided. Their precious quarterback would not be going to jail.

"He was going to rape her, you know. If I hadn't showed up, he—he wasn't going to stop, no matter how much she resisted." God, just thinking about the possibilities of what could have happened made him vibrate with fury all over again.

"We're aware the two had a slight misunderstanding."

Logan's jaw clenched. He was surprised he didn't crack a couple teeth he gnashed them together so hard. "Misunderstanding?" He'd seen no such thing. Paige had been screaming behind the hand over her mouth, and Wade had been—

Probably shouldn't let himself think about that again.

"Miss Zukowski realizes Wade had no intention of hurting her, and Mr. Wade realizes he scared her needlessly. She didn't press charges, so there's no need for anyone to go to jail."

Logan just stared at them, disbelieving, wondering if she'd really said that or if they'd even talked to her. It seemed incomprehensible that there would be no justice for Paige. Had they not seen the trembling tears in her eyes, the way she'd shaken with fear, the torn strap of her dress, the fresh marks on her already bruised face?

"Can I go, then?" he growled, wanting to be as far away from this party and these people as he could possibly get.

"Not just yet. We've got a couple more questions, Mr. Xander." The two officers closed in on him as if they were about to apprehend him. "It's been brought to our attention that you're known for brawling where you come from. That a *death* actually occurred from one of your high school scrapes."

So, someone from the grief group had talked, huh? He should've expected that, but for some reason, the news caught him off guard.

"Yeah?" He rumbled out his answer, glaring at both cops, daring them to cuff him.

"We don't want that kind of reputation here at Granton. If we learn of you getting into any more fights, for *any* reason, you're out of here. And we don't just mean out of the party. Got it?"

A tremor of fear shivered up his spine. Kicked out of school for preventing a rape? Yeah, he got it. With a silent nod, he brushed past them, no longer caring if they had any more questions.

They didn't call him back, so he figured they were done "warning" him.

He wanted to howl at the moon, beat on his chest, do *something* savage and primal. The campus cops could intimidate him as much as they liked. He deserved a little dirt. But no punishment for Paige's attacker made him seethe.

Paige left her coat at the fraternity house. She didn't even notice the cold until Grammar Hall and the promise of a safe haven came into view. Then she finally started to shiver.

Keeping stride beside her, Mariah cast her a quick, assessing glance. "Almost there," she said.

Paige nodded, letting Mariah know she'd heard and would keep herself together until they made it to their room.

Einstein lurked in his usual spot and darted into the foyer as soon as Paige came through the door. Without meaning to, she gasped and shied away from him.

Freezing in place, he looked her up and down, his gaze pausing on her chest where she physically held up the top of her dress. "What happened?"

Mariah snorted. "Dorian Wade happened. The bastard." She bustled inside behind Paige and manually took Paige's shoulders to aim her toward the staircase.

Paige couldn't stop staring at Einstein as Mariah nudged her along. He didn't look real, his mouth falling open and eyes shocked.

"Dorian Wade? The star football player?"

"Yes! The *star* football player," Mariah snapped as she prodded Paige up another step. "He just tried to rape Paige."

The word had her shuddering. Hearing it aloud made is suddenly real. Oh, God. She'd almost been—

She couldn't even think the word.

"*What!*" Einstein scurried after them, following them up the stairs. "Are you okay, Paige? What happened? Did he hurt you?"

"Does she freaking look okay to you, kid?" Mariah waved him back. "Go back to lurking in your creepy little hole. She wants to be left alone right now."

It wasn't until after he'd disappeared that Paige blinked and glanced at her roommate. "You didn't have to be so mean to him."

Mariah snorted. "What? He's an eerie little freak that needs to grow up and learn how annoying and weird he is."

"He's not annoying. He's just lonely."

She understood loneliness. Too well.

"And you're totally wigging out," Mariah said, clutching Paige's arm to keep her upright when her shaking knees turned to noodles.

Paige shrugged Mariah away. "I'm okay." But as soon as she spoke, she shivered and huddled her shoulders deeper over her torso, preserving as much body heat as possible.

Mariah stopped touching her but lingered close enough to catch her if need be as they inched down the hallway, Paige leaning on the wall for support.

"Here. I think I have my key." Being uncommonly helpful, Mariah surged in front of her to take care of the lock. After she disappeared into their room, Paige followed, going straight to her bed and slumping down. She kicked off the shoes Mariah had loaned her and hugged herself, rocking back and forth.

Shoving open the bathroom, Mariah hurried inside only to pound on the opposite door. When neither Bailey nor Tess answered, she cursed. "Where the hell are Larry and Curly? Aren't they always around?"

"They left for the weekend. Went skiing," Paige automatically answered before squinting over the comedy reference. "The Three Stooges? Does that make me Moe then?"

Her roommate didn't bother to answer. She let out a weighty sigh, set her hands on her hips, and studied Paige with an expression that clearly said, *What'm I supposed to do with you now?*

Paige burst into tears.

Mariah cursed again and began to pace.

"I'm okay," Paige tried to reassure her, though she couldn't stop crying and she couldn't stop shaking. "I...I think I'll just...I'm going to take a shower and...and scrub my skin raw."

"Okay." Mariah nodded. "Okay, good. I'm just going to…" She glanced longingly at the door.

Paige gave her a wobbly smile. "Yeah. Thanks for bringing me home. You can go."

Hesitating, Mariah frowned. "You sure you'll be okay alone?"

"I'll be fine." She'd rather be alone than have Mariah hover over her, frowning all night, that was for sure.

Left alone, she took the longest shower she'd ever taken.

When she finished, she dressed in long sleeves, covering as much skin as possible, wanting every inch of flesh protected. But even in her long, baggy pants and turtleneck, she felt exposed, still remembering the air rushing up the back of her thighs, baring her to the world.

She dragged a sweatshirt over the turtleneck and wrapped a fleece throw blanket around her shoulders, but no matter how many layers she piled on, she still felt unprotected and cold, frozen to the bone.

She recalled the feel of Dorian's breath on the back of her neck, moist and sticky. Shoving the memory into the back recesses of her mind, she grabbed her toothbrush and toothpaste and scrubbed the taste of his beer and her strawberry Jell-O shots from her taste buds. She almost wished she'd had enough alcohol to be drunk right now; maybe that would numb some of the fear and creepy, there's-a-spider-crawling-all-over-me sensation she couldn't shrug away.

After brushing her teeth a couple more times, she paced the floor. But her knees still kept going loose and unstable, so she curled up on her bed and grabbed the remote to turn the TV on. After flipping through a dozen stations, she settled on an old episode of *Dirty Jobs*. She'd just lowered the volume and was staring vacantly at the screen when a soft knock came on her door.

She didn't feel like talking to Einstein. But she didn't want to brush him off either.

Closing her eyes briefly and bolstering her resolve, she pushed from her mattress to cheek the peephole.

Her breath caught when she saw a familiar pair of blue eyes staring back.

Chapter Twenty-Eight

Fingers fumbling as she unlocked her door, Paige yanked it open to gape at Logan.

He lifted his face, looking apologetic. "Mariah let me into the building when she was leaving. She said to give you a couple minutes to get cleaned up before knocking."

Silently, she shifted aside to permit him entrance. After he stepped past her, she shut the door and locked, then bolted, it.

When she turned around, she found him watching her.

"I just came by to see how you were doing." Blue eyes analyzed her face, and he exhaled harshly. "He did hit you, didn't he? You're already starting to bruise."

He stepped toward her, lifting the tips of his fingers to her still-throbbing cheek. She winced and skittered a cautious step back. "It's fine," she rushed to say.

He froze, his expression wounded as his gaze darted to hers. Dropping his hand, he swallowed hard. "Sorry."

She licked her cracked lips and tried to think up something to say to make him feel better. "He…he didn't hit me."

She decided against explaining that the newest bruise had actually come from the wall when Dorian had shoved her against it and pinned her there while he'd thrust her dress up around her waist.

She shuddered, telling herself to stop thinking about that already.

Logan went beet red. "The police told me they talked to you. Did they really talk to you?"

She winced as that disturbing conversation wavered through her brain and gave a slight nod. "Yeah. We talked."

He narrowed his eyes. "You didn't really tell them it was a misunderstanding, did you?"

That hadn't been her word, but she'd known that's what the cops had wanted her to say. They'd led the questioning so that all she needed to do what nod and say, "*Sure. That's what happened.*" They didn't want their school embroiled into any media-covered scandal any more than she wanted to revisit what had happened. It had been so much easier to simply agree with them and let it all drop.

"Paige, you didn't. Christ, he wasn't going to stop, and you know it."

She sat on the edge of the bed and tried to stop shivering, briskly rubbing her palms over the tops of her thighs. He knelt in front of her, his eyes reflecting all the pain and anguish inside her.

"You should go back to the police and tell them the truth. I'll come with you."

When he reached out as if to take her hand and lead her to the authorities right then, she shook her head vigorously. "No. No, I don't want to drag this out. I just want it to be over."

"But—"

"Please," she whispered.

He clenched his teeth and closed his eyes. "I am so sorry, Paige. This is my fault. I should've checked on you sooner. I should've... Damn it, if I'd have known he wasn't going to be punished, I would've hit him harder."

But as soon as he spoke, he cringed. "God, I didn't mean to say that. After what happened with...your brother, I didn't think I'd ever want to hit anyone else again. But when I saw you struggling against him, with your skirt...I got over my aversion real quick." He shook his head, his lashes lifting so he could look at her from tortured eyes.

"It okay," she assured, her throat burning and sore from screaming a short time ago. Still feeling Dorian's hands on her, ripping down the front of her dress and touching her where she hadn't allowed him to touch, she hugged herself, protecting her chest, even though she knew the threat was gone. "I'm actually glad you got over it."

Logan's attention drifted to her trembling hands, and he cursed under his breath. "What am I doing?" he muttered and pushed back to his feet to run his hands through his hair. "I came here to make sure you were okay, not talk about...about that."

"It's okay," she whispered, wondering how many times it'd take her to repeat the sentiment until she began to believe it.

When he stalked across the carpet and back, she gave a small smile. Her floor had definitely seen its fair share of pacing tonight. But she liked watching Logan pace. The way he looked so concerned and agitated all on her account made her feel...loved. With Mariah's irritated mumblings as she'd paced, Paige had just wanted to be alone. But with Logan here...

"Will you keep me company for a little bit?" Her chin trembled when she realized she'd probably burst out crying if he said no. "I don't want to be alone."

His eyes widened, but he didn't say anything, only nodded and gingerly settled himself on the floor across the room from her.

Unable to take her eyes off him, afraid he'd disappear if she looked away, she rubbed her hands up and down the sides of her arms, keeping them crossed defensively over her chest, but she still felt chilled through two layers of clothes.

Silently, Logan leaned back against a bare patch of wall next to the bathroom. With his hands stuffed deep in the front pocket of his hoodie, he looked like he was as drawn into himself as she was with her arms fastened securely over her chest.

What a pair they made.

He turned his attention to her television and stared vacantly at the commercial playing. She studied it too. It didn't even occur to her to turn up the volume. As they watched in silence, she felt safe with him keeping a quiet vigil over her. She didn't think anyone else could've made her feel any safer.

"How far did he get?" he finally asked.

Paige closed her eyes and tried not to remember, but it kept rolling through her head like an awful horror movie stuck on replay.

"Right...right after..." She wasn't sure if she could say it aloud. But when she opened her eyes, Logan was watching her with an intent expression, letting her know he wouldn't leave it alone until she told him everything.

Gulping, she tried again. "Right after I heard him unzip, he pulled my skirt up. He was…he was trying to remove my underwear when you arrived."

"He'd already unzipped?" His voice cracked as he spoke, the muscles in his upper arms occasionally twitching under his long sleeves.

Paige glanced away. "Didn't you notice his fly hanging open while he was slumped on the ground?"

"No." He looked stupefied. "Thank God. I probably would've killed him." As soon as the words cleared his throat, he winced and thumped his head back against the wall. "I didn't mean to say that."

She knew he hadn't. She opened her mouth to tell him so, but his gaze traveled to the picture sitting on her desk of her and her brother.

"I never should've hit Trace." His face filled with hot color. "I never should have messed with his girlfriend. I never should've… God." He bowed his head nearly between his bent knees. "He could still be here today. He could've been at that party and been the one to save you, but…I took that away from you, and I don't know how to bring him back."

When he looked at her, tears filled his eyes.

"I don't know how to undo this," he confessed on a harsh whisper. "I try. I try so hard to be good, to work hard at my job, to study all my assignments. But none of it matters, not how many cancer clinics I volunteer at or bloody fingers I patch up. He'll still be gone. And he should be here, right now, instead of me. He could go to you and put his arms around you and just…hug you. I know that's what you need. You need someone to hold you."

"Logan."

She said his name because she didn't think she could listen to any more of his gut-wrenching words. Her heart broke. For him. For herself. For their situation.

But when she slid from her bed to approach him, he surged off the floor, shaking his head as if he couldn't bear her kindness.

"I should go." He turned toward the door without a farewell.

She held herself tight, standing lonely in the middle of her dorm room. He reached for the doorknob and even wrapped his hand around it. But he didn't turn the handle, and he didn't leave.

Instead, he swerved slowly back around, looking apologetic and defeated. "I can't go," he confessed, his red-rimmed eyes lost and tormented. "I'm just going to hold you, okay? You need some comfort. So, just…pretend I'm someone else. All right?"

But she didn't want anyone else. She only wanted him. "All right."

When he caught her shoulders and nudged her gently against his chest, she closed her eyes and sank home. Solid and real, he closed his arms around her and tucked his face close to her hers, kissing her hair. "You're going to be okay."

She breathed in the scent of his hoodie, and listened to the steady thud of his heart through his chest. It was delicious and warm and just what she needed. He felt so different from the bulkier Dorian Wade, and that difference mattered.

Logan was safe.

Yet his steady, supporting, sheltering presence made a dam burst inside her, splintering apart all the emotions she'd been holding back since her last sob fest.

She cried some more.

Each teardrop fell for a different reason. A few dozen for the night's events. A handful more for the loss of her brother. She even shed tears for her mother and her father. For Kayla. She cried for Logan and all the misery he'd been through since making a horrible mistake three years ago. But mostly she cried for their lost relationship.

Logan held her through it all, a silent fount of protective support. When she lifted her face from his shoulder, she felt drained.

"I want to lie down," she slurred.

He nodded instantly. "Okay."

He shifted them to the bed until he was easing her down. When he tried to step back so she was lying by herself, she tightened her hold on him. "No. Please. Stay."

Again, he nodded. As he hesitantly stretched out on the narrow mattress beside her, she curled close. Trusting him implicitly, she relished the feel of the blankets at her side and his warmth at her cheek.

She nestled close. "I didn't think I'd ever feel warm again. I was so cold."

He rubbed her arm, warming her even more. When she used his shoulder as a pillow, he kissed her hair.

"Rest," he murmured gently. His breath on her cheek didn't feel at all like Dorian's had because it was warm and scented with Logan's dragon-defeating spearmint gum.

Smiling with the memory of their morning together at the children's ward, she closed her eyes and relaxed against him, soothed by his presence. He coaxed her into sleep, stroking her arm through all the layers of clothing separating them.

"Don't leave," she mumbled, her brain already fogging into a lovely oblivion.

She woke once in the night to a nightmare. Phantom hands groping her, crawling up her skirt, nipping at her neck. Cold air seizing her thighs.

Paige whimpered and flailed. When she struck something solid and fleshy, she slashed toward it again, intent on defending herself.

A grunt and curse followed, and suddenly it was gone. Then something grasped her shoulders. "Paige. Paige, wake up. You're having a nightmare."

The dream didn't let her go easily. Her brain kept dragging her back into the dark torments of hands over her mouth, arms pinning her own immobile. She cried out, afraid.

"*Paige!*"

She gasped into consciousness and was instantly hugged to a solid, familiar chest. "It's okay," he assured her, smoothing back her hair. "Just a dream. You're okay."

She gulped and panted as she tried to regain her sanity. Logan disappeared for a second only to reappear and thrust a cup of water into her hand. She drank gratefully.

It cleared her brain until she could think rationally. "Did I hit you?"

He ran his fingers over his hair stubble and shook his head. "Just my arm. I'm fine. Are *you* better now?"

She nodded and returned the empty cup to him. He straightened and carried it to the sink where he must've found it.

All the lights blazed in the room. She soaked up his face, immediately feeling better. She wanted to reach out and smooth her fingers over his buzz cut as she'd just watched him do.

He was so *Logan*, and she was so relieved he was here.

"I should probably go." His blue eyes looked worried as he backed away from her.

"What? No!" She launched herself off the bed and clutched him close, clinging shamelessly. "Don't leave me *now*."

"Okay, okay." He patted her hands, reassuring her. "I'll stay. No problem." But his gaze strayed toward Mariah's side of the room. "Do you think your roommate would mind if I crashed on her mattress?"

The idea of him anywhere near Mariah's bed sent irrational jealousy through her system. In fact, the idea of him anywhere right now, except wrapped around her, sounded downright intolerable.

"I promise I won't punch you again in my sleep," she blurted.

His eyes flared wide with surprise. Then he sputtered out a laugh. "Paige, you can punch me in your sleep as much as you need to. I just thought you wanted me out of your bed. I mean, I scared you and caused you to have a nightmare by being beside you, making you think I was him."

She frowned. "No." Shaking her head, she tugged him closer. "No, you didn't cause the nightmare. I swear. *He* caused it. Not you. I don't think of any of that when you're holding me. So come back to bed. Make it go away again. Please."

He shook his head, looking amused. "You don't have to beg, you know, because honestly, there's nowhere else I'd rather be."

"Good." She tugged on him harder.

As they settled back on the mattress with him spooned on his side behind her, she curled up her knees so he could do the same.

He rested his face by the back of her neck, his breath stirring her hair with a pleasant spearmint warmth.

"Do you want the lights off?"

She shook her head. "No."

"Okay." He relaxed his muscles, and all was right in the world again. Snuggled into him, she closed her eyes and sleep immediately claimed her.

At some point during the night, she managed to wiggle around on the two foot of mattress space she had until he was trapped between her and the wall and she was facing him. Though they were both still fully clothed, their legs had intertwined so their knees bent in toward each other to stack his leg, then hers, then his, and hers again.

Paige blinked against the sunlight pouring through the closed window blinds and untangled their limbs before she sat up.

She glanced down at Logan still asleep on her mattress, and drank in the sight he made first thing in the morning. With the way his lashes rested against his cheek and the start of a beard stubbling his jaw, he was art. Her gaze drifted down to wide shoulders and the crook of his elbow where he bent it to rest his face on one hand. Slim waist, long legs—he really was beautiful. When she reached his feet, she was startled to find he still wore his shoes.

Paige was tempted to tug them off for him but was too afraid to wake him, so she quietly slipped off the bed and tiptoed to the bathroom. Once finished in there, she washed her hands back in the bedroom and was halfway through brushing her teeth, when she checked on him in the mirror to find him exactly as she left him, but with this eyes opened as he watched her.

She whirled around, the bristles of her toothbrush still scrubbing on her molars.

"G'morning." His raspy voice was just as appealing as the rest of him.

"Hi," she muffled out, her face heating as she turned back to the sink, spit, and quickly rinsed, unnerved by the fact he was watching her take care of her morning ablutions.

As she filled her cup and drank some water, he asked, "Can I have some of that?"

Her gaze met his in the mirror mid-swallow. He still lay tucked up on his side on her mattress, but his alert eyes looked as bright and blue as a cloudless sky.

Paige lowered the cup from her mouth. It was three-quarters full so she turned to him and shuffled the few feet to the bed to hand it to him.

"Thanks." His warm fingers brushed hers as he accepted, sitting up when he did so.

She watched his strong, tanned throat work as he swallowed. Feeling the need to fidget as she stood beside the bed, she sat next to him on the mattress. And suddenly he seemed a lot closer, and the closeness actually comforted her.

With a refreshed sigh, Logan leaned sideways to set the empty cup on Mariah's desktop. Then he studied Paige, his lips tipped in a sleepy smile. Lifting his fingers, he sifted a few strands of hair away from her cheek. "Your bruise is darker." He didn't touch the offended area, just studied it from sympathetic eyes. "It almost matches the one your dad gave you on the other side."

She caught sight of his knuckles as he moved his hand back. "You're a little banged up yourself."

He looked down and frowned. "It looks like *I'm* the one who hit you."

Paige didn't like how bothered he appeared by that observation. It occurred to her how this was the last thing to ever touch her brother alive, these very knuckles that had defended her only a few hours ago. She grazed them gently with her fingertips; she wasn't horrified by them in the least. Glancing up to meet his gaze, she brought his bruised, scraped hand to her mouth and gently kissed the warm, battered flesh.

He closed his eyes and drew in a sharp breath.

Her fingers ran gently over his before she trailed her touch down along his palm and reached the hem of his hoodie. Bunching the fabric out of her way, she exposed the scars on his wrist and kissed them too.

When his lashes flickered apart, he looked dazed and half-drugged.

She felt his desire mirrored from every organ in her body.

Needing her mouth against his more than she needed her next breath, she leaned forward, straining until she reached him. His lips parted, but he didn't move to meet her. He watched her, his eyes hopeful and wary in equal measure.

"Paige." He was going to tell her to stop; she could tell by the cautious inflection in his voice. She understood his reasons for stopping perfectly. After the night she'd had, after everything stacked between them, kissing him was the height of stupidity.

But it was the only thing she wanted.

Closing her eyes, she rested her cheek on his shoulder. He wrapped his arm around her and tugged her close until they were sitting hip to hip. She set her hand over his heart and grasped a handful of cloth.

"I let him kiss me last night," she admitted, her voice low and ashamed.

Logan's chest heaved under her fist, and his arms tightened around her, but he didn't interfere. He let her talk.

"I wanted…I wanted to move on, to get over this, whatever it is…this thing I have for you. So I let him kiss me, hoping…" She shook her head and burrowed closer. "But the only moment it was any good was when I pretended it was you."

A choked sound tore from his chest, echoing through the ear she had pressed against him. His shifted so he was cupping her cheek in his palm. Then he ducked his face until his nose brushed her jaw.

"It doesn't seem to matter how wrong it is or how much I fight it, I'm drawn to you. I can't get you out from under my skin." She tipped her face up just enough to align her mouth with his. But when she began to lean forward, he tightened his hold on her cheek, staying her.

"It's too soon." His fingers stroked their way down her throat. "After last night, you need time to—"

"No." She squeezed his wrist. "You don't understand. He touched me where—" With a shudder, she shook her head, unable to go *there*. "He made me feel vile, Logan. And the only person I want to wash his touch away is you. I think you're the only person who *can*."

Deciding there was only one way to keep him from speaking out another warning, she pressed her mouth to his, smothering any more protests.

He jolted and made a sound of objection deep in his throat. But a split second later, he sighed and caught her by the back of her neck to keep her from pulling away. She opened her mouth, and he was right there with her, tasting and exploring.

She moved closer, climbing into his lap. He caught her hip to keep their bodies from getting too close even as he groaned his satisfaction. One long, deep, wet kiss later, he broke away and tugged her back just enough to look into her eyes. The awe in his expression affected her with a tight pinch in the center of her chest. He really did love her; it shone from every pore in his body.

"I can't believe we're doing this." His whisper sounded desperate, as if he expected her to return to her senses and abandon him any second. "Are you sure you're okay?"

"I'm fine," she whispered back, resting her forehead against his as she ran her fingers over his unshaven jaw. "This isn't wrong."

His blue eyes glittered, and his rickety answer came in unsteady wheezes. "The fact that you even had to say that—"

She kissed him again, muffling his arguments. He arched under her, sinking all ten of his fingers into her hair. She cupped his head, delighting in the stubbly texture of his buzzed hair against her palms.

Their mouths worked in harmony, and heat built between them. She wasn't sure why she kept moving against him, but the friction felt really good, so she kept doing it, the slide of their bodies ignited a fire in her she didn't want to bank.

Wrapping his arm around her lower back, he tugged her close until she was tucked flush against him. Their lower parts bumped against one another, and the shock of the sensation made her gasp.

He cursed. "Shit. Sorry. I forgot."

But when he tried to scoot her back away from the warmest part of his lap, she tightened her thighs around him, resisting. "No, it's okay. I'm fine."

In her mind, she felt the cool air from Dorian lifting her dress and the rough texture of his fingers as they moved up her thigh. But the warm, firm security of Logan under her helped.

She wasn't about to let him retreat and take away the only thing helping her, so she cupped his face, dipped her head, and kissed him again.

His resistance was futile. He met her lips eagerly and even pushed his hips against hers — though that part was probably an unconscious action. But God, he could kiss her forever, and she'd die a happy girl. He felt so good against her. Solid. Real. Logan. She wanted more.

Needing to experience her flesh against his, she worked her hands under his hoodie and another shirt and smoothed her palms flat against his back. His skin was warm and soft; she couldn't stop touching him.

Murmuring an incoherent sound of pleasure, he tried to return the favor and buried one hand under the back of one of her sweatshirts. When he encountered more cloth, his fingers burrowed past that, only to find more.

Finally, he lifted his face. "How many layers are you wearing?"

She laughed, even though her nerves jittered with fear and excitement. "Too many."

Gathering the hem of two of the sweatshirts, she tugged them off over her head. After tossing them aside, she wrapped her arms around his neck and pulled him close so she could nuzzle her nose against his.

"Better?"

He merely groaned as his warm fingers slid up her spine. Throwing her head back, she groaned too.

He'd just begun to kiss his way down her jaw to her neck when the handle to her room jiggled and the door flew open. Paige hopped off Logan's lap and stumbled backward away from him.

"Oops." Mariah giggled and covered her mouth, though her eyes above her hand danced with delight. She dropped her fingers to smirk, not even bothering to back from the room to give them privacy. "Well, this is interesting," she cooed, reveling in the moment. "The two virgins of Granton are making out in my dorm room. I knew I'd eventually rub off on you guys."

Logan cleared his throat and pushed off the bed, coming to his feet in one smooth, liquid move. He glanced toward Paige before running his hand over his short hair. "I, uh, I'll talk to you later."

Before Mariah could even pull the door shut, Logan grabbed his shirt and hoodie and streaked past her and shot into the hall.

Paige stared after him, dazed, embarrassed, and yet her body was pleasantly drunk off the arousal he'd stirred inside her.

"Well. I guess you're already over your near-rape," Mariah said, her voice dry as she strolled to her side of the room. "And thank God. I don't think I could deal with a roommate who wigged out all the time the way you did last night."

Paige scowled at her, irritated that Mariah had no more empathy than she did, and even more irritated she'd interrupted Paige's delicious moment with Logan.

"I'm taking a shower," she muttered, pushing to her feet. She grabbed a fresh bath towel and escaped into the bathroom.

Chapter Twenty-Nine

Freshly showered, Paige collected her purse, keys, and a borrowed coat from Mariah. She hurried outside to the parking lot where she found her car. Climbing behind the wheel, she started the engine and backed from the parking spot.

She had no destination in mind. She just knew she needed to get out for a while, away from campus, away from Mariah, away from anything to do with Dorian Wade and all the thoughts about what she was going to do concerning Logan.

After last night, so many things were no longer important. All the mental walls she'd thrown up to keep him away had crumbled. All her reasons for staying away felt stupid and petty.

She just wanted to be with him.

Nothing else mattered. Well, nothing except the opinions of two very important people in her life.

When she turned onto the interstate that would take her home, she realized she'd been heading this way all along.

Too many hours later, she pulled into the Hashmans' driveway. It struck her then that she had no idea if her best friend would be home, or if she'd even want company. But Paige slid from the car anyway. She was already here. She might as well find out.

As much as Kayla had talked about moving out and finding her own place, Paige couldn't picture her living anywhere else. This house right here equaled Kayla.

Knocking on the front door, she was surprised when Kayla herself answered. "Oh my God! *Paige?* What're you doing here? Wha — oh my God, where'd you get a new bruise? And don't tell me a laundry basket this time."

Paige managed a weak smile. "Can we talk?"

"Of course. Come in." Kayla dragged her over the threshold and into the living room. "What happened?"

Paige glanced around, checking for either of Kayla's parents.

"They went grocery shopping," Kayla answered her unspoken query. "But let's go to my room anyway."

Once they reached Kayla's domain, Paige bypassed her favorite spot in front of Kayla's vanity, not wanting to look at all the bruises on her face. She collapsed onto the bed.

"Now." Kayla breathed out a steadying breath. "Who hurt you and where can I find him?"

Closing her eyes, Paige grinned. "I love you so much." Nothing else mattered, not who Kayla had kissed three years ago, not who Paige had kissed this morning, not anything. She loved her best friend and needed her.

Kayla sat beside her and smoothed Paige's hair behind her ear. "And I love you too, sweetie. Now talk."

"I don't even know where to start."

Kayla laughed. "Where else? At the beginning. Duh."

With that practical advice hanging in the air, Paige rolled her head along the mattress until she was facing her friend. "Do you think it's possible to forgive someone for what they did and move on as if it never happened? I mean, if it was something *so* bad it changed your entire life forever, and what they did could never be undone, but you knew they never meant any harm and were sorry for their actions?"

"Wha…" Kayla paused to lick her lips nervously. "What's this all about?"

Paige closed her eyes. "Logan Xander goes to Granton."

Kayla cursed long and fluid. "He *what?*"

"He goes to Granton. And he works with me at The Squeeze. And we're in the same grief group. And I pretty much see him all the time."

"Oh, God." Kayla moaned and clutched her stomach. "He told you, didn't he? He told you I kissed him that night."

Wait. Kayla had kissed *him?*

Paige sat up and stared at her, wide eyed. "He never said that you had *initiated* the kiss."

What the hell? *Kayla* had kissed *him?*

Kayla squeezed her eyes shut. "I'm so sorry, Pay Day. I…he…" Tears immediately gushed down her cheeks. "I…I…"

Again, Paige reminded herself how much she loved her best friend. Nothing else mattered.

"You were drunk," she tonelessly echoed Logan's explanation. But she still couldn't wrap her mind around this new development. "And he came on strong."

"He was so nice," Kayla wailed. "And cute. And Trace couldn't stop talking about *Granton.* He was going to leave me behind, and I was feeling s-sorry for myself. Then, suddenly, there was this cute boy flirting with me, and…I don't know. I wanted Trace to see us. I wanted him to appreciate me more so he wouldn't leave me."

Paige covered her mouth as she listened. She could hurt her best friend by telling her Trace had never meant to leave her; he'd wanted to marry her. Or she could let the past stay in the past.

"I never imagined it would end up like that. I never thought they'd fight and Trace would — "

"Hush," Paige whispered. She wrapped her arms around Kayla and held her tight. "Don't. It's okay. I forgave you the night I learned about it."

"But he died thinking I — "

"No," Paige cut in sharply. "Enough. It's over. It's past. You're my best friend, and I refuse to lose you over something neither of us can control now."

Kayla squeezed her hard, her body trembling without any semblance of control. "You're the best friend I ever had."

"And you're mine," Paige promised her.

Sniffing, Kayla sat back and sent her a watery look of entreaty. "So, you really think you can move past this as if it never happened?"

Paige's mouth fell open. "Oh! Actually, I wasn't talking about you when I said that. I…" She began to wring her hands. "Of course

I can move on like it never happened with you. I was talking about Logan. I…he…I really like him, Kay Kay. I like him a lot."

Kayla blinked once, digesting. Then her eyes flooded with horror. "Paige, no. You can't."

"But—"

"Did he give you that bruise?"

"What?" Paige shook her head. "No, of course not. He actually—"

"Look, I know how charming he can be," Kayla spoke over her. "I fell for his lines too, remember. He can't be trusted. Please don't let him use you. He could hurt you so easily. Just think about how much he's already hurt you, hurt all of us."

Frowning, Paige lifted her hands to hush her friend. "No, just stop. Please. He's never used a line on me."

Kayla heaved in a long sigh, the one she made right before she started a long-winded, parental lecture. "Paige, listen to me."

Paige grasped both of her hands insistently. "No, you listen. You don't know him the way I do. You haven't seen what he's like now. Trace's death changed him. He…he's not charming at all."

Kayla lifted an eyebrow as if to ask, *then why the heck do you like him?*

Paige flushed. "I…he…he's quiet and serious and intense. And when he manages to smile, it almost hurts to look at him because he's still so tormented. But I get him. I understand the most elemental part of him because it's like…it's like seeing…me. And…and…he likes me too. A lot."

"I…" Kayla shook her head and gave a nervous laugh. "I don't know what to say. I just…this is the last thing I ever thought to hear come from your mouth. You've never really liked a certain guy before."

"Well, I like *him*." Paige took a deep breath and plunged in. "I'm pretty sure I love him."

Kayla's mouth dropped open. "Okay, *that* is the very last thing I ever thought I'd hear you say. Wow." She shook her head as if to clear it. "But seriously. Wow. You've never even talked about liking a boy before. And now suddenly you're in *love* with *Logan Xander?* You certainly don't choose the easy path, do you?"

Paige bit her lip and shook her head.

"Well, okay." Kayla squeezed her eyes closed before she opened them and shrugged. "I guess I can say one thing for him. After…

after it happened, he stayed with me…with Trace and me. Everyone else took off, even Trace's friends. They just disappeared, scattering as soon as it happened. But Xander fell onto his knees on the other side of Trace and used his cell phone to call the police. He didn't budge once as I bawled all over Trace's body, not until help arrived. He even reached out and closed Trace's eyes. I think I appreciated that more than anything."

Paige pulled Kayla into a hug. "He's a good person. No matter what happened three years ago, he's paid for it for too long. And I think I help heal him."

Kayla nodded. "Well, then, I think if you really want to be with him, I'll support any decision you make." Then she winced. "But I wouldn't tell your dad about it for a while if I were you."

Paige snickered. "No, I hadn't planned on it quite yet either."

She stayed with Kayla and talked for almost an hour. But since she was scheduled to work that evening, and there was one more stop she wanted to make before leaving the county, she hugged her friend goodbye and headed out.

When she arrived in Village Heights fifteen minutes later, she stopped at a gas station to borrow a telephone book. After she found the address for Roderick Xander, it took less than five minutes for her to pull to the curb in front of a stately, two-story estate.

Wringing her hands, she walked slowly to the front door and rang the bell. She almost expected a servant to answer, so when Logan's father pulled the door open, she took an immediate, leery step back, not prepared to jump into this quite yet.

"Can I help you?" he asked.

"I…yes. Hello. I…I'm Paige Zukowski. My brother was—"

"We know," he bit off abruptly, his eyes chilling. "And you've come to the wrong place. We don't know where he is."

Paige frowned. "Where…who is?"

"Logan. If you're here to see to him, he's not here."

"Oh. I know that." Paige fumbled a moment, not sure how to proceed. "I mean, I know he's not here. But that's not why I'm here. I mean, it is. Kind of."

The words sounded bumbled on her tongue. Even Mr. Xander cocked his head, looking bewildered as he studied her. When his wife appeared beside him, setting her hand on his arm, Paige glanced at both of them and started again.

"I'm sorry. I realize I'm messing this up. I just…I didn't come to see him. I came to talk to you. To the both of you."

"We don't have anything to say about that night," Mrs. Xander said, her voice chilly and strained. "I'm sorry."

When she began to shut the door, Paige threw out her hand to block it. "No. Wait! Please. I know you kicked him out after helping him with his legal matters, and I…I…I just wanted to let you know I think you made a big mistake in doing that."

Logan's parents paused in shutting the door and opened it wide again. "Excuse us?"

"He's your son," she said simply.

When Mrs. Xander covered her mouth with her hands, clearly affected, Paige turned beseechingly to her. "He might've messed up and made a few wrong decisions that night. But you're his parents. His *family*."

She glanced toward his two brothers who'd crowded together at the end of a curving staircase. "It was your job to help him get back onto his feet and move past this tragedy. I just can't understand how you could turn away from him. He's not a bad person, and he paid for what happened. More than he should have. And he's still paying for it. He needs you, but you treat him like he's dead. And that's wrong. If I had the chance to see my brother just one more time, I'd take it in a heartbeat. Do you want to lose any chance you might have to ever see Logan again? Honestly?"

"How dare you!" Logan's father rumbled as he reached for his silently sobbing wife and pulled her into his arms. Glaring at Paige, he sneered. "How dare you come into *our* home and tell us what to feel. You have no idea what our lives have been like these past three years. You know nothing, little girl."

Paige cowered a step back, sufficiently put in her place. "You're right," she said, wiping her damp palms on her thighs. "I don't know what you have been through. I'm sorry for barging onto your property and insulting you. But I needed to say that." She began to turn away. "I'll leave you alone now."

No one stopped her, no one contradicted her, no one argued with her opinion or even thanked her for coming. They merely glared after her as she strode down the sidewalk.

She wasn't sure if she'd accomplished anything from her visit, but at least she felt better about saying her piece.

Chapter Thirty

Paige barely made it back to Granton in time to make her evening shift at the juice bar. She clocked in and was wrapping her apron around her waist as she breezed into the front.

Seeing Logan made her pull up short. She usually worked Saturday nights with Bella. "What're *you* doing here?"

He looked as equally shocked to see her. "Gus called me in to work because he said someone else couldn't make it. I thought that someone else was you. What're *you* doing here? After last night, you should take some time off." He sounded very stern and fatherly. "You need to rest."

"Last night?" She stared blankly until it struck her what he meant.

Wow, for a while, she'd actually forgotten all about Dorian Wade. At least there was one bright side to her busy day. With so many other things to deal with, she could forget for a couple minutes about being attacked less than twenty-four hours ago.

"I feel fine," she said. Brushing past him, she smiled at the approaching couple and took their order.

Logan hovered behind her and hurried to make the smoothies the customers wanted before she could. As soon as they paid for their order and walked back out the door, leaving Logan and Paige the only two people in the shop, she turned back to him.

"Has it been this quiet all evening?"

He shook his head and sputtered out a sound of confusion as if he couldn't believe she wanted to talk about *work*. "I've only been here ten minutes, but yeah."

She frowned. "Huh. That's strange. I wonder where everyone is."

As if to ease her worries, the bell over the door rang, admitting new customers. A group of about half a dozen students entered. But when they saw Paige and Logan at the counter, they quieted immediately and appeared almost leery about approaching.

"Welcome to The Squeeze," Paige called with an overly friendly smile, inwardly wincing because she sounded way too syrupy-sweet. "What can we get you?"

Most of the group got into her line, but a couple stragglers went to Logan's register. Logan and Paige filled their orders within a couple of minutes. After paying, the group moved as one big cluster to a high round table, but no one sat. They whispered among themselves for a few minutes, casting glances toward the counter before they exited the shop en masse.

Once again, The Squeeze was left empty.

"Okay, this is beyond bizarre," Paige said, watching them flee. "What the heck is going on?"

Logan sighed and rubbed at the center of his forehead. "I think word has gotten out about me." Ducking his head, he added, "About my past."

Paige whirled to gape at him. "What? What makes you think that?"

Though he kept his face lowered, he raised his eyes. "The campus cops. They brought it up when they were questioning me last night after the fight. They inferred that if I was involved in another physical altercation on campus, the university would…expel me."

Paige's heart felt like it literally plummeted into her stomach. She covered her mouth, unable to believe her ears. "Oh my God. Who do you think told them?"

He shrugged, glancing away. "I don't know. It doesn't matter."

Why wouldn't he look at her? "You don't…you don't think it was me. Do you?"

Blue eyes veered back. "No. Not at all. You would've said something a long time ago if you were going to talk. It must've been someone from the grief group."

At the front of the store, the door swung open. Paige whirled around to watch two girls begin to enter. But when they saw Logan, their eyes grew large. Jarring to a halt, they gawked at him before scurrying backward and out the exit.

Paige's mouth fell open. "Oh my God. I cannot believe this. It was three years ago, people. And it was an *accident*."

Opening her mouth to rage about the treatment he was getting, she spun to Logan and froze when she saw his pale features. He looked downright haunted.

Sending her a tremulous smile, he said, "Yeah. Well, not everyone has your ability to forgive and move on."

She couldn't handle seeing him so crushed. She stepped forward to hug him, let him know she wouldn't abandon him, but the business phone rang, stalling her.

Logan jerked, and then rushed to answer. "You've reached The Squeeze. How can I help you?" He pulled back as if startled to hear whatever he was hearing. Paige shifted closer, focusing on his face. "Yes," he answered before shaking his head. "No. Actually, it's not at all…okay." His gaze slid to her, the expression on his face unreadable. "Okay. I will. Okay. Bye."

He hung up and continued to stare at Paige.

"Well?" she demanded.

He blinked as if…well, it was still hard to read him. But he appeared to be somewhere between perplexed, upset, and worried. "That was Gus," he said slowly. "He said to close shop and lock the place up."

Paige's mouth dropped open. "What? Why?"

Logan shrugged. "He didn't say."

"And you didn't ask?" Paige was furious. The angst in his eyes told her why he hadn't. "You think it's because of you."

His gaze said yes, but his lips said, "I don't know, but he wanted to make sure I walked you home tonight."

Paige blinked. "Huh?"

Logan shook his head and lifted his hands. "Look, I have no idea. But this is really weird. I'm not getting good vibes. Let's just do what he says and get out of here as fast as possible." Turning away, he opened the cash drawer and began to clear out the register. "Can you get the front door?"

Paige stared at him a moment before she let out a sigh. "Yeah," she said and left him to his task.

As soon as she locked the door and flipped the *Open* sign over, an upbeat hip-hop melody filled the air behind her. She looked back just in time to see Logan lowering his arm from the radio clock above the juice machine.

Grinning because he'd remembered how much she liked to work to music, she hummed along to the popular tune and found a broom to sweep the front parlor. Logan stayed behind the counter, starting the sink water, looking uptight and concerned. As he added suds, Paige twirled her broom, dancing with it as she swept. She glanced at him, hoping he was watching, hoping her silliness would help loosen him up.

He was, and his gorgeous half-smile tugged at his cheeks. Shaking his head, he returned his attention to the dirty dishes, but at least his shoulders looked more relaxed.

Though she put on a façade of being perfectly fine, her body remained tense and braced. Something eerie was going on, and it involved Logan somehow. But for Gus to request that Logan see her safely home suggested something else entirely.

She shook her head as she stowed the broom away and moved behind the counter to help Logan with the finishing touches.

When Jason Mraz's song *I Won't Give Up* came on over the radio, they were nearly done with clean up.

Paige sucked in a long breath. She needed something to distract her nerves. And she needed a reason to touch him again. Grasping onto this excuse, she swirled to him with a coaxing smile. "This is my favorite song." Drawn toward him as she'd never been drawn to anyone, she held out her arms. "Dance with me?"

He hesitated, though the temptation was clear in his gaze. Shaking his head lightly, he gave a soft chuckle. "We don't have time."

She batted her lashes. "Come on. There's always time for one dance." When he didn't immediately give in, her expression turned serious. "Besides, we need to talk…about last night. And this morning."

If anything, that only made him look more wary. So she went back to coaxing. "Please. I want to dance with you."

He shifted toward her, then stopped himself. "I don't know. It's been too long since I last danced with anyone."

Her smile bloomed wide. She was breaking him down. "You can't be any worse than the broom."

His grin flickered. "Don't be so sure. The broom couldn't step on your toes."

"You can step on my toes all you like." Dropping her playful humor, Paige swung toward him and stopped sweet-talking. Without saying a word, she wound her arms around his neck. "Just hold me, and I'll do the rest."

Closing his eyes, he gulped audibly and pressed his forehead to hers. As she swayed into the slow rhythm of the song, he moved with her, his hands clinging to her waist.

Mraz crooned through the quiet juice bar, asking how old their souls were. And Logan tugged her just a little closer.

"Whatever is going on, whatever reason Gus wants us to close early, I'm going to stay by your side, okay?" she promised him. "I won't let you face any ostracism alone."

Logan shuddered. "I went back to your room today." As he lifted his face to kiss her hair, his jaw scraped gently across her temple. "You didn't answer your door. I thought maybe you didn't want to see me, that you might regret —"

"No." She pressed her cheek to his, needing the skin-to-skin contact. "No, that wasn't it at all. I really wasn't there. I went home. To talk to Kayla." She decided not to mention the visit to his parents' house.

Logan's brow puckered in confusion as he pulled back enough to study her face. "You drove all the way to Creighton County... and back? Today?"

She nodded. "I wanted to clear the air between the two of us."

"And?"

Paige grinned. "And we did."

His shoulders sagged as he exhaled. "Good. I'm glad you didn't... I'm just glad." His hold on her tightened fractionally. "Your ability to forgive astounds me, you know."

Mraz continued to serenade them, promising not to give up, even if the skies got rough. Licking her lips, Paige added, "And I wanted to get her take on the idea of you and me...together."

His body stiffened as he stopped dancing. Studying her intently, his face went a sickly gray.

"I want to be with you, Logan." God, she'd hoped her voice wouldn't break when she said that, but it sounded rougher than sandpaper. "And I want everyone else to accept it."

A ripple surged through him, making him shiver. "Did she?" he whispered. "Did she accept it?"

Paige's smile trembled as she bobbed her head. "Yes. After a little convincing, she said she just wanted me to be happy."

"And your dad?" he pressed, his voice barely audible.

With a shrug, Paige made a face. "Right now, I'm not really concerned enough about his opinion to ask for it." Later, she would be. But for now, she wanted Logan more.

His eyes darted around the room as he turned his face from her. He looked like he might be going into shock. "I…" His breathing grew winded. "Oh, boy. This is a dream, isn't it?"

Paige's soul sang with pleasure as she beamed at him. "I don't think so. I feel pretty awake."

When he just stared at her, appearing too dazed to speak, Paige cupped his face in both her hands. "Logan…"

His lashes flickered as he swayed toward her. When his head dipped, a persistent tap started on the glass window front of the store.

Paige yelped and spun around. Two uniformed officers were loitering right outside the entrance of The Squeeze. One man, lowering the butt of his Maglite he'd used to knock on the window, motioned for her and Logan to come let them in.

She gulped, dread icing her skin. "What're the chances they just want a smoothie?"

"They don't look very thirsty." Dropping his hands from her, Logan strode around the counter and went to unlock the door.

The two officers stepped inside.

"We're looking for Logan Xander. We were told he might be working here tonight."

Logan exchanged a glance with Paige and turned back to them. "I'm Logan."

She creeped out from behind the counter to join the group. This could only be about his fight with Dorian. But the campus police had already questioned everyone last night. If Logan was in any trouble, wouldn't they have done something about it then?

Checking out their uniforms and patches, she realized they worked for the city, not the university. Maybe a different law enforcement agency wanted to take different measures.

She itched to reach out and touch Logan, just to reassure him and herself everything was going to be okay. But by the stiff, formal way the men stood, soothing touches seemed forbidden. Curling her arms around her body, she hovered just beside Logan as one officer pulled out a notepad and the other asked if they could question him.

"Mr. Xander," he started, his voice brooking no room for jokes. "Were you aware Dorian Wade died in his dorm room late last night?"

Chapter Thirty-One

Paige gasped aloud. The two cops glanced her way. Staring back, she stumbled in reverse until she sank into a nearby chair.

Sheet white, Logan stared at her for the longest time before he turned back to the cops.

"No." He shook his head. His voice sounded too hoarse to be healthy, and he looked as if he might pass out. "No, I…I…I had no idea. Oh God, how did he die? Was it some kind of blood clot? I hit him so hard, I…" Losing his voice, he bowed his head and bent his shoulders in over his body.

No, no, no. This wasn't happening. If another person died after getting into a fight with him, Logan would lose it. And she would lose him to his own self-torment.

"He was shot at close range…four times," one of the cops said.

"What?" Paige sprang to her feet, not expecting this answer at all. "*Shot?* With a *gun?*"

She wished it had been one of those moments when someone would roll his eyes and snicker, saying, "No, he was shot with a *spoon*." She needed a comedic break right about now. But no one even cracked a smile. The seriousness of the situation ricocheted through her with a full-body tremble.

Dorian Wade had been shot with a gun.

And killed.

The same night he'd tried to rape her.

"Oh, God," Logan repeated, straightening. He blew out a relieved breath. "Oh, thank God."

When both policemen frowned, he flushed. "I mean, not thank God he's dead. Just…that I didn't kill him from our fight. I just—" He shook his head as if realizing he should stop talking before he incriminated himself further.

"When was the last time you saw the victim, Mr. Xander?"

"Last night," Logan croaked. He looked as if he were about to empty his stomach. Paige wondered how he was still standing. "At the…at the party."

"At the fraternity house where you engaged him in a fight?" the officer asked.

Logan nodded, closing his eyes.

"You didn't see him again after that?"

This time Logan shook his head. "No."

"Where were you from between midnight last night and six this morning?"

When it struck her where he'd been, Paige gasped again. Both officers turned toward her. She slapped her hands over her mouth and gaped back before quickly lowering her fingers.

"He was with me," she admitted, shocked she was actually his alibi.

This seemed to take the men by surprise. "And you are…?" The cop asking all the questions shifted intimidatingly closer to her.

"Paige Zukowski." Her voice was small as she answered.

The uniform taking notes paused halfway through his writing and looked up. "You're the…"

"The girl Dorian attacked," she finished. "Yeah."

Logan shifted protectively closer to her, and she shared a quick look with him before turning back to the officers. "I…we…after Logan saved me from…from…well, you know, my dorm mate brought me home. Logan showed up almost immediately to see how I was doing. I was pretty shaken, so he stuck around the entire night and took care of me."

This time, the two cops shared a glance with each other, both looking entirely too suspicious for Paige's comfort. In unison, they turned back to her. "And you two just happen to work together?"

Paige couldn't help herself; she sent a telling look from The Squeeze apron around her own waist to the one wrapped around Logan's. "Uh... yeah," she answered the obvious.

The cop with the pen took notes as the other motioned between them. "What is the nature of the relationship between you two?"

Paige's cheeks burned with heat. When she realized Logan had turned to her expectantly as if he also wanted the answer to that question, she cleared her throat. "Um, well...I'm not too sure yet. It's kind of undefined at the moment. I mean, I started out really, *really* not liking him. But then he was okay, you know. And I just couldn't hate him no matter how hard I tried. And now...now he's just...amazing and—"

When she lifted her face, she caught Logan's gaze. He looked so hopeful she whirled back to the officers before she did something embarrassing like throw herself at him. "I guess you kind of inter-rupted us mid-transformation between relationship statuses."

Both cops stared at her as if she was loony.

Logan cleared his throat. "You can just say we're coworkers."

The cop scribbled that down.

Nothing about the situation was funny, but Paige grinned anyway.

"Can anyone else verify this alibi?" One cop asked, making her grin die a quick, ugly death. "Did anyone else see him in your room all night?"

Her mouth fell open. They didn't believe her? Shocked, she was too busy gaping at them to immediately realize she hadn't answered the question. Then she snapped her fingers.

"Ooh! Yes, my roommate can. She let him into the building when he arrived." At least, that's what Logan had told her. She sent him a swift glance. "Right?" When he nodded, she returned her attention to the cops. "Then when she came back in the morning at about... eight, eight-thirty, he was still there."

Another blush scorched her cheeks. "She actually thought we'd... you know." Motioning between Logan and herself, she managed a nervous laugh. "But we hadn't."

"I don't think they really care about that part," Logan murmured beside her, looking amused.

She rolled her eyes. "Trust me, everyone always cares about that part."

He stared at her a moment before his lips twitched. It was so charming, she wanted to throw herself at him again and kiss him all over his sexy mouth.

Clearing her throat, she forced her gaze back to the officers, who were also sporting entertained grins they were trying to hide.

"So, you two were together, alone in your dorm room from…?"

"From about eleven last night to eight this morning, I guess." Wow, had it only been this morning?

The cops nodded, finally looking satisfied with one of her answers.

"Okay. I think that's about everything we needed to know. Oh, one more thing." They focused on Logan. "Do you own a gun, Mr. Xander?"

Logan shook his head. "No."

"All right then. Thanks for answering our questions. We'll be in touch if we have more. You two stay safe. There's an armed murderer out there on the loose."

Paige shivered as she watched them leave. No wonder Gus had called. It hadn't had anything to do with Logan's past it all.

Things had just gotten real.

The Squeeze was deathly silent after the cops left.

"Logan?" Paige said as he locked the door. He looked so tense she grew worried about him.

He closed his eyes and shook his head, waving his hand to keep her away. "Thanks for the alibi," he rumbled.

"I just told them the truth." When she took a step toward him, he flashed his eyes open. The wild gleam in them warned her to keep her distance. She skidded to a stop.

"Well, thank you anyway." He turned away. "I'm going to stock up on supplies, and then we should go."

After he disappeared into the back, she stared at the spot where he'd been standing. Shaking her head, she hurried after him. "Logan—"

He put up a hand again to stop her from approaching any closer. "I can't..." He wouldn't look at her. "I don't want to talk about it, okay?"

"Okay," she whispered, not wanting to push.

Logan cleared his throat. "I'm not...this isn't..." When he glanced to her, he shook his head and sent her an apologetic look. "Forget the supplies. I should get you home and safe as soon as possible."

His words sounded so final, as if he felt it was the last thing he'd ever say to her. It scared her. Even though he was going to escort her home, she didn't want to leave the juice bar until they settled this. Following her body's natural instinct to race after him, she caught him as soon as he reached the time clock.

"Logan, wait." Grabbing his arm, she spun him around, and he let her. Hugging him tight, she pressed her cheek against his chest and clenched her eyes shut. "I won't give up on you," she said, meaning it from the bottom of her soul. "I can't."

He shuddered and hugged her back. "Paige, we can't...this isn't... God!" He squeezed her back and pressed his face against her hair as a full-body tremble seized him. "I killed someone. I killed your *brother*. And people here know that now. Whenever anyone else dies, I'm going to be the first person they look at. I'm — "

"No," she insisted, shaking her head hard and tightening her grip.

"Yes." He grasped her arms and pulled her back so she'd be forced to look at him. "Don't you get it? Every bad thing that ever happened to you originated with *me*. Your brother, your mother, your father. Even your best friend. It's like bad things just follow me around so they can attack *you*. I'm a...a bad-thing magnet."

She couldn't help but smirk. "A bad-thing magnet?"

He shook his head. "I don't know. My brain is fried. I couldn't think up another term at the spur of the moment."

This time, she grinned full-out. "I think my first gift to you is going to be a thesaurus."

His eyes went moist. "How can you smile and tease at a time like this? It's like..." He shook his head. "It's like you're pure sunlight and I'm darkness. You are so amazing, you don't even realize. You've been so good for me. I need you like I've never needed anything. But I'm just *bad* for you. I hate that."

When he closed his eyes and bowed his emotion-ravaged face, Paige wrapped herself around him again. He shook his head, but the rest of his body went into some strange kind of conflict. His arms came up between them as if he wasn't sure if he should push her away or pull her against him, but the rest of him swayed close.

"You're not bad for me." Making up his mind for him, she folded her arms around his neck. "You're *not* bad for me."

When she kissed him, he resisted for a second. Just a microsecond. Then he groaned and tilted his chin to fit their mouths more firmly together.

Paige cradled his face in both hands as he cupped her waist. Lifting her off her feet, he swept her around until her back met the wall. Snuggled between him and another solid surface, she climbed him, hooking one leg around his waist.

He opened his mouth against hers and kissed her desperately.

Heat and energy and a crackling electricity curled through her. "I don't want to be away from you right now. Especially at night. You're the only one that brings me peace. Please. Come back to my room with me." She panted between long liquid kisses. "And stay."

"Yes," he said, and he kissed her again. "Yes." And again. "Yes."

Chapter Thirty-Two

Paige was kind of glad it was so cold out; it gave her plenty of reason to snuggle as close to Logan as humanly possible on their long walk to Grammar Hall, a walk that suddenly didn't seem long enough because it was filled with stolen kisses and straying hands. It felt as if she'd snagged a chunk of time and was able to keep it separate from everything happening around them. In this moment, they existed in their own little bubble. Just the two of them.

When her dormitory appeared at the end of the block, she let go of his hand and put a foot of space between them.

"We probably shouldn't touch when we go inside. My friend, Einstein, hangs out in the entrance a lot and gets insanely jealous when he sees other guys around me."

When Logan wrinkled his eyebrows and cocked her a strange look, she tried to explain. "I don't want him to do anything to you. He's scary smart on the computer. And one time, this guy simply smiled and said hi to me when he passed by the common's room where Einstein and I were doing homework. They next day, I heard he'd had a bunch of problems because his transcript suddenly disappeared out of the system. He had to drive home and manually retrieve it from his high school and was lucky he didn't need to repeat all the classes he'd taken last semester. I didn't ask, but I had a bad feeling Einstein was behind that."

With a frown, Logan shifted closer to her and grasped her hand, holding tight enough that she couldn't let go. "That doesn't sound good. Paige, if this kid is so obsessed with you—"

"He's harmless," she assured, leaning against him since he seemed to want to ignore her warning to keep his space. "Einstein is just—"

"He sounds disturbed. Like really—"

"He has his issues. I know that, okay? But he also needs a friend. He'll never get better if no one befriends him."

With a surrendering sigh, Logan wrapped his arm around her, sealing her to his side. He kissed her temple. "You have too good of a heart, do you know that?"

She smiled and snuggled close, then tipped up her face for a kiss, which he gladly obliged. But as they approached her building, she held her breath and her joints stiffened with anxiety.

Keeping an eye out for Einstein as she unlocked the door, she eased inside the foyer with Logan unwilling to let go of her hand.

Einstein didn't appear.

Her shoulders fell with relief as she exhaled, but she just as quickly frowned. "Hmm. I wonder where he is." Biting her lip, she glanced up at Logan. "Do you think he's okay? With a killer on the loose—"

He shrugged. "I'm sure your little friend knows how to take care of himself and stay safe."

"You think?"

"From what little I've seen of him, I think he knows exactly what to do to survive."

Paige wanted to keep defending Einstein. She knew he had problems, but what person didn't? Except Logan went and buried his nose into her hair, distracting her. He kissed her temple as they ascended the stairs.

"Though I have to admit," he murmured, "the kid does have great taste. If I had to pick one girl on campus to become unhealthily obsessed with, I'd pick you too." When Paige turned them down the hall toward her room at the top of the steps, Logan pressed his mouth to her jaw. "Actually, I think I'm already unhealthily obsessed with you."

When she paused in front of her door, she looked up at him before digging her key from her purse. "Unhealthily?"

He pressed his forehead to hers. "Yeah. After last night, I know you need time and space to get over what happened, but I can't keep my hands off you. I'm still just so amazed you're letting me touch you, that you *want* me to touch you."

With the reminder of what had happened less than twenty-four hours before, Paige shook as she tried to fit her key into the lock. "Wow. So much has happened today, that feels like ages ago."

He covered her hand to help her unlock her door. "But it's still only been a day." He turned the handle and then preceded her into her room, turning on the light and glancing around before he fully let her in.

Grinning, she shut and locked them inside alone before grasping his arm and whirling him around to face her. When she looped his neck with her arms, he caught her waist and let her lean flush against him.

"Were you checking out the place for bad guys before you let me come in?"

His blue eyes glittered as he kissed the end of her nose. "Maybe."

She let out a big, dramatic sigh. "My hero." Stepping up onto tip-toes, she pressed her breasts against his chest and fused their mouths together.

The man must be the best kisser on the planet. Strange, amazing things happened to her when his lips touched her. Then they opened and his tongue tangled with hers, and she moved into him enough to make him stumble backward. Using her momentum, she corralled him toward her bed until the backs of his legs bumped the edge. When he lost his balance and went down, she happily went with him, landing on his lap as soon as they hit the mattress. Smothering any possible protests with another soul-searing kiss, she plastered herself to him.

He was all in, kissing her back just as heartily until she let her hand wander between their bodies so she could explore him through his jeans. Then he rocketed backward, tearing his mouth from hers.

"Wait, wait, wait," he panted. "We need to slow down. Jesus. We need to *stop*."

"Why?"

"You're not ready. It's too soon. I—"

"I'm ready." She assured him, caressing his face and kissing her way along his jaw.

He drew in a heavy breath, and his body tensed under hers, but when she slid her hand down his ribcage and toward his lap again, he caught her wrist. "No. You're not. I Googled this today, and rape victims have to go through a bunch of steps before they can heal. There's fear, shock, disbelief, denial, a complete breakdown of out-of-control emotions and anxiety along with depression. And then you can finally accept and move on. You—"

"Oh my God." Clutching two handfuls of hair, Paige clenched her teeth and scowled at him. "You just won't give up about this, will you?"

"No. I know you, Paige. You're not over it. You're just pushing it down, and that's not healthy."

"Okay, fine." She blew out a disgusted breath. "Let's see. What did you list? Fear? Check; I definitely experienced that already. Shock? Oh, yeah. I've had some of that too. Disbelief? Totally. Denial?"

When he arched his eyebrow, she rolled her eyes. "Oh, shut up. So, I'm pushing it down. Would it make you feel better if I had a total breakdown and freaked out on you right now?"

With a shrug, Logan gifted her with a small, amused smile. "Maybe."

She shoved him in the arm. "Thanks." He laughed and caught her hand, and she leaned forward to rest her forehead on his shoulder. "You do realize I wasn't really raped, right?"

He stroked her hair, tangling his fingers through the long, dark tresses. "It was close enough." Then he kissed her temple. "Too close."

Her sigh was long and sad. Logan continued to brush her hair with his hand, and it lulled her into a warm sense of security. "So much has happened all at once. It's impossible to take it all in. I need a break, just a little time out to do something normal and memorable. Last night, Dorian Wade was alive and scary. Today, he's…gone. What if tomorrow it's you or me?" Lifting her face from his sturdy shoulder, she met his gaze. "I don't want to die with what he did to me being my sole source of experience with sex."

Logan's face drained of color. "You're a vir—" He squeezed his eyes closed and pinched the bridge of his nose. "Oh, thanks. No pressure or anything there. It's been three years for me. I'm not ex-actly on the top of my game here, and I want you to have the best."

She grinned and set both hands on his thigh to knead at the muscles bunching under her fingers. "I have a feeling you'll rise to the occasion."

Dropping his hand to study her, he shook his head. "I don't have anything. No protection." Just as soon as he said that, he hissed out a breath and pressed a fist to his forehead. "I can't believe I just said that. I'm not considering this. It's not going to happen. You're not ready."

But the more convinced he was that she wasn't ready, the more she felt ready because she knew she could trust him implicitly. The "protection" aspect caused her a moment of pause, though. She bit her lip before an idea struck. With a gasp, she leapt off him and hurried to Mariah's side of the room. Hitting pay dirt with the first drawer she opened in her roommate's desk, she yanked out the foil package she found lying inside and whirled around to wave it victoriously.

His blue eyes flared as he stared at the condom. Then he slowly shook his head and whispered an obscenity. It was like watching the walls of his resistance crumble to dust. As she moved toward him, feeling powerful and excited, plus a little nervous and scared, he looked up.

"You know what you're doing, right?" he croaked. "You're asking me to deflower Trace Zukowski's little sister. Paige—"

She pressed her fingers to his lips and drew in a sharp breath. Hearing her brother's name caused her a moment of pain. She pictured him in her mind and bit the inside of her lip. But then she focused on the man sitting on her bed, his expression tormented as he watched her. And loved her.

"No," she said. "I'm asking you to make love to the woman you claim you love and to help her heal from a horrible event."

He shuddered and blinked a few dozen times. "You have to be sure about this, Paige. You have to convince me without a doubt that you're ready."

Before she could respond, he reached out and grabbed her between the legs. Paige yelped and jerked away from him.

Narrowing his baby blues, he lifted an eyebrow. "I'm not convinced."

"Well, you caught me off guard. Damn it." Knowing he'd done that on purposed to prove his point, she set her jaw hard and scowled at him. But she wasn't going to give up. Grasping his wrist, she led him back to the spot he'd just touched, more slowly this time. Gently, she fit his hand into place.

As he sucked in a breath, she bit her lip and threw back her head.

The warmth of his palm seeped through her jeans and panties, making the muscles in her stomach clench as she used her hold on his wrist to rub him lightly against her. Immediately, her breasts tingled, and an electric pulse shot up the insides of her thighs. With a little moan, she shifted closer so she could use his hand more freely to grind over the sweet spot.

"See," she panted, forcing herself to focus on his face. But when she saw the way his eyes had widened and his frame had frozen with either shock or horror, she flinched. "What's wrong?"

It took him a second to tear his attention from his hand and lift his face. "I don't think you realize just how incredibly hot it is to watch you touch yourself…with *my* hand."

Using the hand between her legs, he drew her closer to snag the condom from her grasp. Then he tipped his face up for a kiss. Paige leaned down to meet him, and he tumbled her back onto the bed as soon as their mouths met. Without untangling his tongue from her, he tucked her under him on the mattress and took control of his grinding hand. She arched under him.

When he abandoned her lips to run his own down her throat, he groaned. "You asked for this."

Oh, yes, she had. And she didn't regret it at all. She loved the way his large protective body covered hers, how his mouth cherished her, and his hands worshiped everything they touched. When he sat up long enough to pull his shirt over his head, she sat up with him to stroke his bare chest, loving the way he let her curiously explore every inch.

Relishing the reverent look in his eyes when he helped her remove her shirt, she felt adored. They removed her bra in a united effort, and it seemed more meaningful to her that they did it together. He fitted his mouth over her breast as he unzipped her jeans. She moved with his every touch, bowled over by it all. This was really happening. She was with Logan, and they were going to go all the way.

She scissor-kicked her legs to assist with the removal of her jeans, then grinned at him when she went for his. He touched her face as he let her slide his pants down his powerful thighs. Once they were both stripped completely, she met his gaze to find him staring back, his eyes glittering with a euphoria she'd never seen on his face before.

"Want to help me with this?" he asked as he tore open the condom package.

Intrigued by the process, she scooted in to watch as he pinched the tip of the latex and rolled it into place. When she reached out with a shaking hand, he let her finish. Once he was covered completely, she let her fingers wander back up the entire length.

Logan shuddered and groaned. "You can be less gentle," he said. "Here."

After he showed her what he liked, she kept her fingers curled around him and pumped from tip to base. He buried his hand in her hair at the nape of her neck and pressed his forehead to hers. A couple more strokes later, he moaned. "Your turn." Nudging her back onto the mattress, he asked, "What do you like?"

Paige shook her head. "I have no idea."

"Right." He met her gaze and grinned. "First time." Studying her face with a thoughtful expression, he suggested, "How about I experiment a little, and you give me a yea or nay?"

Not sure how else to do it, she bobbed her head.

What followed was a whole lot of yeas and nary a nay.

Logan hit a very enthusiastic yea when he bent his face between her legs and licked. Paige gasped and arched. She tried to clutch his hair, but ended up cursing. "Damn it. You need longer hair."

"Sorry." He grinned as he crawled back up her body. "I'll work on that." Slotting his hips into place, he interlaced their hands and held them in place by her face as he rested his upper body weight on his elbows.

She felt him down there as his blue eyes watched her. "Are you ready?"

Still throbbing from the sweet torture his tongue had put her through, she nodded, as eager as she was nervous to experience what came next. Logan's grip on her hands tightened, and he rocked forward. They stared at each other, and she absorbed the expression on his face as he seemed to do the same to her. Watching his eyes go unfocused and his cheeks ruddy from pleasure was overwhelming. It was almost as powerful as feeling him press into her for the first time. The pressure and stretching was the most indescribable sensation.

Once he was seated deep, he paused and let out a breath. It gave her enough time to grow accustomed to the feel of his body joined with hers.

"You okay?" he asked, his voice strained.

Paige didn't think okay was quite the word she needed, but she said, "Yes. Yes, I…that wasn't so bad at all." She'd been braced for tearing pain.

He choked out a laugh and pressed his forehead to hers. "What every guy aspires to be. *Not so bad.*"

She flushed. "I mean—"

"Shh." He kissed her lightly. "It's fine. This way, we only have room to improve." Then he pulled out and eased back in.

Paige arched and squirmed as he seemed to hit every nerve ending inside her. "Oh," she gasped in surprise and felt the need to move with him as he did it again. "Better."

Amusement lit his face. "Is it? How about this?"

He shifted slightly and came in at a different angle.

With a moan, she bit her lip and nodded. "Mmm hmm."

"And this?"

"Oh yeah." She wrapped her legs around him and tightened her fingers in his grip. "That. Do that. But faster."

"Like this?"

Losing the ability to voice her opinion with intelligible words, she merely clung to him, enthralled until there was nowhere higher he could take her. Plunging off the zenith of her pleasure, she swept him over the edge with her, and together they seemed to free fall into oblivion.

"I told you, you were totally ready."

At Logan's smug-sounding comment, Paige cracked a tired smile and lightly poked her elbow back to nudge him in the gut. "Oh, yeah. You called it. Liar."

Spooned behind her, he let out a quiet oomph and then chuckled before he kissed the back of her hair. "Seriously, are you okay?"

She hummed out a sound of contentment. "I am so far from okay, it's not even funny. I'm too elated, overjoyed, gratified—" she yawned "—and exhausted to be a measly okay."

"Good. I am too."

Feeling a little smug herself to hear such a positive report, she closed her eyes.

Since neither knew if Mariah might try to pop in at some point in the night, they'd reluctantly crawled back into enough clothes to be decent. But Logan's fingers had no problem finding their way inside her oversized t-shirt that stretched down to her knees. When he cupped her breasts and flicked an expert thumb over her nipples, she moaned with pleasure.

"Want me to raid my roommate's drawers again for a little something-something?"

He groaned and pressed into her from behind. "Don't tempt me." Then he just as quickly added, "I don't want you to get into trouble with her."

Paige snorted. "Don't worry. If she knew what I wanted to do right now, she'd probably run out and buy me an entire case of condoms."

"She would, would she?"

"Oh, yeah." She rolled around to face him. Though she could barely see him in the dark room, her lips found his without a problem.

He didn't break away until her hand smoothed down his bare chest and discovered the waistband of his boxer shorts. "We probably shouldn't," he said, his voice strained as he caught her wrist. "You have to be sore. I don't want to hurt you."

Wiggling her fingers, she tried to break free to tempt him some more. "I don't mind. Really."

"But I do. Please, Paige." His lashes fluttered against his cheek. "Let me be a gentleman, this time at least." Then he set his mouth by her ear and whispered, "because I have a bad feeling that after I'm sure you're healed, I'll be attacking you every chance I get."

Though the last part of his explanation heated her to the core, the importance of his wanting to be a gentleman struck her as special, showed her how much he cared and wanted to treat her right. She honestly didn't mind a little soreness, but she sighed and kissed his chin.

"Oh, all right."

She let him work her back around until they were spooning again. When he returned to stroking his hand down her arm, she relaxed against him. "What time is it?"

She felt him lift his head off the pillow before he said, "Just after two," and then he nestled his face back into her hair.

She let out a sad sigh. "I wish tomorrow didn't have to come so soon. I wish we could stay here like this until…I don't know. For a long time."

"All right then. I forthwith suspend time until the lady wishes to move on."

Wrinkling her nose, she laughed. "Forthwith?"

"What? What's wrong with forthwith?"

"I'm definitely getting you a thesaurus. No one uses *forthwith* anymore."

Logan chuckled with her. "Did anyone ever?"

She shrugged. "I don't know. Maybe in the eighteen hundreds."

"While drinking tea and eating crumpets in the blue salon," he suggested, affecting a British accent, which made her giggle.

"And talking about dukes and earls who might be attending the upcoming masquerade ball," she added.

He played along, building to the story. And she felt the need to outdo him until soon they had a ridiculous tale created that no longer had anything to do with the word forthwith.

They talked deep into the night, teasing and whispering, kissing then touching. By the time Paige drifted into a dreamless sleep, she felt happier than she could ever remember feeling in her life. Just before unconsciousness claimed her, a pair of warm lips pressed against the back of her head.

"I love you," he whispered.

And that was all she needed to feel content.

Chapter Thirty-Three

"Paige, you will not believe—" The bathroom door to Paige's room flew open and Bailey exploded inside with Tess hot on her heels. "Dorian Wa—oh my God. Paige is in bed with a guy!"

Jerked from a deep sleep, Paige sat straight up, making her covers slide down to reveal the Minnie Mouse t-shirt she'd worn to sleep. Beside her, Logan lurched sideways and tumbled to the floor.

When he landed with a thump, Paige scurried forward to peer over the edge. "Are you okay?"

Lying flat on his back, he groaned and opened his eyes. "Does everyone blow in here like that each morning without knocking first?"

She winced. "Actually, no. I think you've just gotten lucky." She held out her hand to help him up.

As he accepted it, Bailey shifted around them, studying him from a different angle before her eyes flared. "Hey, you're that hot designated driver guy."

He grunted out an unintelligible sound and rubbed the shoulder he'd landed on as he scowled at her. "Yeah. G'morning to you too."

"Pai-aige!" Tess looked pleasantly scandalized as she put two syllables in Paige's name. Eyes glittering with glee, she rubbed her hands together. "Did you get drunk and need a ride home last night?"

Both Logan and Paige ignored the intruders as they gazed at each other.

Reaching out, he caught a piece of her hair and smoothed it down, his expression full of adoring amusement. "I should probably go."

She nodded glumly and watched him glance around the room until he spotted his jeans draped over the back of her desk chair. Her greedy gaze gobbled up the muscle tone on his legs and the sleek line of his vertebra as he kept his back to them and jerked his pants on, tugging them up over his boxer shorts.

Paige licked her lips, remembering how she'd clutched that very back last night before she realized she wasn't the only one taking in an eyeful.

Scowling at both her suitemates as their stares followed every move Logan made, she stepped partially in front of them to block their view and crossed her arms over her chest.

Lifting an eyebrow, she asked, "Do you mind?"

Bailey shifted to the side so she could peer around Paige's shoulder. "Not at all."

"Me neither," a blushing Tess piped up as she dodged to the other side of Paige for her own peek.

Giving up on them, Paige sighed and turned just in time to see the last bit of Logan's golden back disappear as he slipped on his shirt. When he glanced at her with a nervous, uncertain smile, she melted. His blue eyes asked if she was okay, if she regretted anything, if she wanted to see him again.

She loved how much he cared. Smiling her reassurance, she took his hand. He squeezed her fingers before his shoulders eased and he breathed out a silent, relieved breath.

"I guess I'm going then," he said.

She followed him to the door, where he crouched down to pull on his shoes. "Do you have to work today?"

"No, I…" Shoving his foot into the last shoe, he stood and cast her suitemates a cautious squint. They watched him avidly. "I have a feeling you and your friends need to talk, though."

Paige glanced at Tess and Bailey who both bobbed their heads in vigorous agreement. She sighed. "Yeah." And she had a lot more to tell them than Logan realized. "It might take a while too." She sent him an apologetic grimace.

"That's fine. I'm going to head home and grab a shower. I think I left my cell phone at The Squeeze, so I might pop in there to get it, and make sure we didn't leave too much of a mess last night while I'm at it. Is…" He cast their audience a discreet look before turning back to her. "Is it okay if I stop by later?"

Without answering, Paige grabbed the front of his shirt with both hands and yanked him against her for a goodbye kiss. When his mouth captured hers, she felt home.

Soon, the meeting of lips turned into something too deep for prying eyes, so she regretfully let go of his shirt. He took a step away from her, looking dazed as he struggled for air.

"Okay, then. I'll take that as a yes." He returned to her just enough to press his forehead to hers and nuzzle their noses back and forth.

"I think that was a hell yes," Bailey piped up.

Logan grinned as he pulled back. Paige's hand caught his and their fingers naturally interlaced as he nodded to her suitemates and then opened the door to the hall. His eyes were soft and content.

"Bye."

"Bye," she whispered back, not letting go of his fingers until the very last moment. The door closed gently before she turned around, floating on a cloud of ecstasy—

And found both her friends gawking.

"What…" Bailey couldn't speak beyond that.

Paige blushed. "Um…that's a long story. You go first. What were you saying when you came in?"

Bailey and Tess exchanged glances, both looking confused as if they'd already forgotten what they'd been so excited to share.

"And what're you doing back on campus so early?" Usually they didn't roll in until after sundown on the Sunday before the week started. But it couldn't even be eight a.m. yet. "Didn't your ski trip go okay?"

"Oh!" Tess finally brightened. "Yeah. No. I mean, my dad broke his ankle, and we had to leave early. But he's going to be fine. We heard about Dorian Wade on the news so we hurried back to find out what was going on here. Did you know he was found—"

Paige blanched. "Yeah, I know." Scrubbing her face with both hands, she sighed and slumped onto the edge of her bed.

Had it only been two nights ago that the whole debacle with Dorian had started? It didn't seem possible. It felt like ages had passed. Things were moving too quickly. She didn't know if she could keep up.

"I have a lot more to tell you than you'll believe," she admitted.

"Start with Logan," Tess demanded, plopping down beside her. "And don't leave out a single detail."

"Especially the juicy ones," Bailey added, landing on her other side.

"Actually, I think I need to start three years ago." Paige groaned and dropped her hands. "But first, tell me what they said on the news. Do they have any suspects for who shot Dorian?"

Tess gasped. "He was *shot?* With a gun?"

"No, with a paper clip," Bailey muttered. "God, Tessie. Really?"

Tess ignored her and never took her wide-eyed gaze off Paige. "Holy crap. How do you know he was shot?"

Paige winced. "The cops told us. When they came to question Logan and me."

Bailey waved her hands. "Wait, wait, wait! Why would the cops question you and Logan? Maybe you should start with that story first."

"No!" Tess grabbed her wrist. "Start with the bedroom details first. I want to know how long you guys have been *sleeping* together."

Paige blushed hard. "I don't know if I can. It's so surreal. I still can't believe this is actually happening. But, oh my God, you guys. It was sooo…" She grinned and sighed. "He kept telling me I wasn't ready, especially after Friday night. But I kept pushing and—" With a gasp of clarity, she glanced between her friends. "I'm no longer a virgin. Oh, wow. I can't…this is all just so…I don't know how to explain it. It was amazing, and I feel so alive and exhilarated and…and…but then I'm also kind of nervous and afraid that my dad is going to disown me, and I'll lose my friend Kayla. But it was still so worth it." Cupping her face in her hands, she gave a little moan. "I can't process everything."

When both her friends stared at her as if she was insane, she blushed. "What?"

Bailey blinked. "I'm in shock we're even having this conversation."

"What brought you two together?" Tess asked.

"Oh, right." She still had to tell them everything. Blowing out a breath, Paige collapsed backward, landing with a plop on the mattress. Bringing her knees up to her chest, she hugged them hard and swallowed her apprehensions.

"There's a lot I haven't told you guys," she confessed. "About me. About my family. About before I came to Granton. And it started three years ago. With my brother."

Almost two hours later, Paige had changed into some day clothes and told her friends the entire history of her and Logan. Feeling drained, she slid off the bed and approached the sink to wash her hands. She had no idea why the urge came over her, maybe she needed to physically rinse away her anxieties.

On her bed, Bailey and Tess remained mute, much as they had been through most of her story. Feeling their gazes, she studied her reflection in the mirror. Other than her tousled hair full of bed-head — yeesh, no wonder Logan had appeared so amused when he'd touched her hair — she looked exactly like herself.

It was strange how the world around her seemed to be falling apart and her features hadn't altered even a tad — well, except for the pair of nifty bruises on each cheek.

Needing something to do as she received her friends' inevitable reactions, she snatched up her brush and pulled the bristles through the dark strands as she turned to face Bailey and Tess.

"So what do you think?"

Bailey's mouth moved, but nothing came out.

"Which, uh, which part are you asking about specifically?" Tess pressed her hand against her forehead. "There's kind of a lot to digest here, and...and respond to."

"I guess, right now, I just want to know if I'm still your friend." Paige dropped her brush to her side, her eyes imploring them to forgive her. "I should've been up front with you and told you about my mom...and Logan a long time ago. But I was just so..." She winced. "It was just so hard to talk about. I was so mad at both of them, blaming them for things they didn't need to be blamed for, needing to put my miseries on *someone's* shoulders. I couldn't even talk about it at my grief group, but — "

"Shh, shh." Tess swept off the bed to hug her. Pulling Paige close, she said, "We aren't mad, I swear. You just needed a little time before you could talk about it, is all. We still love you, don't worry about that."

"Speak for yourself," Bailey muttered. "These are exactly the kind of exciting details I want to know as soon as I meet a person."

When Tess scowled at her, she grinned. "Just kidding. I love you too." Opening her arms, she joined the group hug.

So very glad she'd found these two women, Paige sighed and rested her cheek on Tess's shoulder. "And what about Logan?" she asked. "Do…do you think I'm awful for…for falling for him?"

Bailey wrinkled her brow with the confused frown. "Why?"

"I…" Paige blinked, wondering about that herself. "I don't know. I guess I just hated him for so long without even knowing him. I actually spit in his face when he came to Trace's funeral, and he was probably there to apologize." Groaning, she covered her eyes with both hands. "Oh, Lord. I just remembered that. I'm surprised he didn't hate me right back all these years. I blamed him and thought everyone else did too. I thought everyone would be scandalized if we ever got together."

"Well, what do you think your brother would say if he were here right now?" Tess asked.

"I'm not sure. He wasn't the vindictive type. I couldn't see him blaming Logan for causing his death." She winced. "Maybe for kissing Kayla. But she was there and didn't blame Logan afterward. It was clear to her he never wanted to permanently harm Trace. But I just…" She blew out a tired breath. "Thinking about it gives me a headache."

"Me too." Bailey rubbed her own temple. "I'm telling you, if I had to deal with as much as you have, I'd have a prescription for Xanax by now."

"No, you'd be in a loony bin by now," Tess corrected.

As the two roommates scowled at each other, squabbling over which one of them could take on more stress without breaking, Paige grinned. No matter what, she knew she could always count on these two for a smile.

Before she could tell them how much she loved them both, her phone dinged, telling her she had a text. Thinking it might be Logan, she instantly forgot about Bailey and Tess. She hurried to her desk and heard two dings from Bailey and Tess's room before she could check the message.

"That's weird," Tess said, disappearing into the bathroom. "Hey, I wonder if it's A."

"Oh, Lord." Bailey groaned as she followed Tess into their room to fetch her own cell phone. "I'm officially cutting you off from *Pretty Little Liars*, starting now."

Paige opened her phone to find a text alert from the University.

"It must be about Dorian," Bailey mused aloud when she and Tess returned with both their phones.

All three of them checked their shared message simultaneously, Tess reading hers aloud. "Police are pursuing an armed gunman on the west end of the campus. *Oh my God.*" She gulped before reading the rest. "School officials advise everyone remain inside with locked doors, and stay away from the west side of the university completely."

A cold arrow of dread sliced up the back of Paige's neck.

An armed gunman? That didn't even seem possible.

"What the hell," Bailey breathed. She raced to the window and yanked up the shade. Students were running—sprinting actually—for any building closest to them. It was bizarre to watch, like a tiny stream of ants seeking cover from an invisible giant shoe stomping down on them.

"This isn't happening." Tess grabbed Paige's hand and held on tight.

"Just…calm down," Bailey said, her rational voice grounding Paige. "We're a good distance away from the west end of campus. We're safe here." Then she pointed at Tess. "Go lock the door. To our room too."

Tess let go of Paige's hand and raced off, immediately obeying.

Bailey found the remote control for Mariah's TV and clicked it on. Paige just stood there, dazed. Her mind racing, she tried to orient herself, remembering what was on the west end of campus. She couldn't think, couldn't map out the buildings in her head. She grabbed her skull in both hands as the TV popped on. Instantly, an aerial view of Granton from a helicopter's perspective appeared on the screen.

"It's still unclear who the gunman is," a news reporter's voice told them. "Authorities are vague on details, but we can see from this vantage point, there have been injuries if not loss of life."

Bailey approached the fifty-inch screen as if in a daze. She pointed to a shadowed blob lying on the ground in the middle of a deserted street. "Is that…is that a *person?*"

Tess returned to Paige's room and neared the television with Paige to gather around Bailey. Before they could decide if it was a human being lying in the middle of the road or not, a blast of light appeared from an alleyway, preceding a dark figure, holding what could only be a massively huge gun.

"Oh my God!" All three girls screamed and clapped their hands over their mouths.

"He's shooting," Tess gasped.

"It looks like we have a visual of the shooter." Even the reporter's voice took on an anxious edge as the camera zoomed in, but it couldn't focus enough to give any details of the person with the gun except for a dark outline. "It impossible to tell from this distance if we're dealing with a male for female. But the gunman is still very much on the loose and firing his or her weapon."

"This isn't happening, this isn't happening," Tess chanted.

"Where *are* they?" Bailey asked, squinting as she eased closer. "Is that…is that the food court?"

The food court?

Paige forgot to breathe as she studied the buildings instead of the dead person lying on the ground. It *was* the food court, less than a block away from The Squeeze.

"*Logan!*"

She didn't think, she just moved, lunging for the doorway. Bailey caught her just as she unbolted the top lock. Hooking her around Paige's waist, she hauled Paige backward, Tess joining in to the assist her when Paige resisted.

"Paige! What are you doing? Are you insane?"

"He's out there." She struggled harder against both girls. "Let me go! Oh my God, let me go." When a sob hiccupped from her throat, she wiggled and twisted with more fervor.

Bailey cursed and Tess ducked when Paige's elbow inadvertently swung her way. Finally, her suitemates propelled her backward enough to tackle her onto Mariah's bed.

"You…are…not…leaving…this room." Bailey panted, out of breath.

Tess stroked her hair in a soothing manner. "Just relax, sweetie. Logan is fine. He's just fine."

Paige only tensed harder, trying to buck her friends off her. "How do you know that? He said he was going to—"

"Well, you're not going out there to check on him without thinking. God, Paige, *think!*" Bailey sat up and off her, brushing her multicolored hair out of her face. "You didn't even try his cell phone first."

"Yeah, that's a good idea." Tess sat up too. "Let's just call him and have *him* tell you he's okay."

"Okay." Paige wheezed out a breath, forcing herself to calm down and think logically. But her body just wouldn't unwind; alarm warnings were going off all over inside her. Logan was in trouble; she just knew it.

She couldn't lose him. She'd already lost too many people in her life. Not Logan too. She still itched to dash for the door and physically find him.

But she did the rational thing first. She called his cell phone with fingers that could barely dial through all the shaking.

"He's not answering." She squeezed her eyes closed. "Why isn't he answering?"

Tess bit her lip and glanced at Bailey before saying, "Maybe he hadn't gone to the juice bar yet to pick up his phone."

Or maybe he was that shadowed figure lying in his own blood they wouldn't take off the screen of her television.

Her whole body began to shake.

The gunman had disappeared down another dark alley and was out of the view of the camera, but the motionless figure in the middle of the street hadn't moved, would probably never move again.

Tears flooded her lashes. "Logan, where *are* you?"

Chapter Thirty-Four

Paige escaped through the bathroom.

After she, and Tess, and Bailey called every possible place Logan might be with no answer from any of them, she went into the bathroom, telling her friends, she needed a moment alone. But as soon as she closed the door to her room, she opened the door to theirs.

She unlatched all the locks with trembling fingers, trying to be as quick and silent as possible so her suitemates wouldn't hear. And finally, she was in the hallway, free to find Logan. A few doors opened, big round, scared eyes peeking out, asking her what was going on. But she didn't pause as she rushed for the exit at the end of the hall. She took the stairs two and a time and pushed her way outside within seconds.

The world was eerily quiet, the campus lawns totally deserted. In the distance, she saw the news helicopter hovering over the food court district and headed that way.

She raced down the street, keeping close to the bushes and trees for cover. When she neared the west end of campus, her breathing escalated.

Scared to death, she plowed forward anyway, more afraid she'd never see Logan again than actually encountering a madman with a huge gun.

Reaching out to touch the solid surface of Jamison Hall, the arts department building, she slowed her pace with growing hesitance, not sure how to creep up to The Squeeze without crossing an open, exposed street.

She heard a gunshot in the distance, and her heart shuddered in her chest. She couldn't tell how far away the sound was — two blocks? Three? — or how close it was to the juice bar, but she prayed Logan hadn't been —

An arm shot out from the thin alley between Jamison Hall and McCuffrey, the science center, as she began to dart across it. When it wrapped around her waist, she started to scream but a hand clapped over her mouth, muffling the sound. Her assailant dragged her backward into the alley and pressed her against the cold bricks of Jamison Hall.

She began to struggle until his face appeared before her, his azure blue eyes bright with shock and anger.

"What're you *doing?*" he hissed.

"Oh my God!" She leaped at him, beyond relieved to see him, and wrapped her arms tight around his neck, squeezing with a force that made him stumble against her. With the solid warmth of his body reassuring her, she shuddered. "Oh my God. I was so worried. When I got the text alert, I thought you were there…getting your phone. I had to know…make sure you were okay."

Adrenaline made her breaths come in sharp, painful wheezes. It was possible she was even hyperventilating. She wasn't sure. It was hard to think. All she knew was that Logan hadn't been hurt.

That was all that mattered.

Petting his hair, she kept touching him, stroking the skin on the back of his neck, so very, very grateful. Another shot rang out, echoing eerily down the alley. They were coming more sporadically now. Probably fewer people to shoot at. Hopefully.

Logan jerked in her embrace and pulled back to send her an incredulous stare. "Are you completely insane? How could you run *toward* a terrorist killing random people just to make sure I was okay?"

Paige could only stare at him, her mind a scattered mess. She held her breath, trying to control her rickety gasps for air. "What're *you* doing here?" she was finally able to ask, glancing around the deserted alley.

It was quiet now. Too quiet.

Like death.

Logan shook his head and sent her a look as if he couldn't believe she even had to ask. "Don't you know? I showed up at your room but Tess and Bailey said you'd gone looking for me, so I raced toward a freaking terrorist shooting random people to make sure *you* were okay."

A laugh blurted form Paige's lungs. "God, I love you." The words tumbled out before she'd even planned what to say. But she didn't regret them in the least. She wanted him to know before—

Well, before anything else might happen.

His eyes flared with surprise. Then he lunged toward her and held her hard. The hug was comforting and warm. She felt safe and happier than she could remember being in a long time. Logan was holding her. Logan was alive. He dipped his face and kissed her hard, his mouth frantic as it clung to hers.

Another gunshot—too close for comfort—broke them apart.

"We need to get out of here." He grabbed her hand and pulled her tight behind him. Bending his knees into a slight crouch, he inched them cautiously toward the opening of the alley as he ran his free hand along the wall and used it like some kind of guide.

Closing her eyes briefly, Paige leaned in to him so she could inhale his scent from his shirt. Still relieved he hadn't been at work and wasn't the blob she'd seen lying in the middle of the street on TV, she whispered, "Do you know who the shooter is?"

"No."

"How are we going to get back to Grammar Hall?"

"No idea," he murmured only to stop dead in his tracks, making her bump into him.

Paige looked up over his shoulder to see what had stalled him. A shadowed figure blocked their escape, and he had a nasty-looking semi-automatic rifle hooked over his shoulder with a sling.

"Logan!" She hissed and instinctively tried to move around him, worried how much more exposed he was than she. But he became like steel, nearly crushing her fingers as he refused to let her wiggle out from behind him.

"Who's down here?" a shockingly familiar voice called. "More sheep? *Baa.*"

"*Einstein?*"

The gunman reacted violently, rotating the gun around on its sling until he swung it in their direction and held it in firing position. He lurched a step into the alley toward them. Paige yelped out her shock while Logan whisked them nearly sideways, turning their bodies just enough that he could pin her to the brick wall, completely protecting her with his own body as he tucked her behind him.

"Paige?" Einstein called, sounding almost frightened. Lost.

"Oh my God. *Einstein!* What're you *doing?*" She couldn't believe… it couldn't be possible. Just because he'd been a little strange…but he was so harmless.

Einstein stalked close enough for her to see the sweat gleaming on his face. He never once lowered the gun or took his aim off them as his pale brown eyes focused on her. What she'd once thought was an innocent baby face had contorted into the face of an executioner. Dull lifeless orbs stared from his blank gaze. She trembled, experiencing fear as she'd never experienced it before. The stranger before her could kill…mercilessly.

Eyeing Logan up and down, he asked suspiciously, "Who's he?"

"Wh-what're you doing, Einstein?" Paige repeated, her voice wobbling, her fingers digging deep into Logan's arm, wishing he wasn't so visible. "Put the gun down. Did you actually *shoot* someone?"

Taking his gaze off Logan, Einstein looked at her again. His face crumpled into a piteous expression, and his voice whined. "I did it for you, Paige."

"Wha—" She licked her dry, cracked lips, afraid to ask. This was worse than a nightmare. She couldn't even dream up something this horrific. "What did you do?"

Oh, God. What had he done?

"I killed him." A rusty sob grated from his throat. "I killed him because he hurt you."

She gasped, and Logan's muscles tensed against her. "Dorian? *You* killed Dorian?"

Nodding, Einstein gulped. "I killed him." Then a strange gleam entered his dead eyes before he smiled. "And it felt good. It felt like… justice. So I decided to kill them all. Everyone who ever made fun of me. Slaughter the sheep."

Logan lifted his free hand in a surrendering kind of way. "Then why are you pointing that gun at Paige? She never made fun of you." His voice was calm, placating.

It irritated Einstein. Slashing his gaze to Logan, his eyes flared with a rage Paige had never seen her friend turn on anyone. Gritting his teeth, the sixteen-year-old pulled the butt of the gun snug against his shoulder and focused his aim on Logan.

"Paige didn't, but I don't know about you. Who the hell are you?"

He didn't give Logan a chance to answer. The crack of light and explosion of sound that followed dragged a scream of terror from Paige's lungs.

In front of her, Logan jerked backward, bumping into her hard. Then his grip on her hand went slack. His body sagged, beginning to slip down hers like a limp sheet fluttering toward the ground.

"Logan?" She caught him around the waist and slid her hands up to support him by the armpits.

Head lulling against her shoulder, he didn't respond.

"Logan!" This time the scream came from her very soul. *"Noooo!"*

Vaguely, she realized the danger was far from over, but a part of her had gone numb. Logan slumped in her arms. Sounds like a tortured animal rose in her throat, and she tilted her cheek to press it against his temple as she squeezed her eyes closed.

Logan.

"You like him." The words came at her like an accusation.

Paige trembled and lifted her wet lashes. "I love him."

Einstein gaped at her, looking thunderstruck. "I killed for you, and you went out and got a *boyfriend?*"

"Einstein." Her voice sounded hoarse. "Please."

Sobs consumed her, making her chest raw from the pain that tore through her heart. Her arms began to burn from holding Logan's dead weight.

"Please." She had no idea what she was begging for. Life maybe. Logan's life. Einstein's surrender.

Einstein watched the tears slide down her cheeks, a look of awe on his face. Then his eyes widened and horror crossed his expression. He jerked the gun away from her and awkwardly ripped the sling off his shoulder. When she realized he was trying to position the long barrel to aim at himself, her eyes flared open wide.

"Don't. *Einstein!*"

He didn't hear her, didn't even pause.

Squeezing her eyes shut, she tucked her face against Logan's cooling cheek and everything inside her jumped when the next shot blasted a second later. It deafened her, but she still heard the rifle clatter to the asphalt a split second before the body dropped beside it. She didn't have the courage to check, but she knew.

Einstein was gone.

Quivering, crying, panting hard, she shuffled backward until her back met the wall, then she slid down in increments, cradling Logan carefully so as not to jar him. When she was finally seated, his long legs sprawled away from them as she gently supported his head in her lap. His eyes were closed and lips slightly parted.

Even though she braced herself before looking, the sight of his wound still sent a shockwave of electric proportions shooting to every nerve in her body, waking the numb sensors with a zap of terror.

"Logan?" Her voice shook. "Logan, please open your eyes."

Blood pooled from the hole, making the stain on his torn shirt grow bigger. She closed her eyes, prayed not to vomit, and slapped her hand over the area, pressing down hard.

Stanch the blood flow.

He gasped, and his muscles seized. Paige opened her eyes to find his own had opened. Gritting his teeth, he wheezed, "What… where…"

Moaning with relief, Paige kissed his hair, his forehead, the side of his face. "Shh. Don't talk. Don't talk. You were shot. You're going be okay. You'll be fine."

Except she could feel warm liquid life ooze between her fingers. He wouldn't stop bleeding. A chest shot couldn't be good. Couldn't be—

"Einstein?" he rasped, trying to look around but immediately falling still with an injured grunt.

"He's…he's dead." Still too afraid to glance Einstein's way to confirm her own words, she kept her gaze on Logan's as she stroked his face. "It's okay now. It's over. We're gonna get you help, and everything's going to be fine."

The only thing on him he could seem to move was his eyes. He kept shifting them around as if he wanted to assess the situation.

Then he stopped, his glazed gaze landing on her face. "But blood makes you woozy."

Of all the things to say. Of all the things to remind her.

Paige swallowed and gave a quiet nod, refusing to look at her hand pressed against his ribcage. Her stomach was already rebelling, and her head felt heavy. He went briefly out of focus in her vision. She concentrated all her attention on his face, making that the center of her universe.

He looked pale. Pasty pale. And he wasn't breathing so well.

"I won't leave you," she promised, thinking how strange she sounded and wondering why she'd said that. People said such odd things in extreme situations. Her thoughts were so weird.

There was so much sweat on Logan's face.

He covered her hand she was using to bandage his wound as if to comfort her. His fingers felt freezing against her own. "It's okay," he slurred. "You can pass out if you need to."

Paige shook her head, refusing to leave him. Her lashes fluttered as she fought his suggestion.

What sounded like a stampede of clopping boots on concrete invaded her consciousness. She looked up just in time to see half a dozen military-looking men in black combat gear toting long rifles stream into the alley, shouting orders and questions.

"Oh, thank God," she mumbled dazedly — they were saved — just as the blackness swarmed in and enveloped her.

Chapter Thirty-Five

Shifting in her seat, Paige decided the cushions in a hospital waiting room chair lost all sense of comfort after five hours. She straightened and twisted her spine to work out the kinks while she checked the clock on the wall.

Almost midnight. Thank the Lord. She was ready for this day to be over.

Weary yet wired, she pushed to her feet to pace again. Other worried families of other wounded Granton students had gathered in the same room. But she ignored them.

A cooking show began on the television hanging from the ceiling. Since the thought of food turned her stomach, she climbed onto the chair below the TV and turned the channel...for the tenth time today.

Pushing the *next* arrow, the next station in line flipped to CNN. Immediately, aerial footage of Granton sprang onto the screen.

"So far, there are six confirmed deaths, including the shooter, and at least two dozen injuries. Lisa, on the scene, has spoken with authorities and—"

Her vision graying at the fringes, Paige stamped the *next* button again, and no one in the waiting room objected to her hurry. The station landed on a cartoon of a carpenter with talking tools. She left it there.

But *six* deaths?

She stepped off the chair and stared sightlessly at the sea of worried faces surrounding her. It didn't seem possible or real. She wanted to pull her hair and scream and make the day—the entire weekend—start over again…well, except maybe for last night, with Logan.

How could Einstein have done what he'd done?

And how could he say he'd done it for her, putting some of the culpability on her shoulders? She didn't want anything to do with it, didn't understand any of it, just wanted it gone. But mostly, she wanted to see Logan.

When a doctor appeared in the entrance of the room, looking grave, she held her breath. He called a name familiar to her, the name of someone she was sure she'd shared her chemistry course with last semester. A handful of people rose and followed the doctor into a tiny room to the side. The cries and wails that followed had Paige shaking all over.

One more life gone.

Blinking rapidly, she glanced toward the television as if she could still see the emergency vehicles flooding her beloved campus on the screen. She closed her eyes and tried to settle her erratic breathing.

Seven people. Dead. For no good reason.

Realizing news of the shooting had been broadcasting on CNN, a national network, Paige winced, thinking of Kayla, who had no doubt seen the coverage. She was probably worried sick. Paige strode from the waiting room, glad she had something to do while she waited for word from Logan's doctor about how his surgery was going.

She approached the nurses' station. She knew the hospital was busy—Logan certainly wasn't the only gunshot victim with a critical injury who was being treated. But the nurses had been kind to her so far. They'd given her an extra pair of scrubs to wear so she could change out of her blood-splattered clothes. Then they'd let her use the phone so she could call Logan's family because she'd left her cell in the dorm room when she'd snuck away from Tess and Bailey. One more request shouldn't be asking too much.

"The doctor's just finishing up with your boyfriend's surgery," a sympathetic RN told her as Paige approached. "I bet he'll be out in a few minutes to update you. 'Kay?"

Paige blew out a breath, not sure if she was relieved she'd get news soon, or scared to death it might not be positive news. "Thanks." She gulped once more before asking, "Is it okay if I borrow the phone again? I forgot to call my own family the first time and tell them I was okay."

Pity filled the nurse's gaze as she nodded. "Yes, today it's fine. Go ahead, hon."

Paige slid gratefully behind the counter to the phone. She'd yet to mention it to anyone, but she'd found a hole in her shirt when she'd changed into the borrowed scrubs.

A bullet hole.

Actually, one of the nurses had spotted it. For the longest time, Paige had just stared at it, confused. The nurse had searched her for an injury Paige already knew she didn't have. The only thing they discovered was a bruise forming on her breastbone. And suddenly, everything became clear.

The round Einstein had fired at Logan must've passed through him and caught her. She was unharmed only because she'd been wearing her brother's thick, metal cross amulet—now dented and the ruby shattered.

After the nurse had confiscated her old clothes to give to the police for evidence and loaned her a pair of scrubs to wear, Paige kept rubbing the necklace with awe.

She fingered it now as she dialed Kayla's number.

It was a sign, she told herself. Trace had helped protect her, letting her know he wasn't upset with her, so he must approve of her decision to be with Logan.

At least, that's what she chose to believe it meant.

The phone barely rang once before Kayla answered with, "Paige?"

Paige closed her eyes. "Yes, I'm sorry I didn't—"

"Oh, my God. Oh, my God." Kayla began to sob. "I thought you were dead. We saw the news on TV, and I called you immediately, but your roommate answered your phone, hysterical, saying you had run off. She didn't know where you were and was sure something awful had happened. I thought I was never going to see you again. Oh my God, I thought—"

"Kayla. *Kayla!*" Paige laughed as tears prickled her eyes. "I'm fine. I swear to you, I'm okay."

"Oh my God, why didn't you call sooner?"

"I'm sorry, sweetie. I just...everything's been so insane. Logan was shot. I'm at the hospital. He's been in surgery for hours, and I can't...I just can't think straight. I'm sorry."

"You're at the hospital? We'll be there in a few minutes."

"Okay." Paige nodded and closed her eyes, relieved to know she'd soon have her best friend in the world with her. Then her eyes opened wide. "Wait. Did you say a few *minutes?*"

"Yeah. We're in Granton now. We left as soon as we saw the report on TV. God, this entire town is a chaotic mess. They're not letting anyone on or off campus, and no one seems to know anything. We've been driving around the streets, just *looking* for you for the past hour."

Astonished to learn Kayla had jumped into a car to come to her, Paige pressed her hand to her heart. "Who's we?" she asked, expecting to hear Kayla say her boyfriend or her parents had come with her.

But instead she answered, "Your dad and I. Who else?"

Paige blinked. "My dad?"

"Yeah. He's busy driving right now, but he says to tell you he loves you and we'll be there soon."

A tear dripped down Paige's cheek as she nodded. "Okay," she whispered, unable to speak any louder than that. "Hurry." Knowing that support was on its way made her nearly dizzy with relief. She'd been so preoccupied just holding herself together through most of the day, the thought of not having to do so any longer actually drained her.

"I love you guys."

"We love you too. See you soon." When Kayla hung up, Paige stood, frozen in her shoes. When the dial tone blared in her ear, she quickly punched in her dorm room.

Bailey answered as quickly as Kayla had. "Where the hell are you?"

After another five minutes of getting lectured at by Bailey and then Tess for scaring the life out of them, they spent another five minutes telling her how much they loved her and were glad she was safe. If officials weren't sequestering everyone on campus to their dormitories, she had a feeling her suitemates would be on their way to sit with her at the hospital as well.

By the time she hung up with them, she was a watering pot. She was wiping her soggy cheeks when Logan's family rushed down the hall. His parents and two brothers skidded to a halt when they spotted her.

Taking in Paige's wet, red eyes, Mrs. Xander pressed a hand to her heart and hiccupped a sound of agony. "We're too late."

"No." Paige shook her head. "Actually, I don't know. I haven't gotten an update yet."

His mother blew out a breath and nodded, though she looked scared spitless. Logan's family entire family looked shell-shocked.

Logan's father went to the nurses' desk, demanding answers just as the doctor appeared in the hall, striding toward them.

"Logan Xander family?" he asked.

Mrs. Xander reached out and clutched Paige's hand, and Paige held on to her for dear life as she whispered, "Yes."

Paige held her hands against her chest as she cautiously trailed Logan's parents and brothers down the hall to his recovery room. The doctor might have told them he'd come out of surgery very well and was awake and cognizant, but she couldn't actually believe it until she saw him.

Holding back as his parents, then his brothers, went in first, she remained just outside the doorway, eager to catch a glimpse of him.

When his mother whispered his name as she crept close, the figure lying on the hospital bed moved his head to the side and opened his eyes.

"Mom?"

Tears flooded Paige's cheeks as she watched his mother grasp his hands and weep over him. "We were so worried. We'd thought we'd lost you for good, that it was too late."

His dad and brother corralled around his bed, chipping in their own greetings of deep regret, and then thanksgiving that he was alive.

Pressing her back against the hall wall inches from the doorway, Paige listened to the family reunion, so very glad they'd found their way back together. The Xanders didn't do a whole lot of clarifying as to why they'd suddenly let Logan back into the fold, and Logan didn't demand an explanation. All that would no doubt come later, after the shock had worn off. For now, they simply seemed happy to be together again, and Paige was happy they were happy.

"So how many stitches do you have?" one of the brothers asked a couple minutes later.

"Actually, I don't know if they're staples or stitches," Logan said, "and I didn't ask how many. I don't think I want to know."

Paige grinned, thinking that sounded like the perfect Logan answer. Relieved she could listen to his voice and hear him give a Logan kind of response, she closed her eyes and pressed her hand to her heart, sending up a prayer of thanks. She'd come so close to losing him forever.

"I didn't think puncture wounds like a gunshot needed stitches," Mr. Xander mused aloud.

Logan gave a weak chuckle. "Yeah. Well, I guess they had to open me up a little more to operate on a couple things that had gotten nicked."

"Nicked?" Paige echoed aloud. More worried than concerned about privacy and family time, she whirled from the hallway to gape at him through the threshold. "Where did you get *nicked?*"

Was it serious? An important organ he could never use again? Would he have lasting damage, or could it get worse later on?

He glanced up and immediately sucked in a gasp. "You're here." His voice was breathless, his blue eyes alive with emotion. "When you passed out, I didn't know if the bullet had gone through me and hit you or what."

She blanched, pretty sure she never wanted him to learn that's exactly what had happened.

"You were there too?" One of his brothers glanced at her with wide, curious eyes as she slowly edged into the room. "Sweet. What happened?"

Logan shook his head. "Trust me. It was not sweet."

"So what happened?" the other brother repeated. He looked like the older of the two. Caleb, Paige decided, remembering his name.

"He saved my life," she spoke up, her eyes only for Logan. "That's what happened. We were hiding in this alley away from…from…" *Einstein.* Her insides wrenched with misery just thinking about Einstein. "…the gunman, when he found us. Logan lunged in front of me and shielded me with his body."

"Dude." Jake, the younger brother, gawked at Logan in awe. "You're, like, a hero."

Logan shook his head again and winced. "No."

"Yes," Paige countered. "You kept me trapped behind you." She shuddered, remembering those helpless horrifying moments. "You protected me with your own body."

"And you were talking him down until I opened my big mouth," he countered.

She hugged herself. "I don't think so. He was so unstable he would've shot us both." The dull dead look in Einstein's eyes the moment before he'd pulled the trigger would haunt her for the rest of her life.

"Well, however it happened," Logan's mom spoke up, cuddling reassuringly close to her son, "I'm just glad it's over and you're both okay."

"Me too," Logan echoed, his gaze sliding to Paige. She felt warm and cherished under his inspection.

When a soft knock came from behind her, everyone in the room glanced up to see two more people hovering hesitantly in the doorway.

Her father made eye contact with her and moaned out a sound like a wounded animal. "My baby." He charged forward and enveloped her into a large bear hug. "I'm so glad, I'm so glad," he chanted into her hair as he hugged her tight.

Unable to remember the last time she'd *touched* Paul Zukowski, Paige clung to him, noticing he didn't feel as full in her arms as he used to. He'd lost a great deal of weight over the last few years.

Skinny or not, he was holding her now, and she was glad to be in his arms. She buried her face in his neck and shuddered. "Daddy."

"That was too close," he said as he pulled back to look her over. "Too close. I can't lose my little girl. I just…can't." When he cupped her cheeks in his hands, his face went red as he began to cry. "I'm so sorry. I'm so sorry for the way I've treated you. I'll change. I swear to God. Just don't leave me too."

When he hugged her once more, she whispered, "I won't. Not ever."

Kayla crowded in then to make it a group hug, and Paige realized her best friend wasn't just a friend, she was a part of her family. Glad she had her family with her and that they'd progressed to human contact, and Logan's family had come for him, she had a feeling things could only get better from here.

With the support of their loved ones, she knew they could handle whatever happened next.

Chapter Thirty-Six

After her hug-fest settled down in the middle of Logan's recovery room, Paige went around introducing everyone and catching Kayla and her dad up on what had happened in the alley.

The link they shared from three years before stirred up a stilted uncomfortable silence as the Xander clan eyed the Zukowski clan with unease. And Paige's dad narrowed his glare right back at them. But she figured they might as well start getting over the awkwardness now, because if she had her way, she and Logan would be together for a good, long while, and the two families would be pushed together more in the future.

When her father slid a wary gaze to Logan, she held her breath. The two studied each other for far too long before her dad said, "You saved my daughter's life."

Logan glanced at her and then back to her father. He didn't confirm or deny it.

Paul Zukowski cleared his throat and glanced at the floor before he mumbled, "Thank you."

Logan's eyes moistened. With his own nod of acknowledgement, he looked too choked up to respond. Paige wanted to go to his side and take his hand. She needed to be close to him. She needed to touch him for that added reassurance to make sure he was okay. But his family was here. Her family was here. She hugged her own waist, feeling bereft.

Her dad touched her elbow. "We should get going."

When Kayla crowded around her from the other side, she realized they wanted her to go with them. But she shook her head.

"I'm staying."

She knew the exact moment her dad realized what that meant. His eyes flared, and he swerved another glance toward Logan. But he said nothing, schooling his features until she squirmed inside, wondering what he was thinking.

Clearing his throat, he glanced back to her and gave a short nod. "We're going to find a hotel to stay in for a few days. Call us when you need us."

Paige's eyes misted with relief. He may not readily approve, but at least he wasn't going to disown her over it. "Thanks," she choked out.

He nodded again and motioned for Kayla to follow him. Her friend gave her a hard, quick hug goodbye and hurried after Paul. Once they were gone, the Xander family visibly relaxed.

They started talking about the day's events. What was worse, as they gabbed on about the shooting, a silent Logan kept throwing her concerned glances. He knew how much talk of Einstein bothered her. But she was too worried about him to focus her thoughts on her young, troubled, dead friend.

The shadows under his eyes grew darker, and the hollows in his cheeks more gaunt. After his surgery, he must be exhausted.

She shifted surreptitiously closer, stopping just behind his shoulder at his right side. "Looks like you need some rest," she murmured for his ears alone. "Do you want us to clear out and give you some peace?"

"I don't want *you* to," he said softly as he lifted his chin so he could look up at her, his gaze holding hers with a wealth of emotion.

She flushed warm. She wouldn't mind if everyone except her left him alone either.

"Well, I don't know about anyone else," his mom called, lifting her voice above the hushed conversations circulating the room. "But I'm starving. None of us had lunch or dinner, and it's almost one in the morning."

She set her hand on Paige's arm. "Paige?"

Paige opened her mouth to decline. Logan wanted her to stay, so she would stay. But instead of asking her along, his mother merely smiled. "Can we get you anything while we're there?"

Paige blinked, not expecting such understanding. "Umm...no thanks."

Logan lifted his hand. "Could you get her some blueberry muffins and an iced caramel latte?"

Lifting her eyebrows, Paige turned to give him a questioning look.

He frowned back, wrinkling his forehead in confusion. "What?"

"Just how do you know what her favorite food and drink are?" His brother, Caleb, was the one to ask, a mischievous smile tightening his lips.

"Oh, leave them alone," his mother scolded, taking the boy's arm and dragging him from the room. Glancing over her shoulder, she sent Logan a long, assessing look. "We'll be back."

As the last person filed from the room, leaving her alone with Logan, Paige moved down closer to his side. He immediately reached for her. She clasped his fingers eagerly.

She touched his brow, worried about how pale he was, how dark the bruises under his eyes looked.

Grinning, he reached up and grabbed her fingers off his face until he was holding both her hands. "I'm fine."

"But you look—"

"I'll be fine," he insisted. "I'm more worried about you. I know Einstein was your friend."

She winced from just hearing that name. "I *just* got over my brother's death, and I'm still working through my mom's. Plus, you insist I have a near-rape to work through. I think Einstein will have to get in line and wait his turn."

Logan's eyes filled with pity. "You'll get through it," he assured. "You're strong. And besides...I'll be there with you."

She stared at him, feeling settled—complete.

"So your family looked happy to see you," she said, needing to change the subject away from Einstein.

"Yeah." He blew out a breath. "Who knew I'd just have to get shot for them to accept me again?"

Paige let go of one of his hands to nudge his arm in reprimand. "Ha ha," she muttered. "Not funny."

He smiled. "So I guess that ends three years of misery." His blue eyes searched hers. "And begins who-knows-how-many more years of recovering from *this*."

Paige closed her eyes. "So many people died today. Too many people. I can't believe he did it."

Bringing her hand to his lips, Logan kissed her fingers. "Hey, try not to think about that right now. We'll have plenty of time to deal with it all later."

She snorted. "So what do you suggest I think about?"

A sudden grin split his lips wide. "You could always think about me."

Paige rolled her eyes. "I always think about you anyway."

Lifting his eyebrows, Logan looked suddenly interested. "Always?"

"Since the first day I came to Granton and saw you across a crowded classroom," she said, "you've never been far from the forefront of my mind."

"I couldn't get you out of my head either," he confessed. "Even though I knew you hated me, there was something about you. Which makes me wonder, is this poor bed-ridden guy going to get his happy ending and snag the girl, or what?"

Paige gaped at him, unable to believe she saw uncertainty on his face. "Uh..." For a moment, she was too bewildered to speak. "Let's see. I raced toward a bloody massacre to make sure you were okay and defied my own father to stay here with you. Not to mention, you swept in like a total hero, literally stepping in front of a speeding bullet to save my life. Um, yeah, I'd say you snagged the girl."

He closed his eyes, looking satisfied. "Good. That's all I needed to hear."

"Is that so?" she teased, hitching up one eyebrow. "So you didn't need to hear that your entire family was here to see you?"

He opened his eyes. "Okay, that was pretty amazing too. I couldn't believe it when Mom told me you'd gone to talk to them, though. She said you got them thinking so much they'd actually hired a private investigator to find me."

Paige's mouth dropped open. "They didn't know where you were? Goodness, that hadn't even occurred to me. I could've told them that."

He grinned, looking amused by her surprise. "I love you so much."

"And that's what I needed to hear." With a grin, Paige squeezed his hand and immediately loosened her grip when she brushed her thumb over his IV. She tried to pull away, afraid she'd hurt him, but he wouldn't let her go.

Eyes losing their cheerful gleam, he grew serious. "Will you marry me?" When her mouth fell open, he rushed to add, "I mean, someday. Maybe after we both graduate."

"Or sooner." Paige's chest filled with hope.

His breath caught. "Or sooner," he repeated. A grin exploding across his face, he said, "Wow. That right there was all I needed to hear."

"Hey." She fake pouted. "We've both already used that line. You can't get a twofer from it."

He scoffed. "A twofer?"

She nodded astutely.

He grinned, his eyes dazzling to a brilliant azure, the deep shadows under them looking momentarily clear. "Twofer has to be worse than bad-thing magnet and forthwith. As soon as you get me my thesaurus, I'm letting you borrow it. Besides." Placing a hand over his heart, he gave a bad imitation of a groan. "I should get my twofer. I'm wounded and drugged."

Narrowing her eyes, she scowled. "Oh, so we're pulling out the wounded card already, are we? I hope you don't think you can get whatever you want for the next few months just because of a little bullet wound to the chest."

He laughed. A second later, the color fled his face, and he clutched the bandaging over the bullet wound in his chest as his chuckle turned into a real life gasp of pain. "Ouch."

"Oh my God. Are you okay? Don't laugh."

"Sorry," he choked out, breathing heavily.

"Okay, okay. You can use the wounded card whenever you want. Just don't pull your stitches, or staples, or whatever they are."

He chuckled again only to end the laughter on a groan.

"Stop laughing," she scolded, panicking as he panted through the pain.

"Well, stop being funny," he wheezed.

"Okay. I'm serious," she assured him, pulling a straight face. "I'm serious now."

He rolled his eyes and grinned, but at least he didn't laugh again. His gaze taking on an affectionate gleam, he shook his head. "Maybe we should just call a priest to my room. I want to marry you right now. Before you kill me with laughter."

Paige glowed inside even as she folded her arms over her chest. "Trust me. Before I'm done playing Nurse Ratched and making you take all your medicine and drink lots of water, you'll be begging to push the nuptials back a full decade."

He didn't look swayed. In fact, he winked at her. "Bring it."

Epilogue

Paige held Logan's hand as they entered the cemetery. Squeezing his fingers for support, she bumped her shoulder against his until he glanced at her.

"Thanks for coming with me."

He rolled his eyes and tightened his grip. "Where else would I be?"

She bit her lip, pretending to think about it. "Oh, maybe in bed, *resting.*"

It had only been a month since the Granton school shooting. A month since the football quarterback had attacked her and her sixteen-year-old genius friend had killed him in retaliation and then slipped off the deep end and gone onto the shooting spree in one of the busiest sections of campus.

A full month, and nothing had returned to normal. Booths were set up in front of nearly every major building on campus to provide counseling for whoever needed it. A dozen new members had joined the Tuesday night grief group. And emails from university administration flooded her inbox daily about added safety measures they had decided to take around the university.

She felt like a survivor from a war.

And Logan *looked* like a survivor from a war. Though his left arm hadn't been harmed, he wore it in a sling to keep it still. Too much movement, pulling at muscles on his left side, tended to irritate his slowly healing wound.

He'd lost a lot of weight, weight he really couldn't afford to lose. Paige teased that if they ever went back to visit the cancer center, the nurses would probably mistake him for a patient and refuse to let him leave.

Even though he'd been letting his hair grow, it still wasn't long enough for her to skim her fingers through yet. It would be someday, though. And she'd be there to play as soon as it was.

"Resting?" he repeated on a grimace as they approached the tombstone they'd come to visit. "But I can only rest when I know you're nearby."

He wasn't lying. She'd stayed with him every night since he'd been released from the hospital. And more often than not, he woke in the wee hours, sweating and panting from a nightmare. He could only fall back to sleep when she curled up beside him and rubbed his back.

But despite all that, Paige still felt getting past the newest tragedy in their lives was going to be easier for them than recovering from the first one, because now they had each other to lean on.

Pausing in front of Trace's grave, Paige snuggled close to Logan and sighed. "Happy birthday, big brother."

Next to her, Logan shuddered. "It's still so weird to see his name written on a headstone."

Feeling his regret, Paige tilted her face to rest her cheek on his good shoulder. "He's probably up in heaven now, bragging about how he got the nicest, most expensive marker in the cemetery. He'd love his monument. Especially the epitaph."

Under his name and dates, the inscription *That's All Folks* had been engraved in the black marble.

When Trace was fifteen, he had learned that very phrase had been inscribed on the gravestone of Mel Blanc, a famous voice actor, and he'd laughed about it for weeks, saying he wanted something cool like that on his own marker. So Paige had fought to get it on his after he'd died.

She was still glad she'd won that argument. Trace would love it.

"I miss you so much," she told the cold stone. "But I want you to know, I'm happy and doing well. And I'm finally moving on… with my own life." She looked at Logan and grinned.

He pressed his cheek against her forehead and closed his eyes.

After she let go of his hand, she bent and gently laid the bundle of flowers she'd brought with her on the chilly, thawing ground. Spring was just around the corner. It felt like new hope was coming for every corner of her life.

Plucking one of the stems from the bouquet, Paige leaned over the grave next to Trace's and set the single flower on her mother's stone.

"I miss you too, Mom." Smiling sadly, she straightened and turned to face her future. "Ready?"

Logan nodded silently and once again reached for her hand.

She took his fingers, ready for the next phase to begin.

The End

Acknowledgments

Thanks to all my beta readers: Sandra and Alaina, Courtney and Andrea, Shi Ann, Nancy, and Doris.

Another huge round of thank yous to the crew at Omnific Publishing: Kathy, Enn, Micha, Lisa, Kim, Sean, Coreen, and everyone else who helped work on my story that I didn't know about. What a wonderful, professional group of people to work with! I'd gladly work on another project with you.

I'd also like to thank Lisa Filipe, Jean Winters, Kurt, Sandra, Alaina, Adam, Matthew, and Lydia for helping me vote on the cover. Then another hug of appreciation goes to Kurt and Lydia for living with me while I'm lost in writer world.

Lastly, Thanks to the good Lord for spoiling me rotten with way more blessings than I'll ever deserve.